It Was You

JO PLATT

It Was You

San Diego, California

Canelo US
An imprint of Printers Row Publishing Group
9717 Pacific Heights Blvd, San Diego, CA 92121
www.canelobooksus.com

First published in the United Kingdom in 2016 by Canelo. This edition originally published in the United Kingdom in 2020 by Canelo.

Published in partnership with Canelo.

Correspondence regarding the content of this book should be sent to Canelo US, Editorial Department, at the above address. Author inquiries should be sent to Canelo, Unit 9, 5th Floor, Cargo Works, 1–2 Hatfields, London SE1 9PG, United Kingdom, www.canelo.co.

Publisher: Peter Norton • Associate Publisher: Ana Parker
Art Director: Charles McStravick
Senior Developmental Editor: April Graham
Editor: Angela Garcia
Production Team: Beno Chan, Julie Greene

Design: Brianna Lewis

Library of Congress Control Number: 2022939672

ISBN: 978-1-6672-0376-8

Printed in India

27 26 25 24 23   1 2 3 4 5

Fourteen years ago

'Hi, I'm Alice. I'm next door.' I pointed down the hallway to my left. 'There doesn't seem to be anyone else here yet and I wondered if you fancied coming out for a coffee?'

The delicately pretty blonde girl opened the door fully and smiled. 'That'd be really nice,' she said, beckoning me into her room. 'I was just beginning to wonder what to do next.'

'Great.' I followed her inside, where she sat down on a single bed, identical to the one in my room, and began to peel off a pair of long, red-and-white-striped slipper socks.

'I'll just put some shoes on,' she said.

I looked around, noticing the absence of a second bed. 'You're not sharing then?'

'You are?' she asked, slipping her now bare feet into trainers.

I nodded. 'With someone called Miriam, who's studying History. But,' I shrugged, 'as I say, no sign of her yet.' I continued to take in the room, which was already, I thought, looking worryingly well organised in comparison to the chaos I had left behind in mine. 'Actually, maybe I should leave a note for her, explaining that I haven't quite finished sorting out my things yet,' I said. 'Your room is so tidy.'

She followed my gaze. 'I can't claim all the credit for that. My parents stayed for ages to help. I'm an only child, so separation is hard for them.' She looked up at me, before adding more quietly, 'For me too, actually.'

'I'm an only child too,' I nodded. 'So I can relate.'

She smiled and gestured towards a largish box of Geography text books next to her desk. 'They'd still be here now, putting those on shelves, if I hadn't insisted they leave.' She looked around and then picked up a grey rucksack.

'I'm pretty sure my purse is in here,' she said, opening the bag and beginning to rummage.

'My mum and dad weren't half as useful as yours,' I sighed. 'Mum just kept reading recipes out loud from the student cook book she'd bought me and Dad spent the entire time circling all the police stations in my A-Z.'

She looked up and laughed, before delving again into the rucksack, finally withdrawing her hand and triumphantly holding up a purple leather purse. 'Found it!'

'Brilliant,' I said. 'There's a nice café by the water tower on the Downs. We can sit outside.'

'You sound as if you already know your way around Bristol,' she said, standing up. 'I'm from Reading. The university open day was my first visit.'

'I'm less than an hour from home here,' I explained. 'So I've been a few times.'

She walked to the desk and picked up a key. 'That must make everything a lot less daunting,' she said, sounding a little flat.

'Not really. I'm still pretty terrified. Two weeks is the longest I've ever been away from home without my parents.'

Her smile returned. 'Thank you. That makes me feel better.'

We made our way to the door, which she held open for me and then locked behind us. 'And thank you for knocking on my door, Alice.' She placed the room key in her purse and zipped it up.

'Well, thank you for coming for a coffee...' I began, before stopping short, suddenly realising that I didn't know her name. 'I'm sorry,' I said, 'I didn't ask your name.'

'Didn't I say? I'm so hopeless,' she sighed, holding out her hand for me to shake as we made our way down the corridor. 'I'm Lydia.'

Chapter 1

I re-entered the living room of my small garden flat, with a large packet of nuts in one hand and a bottle of red wine in the other, to find Miriam in full flow and Connie and Abs listening intently. 'And I agree with Connie,' said Miriam, closing her copy of *Chronicle of A Death Foretold* and placing it on her lap. 'A perfect example of how less is definitely more. What do you think, Abs?'

'Absolutely,' said Abs, nodding and flipping a long, dark brown plait over her shoulder, before continuing in typically encouraging fashion. 'You're always so insightful and to the point, Connie.'

Connie smiled gratefully, lowering her pale blue eyes, made huge by the bottle-bottom glasses she wore when taking a break from her contacts. Despite, at forty, being twelve years older than Abs, she was far less assured in her opinions. And although she always offered quiet, thoughtful, comments during our book group meetings, she rarely did so with much confidence. 'I'm so pleased you agree, Abigail,' she said, in her soft, Californian drawl. 'You know, I made the same point to Greg earlier this evening and he said he just couldn't see it at all.'

I heard Miriam let slip a quiet sigh, as I stooped to replenish the bowl of nuts sitting on the low coffee table in front of her. Fond as she was of Connie, I knew she disapproved of what she viewed as a tendency to allow herself to be dominated by an over-protective husband; not to mention a highly demanding three-year-old son and a hyperactive Labradoodle.

Miriam cleared her throat. 'Yes, well, husbands and wives often see things differently, don't they?' she said, leaning forward and taking a handful of nuts. 'But that doesn't make you wrong, or your opinions any less valid than Greg's. Goodness knows if I rolled over and just accepted it every time Craig told me I was wrong, I'd never get off the blooming floor.'

Abs nodded. 'I keep telling the kids at school that different isn't the same as wrong,' she beamed. 'We all see things differently. If we didn't, life would be so boring. For example,' she continued, waving her Kindle, 'if we'd all seen this book in exactly the same way, we'd have nothing to discuss.'

'Very true,' I said, holding the bottle of red wine aloft. 'Now, who's for some more of this?'

'Me, please.' Miriam held out her glass and looked up at me. 'And how did *you* see the book, by the way, Alice?' she asked pointedly. 'You haven't said much this evening.'

'I read very nearly all of it, actually, Miriam,' I protested, picking up on the implied criticism: I had a rather confirmed reputation as a non-finisher of the books we chose. 'The best thing was finding out what happens at the end, right at the beginning. Meant I didn't have to read the last page first, like I usually do.'

Miriam sighed and Connie and Abs laughed. 'You are funny,' said Abs, holding out her near-empty wine glass to me. I smiled at her as I topped it up.

'Hmm…' said Miriam. 'Well, I think we need less funny and more reading from you, Alice Waites. May I remind you that we are The Short Book Group because of you – because *you* didn't want to attempt anything over two hundred and fifty pages. And you hardly ever manage even that! What on earth is the point of having an English graduate in our book group if you never read the entire book?'

'Oh, stop getting your knickers in a twist, Miriam,' I said, placing the bag of nuts and the wine on the sideboard and flopping down on the sofa next to her. 'And besides, you're exaggerating. You know, I finish some of them.'

She pursed her lips. 'Well done, you.'

I looked at her. 'You sound just the way you do when you talk to Phoebe.'

'I often think you and my three year-old have a lot in common actually,' she shrugged. 'And I don't just mean a shared refusal to see a book through to the end. How you and my husband didn't get chucked off that English course when we were at uni, I don't know.' She shook her head despairingly.

'That was over a decade ago, you know,' I said tonelessly. 'So I think it might be OK for you to stop telling us off about it now.'

'Gosh, friends for over a decade and you still get on so fabulously,' said Abs, without any hint of irony.

I laughed and Miriam joined in. 'We do,' I said.

'And talking of friends forever,' continued Abs, stretching out in the small blue armchair she was occupying on the far side of the room, 'why are there only the four of us tonight? Where are Jon and Sophie?' She looked at me and frowned questioningly, while still maintaining the broad smile she was rarely without.

'Sophie is sunbathing in Mauritius,' I sighed. 'And not back for another whole week. I really miss her at work. The office is so quiet and David is very down in the dumps without her there to shout at him every five minutes.'

'Wow! Mauritius!' exclaimed Abs, sitting up and leaning excitedly towards me, as if Sophie's holiday was on a par with a moon landing. 'How amazing! Has she gone with Carl?'

I shook my head. 'With Graham. The builder. Carl was the one before Graham.'

'Gotcha.' Abs pushed up the long sleeves of her outsized cream Aran sweater and gave me a double thumbs-up.

Connie nodded thoughtfully. 'I liked Carl,' she said, bending down to retrieve a cup of tea from the floor, her mousy bob falling forward and hiding her face from view. 'I met him only once, but I remember thinking that he had the most wonderfully exotic accent.'

'He was Liverpudlian, Connie,' said Miriam with a frown.

Connie sat up and smiled. 'Yes, it's such a lilting, uplifting accent. So full of optimism and charm. It's why I love Ringo Starr's narration of Thomas the Tank Engine.'

Miriam continued to frown, opened her mouth, as if to respond, before closing it again and smiling resignedly at Connie's appreciation of the Scouse accent. 'Yes, well, anyway,' she said, turning to me, 'while we're on the subject of men, how did your evening with Kieran go?'

Three pairs of eyes looked at me expectantly. I had been both expecting and dreading the question.

I smiled sheepishly. 'I cancelled.'

There was a collective groan.

'You are joking,' said Miriam.

'I know, I know,' I sighed. 'I was a bit frustrated with myself too. But it got to Saturday afternoon and, well,' I shrugged apologetically, 'I just didn't feel like going.'

'Did you feel unwell?' asked Connie. She pushed her glasses to the top of her head, reducing her eyes to regular size, and pulling back her hair to fully reveal pale, slim features, now anxious with concern.

I shook my head. 'No, I went to the Arnolfini with Jane Crane instead.'

'But that's the third time you've stood someone up in the past couple of months,' said Miriam, with a hint of exasperation.

'It's not standing someone up if you tell them you're not coming,' I protested. 'Standing someone up is when—'

'Stop dodging the issue by pleading technicalities,' she interrupted.

I looked at her and sighed. 'I've said I know it's not great, haven't I?'

'So, what's the problem?' she asked. 'Do you think you're still upset over Eddie?'

'God, I really hope not,' I said. 'After all, it's been…' I hesitated, whilst performing a mental calculation, '…well over eighteen months now.'

I leaned back on the sofa and wondered what, or whom, Eddie Hall had been up to since our three-year relationship had reached its explosive conclusion. I had noted, with painful interest, the publication of his second novel. But having proudly resisted the urge either to read it, or to stalk him on the internet, I knew nothing more than that. I loathed him, of course, and couldn't deny that I felt an enormous amount of bitterness towards him, but I was pretty confident that I viewed him as a despicable individual, rather than as representative of eligible men generally. So, as undeniably apathetic as my current approach to dating was, I didn't think I could blame Eddie for it.

I shook my head. 'I don't think that's it. I just...'

'Can't be bothered,' said Miriam.

'Would you *like* to meet someone?' asked Connie, replacing her glasses, interlacing her hands on her lap and peering at me in the manner of a concerned psychiatrist. 'Because, you know, it's just fine to feel happy as you are.'

I smiled at her. 'The thing is, I really like the *idea* of a relationship, Connie.'

'Well, I'm afraid it's going to stay just that – an idea – if you're not going to give anyone a chance,' said Miriam brusquely, reaching once again for the nuts.

I frowned. Although barely a year older than me, Miriam had an irritating tendency to slip into bossy-big-sister mode. This wasn't anything new and had been a recurring feature of our fourteen-year friendship. 'Don't get all Judge Judy with me, Miriam,' I warned.

Miriam smiled and rested her hand gently on my arm. 'I'm not *judging* you,' she said gently, switching seamlessly to kindly-mother mode, 'I'm *caring about* you.'

'Actually,' I said, rolling my eyes at her saccharine tone and reaching for my glass of wine, 'I think I prefer it when you're judging me.'

'Maybe it's just too easy for you to cancel a date with someone you have no connection with,' she continued, now beyond listening. 'Perhaps if they were friends of friends, rather than people you just bumped into at conferences...'

'I didn't meet Kieran at a conference and don't try to turn me into your next project, now that you've finished reupholstering that ottoman,' I said dryly.

She ignored the interruption.

'...then you'd have to at least meet them for coffee when you said you were going to. It'd be much harder to let someone down if they were, say, one of *our* friends.' She glanced at Abs.

'Ooh, yes! Ooh! I've got a friend!' said Abs suddenly, her hand in the air in the manner of one of her more excitable pupils. I looked across at her, then back at Miriam, suspecting a conspiracy. Abs was now grinning at me and fidgeting in her chair.

'Aw, thanks for thinking of me, Abs, but…' I began.

'Tell us more, Abs,' said Miriam, rubbing her hands together theatrically, in order to indicate extreme interest.

I rolled my eyes at the display. 'Like you don't know all about him already,' I murmured.

'His name is Hugh McGlennon,' said Abs. 'He's Scottish, very handsome, very tall, a forensic pathologist and into battle reenactment,' she beamed.

'He sounds very interesting, Abigail,' said Connie, nodding encouragingly.

'So he's either cutting up a dead person or pretending to be one,' I said.

No one appeared to hear.

'The important bit,' said Abs, 'is that he's bought a fixer-upper in Bishopston and could really do with some interior design advice.' She looked at me significantly.

'I don't get it,' I said.

She laughed. 'I might have already told him that you're an interior designer, and so on, Alice.'

My heart sank. I was very familiar with Abs' rose-tinted descriptions of her friends. 'When you say *and so on*, Abs, what exactly have you told him?' I asked wearily.

'Not much. Just that you're thirty-two, highly intelligent, very beautiful and utterly fascinating. So,' she looked at me expectantly, 'what do you think?'

I looked at her blankly. 'I think that you've massively over-sold me.'

'Look,' said Miriam, 'you've just said you're frustrated with yourself over Kieran. So why not make a fresh start by meeting Hugh?'

'Oh yes,' Abs clapped her hands. 'Please, Alice. I could just say you've got some carpenter or plumber contacts for him. There'd be no pressure.'

'Well, I don't know…' I said uncertainly.

'I don't see how it could do any harm, Alice,' said Connie quietly. 'It's just a coffee.'

I looked at her, smiling encouragingly at me, with, I knew, the very best of intentions. She was right. It could do no harm.

'Oh, go on then,' I said. 'I'll go for coffee with Hugh.'

'Yay!' said Abs, punching the air. 'That's the spirit. You've gotta be in it to win it, haven't you?'

'And,' said Miriam, 'if Hugh doesn't work out, I'm sure we have plenty of other people up our sleeves.'

I turned to her. 'Like I said, I'm not your next project.'

She smiled, put her arm around me and opened her mouth to say something but, at that moment, my phone buzzed in my back pocket. 'Sorry,' I said, extricating myself from her cuddle and standing up to remove my phone from my jeans, 'this might be Jon. I sent him a text earlier.' I opened my messages. 'Yes, he's working late so can't make it. That's a shame.'

I smiled sadly and sat back down, as Abs and Connie echoed my disappointment. Miriam, however, remained silent and bit her lower lip. We all looked at her.

'What?' I asked, my face falling. 'What is it?'

'Oh,' she said, looking at each of us in turn. 'I'm so sorry. I thought you'd realised.' She took a deep breath before continuing. 'It was their wedding anniversary today.'

Chapter 2

Miriam was the last to leave and it was almost eleven by the time she rose to her feet and hugged me goodnight. Connie and Abs had left half an hour earlier, each citing an early start the next morning as a reason to get home and to bed.

'Craig'll think I've got lost,' said Miriam, retrieving her grey cloche hat from one of the pegs by the front door in my small hallway. 'Not that he'd care. But anyway,' she pulled the hat down over her short, curly mop of dark hair and reached up to give me a second hug, 'are you ok? I'm so sorry about not mentioning the wedding anniversary sooner.'

'I just can't believe I forgot,' I said quietly, as a renewed sense of guilt and sadness swept over me. 'We were bridesmaids, for goodness sake. What kind of friend does that make me?'

'Oh, don't be so silly,' she said, smiling up at me, her voice breaking slightly. 'Stop punishing yourself, Alice. We all have an awful lot going on. I only remembered yesterday. It's my fault; I should have called you.' She rubbed my arm. 'I suppose I just assumed he'd have mentioned it to you.'

I shook my head sadly. 'I'd been wondering whether something was up, actually.'

'What do you mean?' she asked, her tone a mixture of concern and surprise.

'He's just been so quiet lately. I haven't been able to drag him out for a drink in almost three weeks. He's turned me down twice – said it was work. But that doesn't usually stop him.' I looked at her miserably. 'I was beginning to think I might have upset him in some way.'

'What rubbish,' she tutted, before adding more gently, 'But how about I ask Craig to call him? And maybe the four of us can go for a drink. Or five of us.'

'Five?'

'Romy's planning to visit soon. I'm sure she'd love a chance to catch-up with you and Jon.'

Despite my mood, I managed a smile. Rosemary – or Romy, as she was known to all – was Miriam's younger sister, of whom she was ferociously protective and justifiably proud. She was a woman men adored and women treated with caution; before being won over by her gentle personality and the fact that she was more embarrassed, than flattered, by her hordes of male admirers. Romy and Jon got on very well, and I knew he'd enjoy seeing her as much as I would.

'That'd be nice,' I said.

'Come on,' she said, smiling. 'Don't worry about it. He's fine. He's got through two other wedding anniversaries and he'll get through this one too.'

I nodded again. 'I know. I just feel dreadful for forgetting.'

'Well don't. You're a wonderful friend to him – the best he's got. And the best one I've got too, for that matter.' She kissed my cheek, turned up her coat collar and became suddenly brisk. 'Now, remember to email everyone about the next meeting. Did Abs give you her book choice?'

I nodded. '*Ethan Frome*. I'll email now, before I forget.'

'*Ethan Frome*...' She looked thoughtful for a moment before smiling brightly. 'Don't think I know that one. But I'll let you go and get on with sorting that out. Night, Alice,' she said. And with that, she turned and walked away up the steps and out of sight.

I closed the door behind her and then, still feeling undeniably flat, I fetched my laptop from the kitchen table, returned to the living room, flopped down on the sofa and clicked on my emails. I was surprised to see one from Abs, sent just ten minutes earlier, and I opened it with interest.

From: a.walker@brisecollege.bristol.gov.uk
To: a.waites@mooredesign.co.uk
Subject: Re: This evening

Alice!

You'll never guess what! Got home and had to send out rehearsal schedules for the school play. Hope you can come to that, by the way. All going incredibly, brilliantly well, except that Fagin broke his leg in three places falling off his bicycle last week. Poor sausage. It needed an op to pin it and chances are he'll now have to wear flares, which aren't very Victorian – but hey ho, never mind.

But anyway, was on the computer and thought, I know! I'll email Hugh about Alice! So I did and he replied within five minutes! He's free either next Saturday pm for coffee or next tue or wed after work for a drink. Just let me know which suits best!

Mwa,
Abs
X

I smiled, unsurprised by the fact that she had wasted no time in contacting Hugh. And I would have loved to share in her excitement and enthusiasm, but at that moment found myself unable to summon up anything more than a sense of affectionate amusement at the thought of her making Fagin wear bell-bottoms.

I sighed and decided that maybe bed was the best option right now. I would just send a quick email about the next book group meeting and then call it a day.

I opened a new email and began to type.

From: a.waites@mooredesign.co.uk
To: mims@familymarshall.plus.com,
jon.durham@SynergySolutions.co.uk,
c.golding@skyblue.co.uk,
s.carter@mooredesign.co.uk,

a.walker@brisecollege.bristol.gov.uk
Subject: Book Group

Hi everybody,

It was lovely to see Abs, Connie and Miriam this evening. Sophie and Jon, it was very quiet (Sophie) and unintellectual (Jon) without you. You were missed.

I stopped typing, leaving the cursor flashing mid-sentence, and stared fixedly at the screen, feeling not only low about the forgotten wedding anniversary, but now also conscious of a vague, but growing, sense of emptiness – of something lacking. Worse still, I had no idea what lay behind it.

I thought back to Abs' email about Hugh, and to the conversation about relationships earlier in the evening, wondering if that was what was troubling me. But I found myself genuinely unbothered by the prospect of either dating or not dating. I didn't feel any pressing need to go looking for a boyfriend, but at the same time I didn't mind if Abs and the others wanted to introduce me to their friends; I was happy enough to show willing and see where things led. On top of that I was, I reasoned, fit, healthy and enjoying life. I had a fun job, great friends, a father I adored, and day-to-day I felt busy, fulfilled and relaxed.

So what, I thought, frowning at the screen, was the problem?

I sighed wearily and rubbed my eyes, before deciding not to dwell on feelings I had no hope of resolving as midnight rapidly approached. Instead, I told myself, I would, as my mother always used to recommend, focus on *positive positives* – happy things of which I was absolutely certain – including the fact that I had a caring, well-intentioned group of friends, for whom I was very grateful.

I resumed typing.

Off to bed now, but I'd just like to add that I feel very lucky to have you as friends and I love you very much. I appreciate everything you do for me, including all offers to help me find my Mr Right! Thank you and I faithfully promise not to stand-up any recommended gentlemen.

Alice

X

Then feeling, I thought, a little better, I hit *send* and headed to bed.

Chapter 3

Sophie tutted and picked up the phone. 'Hello, David Moore Interior Design. Sophie Carter speaking. How can I help?'

I looked at her enquiringly, as she rolled her eyes and stuck two fingers up at the receiver. She had returned to work that morning, following her two-week holiday in Mauritius, looking toned, tanned and, I thought, considerably younger than me, despite being the same age. My mood sank a little at the recollection that the only break I had so far booked was an overnight stay with Dad in The Cotswolds in June. I was looking forward to it, and I knew I would enjoy it, but it was hardly two weeks in Mauritius.

I watched as Sophie, with some effort, arranged her features into a smile. 'Oh hello, Eleanor,' she said brightly. 'No. Delivery of the curtains is tomorrow. You'll remember that I did ask you whether you wanted—' She suddenly stopped talking and stared at the phone. 'And a very good day to you too, Ms Black,' she said, replacing the phone in its holder with an angry click. 'God that woman is so bloody rude. She makes me want to scream.' She paused, took a deep breath, picked up her coffee and leaned back in the green velvet armchair in which she was currently lounging. 'It's just a good job we work in such calming surroundings,' she said more quietly.

I smiled and looked around me. She was right. I loved the domestic feel of our small Clifton offices; the cosy-chic lamps, rugs and armchairs chosen by David, reflected not only the warmth and friendliness of his personality, but also the day-to-day working atmosphere.

'We're very lucky,' I said.

'We are,' she agreed. 'But, come on.' She glanced at the art deco clock which took centre-stage on the fireplace to her right, whilst sucking desperately on a small white tube, a nicotine inhaler, which she held in her tanned left hand. 'We've got thirty minutes of lunchtime left before David gets back. Dish.'

I stopped smiling and bit into my chicken salad sandwich. 'What exactly do you want to know?' I mumbled.

She rolled her eyes. '*Everything*, of course. The way Abs tells it, you and Hugh are *mad keen* – her words – on each other. Oh and Miriam said that even if he doesn't pan out, Connie has someone for you.'

I stopped chewing and stared at her. 'What?'

'Connie has—'

'No, no.' I interrupted. 'What did Abs say about Hugh?'

She shrugged. 'She said that you had a coffee with Hugh and that you found him *really* fascinating. I got the impression that he's planning a date for the pair of you. But apparently he's on sabbatical, filming a battle re-enactment in the Highlands with the BBC at the moment, so…'

At this point, I interrupted her flow with a coughing fit, after inhaling a large chunk of chicken salad sandwich in a horrified gasp.

'Christ, are you ok?' Sophie sat forward in her chair, as if about to get up.

I nodded, finished coughing and reached for the bottle of water on my desk. 'I am not *mad keen* on Hugh and he was not *mad keen* on me,' I said, taking a gulp of water. 'In fact, I got the distinct impression he was there just to get the carpenter's phone number and couldn't wait to get away. The pair of us lasted twenty minutes before we made our excuses. The man chops up brains and puts all the little bits in jars. I'm not going to enjoy watching him cut up steak on a dinner date, am I?' I shuddered at the memory of the gruesome surgical details shared by Hugh over coffee, when I had made the huge mistake of asking him to tell me a little bit about his job.

'Oh, cheer up.' Sophie pushed back a stray coil of newly sun-lightened, blonde hair from her eyes. 'It's not like he actually kills the poor sods who end up on his slab, is it? And I don't know what you said to Abs but she thought the whole thing went brilliantly.'

'What?' I looked her in disbelief. 'All I said was that Hugh seemed nice and that his hobby was very unusual. I asked her if she'd ever been to a battle re-enactment and she said no and I said we must go some time. *That was it,*' I emphasised. 'I did not say anything about wanting to see him again. And it was obvious that he wasn't at all interested in me.'

'Not according to Abs,' she smiled. 'You clearly underestimate your charms. Hey, but I tell you what,' she leaned forward conspiratorially, 'he's bloody good-looking, isn't he?'

I narrowed my eyes at her. 'How do you know what he looks like?'

'Because I asked Abs to text me a picture of him, *of course*.' She folded her arms and looked thoughtful. 'He reminded me of that Sherlock Holmes guy. What's his name? Benedict Bumbertwitch – only with less squinty eyes.' She opened her brown eyes to their full extent, giving herself the appearance of a long-lashed owl. 'I'd have certainly given him the benefit of the doubt for longer than twenty minutes.'

I stared at her. 'I can't believe you actually asked Abs for a photo.'

'Anyway, anyway,' she waved a hand dismissively, 'tell me more about that Mr Right email you sent to us all. I loved that. Exactly how pissed were you?'

'I wasn't remotely pissed,' I protested. 'What makes you say that?'

'Oh come off it,' she laughed. 'Telling everyone you love them in a group email? You're not telling me you were sober.'

'I had meant to tell everyone what the next book was. But I was actually just extremely tired,' I muttered, consigning the remainder of my sandwich to the bin, 'and trying to be positive.'

She wagged a finger at me. 'I've said it before and I'll say it again: no texting or emailing when you're knackered or pissed. Remember when you sent Rebecca Warner that gossip about Rebecca Warner's husband being a cross-dresser?'

I eyed her coldly. 'Shut up.'

'I'm just trying to make sure the lesson sinks in this time. But, anyway,' she took another drag on the tube, 'what was actually said about meeting Mr Right at book group?'

'It was suggested,' I sighed, 'that I might show more enthusiasm for dating if I was meeting friends of friends.'

She looked doubtful. 'I suppose you'd be more embarrassed about standing someone up, but more enthusiastic?'

'And then Miriam asked if I thought Eddie was a problem for me. But I don't think he is. At least I hope he's not.'

'Nah,' she said. 'I mean, I wouldn't have blamed you if that shit had put you off men for life but I think...' She suddenly leaned towards me, before just as rapidly sitting back in the armchair and signalling a change of subject with another wave of her hand. 'But who cares what I think? It's probably just bollocks anyway. But hey—'

I opened my mouth to ask her to tell me what she thought my issue might be, but she didn't pause for breath.

'—but, hey,' she sniggered, 'I bumped into that ripped carpenter again this morning. You know, the one we're using on the Eleanor Black project.'

'You were at Eleanor's this morning?' I asked, deciding that I was happy to let the previous conversation, together with its references to Eddie, slide. 'I thought David was down for that visit. She usually insists on seeing the boss.'

'I know. But I offered to pop in and tell her he was sick and he didn't say no. I don't blame him. You know how she's got boobs like watermelons?'

I nodded my acceptance of this description of Eleanor Black's breasts.

'Well,' she continued, 'whenever David goes round, she wears a push-up bra, a low-cut top and leans over him at every opportunity. And then she goes on and on about the trials and tribulations of being an attractive divorcee and how what she needs is a strong man to help her keep all her wolfish admirers at bay. The poor guy's terrified. She was expecting him today and when I turned up she was actually wearing a negligee, for God's sake. Gave me some crap about feeling *under the weather*.'

'Oh no!' I put a horrified hand to my mouth.

'Oh yes, but don't worry.' She took another drag on the tube and then waved a hand in front of her face, as if clearing imaginary smoke. 'I've sorted it for him.'

I experienced a feeling of mild dread. 'And how have you done that exactly?' I asked.

'Easy,' she shrugged. 'I just kept going on about the fact that he's gay.'

'Er…' I hesitated. 'Even though that's not actually a fact and he's not actually gay?'

She nodded. 'Yep.'

I sighed. 'And have you told David you did that?'

'Are you insane?' She looked at me aghast. 'That kind of thing would really panic him, Alice.'

'Yes, it would.' I picked up my coffee. 'I don't know what I was thinking.'

'Anyway, it did the trick,' she said proudly. 'Eleanor said she's happy to deal with you or me in future.' She saluted me with her cup and grinned. 'Another Mad Hatter situation averted.'

Hatty Taylor, or Mad Hatter, as Sophie called her, was David's most recent, and undoubtedly most unstable, ex-girlfriend. As well as funding her art classes, Pilates classes and a Reiki healing course, he had, during their five-month relationship, completely redesigned and refurbished both her living room and bedroom. Her parasitic relationship with him had continued only until Hatty decided that what she really needed in life was a new bathroom, at which point she had dumped David in favour of the owner of the high-end 'Tubs 'n' Tiles', in Cotham. Not that David was unhappy with her decision to end the relationship. He had wanted to do that very thing from week two but had been *anxious regarding the possibility of hurting Hatty's feelings*. When they did finally break up, he had insisted upon marking the occasion by taking Sophie and me out for champagne. I reflected now upon the fact that, in the four years that I had worked for him, he had dated, without exception, only domineering harpies. For some reason, despite his breeding, money, talent and attractive physical appearance – he was tall, dark and, as Sophie put it, anxiously handsome – David seemed to lack the confidence to ask a woman out, and consequently found himself serially manoeuvred into relationships with highly assertive types, unafraid to take the initiative. Sophie had told him on many occasions that she would be happy to act as his agent and deliver the sad news required to end these invariably miserable liaisons, or to *do the dump*, as she put it. But he had always declined her offers – hence her recent, more clandestine, approach to managing his personal relationships.

'Anyway, where were we?' Sophie was looking at me intently, whilst tapping out an impatient rhythm on her desk with her aubergine, manicured nails.

'The ripped carpenter?'

'Ah, yes!' Her face lit up at the thought. 'Plays hockey, he was telling me. God, I bet he's clever with his stick.'

'Perhaps you should go and watch him play,' I suggested, before adding, 'and take Graham along.'

She tutted. 'Oi, you, stop spoiling my fantasy by dragging Graham into this.'

'I thought Graham was your fantasy,' I laughed.

She smiled. 'Nah, Graham and I are just mates, actually. There was nothing going on there. We had a great time away and we enjoy hanging out together but, you know, he's not *The One* or anything.'

I blinked and searched her face for any trace of irony. Sophie never lacked for male company and, from an outside perspective, her relationships seemed happy, fun-filled and, so far as I could tell, always ended, or waned, amicably, with no hard feelings on either side. At no point in the four years I had known her, had it ever occurred to me that she might actually be searching for, or even believe in, the existence of…

'The One?' I repeated, slightly incredulously. '*The One?*'

'Sorry, what?'

'You said about Graham not being The—'

'That's right. You know, I might try two of these at once,' she said suddenly, staring at the tube in her hand.

I dismissed any idea of trying to drag her back to the perfect partner issue, knowing from experience how pointless it was to try and discuss any topic in which she'd lost interest.

'Quitting isn't going well then?' I attempted to sound surprised, but it was a struggle. She tried at least twice a year to give up smoking, without any long-term, or even short-term, success. Her last attempt had ended unhappily with an urgent doctor's appointment for palpitations, resulting from simultaneously wearing two nicotine patches and smoking several cigarettes on a drunken night out.

She shook her head sadly. 'It's like having an itch and not having any hands to scratch it with. Except, of course, I know exactly where my hands are.' She looked towards the window and pointed at the newsagents across the road. 'They're in lots of little packets behind the counter. God, you were so bloody wise never to smoke, Alice. I wish I'd hung around with nice girls like you at school – instead of rolling Rizlas and piercing people's noses for fags behind the gym.' She smiled absently at the memory, before dragging herself back to the matter in hand. 'Anyway, back to finding Mr Right. I wonder if Connie will suggest her friend to you.'

I sighed. 'Well, if she does, I'm quite happy to meet him, assuming,' I added, 'that I haven't already moved in with Hugh, of course.'

Sophie sipped her coffee, peering at me over the top of the cup. 'So, let me get this straight. If Connie phones you up and says...' she switched to Connie's anxious Californian accent, '*Er, I hope you don't mind me mentioning this, Alice, but my friend from Craft Club is very nice and would love to show you his macramé*, you're just going to smile and ask when and where?'

I shrugged. 'Why not? I don't think Connie would point any psychos in my direction.'

Sophie raised a sceptical eyebrow. 'Not intentionally, maybe,' she said, draining her latte and hoisting herself out of the armchair. 'But you do have to remember that she married Greg. Greg who doesn't like her driving after dark. Greg who blows on her tea before handing her the cup. *Greg who fixed stabilisers onto her new bike.*'

'She made him take them off right away,' I pointed out. 'And anyway, Greg may be Connie's type but I'm certain she knows he's not mine,' I protested, with as much conviction as I could muster.

'Well, I for one,' Sophie grinned, 'can't wait to see who she comes up with. What am I saying? I mean, who *we* come up with. You were quite clear about appreciating *all* offers.'

'When I said that,' I said sternly, 'it was on the assumption that no one would take the opportunity to set me up with a creep for their own entertainment.'

'As if I would do that.' She picked up her bag and began to search for something. 'But seriously though,' she said, a little distractedly, 'what about my plasterer, Wayne? Remember him? We ran into him in Pizza Express that time.'

I stared at her, appalled. 'The ginger guy with the criminal record and unintelligible accent?'

She took a small box from her bag, extracted a second white tube and looked up at me with a bemused expression on her face. 'He's from Southmead, Alice, not the bloody Ukraine. And he's lovely, Wayne, and well and truly back on the straight and narrow. And he's newly single.'

'Sophie,' I began, 'I don't want you—'

'Oh for Christ's sake, I'm joking,' she interrupted, laughing. 'Unlike Connie, I am fully aware of your type – even if I don't always approve,' she added pointedly. I shuffled some papers on my desk and ignored this further reference to her dislike of Eddie. I was aware that she had found him less than charming whilst he and I were together, and I couldn't fail to admit that she had ultimately been proved right. Her insight, coupled with a determination to tell the unvarnished truth, even when in danger of being shot as the messenger, was an aspect of our friendship which I both valued and feared. 'I'm not going to suggest anyone at the moment,' she continued. 'So you'll just have to see who Connie comes up with – if, as you say, things don't work out with Hugh. And then, of course, Jon might want to pitch you an idea or two.' She popped the two tubes into her mouth and sucked.

'Well, he's got a chance to do that tonight if he wants,' I smiled. 'I'm meeting him for a drink, with Miriam and Craig. Ooh and Romy,' I added.

'Romy's visiting?' mumbled Sophie, a plastic tube now hanging from either side of her mouth.

I nodded and then pointed at the tubes. 'Are you sure that's not worse for you than an actual cigarette?'

She shrugged and removed the tubes. 'Maybe, but at least I don't stink like an ashtray at work.'

'You've never smelled like an ashtray,' I said. 'But anyway, fancy coming out tonight?'

She shook her head. 'It'd be nice, but I'm still a bit jet-lagged.'

'Thought you might be.'

She didn't reply, but instead frowned at me.

'What?' I asked. 'Have I got something on my face?' I put a hand to my mouth.

She shook her head. 'I was just thinking that I'm very interested to see what happens next with you and Hugh.'

I laughed. 'You're making me feel like a docu-drama.'

'Well, you're very interesting viewing right now, Alice. And you never know,' she said, turning away from me and towards her screen. You've only just been introduced to Hugh and when have you *ever* known which way a relationship will go based on a first encounter?'

Seven years ago

'And this,' said Lydia 'is Jon.' She looked up affectionately at the tall, dark haired man by her side. He smiled down at her with equal affection, before placing an arm around her shoulders and planting a kiss on the top of her head.

'It's just so lovely to finally meet you, Jon!' said Miriam, stepping forward and standing on tip-toe in order to simultaneously deliver and receive a kiss on the cheek.

'Hello, Miriam,' he said, 'and Alice,' he added, turning to me.

I hugged and kissed him in my turn. 'Hello,' I said. 'Miriam's right. It's great to finally meet you. We've heard such a lot about you from Lydia over the past six months.'

'Seven months,' corrected Miriam.

I looked at her. 'Thank you, Miriam. Seven months,' I said, turning back to Jon. He was smiling at Miriam and me, clearly amused. 'And, of course, congratulations on your engagement,' I added.

'Yes,' beamed Miriam. 'And I can highly recommend married life.'

Jon nodded. 'I'm an exceptionally lucky man,' he said, looking at Lydia in a way which made it clear that this was not simply a throw-away comment. 'And I'm sorry I missed your other visits to London. But, fingers crossed, from next year, my weekends of working away will be a thing of the past.'

'Ooh, yes!' Miriam clasped her hands together excitedly. 'And then you'll be back in Bristol, Lydia!'

'I can't wait,' said Lydia. 'I've really missed Bristol. And you two. I bore Jon rigid with tales from our house-sharing days.' She reached out to us for a three-way hug.

'Poor Jon,' said Miriam, turning and placing a hand on his arm as we released each other a moment or two later. 'You'll be sick of having three women in the house by the end of this weekend.'

He shook his head. 'Lydia talks about you both so much, it feels like you're here most of the time anyway,' he smiled.

'Well, I wouldn't rely too heavily on the accuracy of anything she's told you,' I sighed. 'She never has a bad word to say about anyone. It's her only flaw.'

Lydia shook her head and Jon laughed. 'So she has a flaw?' he said, placing his arm around her once again and drawing her to him. 'That's a relief. I've been desperately trying to find fault with her. You know, just to reassure myself that I'm actually worthy.'

Chapter 4

'Hello, Mr Durham.' I had spotted Jon immediately on entering the already busy bar of The Cambridge Arms. He was sitting with a pint at a large corner table, clearly absorbed in whatever he was reading on the phone he held in his left hand.

He looked up at the sound of my voice and smiled. 'Hello, Ms Waites,' he said, standing up to kiss me, before pointing to the glass of red wine in my hand. 'I see you stopped en route.'

'Trying to be efficient,' I said, as I draped my coat over the back of a chair and sat down opposite him. 'Well, for someone so very busy, you're here awfully early.'

He sat back down, tucking his phone into an inside pocket of his dark grey suit. 'Miriam scares me,' he said. 'And she told me not to be late.'

I nodded. 'Same.'

He held out his pint to me and I clinked my glass against his.

'So,' he smiled, 'what have you been up to?'

I sighed heavily. 'Nothing I haven't already told you about by email. I'm more interested in what *you've* been up to.' I prodded his arm. 'You've been so quiet.'

'Just busy.' He looked down at his pint. 'Come on. Which sofa did you go for? Patterned or plain?'

My eyes widened. 'So you *do* read my emails.'

'Actually, I get Geraldine to précis them for me,' he said, sipping his beer and then returning the glass to the table. 'I've added it to her job description. She drew my attention in particular to the one about Mr Right.' He raised his eyebrows.

'God, that,' I laughed.

'Yes, that,' he said.

'There had been a conversation about dating,' I explained. 'They want to put forward a few suggestions and I don't mind.' I smiled and shrugged. 'Just have to see what happens.'

He nodded and put down his beer.

I took my first sip of wine.

'What is it?' I asked, after a moment.

He looked up. 'What do you mean?'

'You're doing that thing with your hair that you do when you're thinking really hard about something.' I pointed at his now tousled hair.

He frowned. 'What thing?'

'You know. You run your hand halfway through it, leave it on the very top of your head for a second, and then complete the run-through.' I demonstrated on my own hair.

'I didn't know I did that,' he said, studying his hand, as if it was a newly-sprouted appendage.

'Well, you do,' I said simply. 'All the time. And now it's all sticking up.' I reached across the table and patted down his hair.

'Thank you,' he said. 'I was actually just trying to remember what we were talking about.' He picked up his beer. 'Before the dating thing.'

'Sofas. And I went ahead and bought the patterned one,' I replied. 'Ooh, but actually, I do have some properly interesting news. Happened yesterday,' I added excitedly.

'Yes?' he looked at me enquiringly.

I smiled but said nothing.

He affected a bored expression. 'I've told you before that the whole pauses-to-build-the-excitement thing you do, just doesn't work with me.' He raised his beer unhurriedly to his lips, before replacing it on the table without taking a sip. 'OK, so it works a bit. Hurry up and tell me your news.'

'I got a pay rise,' I said.

He grinned. 'That's brilliant.'

'I told David that I didn't think I deserved another rise but he wouldn't listen. He's too nice.'

'Not at all,' he said, shaking his head. 'He just recognises how good you are at choosing cushions.'

I tutted and he looked down at his pint and laughed. 'You're very good at what you do and David doesn't want to lose you. The pay rise is a business decision, not a favour.'

'Thank you,' I said, touched by the compliment.

He looked up at me and smiled.

'There they are!' Miriam's voice rang out across the bar and I turned to see her hurrying towards us, beckoning Craig and Romy to follow.

At my side a moment later, she bent down and encased me in a crushing hug, before turning to Jon. 'And how are you, Jon?' she asked, kissing him on the cheek. 'My goodness, you look so handsome in your work clothes. And out of your work clothes too, of course.'

'And when have you seen him naked?' asked Craig, smiling but looking exhausted. He was, I thought, completely unrecognisable as the affable student I had sat next to at my first university lecture, fourteen years earlier, and bonded with over a shared, shameful reliance on synopses of the various works we were supposed to be studying. I had then, a few weeks later, introduced him to my History student roommate, Miriam, and the rest, appropriately enough, was history.

'Hi, Jon. Sorry I'm so under, or over, dressed,' continued Craig, gesturing at his faded jeans and blue and white floral shirt. 'But it's good to see you. Clothed.'

Jon smiled. 'Great to see you too.'

Miriam threw Craig a withering look and then immediately transferred her attention to Romy. 'And here she is,' she said, her gaze transforming from irritated to adoring in an instant, her hands extended, as if presenting a work of art for admiration.

Romy flashed a shy but dazzling smile and raised an alabaster hand in general greeting. 'Hello,' she said.

'Romy,' I stood up and gave her a hug, 'it's so good to see you. You look great.'

'You too, Alice,' she replied, hugging me back, before removing a scrunchy from her wrist and casually bundling her long red curls behind her head. She looked, I thought, absolutely beautiful, and exactly as Miriam would have done, had she been a redhead, four years younger and two stone lighter. 'It's been way too long,' she continued, making as if to sit down next to me. 'I want to hear all about…'

'Oh, Romy,' said Miriam. 'Do you mind if I sit next to Alice? I need to talk to her about the mouldy blinds in the top floor bathroom.'

'Lucky old Alice,' muttered Craig.

'Whilst Craig,' said Miriam pointedly, 'goes and gets everybody a drink.'

'Thanks, but I've barely started this one.' I nodded towards my glass.

'That doesn't matter,' said Miriam, turning to Craig. 'He will still get you one, won't you, Craig?'

They exchanged a look, before Craig sighed, saluted and clicked his heels together. 'The usual for everybody, I take it then,' he said and headed towards the bar.

'So,' said Miriam, returning her attention to the table and beaming once again, as Romy moved to sit next to Jon, 'isn't this nice?'

Chapter 5

As Jon closed the taxi door and gave the driver our addresses, I leaned back in my seat and groaned.

'Dear God,' I said simply.

He laughed. 'Not your best evening ever, then?'

'Well, it was OK for you. You got Romy.'

He nodded. 'Yes, that was OK, actually.'

'Whilst I got Miriam and Craig.'

'There did seem to be a degree of tension there.'

'A degree? There's less tension in the Clifton suspension bridge. I mean, I know they always bicker a bit but honestly.' I slumped in my seat and stared miserably out the window. 'Did you hear the argument about him never putting his pants in the laundry basket?'

'I did.'

'And then the one about him always leaving the lid off the Lurpak?'

'I think I missed that one.'

'Lucky you,' I muttered, 'because that led to him calling Miriam *The Butter Mountain* and then things *really* kicked off.'

I turned to Jon to find him clearly on the verge of laughter.

'I'm sorry,' I smiled. 'I'm being grumpy, aren't I?'

'It's OK,' he said, now laughing. 'You did draw the very short straw tonight.'

'Hmm... Anyway, never mind about that.' I sat up and adjusted my seatbelt. 'I've missed both your correspondence and your company. So what's been keeping you away from me? Work?'

'Mostly,' he said but looked so immediately exhausted at the thought that I decided not to press him for details, guessing that perhaps his recent wedding anniversary might also feature in his list of pre-occupations.

I nodded and he looked at me for a moment, before taking a deep breath and saying, 'And now *I'm* being grumpy. Sorry. So, tell me, how are the cushions?'

I groaned. 'For the last time, my job is not just about soft furnishings. It is a highly complex mix of activities.'

He nodded slowly. 'You see, I keep forgetting that.'

'And just because it doesn't involve…' I hesitated, 'the things which your job involves.'

'Such as hard facts and easily defined concepts and roles?'

'Yes. Just because mine is more about other things.'

'Such as cushions.'

He was now smiling broadly, an expression which put him at his most attractive. When he had laughed with Romy in the pub, they had reminded me of the kind of couple featured in the many home furnishing magazines which littered our office. I could see them now, sipping coffee together in a room of steely blues, decorated to perfectly match and complement his eyes – save, of course, for the tiny, stray fleck of hazel which had somehow found its way into his left iris. And on the walls, autumnal oils, hung to accent Romy's long red curls, as she sat next to Jon, smiling up at him: a perfect couple, in a perfect room.

'And now *you're* thinking,' said Jon suddenly.

'What?' I blinked, his comment dragging me back to the moment.

'You're twisting your mother's wedding ring.' He looked down at my hands. 'You do that when you're thinking.'

'Oh.' I stopped twisting the gold band and looked up at him.

'Plus you were frowning and staring at my mad eye as if you wanted to dissect it,' he said. 'A sure sign of deep thought.'

I smiled. 'I was thinking about…' I began and then hesitated. Discussing Jon's perfect partner, even if only in terms of aesthetics, was something I knew neither of us would enjoy, and I felt my mood dip a little at the thought. 'I was thinking about decor,' I said. 'What a shocker.'

He frowned and offered me a half smile. 'I'm going to believe you,' he said after a moment.

'Hmm...' I adjusted my seatbelt for a second time.

'And while I know I should ask you more about your latest interior design ideas,' he turned his head and opened the window, as the cab came to a halt, 'fortunately for me, you're home.' He pointed to the tall, Georgian, Redland house, the basement of which was my garden flat.

'So I am,' I said. 'Fancy a coffee?'

He checked his watch. 'Bit late for me. Early start tomorrow.'

'OK.' I smiled and leaned over to kiss his cheek, before opening the door of the taxi. 'But let's not leave it so long before our next drink.' I looked over my shoulder at him. 'And next time I could drag David and Sophie along.'

'Or Mr Right,' he said. 'If you've found him by then.'

I climbed out onto the pavement, closed the door of the cab and bent down to look back in through the open window. 'You never know,' I said. 'And I have a feeling they're lining them up for me. But,' I sighed, straightening up and stepping away from the cab, 'even if I haven't found him by then, I've always got my friends, haven't I? And I'm *very* fortunate on that front – present company excepted, of course.'

'Of course,' he said, 'I didn't think for a moment you were referring to me.'

'Not for a moment,' I smiled and then, as he offered me a wave and the cab pulled away, I turned and headed down the steps to my flat.

Four years ago

'Yes, I know we'll always be friends,' said Miriam with a sigh, 'but things are bound to change and I just don't want to spend every evening stuck at home, with only Craig and a pair of leaky boobs for company.'

I held up a hand. 'Too much detail,' I shuddered. 'Way too much.'

'I'm serious, about this, Alice,' she insisted, patting her barely perceptible bump. 'When he or she is born, I won't be popping into wine bars on a whim anymore, will I? So I'd just like a regular thing on the calendar to look forward to. I'm not even thirty,' she sighed. 'I'm not ready for my brain to turn to mush.'

'I think a book group is a lovely idea,' said Lydia, handing us each a mug of peppermint tea, as she returned to join us at her kitchen table. Miriam had just started to suffer from morning sickness and the smell of coffee and black tea were triggers which, she told us, had led to her spending half an hour in the loo at Costa the day before. 'I don't read nearly enough.'

'Of course I'll join in,' I said, 'if it's what you really want to do. But does it have to be a book group? Discussing literature is going to give me distressing flashbacks to university tutorials.'

'Well, maybe if you and Craig had read a few more of the set texts, the tutorials wouldn't have been quite so distressing for you both,' said Miriam scathingly.

'What about something similar… but different,' I suggested, ignoring the dig. 'A pudding club, maybe? That'd be just as comfortingly geriatric as a book group. But with cake.'

Miriam fixed me with a stare. 'Firstly, you can't bake. And secondly, you know full well that I am not aiming for geriatric.'

'A puzzle club then?' I offered. 'Dad has an amazing jigsaw of The Flying Scotsman.'

'If you're not even going to take this seriously...' Miriam began, but Lydia held up a hand.

'How about we just read short books?' she said. 'To start with at least.' She looked at Miriam. 'You're going to be rushed off your feet, and,' she turned to me, 'you'd be OK with a novella or two, wouldn't you, Alice? Two hundred pages or so?'

I looked at her and smiled. 'That's a great idea.'

'Wonderful!' Miriam beamed, putting down her mug. 'Now,' she fidgeted excitedly, 'I thought that to start with we could each just invite one person. It doesn't have to be someone we all know.'

Lydia nodded. 'It'd be nice to introduce new people to each other.'

'I was thinking of asking a friend of Romy's who's just moved to Bristol. I'm pretty sure she'd be keen,' said Miriam.

Lydia looked thoughtful. 'I might bring along someone from work,' she said. 'Although, I've got a lovely American neighbour, who's due about the same time as you, Miriam.'

Miriam's face lit up. 'That would be great! Ooh but,' she laid a hand on Lydia's arm, 'it's got to be your choice, not mine.' She looked at me. 'How about you? Any ideas?'

I shrugged. 'Not off the top of my head. But I'll think about it.'

'You do that,' she said, still smiling broadly. 'And in the meantime,' she picked up and raised her cup of peppermint tea, 'here's to The Short Book Group.'

Chapter 6

'Hello, darling! Come in! Just wait 'til you see what I've cooked up for you today.' Dad stood in the open doorway; a wooden spoon in one hand, a blow-torch in the other and his face shiny with sweat. His still-thick, grey hair appeared slightly damp and my mother's floral pinny, which he always wore when cooking, was splashed with a variety of substances.

He lived in Chippenham, a market town less than thirty miles from Bristol and we tried to meet for Sunday lunch at least once, and often twice, a month, taking it in turns to host. My lunches were usually some form of easy roast, with an accompaniment of standard vegetables. He had, of late, been altogether more adventurous, often with slightly unpalatable results.

'I'd be happy to wait forever,' I said, 'if today's offering is anything like your broccoli soufflé.'

He chuckled. 'You're my harshest critic, you know. Everybody else loved it.' He gave me a side-long glance and winked.

'Please tell me you haven't made it for anyone else.'

He put an arm around me and shepherded me into the hallway. 'I confess, I haven't. Not my favourite dish. Here, let me take that for you,' he said, relieving me of my coat, hanging it on the hat-stand and peering down at me over his glasses. 'Now, let me look at you.'

I sighed.

'None of that,' he said. 'As your father, it is my job to make sure you're looking after yourself and,' he pushed his glasses up his face and attempted to look stern, 'you're looking a little thin, darling. Mind you,' he smiled, 'with your cooking, that's hardly surprising.'

I kissed his cheek. 'How dare you.'

'I dare, because I have to eat it.' He winked again. 'Now, come into the kitchen and I'll show you what I'm up to. You might learn something.'

We walked along the hallway, past its memory-hung walls, towards the kitchen. Just before we entered, he paused and pointed up at a photograph of my mother as a young woman. She was sitting at a table, her head resting on her hands, whilst smiling mischievously up at the photographer – my father.

'I was thinking,' he said, 'that you should take that one with you. You look so like her these days.' He gazed up at the framed black-and-white print and then at me. 'Same smile, same elfin nose. Yes,' he sighed, 'very like her, except for the hair. She had curls, of course. But it was the exact same shade of auburn: to the shoulder, like yours. And the same darkest brown eyes.' He turned to look at her again. 'The very image…' he murmured.

'Why don't I take a copy,' I said, touching his arm, 'and then let you have it back? It'd be a shame to break up the group.' The picture sat amongst relaxed portraits of Dad and other university contemporaries. Mum had told me they were all taken in the summer of 1963.

He tore his eyes away from the picture and smiled at me. 'Yes. You're right. Let's get a copy.' He slapped a hand to his forehead. 'Now, why didn't I think of that? That's age, you see.'

I laughed and looked again at the photograph. My mother had died nine years earlier. Her loss was, of course, devastating for Dad and myself. But as well as taking comfort in each other, we had each benefitted from the support of friends and wider family. I, in particular, had Miriam and Lydia, with whom I was sharing a house at the time. As for Dad, he not only determinedly accepted invitations to dinner from work colleagues and existing friends but also made the, in my opinion, very brave decision to make new friends and take up new hobbies. This pleased but surprised me at the time, as Mum had definitely been the more sociable and outgoing of the pair. And it was some time before I would learn that his new-found enthusiasm for socialising was not, as I had assumed, a personal coping mechanism. He did it, initially at least, entirely for me. Several years after her death, he explained that he had been determined not to give me cause for concern about whether he was lonely or depressed. And it was for this reason alone that, just a few months after Mum passed away, he joined a local choir and the widow and widowers' club of which his neighbour, Trevor, was a member. As it turned out, his decision was beneficial to us both. It provided me, as he had hoped, with peace of mind that he was not home alone every evening, and the various widow/widower events of walks, talks, dinners and quiz nights provided him with regular, welcome distractions from the fact that Mum had gone.

Nine years on and he rarely spent an entire evening at home. The choir accounted for just one evening out of seven, but the club, whilst officially only a once-monthly meet, afforded an extraordinary number of spin-off social events. And Dad was in particular demand – he and Trevor being two of just four widowers amongst over a dozen or so widows – and it was an unusual week when he wasn't attending at least one wedding, birthday party or dinner in the role of platonic male escort.

He mentioned one of his club friends now, as he took my hand and led me into a steam-filled kitchen. 'Today, I am cooking one of Hilary's favourite recipes,' he said. 'It involves steaming.'

'No kidding.' I removed my cardigan and fanned my face with my hand. 'It's like a sauna in here. My pores are gaping. And what,' I gestured towards the blow-torch still in his hand, 'is that for?'

'Oh, this,' he said, placing it on the kitchen island, 'is for the crème brûlée. I'd just fetched it from the shed when you arrived. They used one on *MasterChef* the other day. It all looked very easy, so I thought I'd have a little go.'

'Right.' I opened one of the low cupboards to check that the small fire extinguisher I had bought for him a couple of months earlier was still easily accessible. 'Tell me about lunch.'

'Well,' he began, his eyes dancing at the thought, 'I'm steaming fish in the oven and vegetables on the hob.'

He talked for several minutes about where to find the best sea bass and the perils of adding too much ginger, with me tuning-in only when a food item capable of hospitalising us if incorrectly cooked, was mentioned. In preference to focusing on the culinary details, I took the opportunity, while he was distracted, to assess his physical state. I had been concerned to find him looking a little leaner, and sounding a little down, when we had last lunched. But I was relieved to see that he now seemed fully-recovered; he appeared to have regained any weight he might have lost and his energetic air had returned.

'And you said this is a friend's recipe?' I asked.

He dipped a teaspoon into a greenish sauce and prepared to taste. 'Well, it's actually an adaptation of one of Hilary's recipes,' he replied, removing a lid from a pan and releasing yet more water vapour into the already heavily saturated atmosphere. I ran a hand through my hair, as it began to admit defeat and frizz.

'Oh,' I said, experiencing a slight anxiety about the nature of his adaptations. 'Is she a keen cook?'

'Yes, she is.' He leaned over the pan. 'And a very keen walker: Mendips, Gower, Cotswolds. But anyway...' He cleared his throat. 'Did I tell you that I've made myself some marvellous new slipper insoles from the bathroom linoleum offcuts? They insulate and they're non-slip. Oh, and Robert across the road has offered to take me out on his new motorcycle.'

He spoke rapidly and although I was well-used to his mid-conversation subject changes, three topics in a single breath was exceptional, even for him. I chose a subject.

'When you say Robert, you don't mean Odd Bob, do you?'

'I mean Robert at number 21,' he said, 'with the special friend.'

'The special friend *in his head*,' I clarified.

He nodded absently, distracted by the ongoing tasting process. 'That's right.'

I felt sure there must be some misunderstanding. 'And he's got a motorbike? A real one? Not just imaginary?'

He looked at me. 'Of course it's a real one, darling. Otherwise he wouldn't have been able to invite me to ride on it with him, would he?' He smiled. 'It's white with a blue stripe.'

I was horrified. 'But he was banned from driving on the grounds of insanity, wasn't he?'

'His moods do tend to go up and down a little bit but he's not been banned from riding a motorcycle.'

I took a deep breath and spoke slowly in an effort to keep my voice calm. 'Dad, last year he set fire to his shed, rather than dismantle it. That's not normal behaviour.'

'But you can see his logic, can't you?' he smiled. 'He simply reasoned that it was much cheaper than hiring a skip.'

There was a pause, during which he recommenced tasting and I experienced a rising panic over the possibility of my father careering around Chippenham with a man who regularly shopped in his pyjamas.

'We're never too old for anything, you know,' said Dad quietly, staring thoughtfully down at the cooker.

I looked at him and frowned. 'What on earth are you talking about?' I asked, prodding his upper arm. 'My objection has nothing to do with time of life and everything to do with the fact that Robert has an unhealthy fascination with fire and a distinct look of Norman Bates about him. I don't mind you having a ride on a motorbike – just not that one and not with him.'

He looked up at me, appeared confused for a moment and then smiled. 'Oh I'm sorry, darling. My mind had wandered. Of course I know you're quite right about Robert and the motorcycle.'

I felt relieved and kissed his cheek. 'And I agree with you completely,' I said. 'It's never too late for anything.'

He replaced the various pan lids, turned and hugged me. 'You are your mother's daughter, you know,' he said. Then he looked down, returning his attention to the hob. 'Now,' he continued, suddenly brisk, 'I think this is ready. Let's go and eat.'

–

Lunch was edible, although we both agreed that consumption would have been entirely possible through a straw, due to over-steaming.

'I must check those timings with Hilary,' said Dad, as he sat down in an armchair and accepted the cup of tea I had made for him. 'Thank you, darling. Yes, I'm not sure the spinach should have been quite so…'

'Liquid?' I suggested, sitting down on the sofa and sipping my own tea.

'You'd like Hilary, I think,' he said. 'And I've managed to mend the Hoover.'

For some reason, I felt vaguely unsettled by yet another hasty change of subject, but the opportunity to dwell was snatched away by his next enquiry.

'So, what are you up to over the coming week? Any *plans*?'

I sighed at his emphasis of the word '*plans*'. I knew full well what he meant. 'I haven't got a date. If I did have one, I would tell you.'

He looked puzzled. 'But what about the nice Scottish undertaker you mentioned?'

I smiled. 'Oh, Hugh. Well,' I hesitated, before deciding that I didn't wish to extend the topic, 'he's away at the moment.'

'And what about when he gets back?' he persevered. 'Is he a nice boy?'

'I've only had one quick cup of coffee with him,' I began, determined to restrict myself to fact-based objectivity, 'but he wasn't unpleasant. He enjoys battle re-enactment.' I placed my cup of tea on the coffee table beside me. 'And cutting up dead people,' I concluded.

Dad's eyes twinkled. 'Well, that all sounds most promising.'

'Doesn't it just.'

He smiled. 'You mustn't be afraid to embrace the new.'

I shook my head. 'No,' I said, 'I mustn't. And I promise I will. After all, you certainly embrace it.'

'What?' He physically jumped, causing his tea to slop from cup to saucer. 'Whatever makes you say that?'

'Well, you do!' I exclaimed, amused by his reaction. 'You're so busy and so eager to try new things. It's wonderful. I love to see you booked-up and surrounded by so many friends.'

'Oh, I see,' he said, nodding. 'Silly me. Look what I've done with my tea.' He tipped the contents of the saucer back into the cup and turned to look out of the bay window behind him. 'Yes, I'm very blessed,' he said after a moment, smiling and raising a hand as the young family who lived next door walked past. 'But I do miss your mother,' he said, 'every day.'

I said nothing, but instead picked up my tea and blinked back a tear. He turned to look at me. 'Oh, I'm sorry, darling. I don't mean to upset you.' He looked anxious. 'I'm not at all unhappy. I just mean I *think* about her. I *remember* her. Remember is a better word.'

I smiled but he still looked uncomfortable, before embarking upon what seemed like yet another swift change of subject.

'So, I've been meaning to ask you,' he began. 'How is Jon?'

'Jon?'

'Yes, Jon.' He shifted in his seat. 'How is he getting on?'

'He's well, but very busy at work,' I said. 'I saw him a couple of weeks ago for a drink and he'll be at book group on Tuesday.'

Dad nodded, smiled, took a breath as if to speak, exhaled and nodded again.

I felt intrigued. 'What brings him to mind?' I asked.

He drank his tea. 'Oh, no particular reason. Although, you did mention that it was his wedding anniversary recently. I remember having a long chat with him a good while ago: it was at your book group dinner, I think. Such a lovely chap. And a very handsome fellow. We have a lot in common.'

I laughed. 'Yes, both lovely and very handsome.'

He looked at me and smiled. 'That's not quite what I meant, darling.'

'I know. But it's true just the same. And like you, he's not short of admirers – or so his PA says.'

He looked at me over the top of his teacup. 'You've not talked to him about it?'

I shook my head. 'But I'm sure he'd tell me if there was anything to tell.'

He said nothing, his expression remaining uncharacteristically serious.

'You mustn't worry about him, Dad,' I reassured. 'He's like you. He's not at all unhappy.'

He nodded slowly, as if deep in thought, and then smiled. 'Well, how could he be anything but happy, with you for a friend?'

I rolled my eyes and smiled, and then, deciding that a change of subject and mood might now be a good idea, I asked, 'So, how about a walk?'

He gasped and looked at his watch. 'My goodness. I didn't realise how time had marched on.'

'There's still plenty of time,' I assured him. 'I'm not in a hurry to be away, if you'd like a walk.'

'I would, I would. A leg stretch is an excellent idea,' he said, suddenly standing up. 'I, er, just have to make a two-minute phone call and then we can go and blow away the cobwebs. And while we're out,' he said, getting up and heading into the hallway, 'I can explain the benefits of my new slipper insoles in greater detail.'

Chapter 7

Both my digestive system and my hair had just about recovered from Sunday lunch with Dad by the time I arrived at Connie's Clifton home for our book group meeting two days later. Depositing and locking my bike behind the side gate of the ivy-covered, redbrick house, I made my way back round to the white front door, rang the bell and waited. After just a few moments, the door opened and I was greeted by Connie's husband, Greg.

'Well, if it isn't our Alice,' he boomed, in his Lancashire accent, addressing me, as he always did, as if I was a hard-of-hearing toddler, with an extremely limited grasp of my surroundings. He moved his rimless spectacles to the top of his head. 'Well, and if it isn't my neighbour, Jonathan, too,' he added, looking over my shoulder and grinning broadly.

I turned to see Jon walking up the path towards us. 'Hi,' I said, whilst immediately noting how tired he looked. Despite more than one attempt to drag him out, I hadn't seen him since our drink with Miriam, Craig and Romy. He had continued to protest work as the reason for his unavailability, and I was disappointed to see that the longer office hours were perhaps now taking their toll.

'Hi.' He smiled at Greg and myself and then, as Greg waved us inside, followed me into the hallway.

'Welcome both!' cried Greg genially. 'Of course, I bump into Jon regularly, but I said to Connie last week, I haven't seen our Alice in a long time. How is she?' I glanced down the hallway, just in time to see Connie stick her head round the living room door and offer us an anxious but smiling wave, before almost immediately disappearing again. Meanwhile, Greg wasn't pausing for breath. 'And I forget what

Connie said exactly,' he continued, 'but I got the impression that you're on the prowl for men, Alice.' He made clawing motions with his hands, whilst growling. 'Grrrr… Alice on the hunt. Well, I tell you what. You just think of me as a lame gazelle and we'll see how we go.' He put his arm around me and squeezed hard, revealing, as usual, zero appreciation for both his own strength and the concept of personal space. 'Ah, but you know I'm only teasing, don't you?' He released me from his constrictor grip, but kept his arm extended behind me and poked Jon who was now standing alongside me. 'I say, Jon, she knows I'm only teasing.' He recommenced the clawing. 'Grrrr…'

I smiled weakly.

'How is work, Greg?' Jon asked.

'It's funny you should mention work, Jonathan, because that's another thing I wanted to say to Alice…' He beckoned us to follow him. 'Come into the kitchen and I'll sort you out with some drinks. So yes, another thing, Alice, is that if you're after a man—'

'Well, I—' I held up a hand but he didn't pause.

'I actually work with a very personable one. His name is Stephen and he has a Morgan.' He looked at me significantly.

'Ooh…' I said, uncertainly. 'Wow…'

'Alice doesn't know what a Morgan is, Greg,' said Jon. He had walked over to the bottles of wine and soft drinks already open on the black granite work surface, and was now standing with his back to us. 'You don't mind if I help myself, do you? I'll just grab a drink and go and say hello to everyone, while you tell Alice all about the Morgan.' He poured a glass of red wine and then turned and walked towards the kitchen door. 'And about Stephen,' he added, as he exited.

'Not at all, not at all,' called Greg. 'You carry on, Jon. But yes, Alice, he has a Morgan 4/4, four-seater, with a walnut dash and a five-speed gearbox.' His eyes widened and he nodded at me excitedly. I realised it was my turn to speak.

'Oh, I see, it's a *car*,' I said, smiling.

His smile dropped momentarily and he looked at me, clearly stunned by my ignorance. 'Yes, of course it's a car. And not just any car.'

'No?' I said, trying desperately to appear intrigued.

'No.' He stared off dreamily into the middle distance. 'Its power to weight ratio is—'

'Hey, Alice.' I turned to see Sophie, my saviour in a bright red dress and four inch heels, standing in the open kitchen doorway. 'Stop annoying Greg. Connie's just told me he has somewhere else to be tonight.'

'Oh, my goodness.' Greg checked his watch. 'She's right and now I'm verging on late.'

'Yeah, so come on, Alice,' said Sophie, walking towards me and taking my hand. 'Let Greg get on with getting on, and you come and talk books.'

-

Discussion of *Ethan Frome*, when it began, was lively, with everyone, apart from myself, having read it and loved it. Having read only the first fifteen pages the previous evening, before being too easily distracted from the tale's wintery gloom by a phone call from Dad, I somewhat shame-facedly, took on the role of assistant hostess, hoping to deflect attention from my silence by busying myself topping-up drinks and passing round the nibbles.

And it was as I did a second round with a bottle of red wine, that Connie half raised her hand and coughed lightly, as she always did when wishing to make a point. We all turned towards her.

'I adored this book,' she began hesitantly, in the gentle transatlantic murmur which I always found strangely calming, no matter what she was saying. 'But Zeena seems such a wholly unsympathetic character that I found myself wanting to read it a second time, to see if I could spot one shred of goodness in her.' She cleared her throat and looked down, adjusting the cuffs of her white shirt. 'Because I did have a little difficulty with Ethan's choices and loyalties – no matter what the financial circumstances.'

Abs nodded. 'You're *so* right about Zeena, Connie. I must read it again too, because as far as I can remember, her only show of emotion was over the broken pickle dish.' She wound a strand of her long, dark hair thoughtfully around her finger. 'I teach some very difficult and troubled children, but I do believe there's some good to be found in everyone, if you look hard enough. And it's interesting to think that giving Zeena just one or two sympathetic moments, might change everything for us. If she cared for Ethan, but he still wanted Mattie, how would we have felt then?'

'Well, that would be a totally different story,' said Miriam flatly. 'I'd lose all sympathy for him. We all have faults, marriages aren't perfect, but if one person is trying, then the other person should too.'

'I'm not sure I'd lose *all* sympathy,' said Sophie. 'I mean, you can't always help who you fall for, can you? Even if you think you're happy and even if you're living with a saint. You can't control everything and situations are never black and white.'

'But at the same time,' Miriam frowned, 'you can't just do what you want regardless of the consequences. You sometimes have to set your own feelings aside and think long term and about all the other people involved.'

'Which is what Ethan does,' said Jon. 'It's what holds him back.'

Sophie turned to him. 'I agree with Connie. I was really pissed off with him for holding back.'

I glanced at Connie, who, aside from a little rapid blinking, seemed remarkably at peace with this earthy reinterpretation of her comment.

Jon looked at Sophie. 'So you'd have just gone for it?'

'Me? No.' She shook her head and laughed. 'I'm all mouth and no trousers. But I was still screaming at the page for *him* to just act now and think later, weren't you?'

'It's hard to take a leap when you're uncertain of the consequences,' said Jon. 'Or when you can spot potentially negative ones.'

Sophie looked at him, her head tilted slightly, and then, sitting back in her seat and still gazing at him, she said, 'Yes.'

Abs then said something about the conflicts between head and heart, but as Connie rose to her feet and gently took the bottle of red wine from me, my focus remained on Jon and Sophie, each now clearly deep in thought. And as an unusually sombre Jon thanked Connie as his glass was topped up, I felt frustratingly in the dark and strangely distanced from him. It was a feeling I didn't like and, putting it down to an inability to fathom his reaction to *Ethan Frome*, I found myself for the first time hugely regretting my failure to finish the chosen book.

I was therefore very grateful when, just fifteen minutes later, everyone moved on from Ethan and his emotional dilemmas and financial woes, to the real purpose of the evening – namely the mutual extraction and exchange of as much personal information as possible within a two to three hour period. Sophie recounted, to much laughter and aw-ing, David's near-miss with Eleanor Black, or Mrs Melons, as Sophie now called her. And, as I exited the lounge to make myself a cup of tea, Miriam was updating Abs about Phoebe's progress at pre-school.

I returned a few minutes later, to find Jon and Sophie discussing a recent performance at the Tobacco Factory, whilst the sofa conversation had broadened to include Connie's three year-old son, William, with Connie confessing to Miriam and Abs a difficulty in standing firm in the face of his tantrums. I sat down on a large beanbag to the left of the sofa to listen-in.

'You are such a strong mother, Miriam,' said Connie. 'I wish I had your courage to discipline. And Abigail, you face such challenging issues at school every single day. I know my problems must seem very small.'

'Not at all. I think *you* are just amazing, Connie,' said Abs. 'I get coffee breaks and lunch breaks and my evenings to myself. You're on call as a mother twenty-four seven. I think you're doing a brilliant job with William. You mustn't put yourself down.'

I saw Miriam's lips purse and she gave a light cough.

'How is William, Connie?' I asked.

She shook her head despairingly. 'Well, you know, Greg says it's a zest for life but sometimes I think...' Her voice trailed away.

'That you need to curtail his zest a little,' said Miriam. I knew that she wasn't overly fond of William, or the zest, which had recently manifested itself in him painting the dog green.

'I think that's exactly it, Miriam,' said Connie. 'The other evening, he made a cake on the carpet and I said, "You've made a mistake,

William," very strongly...' There was a slight pause, during which I knew we were each struggling to resist querying the term *cake*, as well as to form a mental image of Connie doing anything *very strongly*. 'And then I put him in his room for a time-out. But Greg said he thought that was overly harsh and that, after all, boys will be boys. So, it was a very short time-out.'

'How short?' asked Miriam. Her tone was clipped.

'Ooh,' Connie studied her lap, 'I would say just one or two minutes.'

'Right,' said Miriam, colouring slightly. 'Well, Connie, perhaps, as you're the one doing the majority of the parenting, and are also the person who has to spend most daytimes with William, you should put it to Greg that maybe he should defer to your judgement in some matters. You must assert, Connie, you really must,' she insisted.

I frowned up at her. Miriam was frequently strident in her opinions, but not often impatient.

'That's just what the instructor says to me every week, when I take Jello to doggy training,' said Connie, looking, I thought, a little cowed.

'Ooh, doggy training. How fascinating!' exclaimed Abs.

'And how is Jello getting on?' I asked, glancing at an unusually stern-looking Miriam, and keen to keep the conversation off parenting.

'Well, he's now doing so much better off the lead,' said Connie. 'And he's stopped menacing elderly people with walking frames.'

'Brilliant!' said Abs. 'It must be amazing to see things progressing like that.'

'Well, yes,' said Connie uncertainly. 'Although, he's still eating a lot of things he shouldn't.'

'Like what?' I asked.

'Well, he does eat his own...' Connie hesitated and pointed downwards '...poop,' she mouthed soundlessly. 'And two weeks ago he ate a fridge magnet and a loaf of bread, still in the bag. That took a visit to the vet to put right. But fortunately, we have pet insurance,' she concluded brightly.

Sophie leaned forward in her chair. 'Did I just hear you say that your dog is eating his own sh—'

I braced myself.

'—his own poo, Connie?' She looked at me and I rolled my eyes at the near miss.

'That is correct, Sophie,' said Connie. 'Apparently, it's not uncommon, you know.'

Sophie's face crumpled and she made a gagging sound. 'I am never, *ever* getting a dog.'

'I sometimes think I'd quite like a cat,' I mused. 'Except I wouldn't want to be labelled *single saddo with cat*.'

'Rather than just *single saddo*?' asked Sophie.

I pointedly ignored her.

'Well,' chipped in Abs with a grin, 'maybe you won't be single for long, Alice.'

'Oh my goodness,' gasped Connie. 'Did it go well with Hugh then?'

I managed a smile as my heart sank. 'We went to a lovely new coffee shop on the Gloucester Road,' I said, deciding to stick to a policy of minimal information.

'Would anyone mind if I had a pretend fag?' asked Sophie, rummaging in her bag. 'And yes, I'm doing very well on the quitting front, thank you very much everyone for asking.'

'Well done you, Sophie,' Abs beamed. 'But, getting back to Hugh…'

Sophie's attempt to divert the conversation having failed, she shot me a sympathetic, side-long glance and commenced sucking on her plastic cigarette.

'…he is just lovely,' continued Abs. 'He has so very many fascinating facets to his personality, it's hard to believe.'

'Yes, it is,' I murmured.

Abs nodded enthusiastically, Miriam pressed her leg into my shoulder and Jon looked at me with something approaching disapproval, before turning to Abs. 'So,' he said, 'remind me how you know Hugh?'

'He studied with Pete at King's,' she explained. 'And Pete is *so* over the moon to be back in touch with him.'

I looked at Abs and wondered, not for the first time, about the criteria she used for judging her partner's levels of excitement. Peter Goodwin was an anaesthetist most notable for his serenity. He and Abs had been together for just over two years and I was always uncertain whether to put his calm disposition down to a refusal to be seen as attempting to compete with his partner's boundless energy and enthusiasm, or to the daily seepage of anaesthetic gases. But, either way, he was placid beyond belief, and the contrast between his own personality and that of his girlfriend was one which I found almost as fascinating as Abs found Hugh.

'And is Hugh an anaesthetist too?' asked Jon, leaning forward in his armchair and smiling at Abs. 'What does he do?'

I looked at him and silently cursed his polite curiosity for extending the conversation.

'Well,' Abs clasped her hands together in childlike delight at an opportunity to sing Hugh's praises, 'his specialty is forensic pathology and he was top of his year in absolutely everything. He's the same age as you, Jon, thirty-five, and he's from Edinburgh originally. And his accent is just *fabulous*,' she continued excitedly. 'He went back up to Scotland when he graduated and then did a stint in London, but he's now in Bristol and,' she turned to me and beamed, 'I thought he and Alice would get on very well and they did! He's so gorgeous, so interesting and so very clever; just like Alice.'

'You are joking,' I protested.

Abs shook her head. 'You're being modest. You and Hugh are far too clever for me. So many things just go completely over my head. Remember when you said he had the personality of one of his corpses,' I shifted uncomfortably on my beanbag, 'and I just couldn't quite tell whether you were joking or not.'

All eyes turned towards me and I felt myself redden. I opened my mouth with the intention of acknowledging my poor delivery, and reassuring Abs regarding her intelligence levels, but Miriam beat me to it.

'For goodness sake, Abs,' she said. 'How can you say that? You're the brightest and most academic amongst us.' She pointed at herself.

'Look at me: intellect stagnating, weight increasing. I'm turning into a full-time frump in a frock. I put this dress on to come out,' she pulled at the neckline of her wrap-around dress, 'and I said to Craig, "I look like a poorly-constructed sausage in this." And he laughed and said, "Yes, you do, actually".' She smiled in an uncertain way and, to my horror, I realised that she was on the verge of tears. There was a general chorus of compliments around the room regarding her appearance and I reached up and squeezed her arm.

'Stop fishing,' I said. 'You know you're fabulous.'

'Oh, it's fine.' She cleared her throat and patted my hand. 'I'm well aware that I'm past my prime. If I ever had one,' she added quietly.

There followed a moment's uneasy silence, which was suddenly, and to my enormous relief, broken by the sound of a duck quacking loudly from Abs' end of the sofa.

'Ooh, sorry,' she said, shuffling forward and reaching into the back pocket of her jeans. 'It's a text. Thought I'd put it on vibrate.' Grateful for the opportunity to focus on someone other than Miriam, we all watched as she extricated her phone and looked at the screen, her eyes widening in excitement. 'Ooh, you'll never guess what!' she exclaimed, looking round the room, before fixing her gaze on me.

A trickle of dread ran down my spine. I wasn't entirely sure what was coming, but I had a sneaking suspicion I wasn't going to like it.

'Hugh…' began Abs, providing immediate confirmation that my early sense of foreboding was well-placed. 'Hugh is back and Alice…' She paused teasingly once again, before delivering a spectacular coup de grace to any lingering hope I may have had that her news might be uplifting, '…he's planning something brilliant for you.'

Four years ago

'Oh, don't look like that,' said Lydia, smiling at me from across the table. 'It's not as bad as it sounds.'

I nodded, avoiding further eye contact by looking around the small, cool basement of the Clifton wine bar, which we currently had all to ourselves. 'I'm just thinking it through,' I said, attempting a smile, whilst feeling stunned; her words having forced a recollection of my mother's cancer diagnosis five years earlier. I glanced across at Miriam. She was smiling, but her expression had taken on a glazed quality.

'Patient recovery statistics for this kind of lymphoma are really good,' continued Lydia steadily. 'And treatment is going to start immediately. Everybody's very optimistic.'

'Of course,' said Miriam. 'You're twenty-eight, young and fit and they're not wasting any time, which is great.' She looked at me.

'When is your first session?' I asked, fighting the onset of tears with a practical enquiry.

'Next Thursday.' Lydia smiled. 'And I'm honestly fine about it. I just want to get on with things now.' She paused and her smile fell a little. 'It's Jon I'm worried about,' she said. 'I reassure him that I'm OK and he tries to look reassured but…' Her breath came in a little gasp and suddenly, the possibility of tears from her, stifled my own selfish ones.

'We'll reassure him too,' I said, reaching out and taking her hand.

'Definitely,' said Miriam. 'You mustn't worry.'

'Miriam is right,' I said. 'Please don't worry, because Jon would really *worry if he thought that you were worrying about him being worried.'*

Miriam turned and looked at me blankly. 'What?'

I smiled. 'I got on a wheel of worry and just couldn't get off.'

Lydia laughed. 'I love you both so much,' she said. And as Miriam and I echoed the sentiment and the three of us enveloped each other in a mutual hug, I maintained my smile, remaining determinedly within the moment, and refusing to think about what may be to come.

Chapter 8

I was feeling much better about all things Hugh by the time I arrived at Moore Interior Design the morning after the book group meeting at Connie's. I still wasn't exactly looking forward to seeing him again, or to whatever he might have planned for the pair of us, but Sophie, I had decided, was right. It would be completely wrong of me to dismiss him after just one, very brief, encounter and I was determined to stick to the promises I had made to my friends and to Dad, to remain open to all new possibilities and, more specifically, not to stand anybody up. Consequently, I was in relatively positive mood as I keyed in the security code, leaned heavily against the stubborn, red front door of the small Victorian terrace house in which our offices were located, and entered.

My sense of well-being, however, was to prove very short-lived.

'Unbelievable! Absolutely un… bloody… believable!' Sophie's voice rang out and reached me immediately, as it did most workday mornings. Usually, however, it was the sound of her raucous laughter, or a high-volume, highly-efficient, first-thing call to a client which greeted me on arrival. Anger was rare.

I walked along the narrow hallway, past Lewis Twinney Legal, the law firm which occupied the ground floor, and up the stairs. I paused and peered in through the partially-open office door, deciding it best to try and discover the nature of the disturbance, or disagreement, before entering.

'Honestly, David!' I could see Sophie, standing by her desk and in full flow. 'What do I have to do? Tell me. What do I have to do? I had warned her off. You were safe. All you had to do was say, "Yes, that's right. I'm gay." But, no.' She threw up her hands in exasperation.

'You're thirty-seven, David. Thirty-seven! And yet still not enough of a man to say you're gay.'

At this point, I heard a brief, low mumbling; not dissimilar to the kind of noise a dog makes when dreaming. I assumed it to be David, attempting to put forward a case. But whatever kind of defence he offered, Sophie was unimpressed. 'Oh don't give me that! That's bollocks. Utter, *utter* bollocks. You are not *drawn* to her. I saw you when you were with her. You did everything but pat yourself down for a piece of garlic and a silver stake. The woman is a bloody nightmare. You know it and I know it.'

At this point, she stepped out of my line of sight and I took a deep breath and entered.

David was seated at Sophie's desk and now leaning back in her chair at a precarious angle. She, meanwhile, was bending menacingly over him, her face just a few inches from his. At around 6ft tall, he usually towered above her, even though she habitually wore heels. She always, therefore, made him sit down for a telling-off. Both turned to look at me as I walked in; Sophie wore an expression of enraged despair, whilst David looked like a man in need of a new pair of trousers.

'Thank God, you're here, Alice,' said Sophie, straightening up.

'Yes, thank God,' said David, adjusting the jacket of his impeccably-tailored light brown suit.

'Will you try talking some sense into him?' Sophie pointed at David. 'Because, you know, I'm really on the verge of washing my hands of him.' She whirled round, stomped over to the hat-stand and unhooked her jacket. 'I need a coffee. A proper one. I'll be back in five.' And, with that, she swept from the office, slamming the door noisily behind her.

I turned to David. He leaned forward, placing his elbows on Sophie's desk and resting his head in his hands.

'Well?' I said.

He looked up at me sadly and opened his mouth to speak, only to be interrupted by Sophie's sudden return.

'Can I get either of you two something?' she asked quietly, poking her head round the door. 'Cappuccino and a croissant, Alice?'

I smiled and nodded. 'That'd be great, thanks.'

She looked at David. 'I'll get you an Americano, David.' She withdrew her head. 'And one of those iced flapjacks you like,' she added, before closing the door once again, this time with a quiet click.

I hung up my coat, placed my bag on the floor by my desk and sat down. David's position and expression were unchanged.

'What happened?' I asked. 'Or do you not want to talk about it?'

He sighed, leaned back in Sophie's chair and addressed the ceiling. 'Eleanor Black phoned me at home on Friday night…'

'Oh, David…'

He didn't pause but instead continued in the manner of an unhappy participant in a school play, desperate to recite his lines, and get it all over with, as quickly as possible. 'She said she was planning a house party for the first weekend in May, when the redesign is complete, and thought I might like to come along and network. I said thank you for the invitation and that I would check my diary. She said: "I didn't realise you were gay." I said: "Neither did I." She said: "Your colleague said you were gay." I said: "There must be some misunderstanding. I am not homosexual." She said: "I have some concerns regarding the Aga. There's a new restaurant on Chandos Road, I'd like to go there. Why don't we kill two birds with one stone?" And, well…' He ground to a halt, concluding his speech with a forlorn shrug.

'Well, maybe it's not too late to get out of it. I could…'

He shook his head.

'You've already been?'

'Yes. We went on Saturday night. Sophie knows because she just took a call from Eleanor confirming that she's free tonight.'

'And had you asked Eleanor if she was free tonight?'

He shook his head again.

'Oh,' I switched on the Mac, 'well, obviously Sophie has already had a go at you – so I'm not going to add to that.' I looked at him. 'But I really don't know why you do it to yourself, David. You're not pretending to be attracted to the woman, are you? Because I've met her and, as far as I can see, she's a cross between a moneyed Bet Lynch and…' I hesitated, before adding in an undertone, 'a viper.'

'I didn't quite catch that,' David transferred his gaze from the ceiling to me, 'fortunately.'

I smiled. 'Look, it's your life but I'm just not certain why you keep going out with women who are… like that. Especially when you could do so much better.'

'Could I?' he sighed.

'Oh, please. You know you could,' I said. 'So, anyway, are you going out with Ms Black tonight?'

He groaned. 'I'm not sure. I've got to phone her now. Sophie's told her that I'm attending a Zumba class…' He paused and looked across at me mournfully. '…with several men friends.'

I laughed and he joined in. 'You know she does it because she loves you.'

He stood up from Sophie's chair and walked towards his office. 'Yes. Tough love, they call it, don't they?' he murmured, before offering me a tired smile, entering his office and pulling the door to behind him.

I returned my attention to my screen but was delighted to be distracted from the task of dealing with emails, within just ten minutes, by the ring of the telephone. I picked it up gratefully. 'Hello, Moore Interior Design. Alice Waites speaking.'

'Hi, Alice. How are you?'

'Hello!' I said, adopting my best delighted-to-hear-from-you-despite-being-clueless-as-to-your-identity tone. 'I'm just fine, thank you. How can I help?'

'Well, er…' The caller hesitated and laughed; a laugh which immediately transformed my smile into a frozen, horrified grimace. 'It's great to hear you sounding on such good form,' he continued. 'I know it's been a while but…' he laughed again, 'I was wondering if you'd be up for a drink. I'm coming to Bristol.'

It was at this point that Sophie returned. She entered the office, having clearly begun an inaudible conversation with me halfway up the stairs. 'I know,' she said. 'It's just that he winds me up. It would have been so easy to say, "Yes, I'm gay." It was on a plate for…' She paused and looked at me; her face a mixture of concern and puzzlement. I sat motionless and in silence, the phone pressed against my ear. 'What is it?' she mouthed, placing a tray of drinks and a brown paper bag on my desk. 'Who's on the phone?'

I said nothing, staring at her dumbly, whilst she gently relieved me of the phone. 'Hello,' she said, 'this is Sophie Carter. I'm afraid Alice has a problem with her line, so she's transferred the call. How can I help?' There was a pause as she listened to the voice on the other end of the line and I watched her expression harden. 'Right,' she said tonelessly, picking up a pen from my desk and beginning to write, 'well, I'll pass that on. No, she can't, I'm afraid. A client has arrived and she's dealing with them now. As I said, I'll pass all that on. Bye.' She hung up the phone, before adding, 'You lowlife bastard.' She walked to my side of the desk, crouched down, took my hand and looked up at me. 'You OK, Alice?' she asked gently. I nodded and she placed the Post-it note, with its scribbled numbers, in front of me. 'That's Eddie's new mobile number and that one is his landline. He's in Bristol the week after next.' She squeezed my hand. 'Are you sure you're OK? I'd be more convinced if you said something. Or blinked, maybe.' She smiled. 'Just a blink?'

I returned the smile and performed an exaggerated blink. 'I'm OK,' I said at last. Although, of course, we both knew that I wasn't.

Three years ago

'Remember when we first met?' Lydia closed her eyes and leaned back in one of the pair of deep red armchairs, which Jon had moved from lounge to bedroom the day before.

I settled myself in the other chair and picked up my mug of coffee from the low, dark wood table which sat between us – another recent arrival from downstairs. 'Of course I do,' I said. 'My first impression was that you were scarily organised.' I sipped my coffee. 'And I was right.'

She opened her eyes and laughed, and for a moment I saw not the frail twenty-nine year-old, exhausted and disfigured by medication, but the smiling eighteen year-old university student, beckoning me into her room.

'I think about it a lot,' she said. 'I was so grateful to you that day. It was such a kind, brave thing to do – to knock on my door like that.'

I smiled. 'I was lonely and desperate.'

She laughed again, before starting to cough. I put down my coffee, stood up and walked the few steps to her chair. 'Here,' I said, 'let me move that pillow for you, it's slipped.' She leaned forward and I adjusted the pillow.

'Thank you, Alice,' she said, as I returned to my chair and sat back down. 'And I don't just mean for plumping my pillow.'

I had been reaching for my coffee but now stopped short and looked up at her, hearing a change in her voice which left me afraid of what she might say next. Unable to speak, I simply shook my head.

'We met with the oncologist on Monday,' she said softly. 'There hasn't been the progress they hoped for. And I just want to enjoy the life I have left.'

I continued to gaze at her; reluctant to accept what I knew she was telling me. I widened my eyes and tilted my head back slightly in a failed attempt to prevent the escape of a tear. I wiped it away, under guise of scratching my cheek.

'But,' she continued, without hesitation, 'I have something important I'd like to talk to you about.'

I found my voice. 'Like that wasn't important,' I said quietly.

She smiled and took a deep breath. 'Jon would like to join the book group.'

I blinked, the shock nature of the proposal providing a fleeting, but welcome, distraction.

'He wants to join the book group?' I echoed, unable to keep a note of surprise from my voice.

'Yes,' she said. 'We've discussed it, and he'd like to join. Not right away but…' she paused, '…maybe in a few months.'

I fought a renewed urge to cry, determined to be supportive, while feeling devastated at the possibility of being so soon without her.

'He's promised me he'll go and,' she looked down at her hands, 'if you're all happy for him to join, I'd love you to encourage him in that if…,' she added, '…if he ever seems reluctant.' She looked up. 'I don't want him to be alone or to feel alone, Alice,' she said, her expression suddenly and agonisingly anxious. 'That's my only worry. My only *worry,' she emphasised.*

I stood up and walked to her for a second time, this time crouching at the side of her chair. 'We'll make it work,' I said. 'I promise you, Lydia. He won't be alone.'

She reached out and stroked my hair; her features softening back into their usual calm. 'Thank you,' she said. 'Again.'

'Thank you*,' I whispered and then lowering my head, unable to be strong any longer, I began to cry. 'I'm so sorry,' I said. 'But I can't pretend this is OK. I can't pretend to myself that you don't matter to me. Even for a moment. Even to be helpful.'*

I leaned forward and we held each other, neither of us saying anything more. We remained that way for some time, before I eventually forced myself to let her go. Reaching for a box of tissues on the bedside cabinet, I took one and then passed the box to Lydia. She took a tissue and dabbed her eyes.

'So, anyway,' I said blowing my nose and sitting down on the bed. 'Have you explained to Jon that the book group is just a cover for getting together and drinking lots of wine?'

Lydia sighed, closed her eyes and leaned back in the armchair once more. 'Oh yes,' she said quietly, now smiling to herself. 'He's quite clear about that.'

Chapter 9

'OK, so you called Eddie back and he said…?' Sophie glanced towards the long bar of The Albion, where David was buying our drinks. We hadn't had an opportunity to discuss Eddie earlier in the day, thanks to the inconvenient scheduling of meetings out of the office, so Sophie had proposed drinks after work. It had been a determined invitation that I hadn't even attempted to refuse, feeling reluctant to go home to an empty flat and dwell on the very brief, and yet supremely depressing, telephone conversation I had snatched with Eddie that afternoon. I had also agreed to her suggestion that we invite David along, confident that he would provide a steadying voice of reason, and prevent either Sophie or myself from becoming over emotional in our analysis of the situation. Nevertheless, despite agreeing to come out, I couldn't claim to be looking forward to the conversation.

'…and he said?' Sophie repeated, looking at me expectantly and then back at David. 'Actually, we'd better wait until David sits down, or he'll just be forever asking annoying catch-up questions. I'll go and hurry him along.' She stood up and went to help him. I couldn't hear their conversation but he shook his head in a faux despairing manner and laughed. In spite of my mood, I found myself smiling at the fascinating and, at times, ridiculous nature of their relationship. He was eminently shockable and she was frighteningly frank. He was both terrified and fond of her in equal measure and she, despite being five years his junior, scolded and protected him as a mother would, whilst at the same time respecting him utterly professionally, and working her socks off for him on a daily basis, as did I. Despite an only partially-suppressed conviction that my job was too much fun to be "proper", I did work hard for David. And our joint efforts as a threesome seemed to pay off; we regularly had to decline offers of work, putting us in the commercially enviable position of being able to cherry-pick our clients.

David and Sophie now returned to the table. He sat down, still laughing, while she handed me a large glass of white wine. 'Here,' she said, sitting down and nudging me amiably with her elbow, 'get that down you and tell us all.' She leaned eagerly towards me and rubbed her hands. But, despite the flippancy of her body language, I knew she was worried. I tried to sound reassuringly unconcerned.

'Well, as you know, Eddie is in Bristol in a couple of weeks' time. He's here on business, and staying for two nights in that boutique hotel on Welsh Back. He wants to meet up there for a drink.' I shrugged. 'That's it, really.' I picked up my glass and took a large gulp.

'And, er...' began David, 'are you going to go?'

They both looked at me questioningly. 'Well, I think I will. I mean,' I took another large draught of wine, 'there's enough water under the bridge. I don't really see a problem.' They exchanged glances in a rapid, anxious manner. 'What?' I asked. 'Why are you looking at each other like that? It would be churlish not to go, wouldn't it?'

'I just think I'd want to know whether he had anything particular in mind to discuss first,' said Sophie.

'Like what? We've got no matters outstanding,' I said, feeling defensive, but not entirely sure of what. 'Maybe he just wants to apologise.'

She rolled her eyes. 'Well, if he does, it'd be about bloody time.'

'And how is that kind of comment supposed to help, exactly?' I asked, now feeling irritated. 'He suggested a drink and I felt I had to say yes, to avoid looking twisted and bitter. That's the situation.'

'Oh, I'm sorry,' said Sophie, placing a calming hand on mine. 'It's just that I really, really hate the bastard.'

'And whilst I might not quite have put it quite in those terms,' said David, shifting in his seat and looking uncomfortable, as he always did whenever Sophie used what he called *coarse* or *man language*, 'I do have to agree with Sophie's sentiment there, Alice. I would be wary of his purpose.'

I sighed. 'He's not exactly my favourite person in the world either, you know,' I said. 'But I don't want to...' I hesitated, uncertain of my feelings, 'I guess I just don't want to live in fear of him. I'd like to be able to shrug him off… to not go into shock when he calls. I think I need closure.'

'And if he turns up and says: *Darling, I don't know what came over me. But now I know it's you I want. Let's try again?*' Sophie avoided eye contact as she spoke, focusing instead on her vodka and tonic.

I shook my head. 'He's not going to say that, Sophie.'

'I was just hoping for an "I'll say no" from you, actually,' she said, looking up at me.

I tutted. 'OK, then. I'll say no.'

She smiled, squeezed my hand and then turned her attention to David. 'And *you* could practise saying that a bit too, you know. It's not that hard. It's just a "nuh" sound, followed by an "o". Very easy.'

'Oh for goodness sake,' said David, sounding as close as he ever did to exasperated. 'I went for dinner with Eleanor once. And I said "nuh", followed by an "o" to early drinks with her this evening, didn't I?'

Sophie's eyes narrowed. 'What do you mean, you said no to *early* drinks?' She flopped back in her chair and shook her head despairingly. 'My God. You're meeting her after this, aren't you?'

'And so what if I am?' said David, attempting defiance. He leaned towards Sophie and I found myself suddenly quite impressed. Sophie too, seemed slightly taken aback. 'It would,' he continued, 'have been extremely rude to say no. And, who knows, her dress sense might improve and her bullish nature might wane and I might, in the future, come to find her attractive.' I groaned internally and stopped being impressed. There was a moment's silence, during which Sophie sat up and eyed David in the manner of a lioness spotting a three-legged baby zebra at just around teatime. I spoke rapidly to prevent a kill.

'Look,' I said, holding up a hand to indicate that no interruptions would be tolerated, 'David has agreed to a less than perfect drinks date, as have I. There's nothing to be done about that now. We just have to try to make the best of the situations we find ourselves in.'

Sophie opened her mouth to raise, I assumed, some sort of objection, but then clearly thought better of it which, to be fair, she often did. 'Yes, well, actually,' she said after a moment, 'I have a plan which might help you with Eleanor, David.'

He looked up from his drink. 'Does it involve me claiming to be gay?' he asked quickly.

'No, it does not,' she said.

'And does it involve me…' he seemed to be searching for words, 'behaving in a manner with another man which might make somebody *assume* that I was gay?'

'No, it does not,' said Sophie, so calmly that I wondered whether that idea had indeed crossed her mind.

'OK,' said David, appearing to relax slightly, 'tell me your plan.'

'Well,' Sophie beamed, 'how about we *all* come to Mrs Melons' reveal party?' She folded her arms and sat back in her chair.

There was a pause, during which David's perpetually puzzled expression deepened. I too was struggling to spot a plan.

I gave up. 'Is that the plan?' I queried. 'The *entire* plan?'

'Of course not,' she tutted. 'I could bring Graham and maybe you could bring Jon.'

'OK, and is *that* the entire plan?' I pressed.

'Pretty much,' Sophie shrugged. 'I really think we could be a big help to David.'

David and I looked at each other. He spoke for us both. 'You want to go to a party with free food and alcohol, don't you?'

'Yes, I do,' said Sophie.

'And so, really, it's not a plan to help me at all, is it?' he said.

'It's a help everybody kind of plan,' she said brightly. 'Alice and I can protect you from Mrs Melons and drop further hints about you being gay and…'

'I don't like this plan,' said David. 'I'd rather you had a different plan.'

She sighed. 'Well, how about we just come along and make it a more relaxed, enjoyable evening for you?'

'Without the gay element?'

'Yes, without the gay *element*.' She emphasised the last word, swapping her usual Essex twang for David's boarding school drawl.

David smiled. 'That sounds rather nice. I'll put it to Mrs Mel… to Eleanor.' He looked at me. 'What do you think, Alice?'

'Sounds good to me,' I said. 'Actually, maybe I'll bring Hugh. Dilute our next meeting a bit.'

Sophie frowned. 'But I thought Abs said he already had something brilliant planned.'

'I missed a call from him yesterday,' I said wearily. 'He left a message but didn't mention any big plan, so maybe I could suggest this. I'd really prefer to see him in a group.'

'But the thing is,' said Sophie, 'I was talking to Jon on the phone the other day and he said he wanted to get out a bit more, now that work has eased up.'

'Did he?' I asked, feeling surprised. I'd heard little from Jon recently and had assumed his work schedule to be as high-pressure as ever.

'Yes,' said Sophie, leaning forwards and looking suddenly anxious. 'But for God's sake don't say I mentioned anything.'

'Of course not,' I said. 'But I'll invite him to the party and then you can still bring Graham.'

'Brill,' she said, relaxing back into her chair. 'Cos Graham says he's very keen to come.'

'And when did he say that?' asked David.

'This afternoon on the phone.'

'But you've only just suggested the idea,' said David, looking confused. 'I haven't discussed it with Eleanor yet.'

Sophie blinked. 'I'm sorry. I don't understand your point, David.'

He sighed and reached for his drink. 'Never mind. I'm sure it'll all be fine.'

'Why wouldn't it be?' said Sophie, beaming at us both. 'It's a marvellous plan.'

Chapter 10

Edward Hall was, when I met him, a twenty-eight year-old reporter with the Bristol Evening Post, covering everything from local fêtes to local murders. In addition, he was the restaurant critic for a free magazine, had just completed his first novel and, on the evening we first met, he was very excited to have had his fourth piece accepted for a national glossy men's mag. I, meanwhile, was twenty-seven, the opposite of driven and clueless as to my preferred career direction.

I had been working at Moore Interior Design for about a week when Sophie's short-lived predecessor, Carrie, suggested a pub crawl, followed by clubbing. I had accepted her invitation reluctantly, having noticed the look of fear in my new boss's eye when she proposed the outing – and this was despite the fact that he hadn't even been asked to join us. However, reluctant to appear boring and anti-social from the off, I had agreed to go along.

So it was that I had found myself, six hours later, sitting alone, and largely sober, in a slightly dodgy nightclub I hadn't visited since my student days. And as midnight approached, I smiled bravely, swayed and waved an arm, in an attempt to show willing, whilst Carrie and her friend, Tara, gyrated on the dance floor and wiped their noses on the backs of their hands in an excited, energetic manner, which suggested they weren't actually suffering from colds.

Just when I had decided to fake an emergency call from Dad in order to engineer an exit, Eddie had flopped down next to me, said, 'I'm not on the pull. I'm just knackered,' and that, as they say, was that.

We were a couple for almost three years, living together in the garden flat I had bought with Dad's help, for two of those. For the first eighteen months of our relationship, I thought Eddie was perfect.

For the next eighteen months, I was increasingly doubtful of that fact and, for the final twelve hours of our co-habitation, I recognised him for the complete and utter shit he really was. And not just a momentary shit. An ongoing, long-term shit.

During our relationship, Eddie was away from home on a regular basis – at least three or four times a month. I suppose if I had been of a more suspicious nature, I might have thought this was unusual for someone with such a local and laptop-based occupation. But he was never away for more than a night or two at a time, and his reasons for absence were always highly plausible and even, as in the case of his regular visits to his last remaining relative, an elderly great aunt in Bournemouth, rather sweet. I had met Great Aunty Mo on a number of occasions and also spoken to her on the phone. She was a lovely, if slightly vague, woman in her seventies. And she was totally besotted with her adoring great nephew, who lavished so much time and attention upon her.

Trips to see Great Aunty Mo aside, Eddie was partial to the odd lads' weekend away and he also wangled and accepted as many invitations to book launches and literary gatherings as he could; the latter with the sole purpose of meeting agents and publishers to whom he could push his novel. As it turned out, it was a tactic which paid off, when he eventually landed a small, but significant, publishing deal for his first book and an advance for a second novel, which, by the time our relationship entered its third year, was already close to completion. He was delighted and I was delighted for him. His work for the national glossies continued to increase steadily, thanks, in part at least, to his determined networking and this in turn enabled him to swap his reporting job for a weekly column. All was rosy – professionally, at least.

On the domestic front, things weren't quite so great. Although I was far from being unhappy, I felt that Eddie was, at times, a little unforthcoming, both emotionally and socially. He seemed to view any enquiries from my friends about his career and friendships as intrusive, rather than interested, and he had a particularly strained relationship with Sophie, despite the fact that, with the exception of the odd encounter at parties, he saw her only when he popped into the office to meet me for lunch. For her part, Sophie rarely mentioned him and it was this striking lack of expressed opinion which made her disapproval so obvious to me. Eddie, on the other hand, was extremely vocal and unequivocal in his dislike of her, his criticisms beginning almost immediately after her appointment, which was just three months after my own. In contrast, I liked her from day one, and what I saw as Eddie's unreasonable prejudice was one of the few issues over which he and I actually argued. On all other matters, any concerns I had over Eddie were largely internalised and, I later realised, unacknowledged.

The end then, when it came, was a shock; our relationship being brought to a sudden and explosive conclusion by one of those coincidences people love to recount in the pub.

The day of the coincidence, Eddie was away. In fact, he had been away for five days, combining a visit to a literary festival in Oxfordshire, with a cycling break with friends. I meanwhile, was treating Miriam to lunch, followed by drinks, for her birthday, which fell the following week. What she didn't know, until the morning of the treat, was that we were lunching not in Bristol, but in London. The change of location had been made just twenty-four hours earlier, when Craig had phoned me to say that he had been offered two seats in a shared box for *The Woman in Black* at The Fortune Theatre the next day. I, of course, said he should take Miriam himself but he refused, claiming that it wasn't really his type of thing. Instead, he wondered if I would mind re-locating our lunch to London, if he sorted out the train tickets. I thought it a lovely idea and immediately set about booking a pre-theatre lunch.

The next day, Craig dropped Miriam and I at Temple Meads at 10.15am and we were in London by half past twelve and sitting down to eat in Covent Garden by one-thirty. From there, it was just a two minute walk to The Fortune and we took our seats in the otherwise empty box in good time for the start of the matinee at 3pm.

'These are great seats, aren't they?' Miriam opened a Twix and leaned forward over the edge of the box. 'I wonder when the others will get here.'

I tapped her shoulder. 'Remind me of Craig's friends' names again.'

'Sharon and Paul,' she said, sitting up. 'Hope they're not stuck in traffic,' she added absently.

'I'm sure they'll be here soon,' I said.

She turned to me and smiled. 'I love this. You always get a little more leg room in a box, don't you? And I've got chocolate.' She gestured towards her Twix. 'Do you want half?' she asked.

'No thanks.' I reached down into my bag and took out a small box of chocolate-covered raisins, 'I've got these.'

'Ooh, lovely,' she mumbled, her mouth now full of Twix. 'But don't they get stuck in your teeth?'

'A bit, but you can pick your teeth while the lights are down.' I opened the box and nudged her. 'Hey and you know what else is great about them?'

She shook her head. 'No, what?'

'They are brilliant,' I tapped a couple from the box into my hand, 'for throwing.'

'Alice!' She put an appalled hand to her mouth. 'Don't you dare!'

'Oh, as if I would.' I popped the raisins into my mouth.

Miriam looked at me.

I looked at Miriam.

'I dare you,' she mouthed.

'Are you serious?' She nodded, returning her hand to her mouth, with a mischievous schoolgirl air. 'OK, but we have to have a plan,' I said.

'A plan?'

'Yes, a *reactions* plan,' I explained. 'We select the target, I throw and then we look at each other and talk as if we're mid-conversation. We do *not* look at the target until a good twenty to thirty seconds has elapsed.'

'You've done this before, haven't you?' she said.

I nodded. 'Yes, I have. But not since I went to see *As You Like It* with the school.'

'Right.' Miriam clasped her hands and looked down eagerly into the stalls. There was now a steady stream of people arriving, creating a useful amount of noise and distraction. 'Let's find a target. How about you try and get it to land in somebody's hair. We need a woman with a bouffant do.'

'OK, but once I've done it, it's your turn.'

'Absolutely,' she said. 'But I do hope we don't get caught and asked to leave. Craig might not understand. There!' she exclaimed suddenly. 'Look! Purple rinse woman. Just there, to your right. About ten rows back – this end of the row.'

'I see her,' I said, tipping a fresh supply of raisins into my hand. 'Now remember, I throw and then we chat. Do not check the target.'

'Agreed,' she laughed. 'Oh no, wait!' She grabbed my arm.

'What?'

'I see an even better one!' Her eyes widened to near-perfect circles.

'Really?' I asked, amused as much by her enthusiasm for the project, as by the project itself.

She turned and placed her hand dramatically on my shoulder. 'Cleavage,' she said solemnly.

'Genius,' I responded, in an equally sombre tone. 'But is it accessible?'

'Oh God, yes.' She returned her gaze to the audience below and beckoned me to look over the side of the box. 'Her boobs look like they're on a tray.'

I leaned forward. 'Where?'

'Immediately below us. Blonde, black blouse with *far* too many buttons undone. Very little throwing required. You could drop it really. Or pop it on the edge and just nudge it over.'

I leaned forward a little farther. 'I don't see her.'

'She's right there. Look, I'll move along one.' Miriam shifted to the seat on her left and I in turn moved along.

'See her now?' She gestured downwards. 'See? She's sitting next to a man who looks… who looks…' Her voice trailed away into a whisper, so that the concluding words of her sentence, '*just like Eddie*', were barely audible. In fact, maybe they weren't audible. Maybe Miriam didn't actually utter them at all. Maybe I just concluded the sentence for myself, in my own head. Because I had already spotted the blonde.

And soon after spotting *her*, I spotted the man who turned, brushed his hand against her cheek and then kissed her with unmistakeable affection. I spotted Eddie.

After that, things seemed to happen either very quickly, or in slow motion. I'm not sure which. I became aware of someone, with impressive projection, standing up and shouting, 'Bastard! Bastard!' repeatedly and very loudly, and of a hush descending upon the assembling audience. I then realised that the person shouting was me.

I remember the momentary look of amusement on Eddie's face, as he tilted his head back to look, along with everybody else, towards the insane woman in the box, before he recognised the nutter as his girlfriend. His blonde companion grinned in scandalised mirth, before turning to Eddie to share her enjoyment of the moment and realising, with one glance at his horrified expression, exactly what was going on. And I remember exiting the box and brushing past a middle-aged couple; the man standing anxiously unmoving, as if made of marble, his hand extended in greeting. He seemed to reawaken as I ran past him, down the corridor towards the stairs, and I heard him calling after me, 'Hello, I'm Paul!' in a manner so inappropriately cheery that I can only assume he was either in shock, or on the spectrum.

A heavily-puffing Miriam managed to catch up with me before I made it to the stalls and somehow convinced me that, actually, the best thing to do would not be to beat Eddie to a pulp with my bare hands but to sit in the now deserted bar and wait until she had gone in search of him. A very lovely, incredibly young, male theatre employee was tasked to sit with me and keep me from both the glassware and the alcohol behind the bar. The poor boy, who looked about sixteen, tried to engage me in a number of topics of conversation, including the musicals of Rogers and Hammerstein. But he gave that up as a bad job, and took to sitting silently with his head in his hands, when I burst into tears during a sudden, unhinged attempt to sing '*Doe a Deer*.'

By the time Miriam returned, without Eddie, I had entered the shuddering, dribbling, hiccoughing stage of despair and my chaperone had poured himself a large Scotch.

She sat down next to me and put an arm around my shoulder. 'He's gone, Alice,' she said, kissing my cheek.

'Are you sure?'

'Yes, I saw him before he left.'

'You spoke to him? Are they…? Is she…?' I attempted to order my thoughts. 'Was it how it seemed?'

I looked at Miriam and realised she was crying. She nodded. 'I think we should just head back to Bristol.' She rubbed my back. 'You must stay with us tonight.'

'I'm so sorry, Miriam,' I mumbled.

'Oh, don't be silly.' She smiled sadly. 'There's nothing whatsoever for you to be sorry about.' She threaded her arm through mine, pushed her chair back and got to her feet, pulling me up with her. 'Come on, Alice. We're going home.'

Chapter 11

As I sat in the chic bar of the hotel on Welsh Back, waiting for Eddie to turn up, it struck me that this would be the first time I had seen him in almost two years, our last meeting having taken place three days after my theatre performance. We had, by then, spoken at length on the telephone, a conversation during which he had explained that the blonde had been a *good friend* for four years and a *very good friend*, for almost two. When I had requested clarification of these friendship categories, it had become apparent that a *good friend* is one in whom you confide, whilst a *very good friend* is one whom you shag senseless at every possible opportunity. It was also explained to me that Eddie's *very good friend*, Philippa Hunter, 'Pip', lived a convenient twenty-minute drive from Great Aunty Mo and was aware of his relationship with me but was, as he put it, *extremely secure in herself and not at all jealous*. He also advised that the last thing either of them wanted was to hurt me.

By way of a retort, I had advised him that anything I chose not to set alight would be in bin bags, ready for him to collect, the following day.

He came. He collected. He went. I later learned from mutual friends that he had relocated, alone, to Manchester, from which I deduced that his attachment to both Great Aunty Mo, and to his *very good friend*, Pip, had waned. But, other than a few subsequent, perfunctory telephone conversations to discuss the various financial and practical issues arising from a broken relationship, I had no further contact with Edward Hall.

Almost two years on then, from this most acrimonious of splits and I had just bought a drink and was sending Sophie a reassuring text, confirming my state of mind as "sound", when Eddie walked into the large, but still relatively empty, hotel bar. I saw him before he saw me and so had the advantage of a few moments to take in his longer mousy hair, his more casual, but undoubtedly more expensive, attire and to note, with some satisfaction, body language which suggested he was not entirely at ease. I felt myself relax a little and raised a hand to attract his attention. He saw me and, after just a flicker of hesitation, smiled and came to join me.

'Alice,' he said, as he reached the table, 'it's so good to see you. You look great.' He inclined slightly towards me, as if for a hug. I didn't budge.

'Hi, Eddie,' I said. 'How are you?'

He straightened up, somewhat awkwardly, pushing his now foppish, locks from his eyes. 'I'm good, I'm good. Right,' he rubbed his hands together and then gestured towards my spritzer, 'well, I can see you're all sorted for a drink – unless you'd like one in waiting?'

I tapped my glass. 'I'm fine with this, thanks,' I said.

'OK,' he looked towards the bar, 'so I'll, er, just get myself one and then we can catch up.'

I smiled. 'Sounds good.'

As he headed for the bar, I finished typing, and quickly reread, my text to Sophie.

> *STOP WORRYING. Am fine – just trying not to fall off ridiculously high stool. Bar not busy yet – just a few couples and one sad guy reading a copy of Heat. Might ask to borrow it if E's late. Got a spritzer. E's just arrived. Looks nervy. Lost weight and his hair is all Hugh Grant. Will text/call later x*

I pressed '*send*', just as Eddie returned to the table.

'So,' he said, sitting down with, I noted, recovered composure, 'how are things with you?'

'Good. And you?'

His reply was lost on me as I continued to take in his sartorial upgrade and the expensive watch, revealed as he removed his jacket and turned back his shirt cuffs, in a relaxed, man-of the-people manner.

'...which was just great,' he concluded, picking up his drink.

'That's nice,' I said, whilst at the same time realising that for me, today, small talk was not going to work. I took a deep breath. 'Eddie, you have never explained or expressed any regret over what you did,' I began, 'and if it's OK I'd like to just cut to the chase and tell you that I'm here only because I thought I should give you a chance to put that right – to say something which might make me feel better about you.' I attempted a smile. 'I'm sorry, but I think that's something we really need to get out of the way.'

'Oh, Alice,' he said gently, leaning towards me. 'Ongoing recrimination and regret isn't helpful.' He placed his hand on mine and offered me a pitying smile. 'I really hoped you'd moved on.'

I looked at his hand and then into his eyes. I searched for the man I had fallen in love with and quickly came to the conclusion that he had never actually existed. He had, I decided, been my own construct. I had been drawn to the journalist, to the author, to the ambition, to the self-confidence and not least to the undeniable ability to charm when required. But the total lack of empathy and, it seemed, of conscience, which was so immediately obvious this evening, had, I decided, always been a problem – I simply hadn't wanted to acknowledge it as such.

I withdrew my hand, picked up my drink and took a sip. 'How is Manchester?'

He leaned back and smiled. 'Ah, Manchester is great. I love it. Working hard on book number three. And it's a great feeling to have the other two under my belt. One is good, two is always better, you know.'

Like women? I managed to resist articulating the thought. I replaced my drink on the table and glanced at my watch, setting myself a target of one hour, before making my excuses.

He was still talking, '...I hope you enjoyed it.'

'Sorry?' I looked up. 'Enjoyed what?'

'My second novel.'

'I haven't read it,' I said simply. He smiled. 'I haven't,' I insisted.

He held up a placatory hand. 'I believe you,' he laughed. 'Anyway, how are *you*? Still at that design place?'

I forced a smile. 'Yes, I am. I'm still very happy there.' He looked mildly incredulous and I lost the battle with my tongue. 'And how is Great Aunty Mo? When did you last see her?'

To my dismay and undisguisable horror, he didn't miss a beat. 'Yesterday morning. She's great. She loves Manchester as much as Pip and I do. It took me a while to find the right house for us all, but Mo has the ground floor and it works really well.'

It was a devastating response; one which immediately converted my rising sense of relief at being free from this man, to a feeling of crushing rejection. When it came to Great Aunty Mo, he clearly felt something remarkably akin to loyalty and love. He was capable of that. He just hadn't felt it for me. And, of course, he was still with bloody Pip.

I nodded and wanted to cry. 'Great Aunty Mo was lovely,' I mumbled.

'She still is. We love having her around. She came to Singapore with us last year. She's incredible – game for absolutely anything. You should have seen her on the flight.'

We. Us. The words sliced into me. I stared, without focusing, at the table and suddenly the prospect of sixty minutes with him seemed like a very painful eternity. It simply had not occurred to me that he would be living a life of domestic bliss. I nodded again and some part of my brain wondered whether he had any concept of what he was doing to me. I looked up at him. He was now relaxed and animated. I realised that he looked genuinely, unselfconsciously happy and that realisation was very nearly the final blow. The *actual* final blow came a second later.

'So, anyway,' he said, still smiling at the thought of Great Aunty Mo on the plane to Singapore, 'I'm pleased you mentioned Mo. It's because of her that I'm here really.' He paused and his smile broadened. 'Pip and I are getting married in September and Mo asked if the lovely Alice would be there. And Pip said absolutely you must come, and I think so too.' He reached for my hand again. 'What do you say, Alice? It would be the perfect way for you to show everyone that you've accepted the situation and moved on, wouldn't it?'

I started to get up and had just picked up my wine glass, with the express intention of emptying its contents over his head, when I felt a hand on my shoulder, gently pressing me back down onto the bar stool, and removing the glass from my grasp.

'There you are,' said David breathlessly, downing the remaining contents of my glass. 'Gosh, I needed that. I'm so sorry to interrupt, Alice.' He turned to Eddie. 'Hello, Edward, how are you? But,' he immediately returned his attention to me, 'my computer has crashed and I have a meeting scheduled with the Harveys in an hour's time. I'll need to present from your laptop.'

I blinked, disorientated by his sudden arrival, the swift change of subject and, not least, by the quite bizarre theft of my drink.

'My laptop? But I—'

'I called you,' said David, 'but it went straight to answer phone. I'm so sorry to interrupt.' He turned again to Eddie. 'So sorry. But it's a very, *very* important pitch for us.'

Eddie waved an amused hand. 'Not at all. You carry on, Dave.'

I reluctantly tore myself away from a delightful, rapidly-forming, mental image of Eddie, lying dead at his own wedding reception, and forced myself to focus on the Harvey pitch. I looked up at David. 'So you need my laptop?'

David wrung his hands. 'I do.'

I shook my head in puzzlement. 'But, David, my laptop is at home and I haven't a clue—'

'Look,' said Eddie, 'this is clearly important. It's fine. You go. We can finish chatting later on the phone. I'll give you all the wedding details. It's just really good to have seen you – even briefly. It's been great, hasn't it?'

'Great?' I returned my gaze, and my attention, to Eddie. He was smiling benignly, graciously, at David and myself. I felt my colour rising. 'Great? It's been bloody—'

'Marvellous!' interrupted David, laughing explosively. 'Bloody marvellous! That's what it's been! Bloody marvellous!' He laughed again.

I stared at him. He appeared to be bordering on mania. 'David, are you—'

'I am, yes,' he said, picking up my handbag and handing it to me with a fixed grin. 'So please come. Goodbye, Edward. Sorry to rush her away but *tempus fugit*.'

Eddie smiled. 'You're clearly the lynch pin of the business, Alice,' he said, as David dragged me across the room. He held his hand to his ear in a telephone gesture. 'Call me!'

David speeded me through the hotel foyer, out onto the pavement and had hustled me a good hundred metres or so along the waterfront before I was able to wrestle my arm from him. 'Hang on,' I protested, shaking myself free and stopping dead. 'I refuse to take another step before you tell me what's going on. Who are the Harveys?'

He looked at me and then glanced back anxiously in the direction of the hotel. 'They are fictitious clients whom I created in order to encourage you to come with me,' he said.

I threw my hands up. 'And you did that because…?'

'Because I thought you were about to either assault Edward with your wine glass or…' he hesitated, gestured towards my eyes and then looked away, '…or get upset,' he concluded quietly.

I opened my mouth to protest, before opting instead for a heavy sigh. 'Well, you were right.' I swallowed hard. 'And it was probably more of a "both" than an "either".'

He smiled. 'Would you like a drink? Somewhere else?' he asked gently.

I shook my head. 'Thanks, David, but I think I'd rather just go home.'

'I understand,' he said. 'My car's in the NCP. I'll drop you.'

'Thank you,' I said, 'both for the lift and for rescuing me from Eddie.' My shoulders sagged. 'And from myself.'

'Come on,' he said, offering me his arm. 'You can tell me about it on the way home.'

I looked at him. 'You didn't hear it all?'

'Well, yes, most of it,' he admitted.

I smiled sadly. 'So maybe instead you could tell me exactly how long you were eavesdropping. And also,' I added, as I linked his arm and we started to walk, 'how Sophie managed to talk you into doing it.'

'Well, as you know,' he sighed, holding up the copy of *Heat* magazine, behind which he had been hiding in the bar, 'Sophie is that rather distressing combination of being frequently formidable,' he looked at the magazine and smiled, 'and invariably right.'

Chapter 12

'And you've definitely ruled out going to the wedding?' Miriam squinted through the glass into the darkened aye-aye enclosure of Bristol Zoo's Twilight World.

'You've asked me that twice already,' I replied tonelessly. 'Once when I got home from seeing Eddie on Thursday evening and you called to see how things had gone. And then again *just forty-five minutes ago*,' I emphasised, 'when you and Phoebe picked me up to bring me here.'

'Oh yes, I'd forgotten.' She tapped on the glass. 'You know, I don't know why we bother with this one. I don't think there's even anything in there.' She tapped again.

'I don't think you're supposed to do that, you know. I'm sure I saw a *no tapping* sign.' I glanced pointlessly around the darkened room.

'Anyway, so long as you've definitely, definitely decided against going to the wedding...'

'Miriam.'

She looked at me. 'Well, I'm glad you're not.' She hesitated. 'And that you've told Eddie that. You have told him that, haven't you?'

'For God's sake. Please stop.' I lowered my voice to a whispered hiss as a woman next to me turned to listen-in, clearly more interested in our conversation than in the elusive inhabitants of Twilight World. 'I'm not going. I texted him last night. That's the end of it. The end of everything. I am no longer remotely attracted to the man, either physically, emotionally or spiritually and he is most definitely not attracted to me. It's finished.'

'Great,' said Miriam, crouching down to speak to Phoebe, who had apparently given up all hope of spotting anything other than tangled branches in the darkness, and was now sitting on the floor, struggling to remove her shoes. 'Don't undo those, darling. How about we go through into the light room and see the rats?' I shuddered at the thought. 'You love the rats, don't you? They can run along ropes, can't they?'

'Whilst carrying over two hundred communicable diseases,' I muttered.

Miriam stood up and tutted. 'I don't know what your problem is with the rats,' she said.

'Me neither. Winston Smith and I are just being silly. Come on, Phoebes,' I said, taking the latter's hand and helping her to her feet. 'Come and show Alice the rats.'

–

An hour later, and we had seen not only the rats but also the penguins, the gorillas, the lorikeets and the pygmy hippos. Miriam and I were sitting on a blanket on the large lawn near the reptile house, eating our picnic, whilst Phoebe entertained herself by running around barefoot and rolling down the small slope behind us, returning to the blanket occasionally, for a handful of Wotsits or a grape. We had been discussing the differences between prairie dogs and meerkats, when Miriam suddenly changed topic.

'Thanks so much for coming with us today,' she said. 'I know you have better things to do with your Saturday.

I lay back, enjoying the unexpected warmth of the April sunshine on my face. 'Like going to Tesco's,' I smiled.

She looked down at me over her sunglasses. 'No, like going on a spa day with Sophie and that other interior designer. The woman with the bracelets and the rhyming name.'

I looked up at her, shielding my eyes from the sunlight with my hand. 'Jane Crane. How do you know about that?' I asked.

'Sophie mentioned it. She didn't know you were coming to the zoo with us.'

'I didn't want to go to a spa,' I said, smiling and closing my eyes. 'You know how I hate being touched.' Miriam laughed. 'And,' I continued, 'I would much rather be here in the sunshine with you and Phoebe. I genuinely like the zoo and you two are my perfect excuse to go.'

'Well, I still think you're lovely to come with us.' I thought I heard her voice catch and I turned to look at her. With her eyes hidden behind sunglasses, it was impossible to guess her mood, but my mind returned to her near tears at the recent book group meeting.

I raised myself up onto my elbows. 'Are you OK?' I asked.

She pushed her sunglasses back up the bridge of her nose. 'Yes, I'm fine,' she said, sounding surprised. 'Why?'

I shrugged. 'You just seem a bit flat at the moment. Not quite yourself.'

She turned her head to look over her shoulder towards Phoebe. 'Do I?' she sighed. 'Probably just my age.'

I waited for her to laugh, or at least smile. She did neither.

'Your age?' I echoed incredulously. 'You're thirty-three, Miriam. Julia Roberts is fifty-five and Jennifer Anniston is over sixty. And look at them.'

'Julia Roberts is not fifty-five,' she said quietly, 'and Jennifer Aniston is mid-forties.' Once again there was no hint of amusement.

'Miriam…'

She turned towards me and at last managed a weak smile. 'Sorry,' she said. 'I know I'm not old. I'm young. I just meant that whatever age I am, whatever stage in life I am at, it's not…' She removed her glasses and began to clean them on her skirt. 'I just don't know where I'm going. Or who I am, for that matter.' She replaced the glasses and stared directly ahead. 'I mean, I know I'm a mother and a wife but I don't want to be defined by my relationship to my family all the time. And what comes next? My days are just running into each other and every one is the same. There's no plan; no forward thinking. Meanwhile, I'm getting older and,' she looked down and patted her stomach, 'fatter, and less attractive and less interesting.'

'None of that is true.'

'It's all true,' she said quietly. 'Do you know what I found myself doing yesterday?'

'What?'

'Well,' she bit her lip before continuing, 'I was packing my bag at the checkout in Sainsbury's and I suddenly realised that I was trying to beat the cashier.'

I frowned. 'I don't understand.'

She sighed. 'I mean, I was trying to pack my items more quickly than she could scan them. My aim was that I should be waiting for her to scan, rather than her waiting for me to pack.' She turned towards me. 'That's what I see as a challenge these days. That was my challenge for yesterday – to beat the cashier.' She shook her head and laughed bitterly. 'Pitiful,' she murmured.

'Not at all. I've done that before,' I lied.

She shook her head. 'That's not true, Alice.'

'OK, but,' I held up a finger, 'I'm going to do it the very next time I'm in Tesco's. Sounds like fun.'

She offered me a tired smile. 'I love Phoebe. I'm so grateful to be a mother but I look at you and you go to work, doing a job you enjoy, working with lovely people and then, at the end of each day, you can do what you like, when you like, with whoever you like. You're a person in your own right. I, on the other hand, get up, take Phoebe to pre-school, do a few mindless secretarial bits and bobs badly for Craig, pick up Phoebe and then spend the rest of the day shopping, cleaning, attending toddler classes or, if I'm really lucky, having a coffee with other women who are in a similarly miserable situation.'

She was now sitting cross-legged, her head bowed once again, whilst she busily decapitated a pile of dandelions she had collected on her lap. Silence, flippancy or a change of subject were not, I decided, options at this point.

'But you're so loved and needed. You've got Phoebe and Craig and I—'

'I wouldn't be without Phoebe.' The beheading ceased momentarily. 'As for Craig...' She left the sentence hanging and recommenced the floral mutilation.

I forced myself to press the matter. 'As for Craig what?' She remained silent. 'Go on, explain what you meant.'

She shrugged. 'Nothing. I'm just being silly.'

I touched her arm. 'Please tell me, or I'll imagine all sorts of things.'

She lifted her head and addressed the middle distance. 'Well, you say I've got Craig but I don't feel I have. Quite a lot of the time these days I feel like a single mother.' She swept the remaining dandelions from her skirt and threw up her hands in a gesture of exasperation. 'He spends more time with his clients than he does with me.'

'We both know he loves you and Phoebe so much,' I sat up and shifted to sit next to her, 'but you should talk to him about this.' At that moment, Phoebe returned to the blanket and grabbed yet another handful of Wotsits. I gently pulled her to me and placed her on my lap. 'Go out for a drink. You know I'm always happy to babysit.' I kissed the top of Phoebe's head. 'You also know how rubbish I am at counselling,' I added. 'I'm used to being the one on the receiving end of your words of wisdom but,' I squeezed her arm, 'please talk to him.'

With her shades still firmly in place, I was unsure whether to interpret the momentary jutting of her lower lip as emotion, or as a rejection of my advice. Either way, the expression quickly transformed back into a smile, as she stroked Phoebe's hair, before suddenly rising to her feet and beginning to gather up the remains of the picnic.

'Anyway,' she said briskly, 'that's enough about me. What I want to know is how things are going with you and Hugh. That's much more interesting. Abs showed me a picture of him.' She stopped packing for a moment and looked at me. 'I had no idea how good-looking he was. He has a gorgeous smile.'

I stifled a groan at the recollection of the torture to come and began to pass the Tupperware. 'Yes, well, I'm not sure I've actually seen him smile yet,' I said.

'So,' Miriam recommenced packing, 'when are you getting together? Anything arranged?'

'Yes, I'm seeing him next weekend.'

'Lovely,' she said, absently, as she zipped up the cool-bag and began to help Phoebe back on with her shoes and socks. 'Doing anything nice?'

I mumbled a reply, whilst folding the picnic blanket. Miriam stopped what she was doing and looked up at me. 'You're doing what?'

I dropped the blanket, flopped back down onto the grass and put my head in my hands. 'He's taking me to a battle re-enactment.'

'Oh, for goodness sake, stop being so melodramatic. Those kind of events can be very interesting. I watched one in—'

'No.' I shook my head. 'I'm not watching it.'

A slow smile spread across Miriam's face. She put her hand to her mouth, in what I knew was a physical attempt to prevent laughter. 'You're…' I watched as she took a deep breath and regained control. 'You're *participating*?'

'Yes,' I said. 'I am participating.'

'In what capacity are you participating?'

'I don't know. I'll find out more this week. But Hugh has my dress size and a costume will be provided.'

'Oh, Alice.'

'I know.'

'And you couldn't say no?'

'How could I?' I sighed heavily. 'He seems to have gone to an awful lot of trouble. And he's so unaware – it was as if he was doing me a favour!'

'Oh my goodness, Alice, that is *so*…' She hesitated. '…so interesting. Which battle will you be—'

'Actually, can we talk about something else?' I put a hand to my forehead. 'Because I'm trying really hard not to think about it.'

'Gosh yes, of course, but…' And at that point, Miriam finally gave in to a fit of the giggles. Phoebe stared at her mother, remaining expressionless for just a moment before sitting down on the grass and laughing along. Confronted by the pair of them, helpless with laughter, I found myself unable to cling to my misery over the battle re-enactment for more than a second or two, before I too was laughing. And, as the three of us sat, happy in the sunshine and leaning against each other for support, I realised that the prospect of a Saturday spent running round a hillside with Hugh did have an upside after all.

Chapter 13

'Dear God, there is just no upside to this.' I articulated the thought, as I pulled back my bedroom curtains and peered out at the blustery, dank and extremely wet day; grim beyond its late April situation on the calendar. I sighed. He would be here in forty-five minutes and I still had to breakfast, shower and check the kit list with which I had been issued. I walked to my bedside table, picked up my phone and re-read the text Hugh had sent earlier in the week.

> *I confirm that I have booked two standard double rooms at The George at a cost of £97 per room. This is inclusive of breakfast on Sunday morning. I will be picking you up at 10 a.m. on Saturday. Do not forget a packed lunch. As discussed, your costume has been arranged and you can collect it on arrival. There will be a number of layers to it but the location is an exposed hillside and depending upon the weather (rain is forecast), you may well need a waterproof to wear when not in character. I suggest you wear walking boots. Any colour is acceptable as your feet will be hidden by your costume…*

I put my phone down, feeling unable to read any further just yet, and headed for the shower.

Forty minutes later and I was dressed in jeans, t-shirt and walking boots and sitting in the living room, cradling on my lap a fleece, waterproof trousers, waterproof jacket and a rucksack which contained my overnight things and, of course, a packed lunch. I sighed and realised that this might be in the running to be my worst weekend away ever. Of course, there had been the time an ex had taken me on a mystery mini-break for my birthday, telling me to pack for lots of walking. I had then spent two days in Paris dressed like a member of the Ramblers Association. That had been pretty bad but, try as I might, I couldn't come up with anything as dreadful as this.

I was just considering feigning illness, either physical, psychological, or both, when the doorbell rang. Deciding it was simply too late for quality artifice, I hauled myself up and, with the air of a condemned woman, bravely resigned myself to my fate.

-

'This is Barry.' After just over an hour's drive, psychologically extended to approximately one year by tedious conversation, Hugh and I had finally reached our destination; the expansive flat summit of a chalk escarpment in Wiltshire. In the distance, I could see the parked motorhomes and pitched tents of the Civil War enthusiasts who would be re-enacting the Battle of Roundway Down for a large (so I had been told) crowd later that day.

'Barry,' continued Hugh, his hand resting on the shoulder of a stout, heavily-bearded man in his late fifties, 'is one of the principal co-ordinators of today's event. It is thanks to Barry, that you are able to join in.'

'Thank you, Barry,' I said, astonished at the level of apparent sincerity I managed to inject into the phrase. 'It's very kind of you and I'm really looking forward to the day.'

'Well, we don't let non-members participate as a rule,' Barry smiled. 'But when Hugh explained the situation and how very keen you were to experience a re-enactment, we of course said yes. Hugh is one of our most experienced, knowledgeable and dedicated members. He has been of invaluable help with the website and with publicity.' He gazed up at Hugh so adoringly that I feared for a moment he might actually kiss him.

To his credit, Hugh looked mildly uncomfortable. 'Not at all, not at all,' he said quietly, whilst fastening his waxed jacket. 'I wonder, Barry, if you could briefly explain to Alice, what she'll be doing today.'

'Delighted,' beamed Barry. 'Well, today, Alice,' he said, 'you will be one of our ladies.'

'That'll make a pleasant change,' I laughed.

Neither Hugh nor Barry seemed to enjoy the joke quite as much as I did, but Barry smiled kindly, whilst Hugh's torso moved in a manner which seemed to indicate a suppressed sigh. 'Sorry, Barry,' I said. 'I'll be quiet. You carry on.'

'How about we talk as we walk?' he said, jovially. 'Let's head over to the tents.'

'I'll say goodbye now then,' said Hugh suddenly. 'You can contact me by phone, if there's a signal. And we could possibly meet for lunch. If not, I will see you at the end of the day.'

'Oh, so we're not going to be together today then?' I asked, looking up at him.

Barry laughed. 'You're on different sides, Alice.'

'We are?' I looked at Hugh.

'I'm a Royalist,' he said, failing to make eye contact and instead addressing my forehead – something which made me want to stand on tiptoe in an attempt to meet his gaze. 'You're a Parliamentarian today, with a Roundhead regiment.'

'Oh, I see.' I blinked, surprised to discover that I was not entirely happy with the idea of separation.

'That's right,' said Barry. 'Now, I don't want to hurry you, Alice, but I've got some artillery to check in a moment, so if I could just get you over to the ladies that would be great.'

'Sorry, yes.' I looked at Hugh. 'Well, I guess I'll see you later, then.'

'You will,' he said, holding up a hand and starting to walk away.

I turned to find Barry already striding off in the direction of a group of women, one or two of whom were now in costume, wearing heavy dresses, aprons, shawls and Puritan caps. I hurried to catch him up and soon he was introducing me to two of my fellow ladies. Each greeted me warmly although also, I couldn't help noticing, with a few sidelong glances at each other.

'So, this is Alice,' said Barry. 'Alice, this is the lovely Val and this divine creature,' he pointed towards a short, rosy-cheeked woman, 'is my wife, Tina. Tina will be keeping an eye on you today and has a costume for you which you can pop on in our motor-home. You've plenty of time. The first skirmish won't kick off for a good couple of hours yet.'

'Hello, Alice,' said Tina, looking, I thought, just a little anxious. 'Now, I think I better say right away that there has been a misunderstanding as regards your costume.' Val solemnly nodded her assent.

'A misunderstanding?' queried Barry, now also looking worried.

Tina turned to him. 'I'm afraid when you told me to add an eight to ten to the list, I thought you meant an age eight to ten.' She looked me up and down. 'The dress I've got would barely cover your knees.'

Relief flooded through me. 'Oh dear, but you mustn't worry,' I gushed. 'I'm more than happy just to watch, you know.'

Barry looked stern. 'Well, I must say I'm rather disappointed. Alice has been looking forward to this for some weeks now.'

'Really,' I touched his arm, 'watching will be very exciting, I've never—'

'I know there's no one at fault here,' continued Barry. 'It's just a silly misunderstanding and I'm as much to blame as anyone but, as I say, I am very disappointed, not to mention a little embarrassed.'

We stood there unspeaking; a sombre circle of four. It was Val who broke the silence. 'There's always Ken's costume,' she said quietly.

'Ken?' Barry appeared confused.

'Ken Lane,' Val continued. 'He's down with a tummy bug so his costume is up for grabs. And what's more he is…' At this point she sucked in her cheeks and described the shape of a long thin rectangle with her hands.

Unhappy with the trajectory of the conversation, I raised a hand, 'Look, I honestly don't want to be a—'

'But Ken is a *man*, Val,' said Barry. 'I know you're trying to help,' he continued gently, 'but I can't hand the girl a pike and shove her into a skirmish.' He turned to me. 'Sorry, Alice, I know you're keen,' I nodded, judging it best to let the mistaken assumption slide, 'but these things are carefully choreographed and it would be dangerous to allow you to participate untrained.'

I smiled. 'I fully understand and—'

'I'm not suggesting Alice actually fights, Barry,' said Val. 'She could just hold the pike and be in costume and that way she can be a character and sit with us. Otherwise she'll be on her own all day and that won't be any fun.'

'But would she really want to dress as a man?' Barry asked. 'She doesn't want to be plodding round wearing heavy boots, a helmet and a breast plate. And the pikes are very heavy.' I found myself warming to Barry. 'That'd be very unpleasant for the girl.'

Tina's eyes glistened dangerously. 'I think you mean *woman*, Barry,' she interjected, 'and of course it wouldn't be a problem. We might be re-enacting a 17th century battle but we're living in the 21st century.' She pursed her lips. 'You'd do well to try to remember that from time to time.'

Barry lowered his eyes and I could, to my horror, see him weakening in the face of a feminist onslaught. Tina pressed home her advantage. 'What do you think, Alice?' She turned to me. 'You don't look one bit like a lipstick and fancy nails kind of woman to me.'

Feeling slightly crushed by this assessment, I scrambled for an avenue of escape from the situation. 'Well,' I said, turning to Barry, who remained my one, slim hope, 'if you're sure there are no health and safety… or insurance… or legal problems…?'

Barry shook his head sadly. 'None that I can think of,' he said, 'so long as you don't actually join in a fray.'

I turned to Val. 'And Ken won't mind? Isn't his costume quite precious to him?'

Val laughed. 'Even if it was, he can't get off the loo right now, so he won't notice it's missing.' My face dropped. 'Oh, I'm only joking, Alice,' she said, rubbing my arm. 'Don't you worry about him, love. He's not that unwell. He just needs to sleep.'

'That's sorted then,' said Tina briskly. 'Disaster averted.'

'Yes,' said Barry, looking, I thought, as defeated as I felt.

I forced a smile. 'Well, thank you for sorting that out for me. I'm sorry to have been such a bother.'

'Nonsense,' said Tina. 'It was our fault and our problem to put right. All's well that ends well and Ken's costume will fit you a treat.

You're actually a very similar build.' Her eyes lingered disconcertingly on my chest. 'Lovely and slim,' she added kindly.

Barry sighed. 'Right, well, I shall leave you ladies – you *women*,' he corrected himself hastily, 'to sort all that out. I'm off to check the artillery.'

'See you later then,' said Tina, kissing him lightly on the cheek. 'And don't worry, I know you're a new man really.'

He smiled fondly at her, raised a hand to the rest of us, and headed off in the direction of a gathering group of men, each of whom was carrying a large musket. Behind them, a second group was busily engaged in manoeuvring a large cannon out of a truck. Despite my reluctance to be there, and my growing horror regarding *participation*, I had to admit to myself that it was all rather fascinating.

'Right then, Alice,' said Tina, interrupting my thoughts. 'Let's get you over to Ken's caravan. He's got his wife Lorraine with him, so she'll sort you out – we won't have to disturb him. We'll just grab the costume and then you can change in my motor-home. Don't want you catching Ken's bug. That wouldn't be any fun, would it?'

I looked at this kind woman and momentarily considered confiding that, actually, vomiting into a bucket in the privacy of a caravan was actually a more appealing prospect than spending the next five hours dressed as a man. But, instead, I restricted myself to what I hoped resembled an excited smile. There was a pause, during which I think both women expected me to speak. However, fearing that any attempt to vocalise might result in tears, I simply broadened the grin.

'You know what,' said Tina at last, taking my arm, 'I don't think I've ever seen anyone quite so excited about a re-enactment.' She turned to Val. 'Have you?'

Val shook her head. I continued to grin. And off we went.

–

An hour later and I was again sitting with Val and Tina, enjoying the cup of tea I had just been handed and scolding myself for having been quite so negative about the re-enactment experience. With the exception of the huge, brown, balloon-like plus fours, which were held up under a long leather waistcoat by a piece of thick twine, the rest of my ensemble wasn't too outsized. The white, collared shirt fitted in the sleeve and Tina had safety-pinned the inside to temporarily take it in. The look was completed by long, grey socks and Ken's boots. The latter were a couple of sizes too big, but even this didn't seem too much of a problem, in view of my sedentary role. All in all, I decided, my attire was nothing to grumble about.

I had, it was true, initially been slightly worried about the accessories: a metal breastplate, secured by leather straps, a Pikeman's pot – an enormous helmet which fell down over my eyes, rendering me both blind and deaf – and, of course, there was the pike itself. I had had no idea that these were so huge. Having imagined it to be the length of an aboriginal spear, I was astonished to be handed a five metre long pole with a spiked metal tip.

'The thing is, you won't have to run around with any of that,' said Val, gesturing at the collection of metal-ware lying on the grass next to me. When you need to be in character, you can just pop it on, stand up and walk a few steps. And, if it feels a bit heavy, I can pop a bandage round your head and you can lie down and pretend to be wounded.' She took a biscuit from the box which was being passed around our group and then offered me one. 'Would you like a digestive?'

'Thank you.' I took a biscuit and looked towards the gathering crowds. 'How many spectators are you expecting today?'

'Several hundred, I should think,' said Tina, looking at the sky, 'I just hope the rain holds off.'

'Will it be cancelled if it rains?' I asked. I might have come to terms with an afternoon of cross-dressing in dry conditions, but I feared my voluminous plus fours would prove the opposite of comfort wear when damp.

'Not at this late stage,' said Val. 'And the BBC are filming for local news.' She smiled and pointed towards a camera crew on the other side of the large designated battlefield.

'I'll just check the forecast on my phone,' I said, reaching into my rucksack.

'Oh, I wouldn't worry too much,' she said. 'A little rain doesn't usually dampen the atmosphere. Kids love the explosions and clashes whatever the weather, and they don't even realise they're being educated.'

'Are the numbers of children ever a problem?' I asked, whilst experiencing a slight sense of foreboding upon seeing heavy rain symbols spread across the afternoon forecast. 'Do any of them ever attempt to join in?'

'Oh no, it's all very secure,' said Tina reassuringly. 'We have lots of marshals to prevent anyone from wandering where they shouldn't. Any injuries are minor – and always restricted to members.'

'So people do get hurt then?'

'Occasionally, but it's only ever bumps and bruises.' Val finished her biscuit and brushed the crumbs from her skirt. 'Now,' she said, 'where's that young man of yours? Royalist or no, he could come and say hello.'

'Oh, Hugh's not my boyfriend,' I said quickly. 'We're just friends.'

'Oh sorry,' said Val, 'I got the wrong end of the stick there.'

'We don't know each other that well at all, to be honest,' I said. 'We were introduced by a mutual friend, who thought we'd get on.'

'Well,' said Tina, 'whether anything comes of it or not, the pair of you will still have had a lovely day out, won't you?'

I smiled and nodded. 'Absolutely.'

She returned my smile, patted my arm and then bent down, and picked up my breast plate. 'What do you say we have a go at putting this on you? See how it feels.'

'OK,' I laughed, handing my phone to Val, 'but you must take a picture of me in the complete uniform, or my friends will never forgive me.'

And then, after an unexpected clap of thunder, it started to rain.

Chapter 14

We retreated into a large white tent, where I remained under cover until the last possible moment; eating lunch, chatting and helping with last-minute costume mends. However, at 2.30pm, thirty minutes before the first skirmish, the last of the ladies exited the tent, sat down around a large cooking pot and began peeling vegetables and talking about food and the state of the nation, in an impressively 17th century kind of way. I, of course, felt that I had no alternative but to join them and so, pike in hand, I stepped outside and into the rain.

Our shelter outside the tent consisted of a brown tarpaulin, draped and secured over four thick wooden poles, each about two metres high, creating a covered area about the size of a large market stall. The ladies sitting in the middle of the space, near the pot, kept relatively dry. However, things were cramped and a combination of the fact that I was standing towards the edge of the tarpaulin, plus a slight side-wind, meant that within ten minutes, my plus fours were soaked and resembling the sort of attire worn by Billy Smart's clowns. They had also doubled in weight and were now seriously challenging the ability of my string belt to keep them aloft. My helmet, although excellent for keeping not only my head, but also my shoulders dry, had the acoustic qualities of a tin drum whenever hit by a drop of rain and, in the end, I was forced to remove it and carry it under my arm. Members of the public ambled past us, hoods up and smiling at the historically accurate conversations of my companions. And whenever I was questioned about my role or uniform, usually by a small child fascinated by my pants, one of my fellow re-enactors would helpfully fill in any details I was unable to supply.

After twenty minutes of standing in the rain and fielding trouser enquiries, I realised I was increasingly desperate for a toilet break. I cursed myself for not thinking to go earlier.

'I'm afraid I need the loo, Tina,' I said. 'I'm sorry, because it's all due to start soon, isn't it?'

She waved a hand. 'Doesn't matter at all,' she said kindly. 'The queues for the Portaloos will be shorter at the moment, so it's actually probably the best time to go. Pop your pike down there and I'll keep an eye on it.'

I smiled my thanks, lay my pike on the ground and hurried off in the direction of the row of green, plastic cubicles, which lay the other side of the battleground. A marshal lifted the red rope, giving me access to the short-cut, and I reached the toilet queue of just four people, in under five minutes.

'I like your hat,' said a small girl of about six or seven, who was standing with a woman immediately in front of me in the queue.

'Oh,' I smiled, looking at the Pikeman's pot under my right arm. 'Do you know, I hadn't realised I'd brought that with me.'

The woman smiled. 'Looks very heavy,' she said.

'It's not too bad,' I replied, 'but it's rather noisy in the rain.'

'You're a girl soldier,' said the child.

'That's right.' I sighed inwardly and then waited for the inevitable follow-up question. It came within seconds.

'Why are your trousers like that?' she asked.

I looked at the woman, who appeared as eager for my explanation as the child.

'Well, things weren't really made-to-measure in those days,' I said. The girl looked at my legs, clearly doubtful that, even in the 17th century, clothes were so poorly fitted.

'The other soldiers' trousers aren't like that,' she said.

'Aren't they?' I sighed again, this time audibly.

'No,' she said. 'Theirs are like…' she paused, 'trousers. Yours are like two big sacks.'

I looked at the woman who, instead of clamping her hand across the child's mouth as Miriam would have done, was actually nodding along in solemn agreement.

'...*and* yours are falling down.' The girl pointed at the string hanging below my jerkin. 'Is that your skipping rope?'

'No, it isn't my skipping rope,' I said. 'It's a special Pikeman's...' I racked my brain for a plausible term, '...binding braid. We all wear them and look,' I continued quickly as the woman appeared intrigued and opened her mouth as if to join the conversation, 'a toilet is free now.' I pointed over the girl's shoulder. 'So that's good isn't it?'

Despite the rain, both mother and child looked disappointed that the close encounter with the poorly-dressed female Pikeman was at an end, and moved reluctantly towards the vacant Portaloo, before squeezing inside and latching the door behind them. A second toilet then became free and I hurried inside.

A few minutes later and I was hastening back to my station as fast as I could, although my progress was now hindered by heavyweight pants, a poorly re-tied belt and Ken's boots, which were proving very difficult to walk in, in the increasingly muddy conditions. With one hand holding up my trousers and the other cradling my helmet, I lolloped towards the battlefield, in the manner of a very wet Quasimodo, focusing determinedly upon the ground, in order to avoid both puddles and eye contact. I eventually reached the edge of the crowd gathered to watch the first skirmish, and then proceeded, with some difficulty, to squeeze my way through the rows of spectators. By the time I reached the red rope and a marshal, my trousers were precariously close to descent, my 'belt' having come almost completely undone.

'Am I still OK to cut across the field?' I addressed the marshal, eyeing and envying his head-to-toe waterproofs.

'Of course,' he said. 'Don't worry, they haven't started without you, love.' He looked me up and down. 'I don't think I've ever seen a woman Pikeman before. Good on you.'

'Sorry,' I panted, 'can you hold my hat, while I re-tie my string?'

'Sure.' He laughed and took the helmet from me. 'Where's your pike?' he asked.

'Someone's looking after it for me,' I replied, untying the twine and re-securing it as best I could around my soaking trousers. 'Thanks so much,' I said, and made to duck under the rope.

'Hey,' he said, 'don't forget this.' He raised the helmet, as if to place it on my head.

'It's OK, I'll carry it,' I said. 'It's a bit big.'

'Are you sure you wouldn't be safer with it on?' he asked.

I looked down at my trousers. He was right. Better that I kept a tight hold on them with both hands. I could always push my helmet back every now and then to check I was going in the right direction. 'OK,' I said, 'could you pop it on for me and do it up?'

'No problem,' he smiled. 'Ah, here's the...' He continued to talk but all conversation was lost to me, as the helmet fell over my ears and the rain began to drum on it.

'That's great,' I said. 'Thanks again.' I struggled under the rope and began to trudge across the field.

I had gone approximately a hundred metres when the sound of what I thought was a clap of thunder penetrated my helmet. It was quickly followed by a second and I tightened my grip on my trousers and attempted to quicken my pace, as much as I was able in Ken's boots. I became suspicious at the third clap and at that point decided to stop hobbling, and get my bearings. The helmet was now fastened under my chin, but I could still tilt it back far enough to afford a decent view of the field.

My first sight was of the happy spectators straight ahead of me and my attention was drawn in particular to one small boy. He was looking to his left, smiling broadly, with his hands over his ears. I followed the direction of his gaze and, to my horror, saw, and then heard, a fast-approaching crowd of men in leather hats, whom I guessed to be Royalists. When I turned to look the other way, I realised that I was now standing just in front, and slightly to the left, of an amassed regiment of Roundheads, striding purposefully towards the opposition. I screamed, allowed my helmet to drop and started to stagger blindly, and as fast as I could, in what I hoped was the direction of the grinning boy.

Expecting at any moment to be squashed, like a tomato in a juicer, between the two advancing groups, it was to my immense relief that I realised from the cries behind me that I had avoided the clash.

I maintained my speed-hobble and managed approximately twenty metres before stopping, exhausted in equal measure by fear and by Ken's boots. After three or four huge gulps of breath, I was unable to resist looking over my shoulder at the apparent mayhem behind me. In the centre of the field, a large group of men were engaged in what looked like an armed, fancy dress, rugby scrum. The noisy group surged backwards and forwards with, every now and then, a member collapsing to the floor and writhing whilst clutching some limb or other. Here and there, pairs broke away from the main throng to perform pre-choreographed hand-to-hand battles. Even though the dodged punches and light wrestling of these staged fights had been described to me in mind-numbing detail by Hugh on the journey up, as I watched now, in such close proximity and with my heart threatening to explode through my chest wall at any moment, the violence looked terrifyingly real.

I bent double, clutching my pants with one hand and holding my helmet up with the other, and desperately tried to calm down. I had just decided to turn and walk the remaining fifty metres or so towards the spectator ranks, when I found myself no longer looking at the grass, but instead lying flat on my back, staring up at the sky. The rain pelted my face and I blinked in confusion, as my brain attempted to compute the sudden shift from a vertical to a horizontal plane.

A man with long, clearly synthetic, hair and a burgundy hat, stood astride me. He quickly fell to his knees and, it seemed to my addled brain, embraced me affectionately before rolling onto his back, so that I was now lying on top of him.

'Aaagh!' He yelled. 'The devil take ye, scum!'

My attacker cuddled me tight and we rolled once more, so that he again looked down on me. He pulled back his right arm and brought down his fist in the mud, about six inches to my left. 'Aaagh!' He yelled before performing yet another caress and roll manoeuvre.

'Stop!' I found my voice at last. 'Stop! I'm not meant to be here!' I cried, struggling to free myself from his determined embrace. I managed to extract my right arm and tugged at my plus fours. 'My trousers will fall off!'

Whether deafened by his sodden wig/hat combo, or simply too caught up in the moment to hear, I wasn't certain. In any case, my words had no effect on him.

'Die!' he yelled. 'Die!' He reached up and tenderly placed his hands around my throat.

I began to cry and, grabbing his wrists, tried frantically to pull his hands away; an action which, I was later told by a nearby marshal, made our battlefield encounter the most moving she had ever witnessed.

And then, suddenly, I was flat on my back, lying motionless in the mud, sobbing gently, as my attacker ran off in the direction of the central melee, hurling indistinct 17th century abuse over his shoulder at me as he went.

How long I lay there I wasn't sure. But I stopped crying, as some sort of primeval survival instinct kicked in and told me that to remain as quiet and still as possible was the best course of action, lest another Royalist should see me as fair game for a second bout of cuddle-wrestling. In addition, after the physical and emotional trauma of someone pretending to kill me, the prospect of a little lie down, even in the mud, seemed rather welcome. And so, staring at the angry sky and feeling suddenly, and very strangely, disassociated from my surroundings, I simply lay there and began to review the day.

On the plus side, I hadn't stood anyone up, I had tried something new and I had, along the way, met some very lovely people.

On the downside… I closed my eyes as brown trousers, outsized helmets, pikes, Portaloos and acrylic wigs danced across my consciousness like drunks at a disco. And, sauntering after them, with a scalpel in one hand and a bit of kidney dangling from the other, came Hugh. Hugh: the biggest, most boring, most inattentive downside of the day. I had been polite enough to accompany him, on the wettest day in April, to an event which held no allure *whatsoever* for me and what had he done? He had effectively left me to rot. Not once, *not once*, in over five hours had he bothered to find me for a chat or even a brief 'hello'. That was, I decided, outrageous. The rain, the mud and my ill-fitting pants were unfortunate, but Hugh was boring, insensitive, self-centred and outrageous.

'Are you OK?' I opened my eyes and saw the outline of a bewigged man silhouetted against the sky. For a moment, I suffered a terrifying mud-cuddle flashback, before realising that this was a different wig-wearer and that my fellow corpses were now all up and walking towards the beer tent. The silhouette crouched down. 'Are you OK?' he repeated kindly and his gentle tone was just too much. I sat up, with the effect that my helmet immediately fell down over my eyes and, with my face half-concealed from view, I started to cry for the second time that day.

'No, I'm not OK,' I sobbed, as I felt a hand come to rest gently on my shoulder. 'My clothes are ridiculous, I'm cold, I'm covered in mud and at one point I thought I was going to die. But,' I paused pushing both hands up inside my helmet to wipe away the tears, 'the worst thing is that after all that, I now have to spend the evening with someone I really don't like and with whom I have absolutely nothing in common. And I don't want to upset Abs but I'm just not sure I can manage it.'

I slumped forward and felt the hand lift from my shoulder, as my companion began to unbuckle the chinstrap on my helmet.

'Well,' he said, removing my Pikeman's pot and then extending a hand to help me to my feet, 'that does all sound a bit grim but, looking on the bright side,' I blinked as my eyes adjusted to the light and I saw Hugh smiling down at me, 'I think we might at last have found several things we agree on, Alice.'

Chapter 15

It was 7pm by the time I finally walked into the cosy hotel bar and discovered Hugh already ensconced in a quiet corner, with his Kindle and an almost-empty pint glass on the table in front of him. He had clearly been there for some time.

He looked up as I approached. 'Feeling better?'

I smiled. 'Much, thanks. Sorry I'm so late down. It took quite a while to wash off all that mud.' I pulled out a chair and looked around the room. 'This is all so lovely,' I smiled, sitting down.

Hugh had booked us into The George, a very pretty local inn, complete with beams, lime-washed walls and huge open fireplaces. The hostelry dated back to the 14th century; one of a thousand facts regarding its history supplied to me by Hugh on our journey from Bristol. And despite my eye-rolling over his historical lecture, and detailing of the practical bases upon which he had selected The George as our accommodation, I couldn't deny that his choice was a very good one. My room was comfortable, the staff were welcoming and the restaurant menu, over which I had already salivated online, held great promise.

He followed my gaze around the bar and nodded. 'Yes,' he said simply, before adding as an apparent afterthought, 'I'm pleased that you like it.'

I pointed at his glass. 'Can I get you another?'

'No, thank you, I'm fine. And there's a glass of Sauvignon Blanc on its way for you.' He raised a hand and I looked over my shoulder to see the barman nodding in acknowledgement.

'Sauvignon Blanc?' I asked.

'You said you were *gagging* for one on the way here.' He switched off the Kindle and pushed it away from him. 'Just before you fell asleep across the back seat.'

'Yes,' I said, smiling my thanks at the barman, as he advanced towards me with a large glass of wine and placed it on the table in front of me, 'it was lucky that you'd planned ahead and brought that roll of polythene with you, otherwise I would have ruined your leather interior. Thank you for this. And cheers.' I raised my glass.

He touched his glass against mine and then replaced it on the table, without taking another sip. 'You find the fact that I brought polythene with me amusing, don't you?' he said.

'Not at all. I...' I hesitated. Before I had fallen asleep in the car, Hugh and I had shared some good-natured, but extremely frank, opinions regarding our compatibility as a couple. I now decided that to lie, for whatever reason, would be a disservice to that honest exchange of views. 'Yes,' I said. 'I do find it funny.'

'And I find it interesting that you find it amusing.'

I smiled. 'It's been an interesting day all round, hasn't it?'

'It has,' he said. 'And I apologise for abandoning you.'

'That's OK. As you now know, I wasn't overly desperate for your company. But only,' I added quickly, 'because Abs had said you were very keen and that made me anxious.'

He sighed. 'Yes, and, of course, she had told me exactly the same thing about you. And that was what was so perplexing about it all. I mean, it was apparent to me within the first ten minutes of our meeting for coffee, that there was no attraction between us.'

Despite sharing this opinion entirely, I realised that the news was not entirely welcomed by my ego. 'Within ten minutes?'

He looked up. 'When I mentioned forensic pathology, you physically recoiled and, I'm sorry, but I have no interest in cushions.'

'Why on earth does everybody think that interior design is all about cushions?' I exclaimed. 'Interior design is about relationships – people with their environment, objects with other objects within an environment.'

He nodded politely.

'You're not interested in those things either, are you?' I said.

He shook his head. 'I'm afraid I'm not. But it's not just that, is it?'

'Isn't it?' I asked, before immediately wishing I hadn't. I was far from eager to hear my unattractive qualities listed like the faults on a car failing its MOT.

'No,' he said. 'A shared professional interest isn't essential for a successful relationship. And I find you interesting in other ways. But we don't find each other attractive, do we?'

I bit my lower lip as it jutted involuntarily. 'Well,' I said, 'my friends think you're very handsome and I can see—'

'You don't find me attractive,' he said.

'Well, it's just difficult to separate—'

'Exactly,' he cut me short for a second time, 'and it's not something to concern yourself over. I don't find you at all attractive either.'

'Right…' I could tell from his expression that he was simply stating fact and that there was no intention to hurt. But although I couldn't disagree at all with his assessment of the situation, it did rather feel as if my self-esteem was being ground into the mud as completely as my torso had been just three hours earlier. 'Er, Hugh…'

'Yes?' He looked up from his beer.

'You're quite right in what you're saying…' I hesitated. 'But some women sometimes find it a little difficult to be told that they're unattractive. In fact,' I continued, 'I'd go so far as to say that *all* women find it *very* difficult, pretty much *all* of the time.'

'Sorry,' he said, frowning. 'I know I'm very direct. My sister tells me regularly that I'm on the spectrum.'

I nodded. 'I think she might have something there.'

He maintained his frown, before suddenly smiling broadly. He pointed at me. 'You're being amusing again.'

I laughed. 'You know, Hugh, the thing is, I would value your sort of directness in a friend,' I said. 'Once I'd desensitised myself to it, of course.'

'And I'd value your…' it was his turn to hesitate, '…your sense of fun in a friend. Just not in a partner. And not every day.' He sipped his beer. 'Not day in, day out. Because I would find that extremely wearing.'

'OK. You've made your point. Now,' I put a finger to my lips, 'shh.'

He smiled again and raised his glass. 'So, it's friends we are, then?' he said.

I clinked my glass against his. 'To friendship.'

'To friendship.'

'And now,' I said, 'are you going to tell Abs, or am I?'

'I have no doubt she'll call you first.' He leaned back in his chair and sighed, as if giving the matter some thought. 'And whilst I would have no difficulty explaining the situation to her, I suspect that my sister would advise that I should let you do it.'

'Oh, God,' I said, 'I'm probably not much better at that kind of thing than you are. I really don't want to hurt her feelings, you know. She's so lovely.'

He looked intrigued. 'Is that why you agreed to come today?'

I nodded. 'Partly. But also because it had been suggested that I hadn't really been giving anyone, including myself, much of a chance on the dating front lately.'

'I see,' he said.

'What *I* don't see,' I said, picking up my wine glass, 'is why on earth you invited me. I would have expected you to give Abs a direct and flat "no", on the basis that you found me completely unattractive.'

He smiled. 'You can blame my sister for that,' he sighed. 'When our first encounter didn't go well, I didn't feel I needed to go into detail with Abigail, because I was certain you felt the same way.' He shrugged. 'I was certain beyond doubt that neither of us would contact the other again. But then Abigail called to say you were keen to experience an historical re-enactment with me. I called Lorna, my sister, to gain a female perspective and, based upon the information provided, she suggested today's event, reasoning that I might be pleasantly surprised and that, if not, we would at least have a chance to discuss things. However, the car journey here was enough to confirm to me that you weren't...' He checked himself, 'that *we* were not ideal together.'

'Not ideal,' I laughed, 'I like that. I might use it when I talk to Abs.'

He saluted me with his beer. 'Feel free.'

I sipped my wine and began to relax. 'So, what *is* your ideal?' I asked, examining his face for any sign that he was uncomfortable with the question, but finding none.

'I often wonder,' he said. 'I've had a number of relationships, most of which have ended amicably. Although, one ex was admittedly disgruntled.'

'Oh?'

'She told Lorna that I had emotionally destroyed her.'

I raised my eyebrows. 'I'm not sure disgruntled quite covers that actually. But never mind, carry on.'

'In Lorna's opinion, I need someone intelligent, kind, passionate and unafraid.'

I thought for a moment. 'Not a bad shopping list.'

'But quite a demanding one.'

'It is and,' I sighed, 'I tick very few of those boxes.'

'Actually,' he said, 'I suspect you tick them all. The problem is that you also have one or two other traits with which I am simply not equipped to cope.'

I held up my hand. 'I don't want to know what they are. So let's just leave that topic of conversation right there.'

'Before you've revealed your ideal?' He looked at me questioningly.

I opened my mouth to respond, before realising that I was totally floored by my own question. Not since being a teenager, and discussing boys with a gaggle of girls in my bedroom, had I described my perfect man. And for some reason, the idea of doing it now wasn't an appealing one. I looked at Hugh to find him watching me with interest.

'To be honest, it's not something I've thought about recently. And I'm not sure I want to,' I admitted. 'Maybe in case he doesn't exist.'

He nodded. 'Or isn't available to you?'

It was a theory which struck an unexpected chord. I toasted him with my glass. 'Thank you for pointing out that second miserable possibility.'

'Sorry,' he said.

I shook my head and smiled. 'Not at all. You've just made me think, that's all.'

'Well, I won't force you to think any more,' he said. 'As it's clearly not something you're comfortable with.'

I laughed. 'You're being amusing,' I said.

'I thought I'd give it a go,' he smiled. 'Just don't expect me to keep it up for any length of time.'

'Takes it out of you?'

'It does.'

'OK,' I said, 'well, how about you tell me about your favourite battle re-enactment instead? Or monologue on your best ever brain dissection? Something like that.'

'Right,' he nodded, 'and what will you be doing whilst I'm talking?'

'I'll be thinking about how to break the bad news to Abs.'

'Perfect,' he said, placing his pint on the table, leaning back in his chair and folding his arms. 'Now, in 2010, I assisted in an autopsy of...'

And while Hugh told his, actually rather interesting, tale of occipital and parietal lobes, I picked up my glass, drank my wine and decided that, all things considered, the day hadn't been so bad after all.

Chapter 16

'Thanks so much for lending me this yet again.' Miriam held up the pale blue silk wrap which she was borrowing to wear to a christening the following day. 'It's so beautiful and,' she gazed at the wrap whilst squeezing her upper arm, 'it hides all this flab.'

'For God's sake,' I sighed. 'You're so self-critical these days. Neither your arms, nor any other bit of you, is flabby.'

Ignoring my exasperated reassurances, she put down the wrap on the kitchen chair in front of her and turned to pick up the two mugs of tea she had just made. She then placed one in front of me and, sipping the other, sat down next to me. 'So, what time is Jon picking you up tonight?' she asked, glancing at the clock above the door into the hallway.

I groaned at the mention of Eleanor Black's reveal party. 'Quite early. Sophie doesn't think we should leave David for too long on his own,' I sighed. 'And Mrs Melons has him there from eight. It's a pain really.'

'Oh, shush. You know you and Jon will have a good time. But you weren't tempted to call Hugh?' She smirked and gave me a nudge.

'Actually,' I said, giving her a look, 'I'd have been quite happy to go with Hugh. We got on fine in the end, last weekend. And we're meeting for drinks next week.'

Her eyes widened slightly. 'You and Hugh?'

'Not just us. Abs and Pete too. So, you know, if Jon hadn't been around tonight, I could have asked Hugh.' I picked up my tea. 'But I'm pleased Jon is coming.' I smiled at the thought of an evening with Jon after several weeks of relatively little communication. 'Sophie told me he felt like he needed to get out a bit more.'

'Really?' Miriam looked puzzled.

I nodded. 'I know. I was surprised by that too.'

'It just doesn't sound like him,' she said. 'And, besides, I don't think he's short of invitations at the moment, is he?' She frowned and pursed her lips.

'Why the lemon lips?' I put my tea down. 'Is there something you're not telling me?'

She eyed me suspiciously. 'I was going to ask you the same thing.'

'I don't know what you mean.'

'I just wondered if Jon had confided in you about… anything.'

I shook my head. 'Nothing. I've hardly heard from him. So, come on, what do you know?'

She hesitated and lowered her voice. 'If I tell you this, you tell no one. And I mean no one. Craig will kill me if he knows I've mentioned it.'

I held up three fingers. 'Dib dob wotnot.'

'Well, on Monday—'

'Monday?' I was appalled. 'You found out something interesting on *Monday*? It's now Saturday! You mean you took a whole five days to tell me?'

'Shh, Craig'll hear,' she whispered. 'I haven't seen you since Monday. Now, do you want to hear or don't you?'

'Of course I want to hear,' I said. 'Get on with it.'

'Well, Craig was at Hotel du Vin with a client on Monday evening and, well, he saw Jon, with a woman. They were having dinner, just the two of them.' She leaned back in her chair and nodded at me in a slow and significant manner. '*Just the two of them*,' she repeated.

'Oh,' I said, momentarily at a loss. I found myself experiencing a strange mixture of extreme surprise and intense curiosity, tinged with a distinct sense of disquiet.

I looked at Miriam.

'Interesting, isn't it?' she said.

We sat in silence for a moment. 'So, did Craig go over?' I asked eventually.

She rolled her eyes. 'He said he couldn't say hello right away as he didn't want to abandon his precious blooming client.'

I picked up my tea again. 'Maybe Jon was with a client too.'

She shook her head. 'Craig said it didn't look like business. Apparently, there was…' She paused for emphasis. '…touching.'

I cleared my throat. 'Who touched whom and how?'

She tapped the table lightly. 'That's exactly what I wanted to know. A reasonable question, you might think. The response I got was, "For God's sake, Miriam, I was discussing a rebrand. I didn't have time to take notes on body language."'

'But he noticed touching?'

'Yes. Apparently, she kept leaning towards him and doing this.' Miriam placed her hand on my arm.

I stared at her hand. 'And what did Jon do?'

'Craig couldn't see. Jon's back was to him most of the time.'

'So Craig didn't speak to Jon at all, then?'

'Apart from as he was leaving,' she added. 'And that was just a brief hello. No introductions.'

'But how did Jon seem?'

She tapped the table for a second time. 'Again, I asked that very question. Craig's response was a shrug.'

I replaced my mug on the table and focused on its remaining contents. 'So, not massively informative then.'

She sighed. 'No.'

'Did Craig say what she looked like?' I asked, my eyes fixed on my tea.

'Oh yes. He managed to note *that*. She was much younger than me, apparently, and very attractive, with long, dark hair.'

I looked up at her. She was unsmiling; her mouth set in a grim line.

'You look very serious about it all,' I said.

'Not really.' She attempted a smile. 'It's just…' she began hesitantly.

'What?'

'Well, this is Jon.'

Neither of us spoke and I took the opportunity to attempt to disentangle my feelings. I felt some surprise and, I admitted to myself, a little hurt that Jon hadn't confided in me over the date – if that's what it was. I had put the lack of phone calls and emails from him down to work, but now it occurred to me that he might have been otherwise occupied – with someone else – and I felt undeniably excluded. I looked at Miriam. She was staring into space with the air of someone listening to a poignant eulogy. I felt my mood sinking and forced myself to seek an alternative, less selfish, perspective.

'I feel a bit odd about it too,' I said at last. 'But, overall, it's a positive thing, isn't it?' I offered.

'I suppose so,' said Miriam, failing either to look or sound reassured.

'Of course,' I persevered, talking as much to myself as to her, 'we're always going to feel we have some sort of special connection or relationship with him, because of the past we share. And I know we can't help but think of him with Lydia.' I took a deep breath, before pressing on. 'But actually, it's not fair to keep defining him, or our relationships with him, by the past, is it? We have to live in the present and he has a right to be happy in the present.'

Miriam said nothing but looked up at me sadly.

'He has a right to be happy,' I repeated quietly, for the benefit of us both.

She nodded slowly and then leaned towards me, her arms extended for a hug. 'It was just a bit of a surprise,' she sighed. 'But you're right. We can't just expect things to stay the same. Situations and feelings change.' She released me and smiled. 'And he's a single man after all,' she added.

'Or was,' I murmured absently. 'I guess maybe we just haven't thought of him as that… until now.' I picked up my tea and then turned my head, distracted by the sound of footsteps in the hallway.

'Bathed and in bed, awaiting a story,' said Craig, entering the kitchen. He walked to the fridge and took out a beer. 'Hi, Alice,' he said, failing to make eye contact with either myself or Miriam.

Miriam stood up and addressed me, whilst looking at Craig. 'Sorry, Alice, I had thought that Craig might read the story tonight. I expect you'll have gone by the time I've finished.' She bent down and kissed my cheek. 'Have a great time at the party. And thanks again for the wrap.' She threw a less-than-adoring glance at her husband, to which he was oblivious, and then left the kitchen.

Craig levered the top off his beer, sat down opposite me and began to drink. He seemed miles away.

I said nothing and eventually he looked at me.

'What?' he said.

'I didn't say anything,' I replied.

'Oh, OK,' he said. 'I thought maybe I'd missed something.'

'I think maybe you have.' He didn't seem to hear me and I stood up. 'Right, well, I have a party to go to.'

This announcement prompted a response. 'Lucky you,' he said miserably.

'God, when did you get so bitter and twisted?' I asked, feeling suddenly irritated.

He smiled. 'It came on gradually.'

'I wasn't entirely joking, you know, Craig.'

'Me neither.' He smiled sadly and opened his mouth to say something more but was robbed of the opportunity by Miriam's return.

'Where's Bunny?' She was standing in the open doorway of the kitchen, looking at Craig. 'Phoebe says she gave him to you before her bath.'

'No doubt she did.' His face darkened once more as he took another swig of his beer, before placing the bottle forcefully on the table. 'So, I'll come and find him,' he said, standing up and brushing past Miriam.

I looked at her. 'Sorry,' she mouthed soundlessly, attempting a smile.

I shook my head. 'It's fine.' I walked across the kitchen and hugged her. 'We need to go out,' I said. 'Soon.'

She smiled and nodded and then walked me to the door. As she opened it, I turned to her. 'You know, I'm not really in the mood for this party and Jon would have a great time with Sophie and David. Why don't you and I go out? Or share a bottle of wine at my place?'

She bit her lip and then hugged me again, so that I couldn't see her face. 'You're lovely. But I'm a bit tired. I'll probably just do a little bit of tidying and go to bed with a book.' She released me from the embrace. 'Something escapist.'

I hesitated, uncertain whether or not to press the matter, before deciding against it and instead giving her a second peck on the cheek. 'That sounds good, actually,' I said. 'I'm jealous.' And then, having never felt less like going to a party, I headed home to get changed.

Three years ago

'I'm going to head home now, Jon.' I looked around the function room, at the few remaining clusters of family members, most of the mourners having already left. 'I've said goodbye to Lydia's mum and dad and to your parents. They're staying with you this evening, aren't they?' I turned back to face him.

'Yes, they are.' He looked at me from hollowed eyes, an attempt at a smile emphasising his slimmer features, a result of his recent tendency to forget to eat. He was, I knew, exhausted – both physically and emotionally.

I looked up at him and hesitated, uncertain what to say. What I wanted to tell him was that his was not the only heart broken and that I too missed her at times more than I could bear. But to say those things seemed selfish and self-indulgent – a thinly veiled request for comfort from a friend so much more in need of comfort himself.

'I'm so sorry, Jon,' I said quietly. 'I do understand in part.'

He bent down to hug me and I placed my arms around his neck, pressing my head against his shoulder and not letting him go until I felt confident I could speak without a wobble.

'I know you're busy,' I said, on eventually releasing him, 'but I'm not. So just let me know if you're free for a coffee, or a drink, or… just anything…' My voice trailed away and I cleared my throat. 'And don't forget about book group at Connie's.' I managed a smile. 'I hope that's in the diary.'

He nodded. 'I haven't forgotten,' he said. 'And I've already read the book.'

'Have you?' I said, my eyes widening. 'That's impressive.'

'Yes,' he smiled again. 'We read it together. There was no way she was going to let me off the hook.'

Chapter 17

'And I've actually read the next book.' I looked up at Jon as he lifted the heavy silver knocker on Eleanor Black's front door and banged it down twice.

'That's quite a departure for you,' he said. 'Is that the first one you've finished this year?'

'Technically, no. Because I did read *Ethan Frome*.' He looked at me, frowning sceptically. 'Eventually. *After* the meeting at Connie and Greg's,' I clarified.

He nodded and turned back to the door. 'And has Greg introduced you to the Morgan yet?'

'To the what?'

'To his friend with the car.'

'Oh, I see.' Our journey to the party had largely been spent catching Jon up on my weekend with Hugh – although, as it turned out, most of the more gruesome details had already been recounted to him by Sophie. For my part, I hadn't quite recovered from the surprise of Miriam's gossip and would have much preferred to spend the drive grilling him about his date at Hotel du Vin. But it seemed an impossible subject to raise and I had therefore decided that, however desperate I was to find out exactly what was going on, I must bide my time, bite my tongue and wait for Jon to mention it.

'Well, Greg helpfully emailed me loads of photos of the car the other day – but not a single one of its driver.' I sighed. 'But no doubt I'll get to meet him at some point.' I nudged Jon and pointed up at the unanswered door. 'Sophie always comments on the size of that knocker.'

He looked at me questioningly.

'Mrs Melons.' I explained, lowering my voice and making a cupping gesture in front of my chest with my hands. 'Big boobs. Large knocker.'

He smiled. 'I can't deny that I'm rather intrigued to meet them – I mean her.' He turned to me and his smile broadened. 'No, you're right, I mean them.' He gestured at the door. 'I'll have another go.'

He brought the knocker down sharply three times and the heavy piece of door furniture was still in his hand as the door itself began to open. Eleanor Black greeted me with what appeared to be a forced and, I suspected, heavily botoxed smile. 'Oh, it's you,' she said. 'I was passing, so I answered myself. God knows where the staff are.' She opened the door further and realised that I was not alone. 'My goodness, I'm so sorry.' Her smile widened, her voice softened and her right hand began to toy with the heavy gold necklace, resembling intertwined earthworms, which sat awkwardly upon her ample cleavage. She was wearing a black and red floral, low cut dress, which looked suspiciously like it had been altered to place as much boob as possible on display, whilst just about allowing her to be able to claim that she was fully-clothed. She looked Jon up and down appreciatively. 'I didn't realise you were with a…' she hesitated, '…a *friend*?'

'Yes,' I said, sliding past her into the hall, 'this is my *friend*, Jon. Jon, this is Eleanor. We've redesigned her kitchen, dining and living spaces for her. The project was an absolute pleasure from beginning to end.'

'Hello,' Jon smiled and stepped inside.

I noticed that Eleanor somehow mistimed the closing of the door, so that she brushed chest-to-chest against him as he entered. 'Sorry, Jon,' she breathed, patting the back of her heavily lacquered, heavily bleached chignon. 'I don't think I gave you quite enough room there, did I? I nearly crushed you.'

'Not a problem, Eleanor,' he said. 'I'm very resilient.'

She inhaled deeply at this response, swelling her bosom and testing the stitching on her dress to the point of destruction.

'Yes,' I said, threading my arm through Jon's and leaning my head against him, 'you're quite hardy, aren't you, Jon?'

Eleanor Black's smile remained in place but her breasts subsided and her eyes hardened.

'Ms Black.'

Our hostess turned her head, as a small, middle-aged woman, wearing a long black apron, ascended the stairs from the lower ground floor. She was accompanied by a tall, good-looking man, whom I guessed to be in his early twenties. The latter was carrying a tray of canapés. 'Are you happy for Damario and Rebecca to start a second sweep, or do you want us to hold back? The bites are going down well.'

A flash of annoyance crossed Eleanor's face. 'I'll come down now,' she said, turning back to face us. 'Caterers,' she breathed quietly to Jon, her smile now back in place. 'But you,' she tapped a hand casually on his chest, 'go on through and get yourself a drink. There's quite a crowd but there's plenty to go round. I shall look forward to catching you later.'

'Thank you, Eleanor,' I said, forcing my way into the exchange. 'That's so kind of you.'

She twitched slightly, as if having forgotten my presence. 'Oh, not at all. I've just seen David and your colleague in the throng near the conservatory.' And with that, she removed her hand from Jon's chest, threw him what I guessed was supposed to be a coquettish smile, and followed the caterers down the stairs.

'The woman is a nightmare,' I muttered, watching her go. 'She was thirty seconds away from unbuttoning your shirt. Poor David.' I looked up at Jon.

'I think the danger has passed.' He nodded his head towards my arm, which was still entwined around his.

I set him free and removed my jacket. 'Sorry,' I said. 'What can I tell you? She brings out my protective, maternal instinct.'

'I felt very safe. Thank you.' He took my jacket from me and hung it on one of the temporary clothes rails positioned in the expansive entrance hall, while I turned and peered towards the rear of the house. It was clear from noise levels, and the groups visible through open doorways, that the party was a large, and possibly over-crowded, affair. I felt some relief at the possibility that Eleanor might actually have some difficulty *catching* us later.

I turned to Jon. 'Shall we go and find David and Sophie?'

He nodded. 'Great idea,' he said.

We walked down the long hallway and into the kitchen, heading towards the crowd occupying the vast seating and dining area, each collecting a glass of champagne from a central, granite-topped island as we went.

David, when we eventually found him, was standing chatting to Louise and Ben Battersby, the former clients who had recommended us to Eleanor Black, their near neighbour. I smiled as we approached. I liked Louise; she was what my mother used to call *unfussy*, and had an entertaining fondness for gossip. She also knew Miriam, their daughters attending the same pre-school. David raised a hand and smiled, as he spotted us heading towards him.

'Alice,' he said, kissing me on the cheek, 'and hello, Jon,' he added, placing a friendly hand on the latter's shoulder. 'Alice, you know Louise and Ben, of course.'

I smiled. 'How are you both?'

'Hello,' said Louise. 'We're just congratulating David on the magnificent job you've done here.' She gestured at the room.

'Thank you,' I said, 'it was a fun project.'

Louise looked doubtful.

'Really?' asked Ben, audibly echoing her scepticism.

'Each project presents unique challenges,' David chipped in. 'But that's what makes it fun, isn't it, Alice?' he added, turning to me.

'Yes,' I said. 'Whether that be the space, or interpreting and managing the expectations of the client.'

'I think we can all guess the nature of the challenge on this occasion,' muttered Ben.

'Ben,' said Louise, her face stern.

'Sorry,' said Ben.

David looked momentarily disconcerted, before settling himself with a polite introduction. 'Oh, Jon,' he said, 'I'm so sorry. This is Louise and Ben Battersby. We helped them with their lounge and playroom last year. Louise and Ben, this is Jonathan Durham. Jon runs a human factors consultancy.'

'I think we might know a few of the same people, Jon,' said Ben. 'Charles Hardwick? He's in ergonomics.'

Jon smiled. 'Yes, I know Charles,' he said, and as the commercial small-talk commenced, I turned to Louise and asked after her daughter, Imi.

'She is doing really well,' said Louise. 'She and Miriam's daughter had a play-date yesterday, actually. With another little girl, Emily.' She paused. 'Has Miriam mentioned Emily?'

I thought for a moment. 'No, I don't think she has.'

'Her father, Eammon, is a stay-at-home dad. Very nice. Phoebe and Emily get on very well together.' She looked at me and paused again, as she sipped her drink. 'As do Miriam and Eammon.'

I looked at Louise and was just about to ask her a little more about Eammon, when she placed a gentle hand on my elbow and, applying near-imperceptible pressure, rotated me away from the men in our group.

'Look,' she said, lowering her voice. 'You tell me to stop being nosey if you want to, but…' she glanced over her shoulder at David, 'he isn't really going out with Eleanor, is he?'

'Well,' I began uncertainly, 'I'm not exactly…'

'Only it doesn't seem like what you'd call a natural pairing to me.' Louise drained her glass. 'I said to Ben, "That's not a natural pairing, Ben." And Ben said, "Why, because David is a very nice person?" And I said, "Well, yes." And Ben said, "You're right."'

I offered her what I hoped was a pained expression.

'Oh, I'm being unfair.' She squeezed my arm. 'Putting you in a difficult position, when Eleanor is a client. But,' she lowered her voice further, 'as I say, it's not a natural pairing.'

'This sounds interesting,' said Ben. We turned to see that the men were now listening-in on our conversation. 'What's all this about natural pairings?' He looked at Louise. 'You're not matchmaking, are you?' he asked, before giving me a wink. 'She's a dreadful matchmaker.'

Louise glanced at David and appeared flustered. 'Ben,' she said, her lips barely moving.

He lowered his head, as if dodging incoming fire.

'I hope you're *not* matchmaking, Louise,' David smiled. 'Poor Alice endured a rather muddy weekend recently as a result of a helpful friend matchmaking. Didn't you, Alice?' he said amiably.

I shot him a glance, which had the effect of making him physically recoil. Jon scratched his upper lip; an attempt, I knew, to suppress a smile.

'Oops,' laughed Ben. 'Put your foot in it there, have you, David?' He seemed to relish the idea that someone, other than himself, had made a faux pas.

'Oh, so you two aren't a couple then?' Louise looked at me, whilst moving her left index finger back and forth between Jon and myself.

I looked at Jon, willing him to share the burden of the attention. Instead, he offered me an amused smile, which I met with a frown.

'No,' I said to Louise. 'But I do love your necklace. Where is it from?' I asked, keen to divert interest from my personal life.

'Sorry for mentioning the matchmaking,' said David. He looked at me anxiously.

'Twice,' I said. 'But it's fine. Nothing like making me sound needy.' I forced a laugh.

Louise put an arm around me and squeezed. 'Being set-up doesn't make you sound needy,' she grinned.

'Well, maybe just a bit needy,' laughed Ben, delivering another wink.

I attempted a smile.

'Hello, strangers!' I turned to discover Sophie standing behind me; cocktail in one hand and yet another variation on the cigarette-substitute theme, in the other. 'Thought you two would never get here,' she said. 'Bloody skivers.' She wagged a finger at Jon and me. Louise laughed and I joined in, delighted to be presented with an opportunity to redirect the conversation.

'Hi!' I said. 'We're not that late. What time did you get here? Where's Graham?'

'Graham?' she said, turning her head towards me in a somewhat concentrated fashion; an indication, I knew, of slight inebriation.

'Oh... he's got a date. I came with David. Was here from the off – sticking to him like glue. I'm like bloody Kevin Costner in *The Bodyguard*.'

David emitted something halfway between a sigh and a groan at this point, before raising a hand to interject. Sophie, of course, ignored the attempted interruption, continuing, without hesitation, her account of the evening. 'So, I just took a ten minute break from driving Miss Daisy,' she waved her non-cigarette at David, 'and met a lovely, lovely man called Henry, who makes puppets. Could be a bit kinky. Not sure yet. How are things at this end of the space? What's the chat?'

'I was just talking to Louise about Imi,' I said.

'And then I mentioned Alice's request for dates.' David smiled apologetically and made a *mea culpa* face.

I stared at him incredulously, whilst making a mental note to slap him at the earliest opportunity.

'You *requested* dates?' Ben guffawed. 'Now that *is* needy!' Louise elbowed him hard in the ribs, causing him to gasp in pain and mutter, 'What the fu—' before a second elbowing cut him short.

'No, actually, I *didn't* request dates,' I said, feeling my cheeks begin to burn. 'And I'm not sure who gave David that impression.' I glared at Sophie before turning back to Louise. 'I'm just happy to meet new people.'

'Euphemism alert!' laughed Ben, clearly recovered from Louise's assault.

'For God's sake, Ben,' groaned Louise. She turned to me. 'I think it's great that you're putting yourself out there. I thought she was with Jon,' she added, nudging Sophie.

I looked miserably at Jon. He was still smiling and I felt suddenly irritated. He, I thought, had divulged nothing – wanted absolute privacy – about his personal relationships. And yet he seemed perfectly happy to laugh along as *my* private life was picked apart at a party.

And suddenly I saw a way to share the spotlight. 'No, Jon and I aren't together,' I said, hurriedly. 'He's actually dating someone, aren't you, Jon?'

I regretted the comment almost before the last word was out.

Sophie's head snapped round. 'Are you, Jon?' she asked, her expression puzzled.

'Ooh, everyone's at it!' laughed Louise. 'I *so* miss my single days and playing the field.'

'Me too,' muttered Ben.

'Are you,' repeated Sophie, punctuating the sentence with a large gulp from her glass, 'seeing someone, Jon?'

'Yes, I am,' he said simply, whilst looking at me steadily. My stomach lurched.

Sophie blinked rapidly. 'Oh,' she said. She appeared totally at a loss; something I had rarely, if ever, witnessed.

Louise's smile faded as she looked from Jon to Sophie and then back again. 'And, er, is that going well, Jon?' she asked uncertainly.

'Yes.' He turned to her and smiled.

I looked at Sophie. She was now chewing on the end of her plastic cigarette, whilst staring expressionlessly at the floor. Louise was eyeing her with obvious concern.

'Well, that's all very... lovely,' said Louise, with exaggerated brightness, 'but it's high time Ben and I stopped tormenting you with personal questions and let you mingle.'

Ben frowned. 'Actually, it wasn't me who—'

Louise cut him off. 'I said it's time for you to *stop* tormenting people now, Ben.' She held up her empty wine glass. 'And I for one need a refill. It's so lovely to see you all again – and to meet you, Jon. And, er, good luck with the dating!' She shot Sophie a last worried look and then turned and walked off in the direction of the kitchen wine supply.

'Right, well...' Ben looked down uncomfortably at the largely untouched glass of wine in his right hand. 'I... well, I'd better keep her company. Best of luck, all.' And off he went.

We stood in unmoving silence, like statues in a particularly busy museum.

'Well,' said Jon after a moment, 'that was fun.'

I looked up at him for any hint of a smile. There was none. He simply raised his eyebrows at me and drank his wine.

David spoke next. 'I'm sorry for raising the subject of…' I held up a hand and he checked himself mid-sentence, '…for raising that subject.'

I shook my head. 'I'm no better,' I mumbled and looked at Jon.

'Let's just find a *new* subject,' he said, looking round the room.

'I'm sorry,' I said.

He didn't reply.

I sighed and tried to recall a worse start to an evening.

Sophie looked up. 'Are you really dating, Jon?' she asked. Her expression was that of a cartoon character who has just been hit in the face with a frying pan.

'Sophie,' I touched her arm, 'he has already said he is.'

She looked at me. 'I'm so confused,' she said. 'And you knew this? How long have you known?'

David stepped towards her. 'Come on,' he said, taking her arm. 'That last cocktail seems to have hit you pretty hard. Let's go and find a sofa and a glass of water.'

She turned towards him and, still looking extremely dazed, said, 'That sounds nice, David. Thank you.'

He smiled down at her, held out his arm for her to link, and together they headed off in the direction of the brand new conservatory, which ran the entire length of the back of the house. I watched them go, noticing Sophie cast a last worried glance at Jon over her shoulder, before forcing David to detour slightly so she could grab a fresh cocktail from a tray carried by the attractive young caterer we had seen earlier.

I turned to Jon. He studied his drink, before looking up at me. 'You've done a great job here,' he said.

'I was just desperate for people to stop asking me about dating,' I said quietly.

He said nothing.

I attempted a smile. 'So, you said things are going well. That's great.'

He remained silent, his expression disconcertingly stern.

'I'd love you to tell me about it all,' I continued, still smiling, whilst feeling increasingly desperate in the face of such obvious disapproval.

'I'm really sorry if I raised it in the wrong way. I know I should have talked to you about it privately first—'

'Or not at all,' he interrupted, his tone abrupt.

My smile fell away. 'What?'

He looked down at me, his expression uncharacteristically lacking in humour and warmth. 'Perhaps you shouldn't have raised it privately or publicly, until I chose to mention it to you. *If* I chose to mention it to you.'

I blinked up at him, completely crushed by an inferred slight regarding the closeness of our friendship, whilst at the same time conscious of a heavy, inescapable irony. Not mentioning his date had been precisely my intention less than an hour earlier. What had happened to that resolve?

'But it's just such a positive thing,' I said quietly. 'It's a shame not to—'

'Don't be disingenuous.' For the first time in our friendship, he sounded irritated with me and it hurt to an unexpected degree. 'You've just admitted that you brought it up to shift the focus from you to me.'

'But it's also—'

'The relationship is not something I want to discuss with you.'

He spoke quietly, but his frustration was obvious. The words hit me like calmly fired bullets. I stared up at him, saying nothing.

He looked at me steadily and, after a moment, I lowered my eyes to gaze, unfocused, into my wine glass.

'Alice,' I heard him say, but I didn't look up. There followed what seemed like a lengthy pause before he spoke again, 'I've spotted a couple of people I know over there. I'm going to go and say hi.'

I opened my mouth to speak but this time he continued without hesitation. 'I'll see you later,' he said. I raised my head and he offered me a distressingly polite smile, before weaving his way in the direction of a small group at the other end of the room. I turned and watched them greet his arrival with delighted surprise.

I stood for a moment, uncertain what to do; my preferred option being to curl up into a foetal position, gnaw on my own fist and bawl.

Jon had dated for the first time in over three years – an undoubtedly huge personal and emotional step. And I had judged it appropriate to raise the matter, in the middle of a party, without warning, in front of people he had never met before. On reflection, I decided "*crass*" was the most appropriate umbrella term for my behaviour.

'Ah, there you are.' I felt a light tap on my shoulder and turned to see Eleanor Black standing behind me. She looked distractingly shiny and I wondered whether the sheen was attributable to alcohol, hostess stress or botox. Quite possibly a combination of all three, I thought. 'There you are,' she repeated, offering me her best smile. 'And where are…' her eyes flickered uncertainly, '…the rest of you?'

'The rest of me?' I asked, genuinely confused by the grammar.

She maintained the smile, but I detected a twitch of annoyance.

'David, and the other one of you and,' she purred, her smile widening to apparent breaking point, 'your friend.'

Ah, my *friend*. Now I understood the charm offensive: the offensive charm. I drained my wine glass, as feelings of misery and guilt over Jon, morphed into ones of impatience and antipathy towards Eleanor Black. She was, I decided, an unfeeling, self-serving, narcissistic, over-sexed harridan and I didn't have it in me to tolerate her company at the moment.

'David and the other one of me are relaxing in the conservatory,' I said. 'I'm just about to join them. Would you like to come?' I extended the invitation, confident of a rejection.

She hesitated; predictably reluctant to be foiled in her pursuit of Jon. 'Right, and how is your friend? I was concerned that he might not know anyone here. Where is he?'

'I think he headed through into the den,' I said, turning and walking towards the conservatory. 'You could try there.'

Escaping Eleanor, I found David and Sophie chatting happily on a sofa in one corner of the crowded conservatory. 'Hello, you two,' I said, when I arrived. 'Room for a small one?'

They looked up and their faces fell, causing me to experience a fresh wave of misery. The evening was turning into a disaster. What had I done now?

It was only when a voice behind me said, 'I think you mean room for two, don't you?' that I realised David and Sophie were looking not at me, but at Eleanor who, despite my conviction to the contrary, had actually followed me into the conservatory and was now standing behind me, awaiting a seat. I had led her straight to David. I considered getting my coat.

'Oh, Eleanor,' David stood up. 'How lovely to see you. We did wonder where you had got to, didn't we, Sophie?'

Sophie folded her arms. 'Oh yes, that's right, we were all wondery wonderment,' she muttered.

Thankfully, Eleanor appeared not to hear. 'Sit back down, David, and I'll sit next to you. And she,' she waved a hand in my direction, whilst continuing to look at David, 'can sit next to your other colleague.'

David sat, as did I.

Sophie turned and gave me a look which I interpreted as mixture of disdain for Eleanor Black and bemusement at the fact that I had brought the child catcher into the nursery.

'So,' said Eleanor, 'I think it's all going rather well.' She pointlessly hoisted up the neckline of her dress, before immediately pulling it down again to re-expose her cleavage. 'Apart from the fact that I now seem to be without a drink.' She looked pointedly at Sophie. 'And I just don't feel I can get up again for a moment. I've been on my feet all evening.'

'Ooh, yes,' said Sophie, glancing at Eleanor's legs, 'your ankles are swelling.'

'I'll get the drinks!' David leapt to his feet. 'Same again, for you, Alice? White wine, Eleanor? And Sophie, I think you're OK for now, yes? Right. Shan't be a tick.'

I could tell that all three of us were slightly taken aback by the speed of his departure and an awkward silence fell as we sat in a row on the sofa; Sophie and I separated from Eleanor by the space so suddenly vacated by David.

Still deflated and distracted by my exchange with Jon, and irritated by Eleanor's pre-occupation with him, I found it difficult to immediately reassume the mantle of business ambassador. It was therefore left to Sophie to end the conversational hiatus.

'I know I'm partly responsible for it,' she said, looking round, 'but your home is looking lovely, Eleanor.' I looked at her, unable to keep my expression entirely free of surprise and admiration at this uncontroversial opener.

'Well, you certainly charged me enough,' said Eleanor.

Oh dear.

I felt Sophie stiffen but she laughed lightly. 'Ah, well, you do get what you pay for.'

'I know what I paid for with the fixtures and fittings, because I can see them and they're useful.' Eleanor offered her a thin smile. 'The value of advice and opinion is harder to quantify.'

Sophie twisted slightly in her seat. 'I agree absolutely,' she said. I experienced an immediate sense of relief and allowed myself to exhale. 'It is difficult to put a value on advice, because, quite often, it is invaluable.' I hoped Sophie would stop there. But, of course, she didn't. 'Take that dress you're wearing, for example—'

'These sofas are soooo comfortable, aren't they?' I said, bouncing slightly.

'What about my dress?' Eleanor looked at Sophie and narrowed her eyes.

'Well, it's a beautiful dress,' said Sophie. 'You've clearly invested there. And you could wear it any number of ways, with any number of accessories. You've chosen to wear it your way.' Sophie thrust her chest forward and pouted. 'Very glamorous. Very Marilyn.'

I glanced at Eleanor and was relieved to see that she seemed to consider this last comment to be a compliment. Nevertheless, I felt the exchange was teetering on the brink of catastrophe and made a second attempt at situation retrieval. 'I've just bought a new sofa. And I actually spent quite a lot of time—'

'It's true that I have a sense of femininity and style which many women envy,' said Eleanor. Sophie nodded, exercising considerable self-restraint. I tensed and prayed for a change of subject. 'And, that being the case, I'm not sure why on earth I would want to take advice from anyone else.' My shoulders sagged involuntarily, as I experienced a sense of resignation to the inevitable.

'It's just all about keeping one's mind open to the possibilities,' Sophie returned.

'Yes, well I've noted lots of sartorial *possibilities* this evening.' Eleanor looked Sophie up and down, her eyes lingering disparagingly on the latter's plain black shift dress. 'And most of them are dire.'

I looked at Sophie, she was now staring unblinkingly and without expression at Eleanor. I leaned forward, placing myself between the two women, summoning up the energy for one last stab at keeping the peace. 'The thing about sofas is that a lot depends upon leg length, doesn't it? I have an incredibly short upper body, so when I—'

Sophie placed a hand on my shoulder and gently eased me back, so that she could see Eleanor. She spoke calmly.

'What I'm saying is that, with third-party perspective, the next time you wore your beautiful dress, you could make it look totally different – like a new dress,' she continued. 'Someone else might suggest you accessorise it in a way you might not have otherwise considered.'

'Rubbish,' said Eleanor dismissively. 'And typical of someone who earns a living charging for hot air. There is nothing anyone could tell me about how to dress.'

'They could tell you to put your tits away,' muttered Sophie.

The comment would have been inaudible to Eleanor, but she sensed a retort and flared nevertheless. 'What did you say?' Her left eye twitched and she looked about to blow. 'I missed your last comment.'

'Did you?' said Sophie. She leaned back on the sofa and looked bored.

I forced myself to look back at Eleanor. She was now red as well as shiny: a buxom tomato.

'Right, here are your drinks,' said David. He was walking towards us, juggling three large glasses of wine. Eleanor and I each relieved him of a glass and he sat back down in the empty sofa space which had been preserved for him.

'Thanks, David,' I said.

Eleanor, the florid, ticking time bomb, nodded at him.

Nobody spoke.

'Gosh, this sofa is comfy,' said David.

'I've tried that,' I said.

He looked at me and frowned. 'What?'

'She has just been very rude about my dress,' Eleanor snapped loudly.

David jumped, his eyes immediately darting to Eleanor's cleavage. 'What breasts?' he said. 'Er, I mean what dress? I mean who's been rude?'

Sophie burst out laughing and, had my mood not been so fatally crushed earlier in the evening, I would no doubt have joined in. However, at that moment, the exchange merely increased my levels of anxiety and irritation.

'Eleanor,' I sighed, 'the dress is lovely. Sophie wasn't criticising it. She was simply using it to illustrate the advantages of a fresh perspective. Don't worry.'

'Don't you patronise me,' Eleanor spat.

I turned to her, astonished by her response. 'I wasn't trying to patronise you. I was simply reassuring you that the dress is fine.'

'Alice,' said David quietly, 'let's just change the subject.'

I drank my wine. 'Why does everybody always want to change the subject?' I said. 'You know, sometimes issues do have to be resolved – no matter what the time or place. Actions have to be explained and feelings expressed. Feelings can't forever be left suppressed and unexpressed, you know.' The words spilled out in an inarticulate stream of tipsy consciousness.

'What *is* she rambling on about?' Eleanor looked at me, whilst placing a red-taloned hand on David's knee.

'I think maybe...' David looked at me uncertainly. 'Do you know, Eleanor, I'm not entirely sure. But what I do know is that Alice is a remarkably bright woman, who usually makes a very good point.'

I felt my lower lip wobble. 'Thank you, David.' I offered him a watery smile and kissed his cheek.

He smiled kindly at me.

'Get off him,' hissed Eleanor menacingly.

Sophie leaned forward. 'What did you say to her?' she asked.

David held up a hand. 'I think—'

'I told her to get off him,' repeated Eleanor, eyeing Sophie dangerously.

'That's what I thought you said.' Sophie's jaw tightened and my sense of foreboding deepened. 'I just don't understand why you spoke to Alice so aggressively and why you referred to David as if he was something you'd picked out at the Sainsbury's meat counter.'

'How dare speak to me to me like that?' Eleanor leaned threateningly towards Sophie. 'May I remind you who has paid your wages for the past two months?'

'David pays my wages. You're a former client who paid a fee for our services, nothing more. I'm sorry if such basic business concepts are beyond you.' Sophie drained her cocktail. 'And even if you had paid my wages, you can't buy respect, you have to earn it. And you haven't earned it – from any of us.' She edged forward in her seat and made as if to leave, but Eleanor reached in front of David and myself, and put a restraining hand on her arm.

'If it wasn't for the fact that David is my boyfriend,' she seethed, 'I would make sure I was the last client your company ever had. You've been an obnoxious little bitch from the start.' She looked at me. 'Both of you have.'

David sat up sharply. 'Eleanor, I won't tolerate—'

'Your *boy*friend?' Sophie stared at Eleanor incredulously. 'You are joking, surely? Firstly, David is all man, so how dare you demean him by using the word *boy*? And—'

'Sophie,' began David, 'let me—'

'And call me a bitch if you want because, actually, yes, I have said some very unflattering stuff about you behind your back but *she*,' Sophie placed her right arm around me and pointed at me with her left hand, '*she* hasn't had a bad word to say about you. And the fact that you are so fucking rude and unpleasant to someone who has never done you any harm just about sums you up. And let me tell you this for nothing, the only reason she and David have anything to do with you, anything *at all*, is because they, and everyone else here,' she waved a hand at the room, 'are just too fucking polite to tell you to piss off. Well I'm not. So piss off! Oh and another thing,' Sophie stood up, 'for fuck's sake put some clothes on!' She pointed at Eleanor's chest. 'Yes, you've got big tits but then so has Simon Cowell and my Uncle Bill's dairy herd. Let me tell you, deary, no one's fucking interested.'

It was at this point I realised that pretty much all conversation around us had ceased; the only noise being what sounded like a faint ripple of anonymous applause from a far corner of the conservatory.

Eleanor Black's mouth opened and closed wordlessly, giving her the appearance of one of the larger puffer fish I had seen with Phoebe at the zoo.

Sophie bit her lip and blinked back what looked suspiciously like tears. She looked first at me and then at David. 'I'm so sorry,' she said quietly, her eyes still fixed on him. 'I think I've let you down.' And with that, she walked rapidly out of the conservatory and disappeared into the blissfully unaware kitchen crowd.

David was staring at the ground. 'Oh dear,' he said.

I looked about me. The various small groups had politely recommenced talking amongst themselves although, judging by some of the smirks and glances in our direction, the recent floorshow was the preferred topic of quiet conversation.

Eleanor Black finally found her voice. 'It is beyond me why you would ever choose to employ someone like that,' she hissed.

David's gaze remained fixed on the floor. 'Because she's excellent at her job,' he said simply, 'and also—'

'That's no justification for—'

'I hadn't finished, Eleanor,' he continued calmly. 'She's excellent at her job and valued by clients for her honesty and straightforwardness.'

'Straightforwardness? Her language is—'

'And I value her for her honesty and integrity also; both professionally and personally. Now,' he looked up at her, 'would it be easier for you if Alice and I left?'

'I... I...' Eleanor stared at David in confusion, as if he was speaking some unknown language.

'Or would you like us to stay?' he asked.

She appeared to collect herself and rose to her feet. 'Stay,' she said, walking away. 'People want to meet you.'

I watched her be swallowed up by the crowd, as David leaned back into the sofa and closed his eyes, clearly as shell-shocked as I was. We'd been at this party for less than an hour and in that time I had been reduced to a complete emotional wreck. However now, I told myself, was not the time to dwell. I had to find Sophie.

I made to stand up. 'I'd better go after her,' I said to David. 'She was very upset.'

He opened his eyes, placed his hand on my arm and stood up. 'No, I'll go, Alice. You stay there and relax.'

Relax? I could only assume that he was existing in some sort of parallel universe.

I tugged at his jacket. 'I meant I was going to find Sophie, David, not Eleanor.'

'I know you did,' he said, turning and walking away. 'So did I.'

Chapter 18

I wasn't certain how long I sat there alone, following David's exit in pursuit of Sophie, but I was already quite far down my second glass of wine, by the time I was jolted back into awareness by Jon's arrival.

'I know I've missed something,' he said. 'I'm just not sure what.'

I raised my head and he looked down at me questioningly, before joining me on the sofa. His appearance was, of course, an immediate reminder of our earlier disagreement and succeeded in lowering my mood even further – something which, up until that point, I would have thought impossible. I returned to studying the contents of my glass and shrugged.

He gestured towards the kitchen. 'A short time ago, Sophie rushed past me looking like she wasn't having a great time. I caught up with her and she said she was fine but had an urgent call to make. And I've just seen David looking like an official mourner. What's happened?'

Reluctant as I was to focus on the situation, I realised I was going to have to update him. 'Well,' I sighed, running a finger absently around the rim of my glass, 'Sophie told Eleanor Black to put her boobs away. Except she used the word "*tits*". And she said also said "*fuck*". A lot.' I looked at him miserably. 'And very loudly. You know the way she does when she's cross.'

'Oh,' he said, clearly trying not to laugh.

I shook my head. 'It's not funny.'

'I think you'll find it is a bit funny.'

I looked at him blankly, envying his apparent ability to firewall all the negative emotions which had been so evident earlier in the evening.

'And if the conversations I've just been party to, are anything to go by,' he continued, 'I'm surprised Sophie didn't get a round of applause.'

'Well, as a matter of fact…' I smiled involuntarily.

He returned the smile and I looked up at him, feeling suddenly torn. I desperately wanted him to be happy and, as I had told Miriam earlier that evening, I accepted that he had every right to be. But at the same time, I now realised that I was having extreme difficulty in being completely selfless about the situation. And the idea of him having a relationship which changed *our* relationship, wasn't an easy one for me. Not only that, I remained undeniably hurt and bewildered that he didn't want to share such a significant part of his life with me.

Meanwhile, he was talking again. 'So, I don't think it's a problem.' He nodded his head towards the kitchen. 'No one in there will have heard anything and Eleanor isn't likely to want to provide any details. Even if it leaked out, most people are just going to be grateful that someone told her to put some clothes on.'

'Sorry, what?' I looked up at him and held up my near-empty glass. 'I'm afraid I'm not focusing very well at the moment. I drank this far too quickly,' I said, trying to smile, before giving it up as a bad job. I sighed, lowered my wine glass and relaxed into misery, instinctively leaning my head against his shoulder. 'I'm so sorry about earlier, Jon,' I said quietly. 'You are such a good friend and I just don't want that to change.'

I felt him suddenly stiffen and I sat up, experiencing an agonising realisation that, however close I thought we were, he clearly now felt differently. Or maybe, I thought miserably, he had always felt differently.

He turned towards me. 'Shall we leave?' he asked. He looked serious and, I guessed, unhappy at the thought of an early exit.

'I wish I could,' I said, taking his suggestion as objective confirmation that my evening was now beyond recovery, 'but I don't want David to feel abandoned.'

He made no response.

'Anyway,' I continued, attempting to pull myself together, 'whatever I do, there's no need for you to leave. I haven't needed seeing to my door in quite a while now. And you know far more people here than I do. Go and enjoy yourself. I'm just going to stay here and keep out of mischief until David gets back. I'll send a few texts and try to find out what's going on.'

'Right,' he said, standing up almost before I had finished speaking. 'I'll leave you to it. But let me know if you do decide to go home. It'll save me looking for you at the end of the evening.'

'Of course,' I said in surprise. 'I wouldn't just…' My voice trailed away as he headed back towards the main kitchen crowd, without waiting for me to complete the sentence.

I sat back on the sofa, heaved a sigh and reached for my bag. Taking out my phone, I texted David.

Have you found Sophie?

I then sent a second text to Sophie.

Are you ok? David was looking for you.

I stared into space, clutching my phone, awaiting a reply. I didn't think there was much more I could do. I began to wish Jon hadn't taken me at my word and left quite so immediately. My phone buzzed. It was a text from Sophie.

I'm fine. Just feeling stupid. Saw David. Now on way home.
Have sister with me tomorrow but will see you Monday. xx

I placed my phone back in my bag, stood up to see if there was any sign of David and immediately spotted him winding his way towards me. He saw me and raised a hand. A few seconds, and multiple *excuse me*'s later, and he was back at my side. I felt a rush of relief at his return.

'Well, I caught her,' he said, as we sat back down.

'I know,' I replied. 'I had a text. How is she?'

'Tearful. It's very strange to see her like that. Usually, she's so…' He made a fist with his hand and shook it at the ceiling.

I nodded. 'Yes.'

'But she didn't really want to talk,' he continued. 'She said she just wanted to get home.'

'She wasn't quite herself all evening.'

He folded his arms and sighed. 'You mean over Jon?'

'You noticed then.'

'I know you think of me as a bumbling idiot,' he said forlornly, 'but that one was hard to miss – even for me.'

'I do not think of you as a bumbling idiot!' I protested. 'I'm the one forever putting my foot in it.'

He offered me a tired smile and then rubbed his eyes. 'I was exaggerating. I just miss social cues sometimes. And I find women particularly confusing,' he sighed. 'Anyway, Sophie was very upset. Kept repeating that she'd let everybody down and wouldn't accept that I didn't see it that way.' He stared at the far wall of the conservatory.

I touched his arm. 'Are you OK?' I asked gently.

'No, I'm not.' He shook his head. 'Because this is actually all my fault.'

'Oh, don't be silly,' I tutted.

'It is,' he insisted. 'And that's what I should have said to Sophie.' He raised a hand to prevent any further objection. 'I shouldn't have engaged in anything beyond a professional relationship with Eleanor. If I hadn't, the argument would never have arisen. In fact, we probably wouldn't even be here.' He looked at me, as if for a response.

'Sorry, David,' I sighed, 'but if you're after relationship advice or top tips on social interaction, you're absolutely talking to the wrong person. I have demonstrated this very evening that I never know when to keep my mouth shut and,' I slumped back wearily on the sofa, 'of course, on top of that, you know that I'm incapable of spotting a total shit at fifty paces. Pardon my man-language.'

He smiled. 'Pardon granted. On the basis,' he added, 'that Edward was, indisputably, a total sh…' He hesitated. 'He was one.'

We sat in silence for a moment.

'I've got to sort things out, Alice,' he said, eventually.

'What do you mean?'

'There are a number of issues to address. However, the first thing I would like to do is leave this party.'

'Oh God, me too,' I said.

He stood up and offered me his hand. 'Shall we?'

I allowed him to hoist me to my feet. 'But I've got to find Jon. He won't want to leave but I must say goodbye.'

'Of course, and,' he paused, 'and we must take leave of our hostess.'

I took a deep breath and nodded. 'Yes,' I said. 'We must.'

Chapter 19

It took us some time to find Jon, but we eventually tracked him down to the front reception room, where he was looking happy and relaxed as he chatted with a largish group, which included Ben Battersby. We walked over to the group and I tapped Jon's shoulder.

He turned, still smiling at whatever anecdote had just been recounted.

'Hi,' he said and then added, addressing David, 'All well?'

David nodded.

'Good.' Jon gestured towards the group. 'Do you know everyone?'

'We're actually just heading off,' I said.

'Both of you?' asked Jon. 'So you don't need seeing to your door?'

David leaned forward. 'Don't worry, Jon, I'll see her safely home.'

'Oh, for goodness sake,' I smiled. 'It's not even eleven and I'm thirty-two years old. But yes, I have David as my escort. So, you can stay and enjoy yourself.'

He nodded and kissed my cheek. 'I'll see you soon. David,' he raised his glass to him, 'I'm pleased everything is OK.'

Whilst David smiled and made some typically positive comments about the evening, I looked up at Jon and had a sudden and unexpected urge to ask him to quit the party, come for coffee, tell me all about his new relationship and reassure me that everything was going to be fine. I wasn't certain what had happened this evening but I felt a distance opening up between us, which I was desperate to narrow.

'Jon,' I began impulsively, as soon as David had finished speaking.

'Sorry, yes?' He had already half-turned away from us to return to the group discussion and he now looked over his shoulder at me enquiringly.

'Well, I just wondered...' I glanced at David, who was now scanning the crowd, I assumed in search of Eleanor. 'I just wondered if... I mean, I know you probably want...'

Jon raised his left eyebrow, looking puzzled and, I thought, mildly impatient. I felt the gulf between us widen. I was making things worse. I shook my head and smiled. 'I'm rambling. I'm sorry. I don't know what's the matter with me this evening.'

'Well, I wouldn't rush to the doctor,' he said. 'You seem pretty much the same as ever to me.'

It sounded like a joke. But it didn't feel like one.

'Ah, you know me so well,' I said, hardening a little. 'Anyway, you enjoy the rest of your evening.'

He didn't speak. Instead, he simply smiled and then nodded a farewell; clearly keen, I thought, not to prompt any further stumbling monologues. I turned to David and put a hand on his arm. 'Let's go,' I said, and we began our search for Eleanor.

We made our way back to the rear of the house and spent two or three minutes looking for her, before deciding she must be elsewhere. Following fruitless forays into the den, the study, the utility room and a return to the front reception room, I was beginning to favour a text-and-run approach to the situation.

'She could be anywhere, David,' I said wearily. We were now standing in the main hallway and I pointed upstairs. 'She might be in the bathroom, or giving someone a tour.'

He nodded. 'I know, but I really don't like to leave without telling her I'm going. You don't have to stay, though.' He took out his phone. 'I'll call you a cab.'

'Put that away,' I said, placing my hand over his phone. 'Of course, I'll stay. Unless there's some reason you'd prefer me not to, that is.'

He looked at the ceiling and blinked rapidly. 'It's just that... I've been thinking...' he began uncertainly, before gathering pace, 'and I believe I need to tell Eleanor, immediately, that I do not want anything beyond a professional relationship with her.' He looked at me. 'I need to be clear with her. And it cannot wait.'

I stared at him. 'You mean you're going to dump her?'

'I'm not really comfortable with that expression,' he said. 'But, yes, I am going to let her go.' He paused and swallowed. 'Whether she wants me to let her go or not.'

I bit my lip. 'But does it have to be right now? Do you think that's wise? I'm not great at this kind of thing but instinct is telling me—'

'Hello, you two!' I turned to see Louise Battersby, waving at us, as she heading down the hallway towards us. 'There's a queue a mile long for the loo back there, so I'm going to make a sneaky run upstairs. Don't tell on me, will you?'

'Louise,' said David, 'I don't suppose you know where Eleanor is, do you?'

She paused mid-flight and considered the matter. 'Well, she said earlier that she had to check on the caterers downstairs. Try down there,' she said, recommencing her climb.

I turned to David with the intention of continuing our conversation regarding the wisdom of dumping Eleanor, a possibly very influential client, at a crowded party – *her* crowded party. But he was already halfway down the stairs to the lower ground floor. I hurried after him.

'David, for goodness sake—'

He looked up at me and put a finger to his lips. He had reached the bottom of the stairs and was standing outside the half-open door to the basement, which was actually guest accommodation, comprising living room, bedroom, shower room and kitchen. The caterers were using the latter as their base, in order to keep the main kitchen free from clutter.

David beckoned to me with his left hand, whilst keeping his right index finger firmly pressed against his lips. I crept down the final few stairs and stood next to him, crouching slightly so that his chin touched the top of my head, our ears turned towards the gap in the doorway.

'I tell people I'm thirty-six and they just can't believe it.' We could hear Eleanor quite clearly, despite the fact that she was using her breathy, rather than her more usual Kalashnikov, tone. 'They all say, "Oh, surely you're not, Eleanor."'

'They say that because she's not,' whispered David. 'She's forty-one. I saw her driving licence.'

I placed my hand across my mouth to stifle a snigger.

'They say that because I look after myself, you see,' Eleanor continued. 'This body doesn't come easy or cheap, you know.' I raised my eyebrows but resisted the obvious joke out of respect for David's current relationship with the woman.

There followed a slight pause, during which someone cleared their throat. 'Ah, yes, I am seeing that, Mees Black,' said a male, heavily-accented voice.

'I know you are…' Eleanor's voice dropped but remained audible. 'I've seen you seeing. You've been seeing all evening, haven't you, Damian?'

'Damario, Mees Black. My name is Damario.' Damario laughed nervously.

'What's in a name?' breathed Eleanor.

More nervous male laughter.

'Anyway, Damian…'

'Damario.'

'Damianario—'

'Eet ees Damario.' He began to enunciate slowly. 'Da…mar…i…'

'Oh who cares what your bloody name is!' Eleanor snapped, before quickly following up the explosion with the most unconvincing attempt at a girlish giggle I had ever heard. 'Of course, *I* care,' she said hurriedly. 'That was just my little joke, Daman… Damar…'

'Da-mar-i-o.'

'Yes, yes, that's right,' she said quickly. 'Now, as I was saying, I know you've been looking. So…' At this point there was a longish pause. '…how about I show you some more?'

I looked at David, my eyes widening. He maintained a blank expression but returned his finger to his lips.

'Eet ees OK, Mees Black.' I detected unmistakeable panic in the voice. 'I seen enough. You are very kindly and attracteev, but I seen enough. Please to you, stop now.'

And, at that point, without warning, David pushed the door wide open. Exposing our presence, and revealing to us an exposed Ms Black.

She was standing with her back to us, her dress unzipped to the waist and pulled from her shoulders. And she was braless; that, absolutely enormous, undergarment lying at her feet on the floor, like a discarded parachute.

I stood up from my crouching position and raised a hand. 'Hello, there,' I said.

She looked over her shoulder towards us, whilst placing her arms across her chest. Her eyes bulged, as her lids opened to their full extent. Her mouth hung ajar.

'We thought you might need assistance,' said David calmly.

'I has not touched her! She ees touching me and I ees not liking eet!' The terrified young caterer wedged between Eleanor Black and the wall began to gabble frantically. 'I try to explain to her but she ees not stopping. I say to stop but she ees not!' He appeared close to tears.

'I was actually talking to you, Damario,' said David. 'We thought *you* might need help.'

The young man slid sideways along the wall to emerge from behind Eleanor. His shoulders sagged and he hung his head in relief. 'Thank you, thank you,' he said.

David walked over to him, extracting a business card from his wallet en route. He handed it to Damario. 'My name is David Moore. This is my card. If you experience any problems,' he looked at Eleanor, 'any problems at all, as a result of what happened here this evening, just give me a call and I will act as a witness for you.' He turned back to the young man. 'Do you understand what I am saying?'

Damario nodded. 'Thank you, Meester Moore. I am grateful.'

'It's not a problem,' said David. 'Now, why don't you get back upstairs? You need have no further contact with Ms Black this evening. And do remember to call me if you experience any difficulty.'

Damario attempted a smile and then, without any acknowledgement of either Eleanor or myself, hastened from the room.

Eleanor slid her arms back into her dress, zipped it up and, still braless, turned to face us, her enormous bosoms settling at somewhere around waist level. Her eyes had shrunk to regular size and I was grudgingly impressed to note that she seemed to have regained some degree of composure. She silently eyed first David and then myself. I felt genuinely relieved that the row of knives, residing on a magnetic wall plate in the kitchen area, was well out of her reach.

'We just came to say goodbye, Eleanor,' said David. His voice remained calm but there was now a look about him which recalled to mind Sophie's assertion earlier in the evening that he was "all man". 'I'm sorry this evening has proved so unpleasant in places. I would be very disappointed if that resulted in any negative impact upon Sophie's reputation or, indeed, upon your own. And I would ask you to bear the latter particularly in mind should you in any way attempt to impugn the reputation of my colleague.' He turned to me. 'Shall we go, Alice?'

I nodded, struck dumb by his air of authority, then led the way out of the basement and upstairs to the front door.

'Do you have a jacket?' David asked, pointing at the clothes rails as we reached the top of the stairs.

'Yes,' I said, 'here it is.' I removed the jacket from its hanger. David took it from me and held it up for me to slip on.

He then wordlessly opened the front door, exiting after me and pulling the door closed behind us. Only when we had walked down the stone steps, crossed the drive and reached the pavement, did he release a huge sigh and permit himself a weary grin.

'Well, Alice,' he said, suddenly regaining the Clark Kent demeanour with which I was so familiar, 'I think that's me off the hook, isn't it?'

Chapter 20

The first thing which struck me upon opening the red street door of our offices the Monday after Eleanor Black's party was the noise – or rather the lack of it. Other than the quiet hum of a printer, just audible through the glass door of Lewis Twinney Legal, I could hear nothing. I checked my watch – eight fifty. Well, perhaps Sophie was running later than usual, or had already gone for coffee.

I trudged up the stairs, opened the office door and entered. Sophie was sitting with her back to me, facing her screen. I looked across to David's office. The door was wide open and he too seemed transfixed by his Mac.

'Hi,' I said, looking at Sophie. 'Morning, David!' I called, raising my voice slightly.

I was greeted by two relatively upbeat-sounding *hellos*, but there were no attempts at supplementary conversation.

'Hitting the ground running this morning?' I said to Sophie, taking off my jacket and sitting down at my desk.

'I think,' she said, turning to face me and lowering her voice, 'it's a case of the Monday after the weekend before.' She jerked her head towards David's office. 'For both of us. There's a coffee somewhere for you.' She glanced around the office. 'Oh look, I've put it down over there.' She gestured to the small bookcase behind my desk, which housed beautifully bound editions of just-for-show classics.

'Thanks,' I said, swivelling in my chair and reaching for the cup. 'So… are you OK?'

She leaned towards me across her desk. 'Fancy lunch out?'

'Post mortem?'

'Exactly.'

I nodded. 'OK. What have you got this morning?'

'I'm out from ten. Shall I meet you at one at Primrose Café?'

I smiled. 'Sounds good.'

David emerged from his office. 'Hi,' he said, walking over to my desk. He offered me a smile which matched his appearance: perfect but exhausted.

'Hi,' I said. 'Good weekend? I mean, good Sunday? A relaxing Sunday?'

'Yes, thank you. And you?'

'Well, I de-cluttered my wardrobe and defrosted the freezer. So that was exciting.' I laughed and was rewarded with two polite smiles. 'You had your sister with you, didn't you, Sophie?'

'Yep.' She stood up. 'Which was as wonderful as it always is. Anyway, I'm going to head off for my ten o'clock. I need to pick up some stuff on the way. See you later!' She held up an index finger to silently confirm our one o'clock lunch, and was gone.

I looked at David. He held out a Post-it note. 'Could you follow this up please, Alice? It's a renovation in Abbots Leigh. I think you'd love it. Give him a call and see what you think.'

'OK. Thanks.' I took the details from him. He placed his hands in his pockets and remained standing at my desk. I looked up at him questioningly.

'I wish she'd shout at me or something,' he said.

'Who? Eleanor?'

'No, no. Sophie,' he said. 'She got in at eight fifteen, brought me a coffee at eight forty-five and worked silently in between. She didn't tell me to get more sleep or to cheer up. She didn't claim to be fed-up of always being the only one bothered to get the coffees and she didn't complain when I did the annoying cough.'

'Not even when you did the cough?'

He shook his head sadly. 'I tried it twice.'

'That's weird. Mind you,' I added, 'she probably thinks you need a bit of peace and quiet after Saturday. You look like you could do with a day off. Is all well? No repercussions?'

'None at all. Except that.' He pointed to the note in my hand. 'It's from an animatronics chap Sophie got chatting to at the party. Henry Stern. Works in film and television. He called me first thing. He was clearly impressed with Sophie's informal pitch and apparently Ben Battersby sang our praises to him too.' He smiled. 'There are more pleasant than unpleasant people in the world, aren't there?'

I nodded. 'Far more. I'll give him a call and arrange a visit. I stuck the note to my phone. Right.' I shifted in my seat and made as if to switch on the Mac, but David didn't move. 'Is there anything else?' I asked.

He looked up, as if surprised. 'What? Oh no, no. Sorry. I was miles away.' He rubbed his chin thoughtfully. 'You know how it is. Things on my mind.'

'Yes, I know how it is,' I sighed. 'But, if you ever want to talk about those things, I'm always happy to listen. I will, of course, constantly drag the conversation back to me and offer no solutions whatsoever, but I can always take copious notes and pass your issues on to Miriam. She loves that sort of thing.'

He smiled and rolled his eyes. I smiled and shrugged. And then he turned and walked back into his office and we carried on with the day.

Chapter 21

On arrival at Primrose Café, I bought a mug of tea and went in search of Sophie. I found her sitting on the upstairs terrace, peering at her phone over the top of her enormous, black, beetle-like sunglasses. She looked up and smiled as I arrived.

'Hi,' I said, 'sorry I'm late. Your puppet guy in Abbots Leigh had a window to see me this morning and I was there a little longer than expected.'

'Ah, Henry, he was nice. Although, he did go on about…' she paused and tapped her phone against her lower lip thoughtfully, '…stimulation through simulation, was how he put it.' She wagged a finger at me. 'So watch out.'

'Well, he was strictly business this morning.'

'Like you'd notice if he wasn't.' She laughed and looked again at her phone. 'And you're not really late. I was a bit early. I ordered you a fish finger sandwich on wholegrain.'

'Brilliant, thanks.' I sat down.

'Sorry.' She nodded towards her phone. 'I'll just be one second.' She tapped the screen. 'There. Done,' she said. 'So,' she took a deep breath. 'First things first: Jon's girlfriend. Who is she and what's she like?' She made the enquiry casually enough, with no trace of the distress she had shown on Saturday night. Her expression now revealed nothing more than intense curiosity.

'No idea, I'm afraid.' I picked up my tea.

'Oh, come on,' she urged.

'I know nothing,' I said simply.

'I don't believe that for a minute,' she grinned. 'You two are as thick as thieves.'

'Not about this,' I said, sipping my tea, my hurt feelings at being shut-out by Jon now resurfacing.

'Ooh, you sound a bit clipped,' she said, still smiling. 'What gives?'

I made a face and replaced my mug on the table. 'We had a bit of a falling-out on Saturday.'

Her smile instantly transformed into open-mouthed disbelief. 'You and Jon?' She laughed uncertainly. 'You're winding me up.'

I leaned forward, placing my elbows on the table and resting my chin on my hands. 'I'm not,' I said quietly. 'It was actually quite bad.'

'Bloody hell, I just don't know what's going on at the moment,' she said, her face aghast. 'And you didn't sort it out yesterday?'

'Things got worse on Saturday when I tried to sort it out.' I looked at her miserably. 'So he hasn't really left me anywhere to go.' She sat back in her chair and looked at me; her eyebrows, just visible above her sunglasses, now knitted in puzzlement. I picked up my tea again. 'It's nothing for you to worry about. It's my problem.'

'And it was over his new relationship?'

'It was over me *mentioning* his new relationship; which I know I shouldn't have done. But then he wouldn't let me apologise and when it was time for me to go home, he was actually quite cutting.'

Sophie shook her head. 'Cutting?'

'He made some dig about me always talking gibberish. I forget his exact words. But he was determined to stay angry with me and by the end of the evening, I just thought fine.' I smiled sadly. 'It doesn't matter.'

'Doesn't it?' Sophie raised her eyebrows in surprise.

'Well, it didn't feel great at the time but if he doesn't want it mentioned then I can do that.' I shrugged. 'He probably won't give it another thought.'

'I doubt that.' Sophie delved into her bag and took out one of her plastic cigarettes, holding it up apologetically. 'Still trying,' she smiled. 'So, who is she?'

'Who?'

'His girlfriend. When did they get together?'

I sighed. 'I really know less than nothing. Jon hasn't told me one word about her. Craig spotted the pair of them in a restaurant. Miriam gossiped to me. That's how I know.'

'And that's it?'

''Fraid so.'

'That's no bloody good.' She banged her fist lightly on the table. 'We need details.'

'Well, my chances of getting any are now nil. And,' I added, noticing Sophie chewing on the end of the faux cigarette, as if formulating a plan, 'I would seriously recommend against any digging on your part. He clearly doesn't want to talk about the relationship.' She continued to chew. 'Sophie?' She looked up. 'I don't think you should ask Jon about his girlfriend.'

'As if I would!' I eyed her sceptically. 'I wouldn't,' she insisted.

'And don't hassle Miriam, either.' At that her lower lip protruded. 'She's got enough on her plate.'

'Like what?'

'Not sure.'

Sophie rolled her eyes. 'You,' she said, 'are *shit* at gossip.'

'I know.' I sighed.

She was silent for a moment and then reached across the table, patting my hand. 'Don't worry about Jon,' she said quietly. 'You'll see him at book group next week, so that'll be a chance for the pair of you to sort things out, if you haven't already.'

I forced a smile. 'I'm not worried about him. I'm sure everything will be fine,' I said, attempting to sound blasé. 'Anyway, enough about me and everyone else. How are you? I was worried about you on Saturday.'

She smiled grimly, put a hand to her cheek and bit her lip. 'God, I made such a tit of myself, didn't I?'

'I don't think anyone saw it like that.'

'Oh, shut-up,' she laughed. 'Having a rant and then running off crying? If that doesn't count as making a tit of yourself, I don't know what does.' She lowered her glasses and winked at me. 'But you're a love for trying to make me feel better.'

I smiled. 'Look, the only person who made an idiot of themselves on Saturday was Eleanor Black.'

Sophie shook her head. 'Can't agree with you there,' she said, repositioning her sunglasses. 'She didn't shout back and, brace yourself, she graciously accepted my apology yesterday.'

My jaw dropped. 'You've spoken to her?'

'Don't sound so shocked. I phoned her yesterday morning. I got her answerphone. So I left her a message. I didn't expect her to call me back but she did.'

'But why did you call her in the first place?'

She looked both puzzled and surprised. 'I was a real bitch to her, Alice, and, besides,' she picked up her coffee, 'I couldn't leave what I'd done hanging over David and the business, could I?'

I blinked. 'And she was OK about everything?'

'Well, she sounded strained, like actually she wanted to kick the shit out of me. I mean, she certainly wasn't Mother Theresa about it or anything. But she said she just wanted to forget about it all and that she would never mention it again. Asked me to tell David that too.'

I looked at her. 'You know why that is, don't you? Has David told you what happened after you left?'

She looked up sharply from her coffee. 'No. I just thought she was being a grown-up and may have some genuine feelings for David after all.' She sighed. 'Made me feel even worse, actually. Thought I may have misjudged her and the situation a bit. I've been doing that a lot lately.' She looked at me and took a thoughtful drag on her plastic tube. 'But anyway, what happened?'

I recounted the tale of Damario, whilst Sophie appeared alternately appalled and delighted. When I finished, she shook her head and grinned. 'That's just…' Her voice trailed away and she leaned back in her chair, tilting her face towards the sky. 'David's just…'

'He's lovely,' I said. 'And his integrity levels astonish me. I just wish he'd find the woman he deserves. And I also wish he could be assertive enough day-to-day, like he was on Saturday night, to find someone good enough for him and go for it.'

Sophie ceased her contemplation of the sky and turned her face towards me again, her eyes still hidden behind her sunglasses. 'He deserves the very best,' she said quietly, 'and nothing less. As do you,' she smiled. 'Oh and look,' she pointed over my shoulder, and I turned my head as a waitress emerged onto the terrace carrying my fish finger sandwich and a salad for Sophie, 'here comes lunch.'

Chapter 22

'Hurrah! It's Alice!' Abs embraced me, pulling me inside for a tight cuddle against one of the many riotously patterned, home-made jumpers she and Pete shared as lounge-wear. This one, I noted, was particularly huge on her, the rolled-up sleeves forming sizable dough-nuts around her wrists.

'That looks warm – for May,' I said, as she released me.

'Oh, you know how I feel the cold,' she grinned, giving herself the air of a slender, wide-eyed Cheshire Cat. 'And this one is my absolute favourite. When I wore it into school, one of the boys in my form asked me if I'd shrunk. And he was serious,' she giggled. 'Pete and I knitted it together and we get in it together sometimes too.'

I held up a hand. 'Enough sharing.'

She laughed again and then turned and shouted in the direction of the lounge. 'Hey, everyone! It's Alice! Yay!'

I smiled. Abs always welcomed visitors, even frequent ones, into her home as if (a) she hadn't seen them for a year or two and (b) seeing them was the best thing that had happened to her in that time.

'I'm sorry I'm a bit late but,' I took off my bicycle helmet and pointed at my bike, now locked to the railings which fronted her maisonette, 'I got a flat, so had to push it part of the way.'

Abs' face fell, as she gasped and put a hand to her mouth. 'Oh my goodness, that's just dreadful. Poor you. Hang on. Pete'll sort this out,' she said, turning and yelling up the stairs at impressive volume, 'Pete! Pete! Alice needs your help urgently!'

We stood for a moment before the silence was broken by the sound of a chair being pushed back on the wooden floor and then of a door creaking open. Slow footsteps were followed, eventually, by an almost whispered response, as Pete made his way unhurriedly down the stairs. I noticed that he didn't seem to share Abs' problem with the cold, as he was tonight wearing navy blue Bermuda shorts, flip flops and a grey t-shirt bearing the slogan 'Run Don't Walk', which sagged a little over his slim frame.

'Oh dear. Is there a problem?' he asked, progressing at the speed of a tortoise and speaking at a similar pace. 'Hello there, Alice.'

'Hi, Pete,' I smiled.

'Yes, yes, there is a problem,' said Abs breathlessly. 'You'll never guess what, Pete.'

Pete's mouth formed a worried 'ooh' shape, but no sound was emitted as he waited for Abs to continue.

'Poor Alice has got a flat.' Abs placed a concerned hand on Pete's elbow, as if to provide physical support, should the news of my puncture prove too much for him.

Pete maintained his silent 'ooh' face.

'I know,' said Abs. 'That's what I said. But you'll fix it for her, won't you?' She turned to me. 'He'll fix it for you, Alice.'

I tried to object. 'Oh no, really, I can—'

'Oh, please let him do it,' she begged. 'He loves that kind of thing, don't you, Pete?' She kissed him fondly on the cheek.

Pete smiled and nodded slowly.

'See?' said Abs. 'See how excited punctures get him?'

I scrutinised Pete for any indication at all that he might not love mending punctures quite as much as Abs was implying. However, finding him looking just as untroubled by the prospect of fixing my bike as he did about every other life event, I decided to relax graciously into the situation.

'Well, if you're sure it's not too much of a bother, Pete, I would be very grateful.'

'My pleasure, Alice,' he said slowly and, so far as I could tell, sincerely.

'Brill,' said Abs. She kissed him again and then took my hand and led me down the hallway.

As we entered the lounge, I was greeted by a chorus of 'hellos' and Sophie beckoned me to come and share the sofa with herself and Miriam. Jon and Connie were seated in armchairs opposite us. I returned everyone's greetings, feeling unexpectedly awkward at seeing Jon for the first time since Eleanor Black's party ten days earlier. We hadn't been in touch at all in that time, other than when responding to a group email Sophie had sent suggesting a foursome tapas evening with herself and David. The matter of our disagreement at the party had never been revisited, and as I sat down and forced myself to make eye contact with him, I realised that, for me, the conversations that night had marked a painful, possibly irreversible, shift in our friendship.

'I'll just run and fetch a dining chair,' said Abs. What can I get you, Alice? White, or red, or a soft drink?'

'Actually, can I just have water, Abs?' I asked.

'Sure,' she said, and disappeared.

'So, I hear you've got a puncture,' smiled Miriam.

I laughed. 'Poor Pete. I'm sure he's got much better things to do with his time. But Miriam,' I said, looking her up and down, 'you look gorgeous.'

She looked pleasurably flustered. 'Do I?'

'Now, if that isn't exactly what I just said to her,' said Connie smiling. 'She looks so beautiful. That top is gorgeous.'

'Oh,' said Miriam, pulling at her blouse, 'this is incredibly old.'

'Well, you look great,' I smiled. 'Have you been up to something special? Not a naughty lunch with Craig?'

Her face darkened. 'Craig hasn't had time for a naughty lunch for over a year now. Not with me anyway,' she added. 'No, I was in Sainsbury's this morning and then I had a play-date in the park this afternoon. Nothing special.'

'Sounds special to me,' said Sophie. 'I wish I'd been in the park.'

Miriam smiled. 'Yes, it was a nice day for it. Phoebe just loves the sandpit, although her friend, Emily, eats the sand. Drives her poor father demented.'

The reference to Emily and her father jolted a memory. 'Oh, I forgot to tell you that I saw Louise Battersby at Eleanor Black's party,' I said. 'She mentioned Emily. And her dad. I forget his name.'

'Eammon,' said Miriam quickly. She shifted in her seat and turned away from me, as if looking for something. 'Now, where did I put my...' she mumbled.

'Here you go, Alice.' Abs re-entered the room, struggling to carry a chair and a glass of water. I stood up and relieved her of the glass. 'Just let me know if you'd like anything else. Now, am I interrupting anything if I quickly sort out a little bit of admin?' She picked up an iPad from the arm of Jon's chair.

'Not at all. You admin away, Abs,' said Sophie.

'Fantastic!' grinned Abs, sitting down. 'Right, well, the first thing is the school production of *Oliver!*'

'Oh yes,' said Connie. 'How are your rehearsals going? How is the poor child with the broken leg? He was playing Fagin, wasn't he?'

'Well,' Abs clasped her hands excitedly, 'he's had his second operation and we did have some mobility concerns, but he's built himself a trolley, which our lovely DT department has made safe. And we've written the stairs out of his scenes.'

'A trolley?' queried Sophie on behalf of us all.

'Yes. I'm so proud of him,' beamed Abs. 'It's just wonderful because he didn't want to be in a wheelchair. He felt it wasn't in the spirit of the times or the situation. And his trolley is just fantastic.'

'Well, that sounds so very intriguing, Abigail,' said Connie.

'But didn't the Victorians have crutches?' asked Sophie. 'Tiny Tim definitely had crutches.'

'The thing is, he can't bend his left knee,' explained Abs. 'So crutches aren't really on. But the trolley is just amazing.'

'I don't get it,' pressed Sophie, looking puzzled. 'Describe the trolley to me.'

'It's about so high,' said Abs, holding her hand out at just below knee height, 'and about a metre and a half long, so he can have his legs sticking straight out.'

'So it's a go-kart,' said Sophie.

Abs looked thoughtful. 'I suppose it is a little like a go-kart, now I think about it.'

'But how does he get around?' Sophie was clearly fascinated. 'How is he going to pick a pocket or two?'

'Well, his head is at perfect pick-a-pocket height and,' Abs sat on the floor, her legs extended in front of her, 'he either propels himself with his hands flat on the floor like this.' She demonstrated. 'Or, during musical numbers, when he has to move and gesture at the same time, Dodger pulls him along on a piece of string. The trolley is on casters, so he can twirl him around beautifully.'

I felt sick with the effort of not laughing and fixed my gaze on a Matisse print, hanging on the wall behind Abs, in a desperate attempt to avoid eye contact with anyone else. However, at this point, Miriam's wine went down the wrong way, prompting a coughing fit which thankfully gave the rest of us something to laugh about.

When the rather disproportionate amusement over Miriam choking had died down, she asked the obvious question. 'Did you never think of perhaps finding someone else for the part, Abs?'

Abs shook her head. 'This child has so many issues,' she said and her smile faded. 'But he is so enthusiastic about everything to do with the show.' She shrugged. 'I just didn't want this to be another disappointment for him.'

'Well, I think the go-kart sounds bloody brilliant,' said Sophie. 'Good for him.'

Abs nodded and her smile returned. 'Anyway, would anyone like to come? And don't worry at all if you can't. Because I know you're all super busy.'

'I'd love to come,' said Jon.

'Fabulous!' said Abs. She looked at me. 'And you, Alice?'

'Of course,' I said. 'It's been on the calendar for months.'

'Oh, thank you. The children so appreciate it and their families aren't always...' Her voice trailed away, as she concentrated on her iPad. 'Two? Is that right? For the Friday?'

'That's right,' I said.

'OK.' She tapped the screen. 'So, Jon, you're coming with Alice, like last year?'

I looked at him and he looked at Abs. 'Wouldn't it be better for you, if we each brought someone else along?' he said.

I nodded and attempted a smile.

'Well,' said Abs, 'obviously the more seats I can fill the better but I don't want anyone to feel they have to buy tickets and—'

'Not at all,' said Jon. 'I had already mentioned it to a friend and she's very keen to come.'

I stared at him, while trying to suppress a rising sense of hurt.

'So you could go as a foursome then,' said Sophie brightly, 'with Alice and her friend on the Friday, couldn't you?'

'Marvellous!' said Abs. 'Thank you so, so much. Anyone else?'

Connie booked a pair of tickets for the opening night, Miriam had to check dates and Sophie already knew she couldn't make it, but ordered a copy of the DVD of the performance. Box office business concluded, Abs moved onto the matter of the book group anniversary dinner. We held one every year, and each member brought along a partner or a guest. I had taken Dad as my plus-one when Eddie couldn't come, and last year I had invited David along.

This year, Abs was in charge of the restaurant booking and, having reserved an upstairs room at Primrose Café, she now needed to confirm numbers, fill us in on menu options and check whether anyone was bringing a friend who had any dietary requirements or, as Sophie put it, was 'fussy'.

'So,' she said, smiling, 'everyone has confirmed they're coming. I just have to check a few plus ones. Miriam,' Abs turned to her, 'you're bringing Romy.'

Miriam nodded.

'It'll be so lovely to see her,' said Abs.

'It will,' I agreed. 'But why isn't Craig coming? Is he working?'

Miriam shrugged. 'I expect so.'

'And Romy's pescatarian…' Abs focused again on her screen. 'Brilliant. Connie, you'll be with Greg.'

'That is correct,' said Connie.

'And Sophie and Alice are definitely coming,' said Abs. 'Each bringing a plus one?'

'Yes,' confirmed Sophie. 'Alice and I are going to toss a coin and whoever loses has to bring David.'

Miriam tutted. 'Poor David.'

'Lovely.' Abs looked up. 'And Jon, did you decide about a guest?'

'Yes,' he nodded. 'I'll be bringing Suzanna.'

I glanced around the room. All eyes were on Jon. The expectation of additional information hung in the air.

I stared down into my glass of water and wondered who, if anyone, would probe further. Under any other circumstances it would have been Sophie. However, she had already ruled herself out by dint of her extreme reaction to the girlfriend bombshell at Eleanor Black's party.

After what seemed like several hours, it was Miriam who asked the question to which we all, I assumed, wanted an answer.

'Suzanna?' she queried hesitantly. 'Do any of us know her?'

'No,' said Jon. 'She lives in London. But I was having dinner with her recently when I bumped into Craig. He may have mentioned it.'

I didn't look at Miriam but her embarrassed confusion was obvious in her voice. 'Ooh… now, did he? Yes, I think he might have said something.'

I placed my glass of water on the floor by my feet and remained silent; unwilling and unable to take any part in the conversation.

'Well, I shall be very interested and delighted to meet her, Jon,' said Connie gently.

'We all will!' exclaimed Abs.

Jon laughed. 'And I'm delighted by your interest.'

I reached down and picked up my book from the floor.

'Gosh,' said Miriam, nudging me, 'you're a bit keen tonight. You haven't actually read it all the way through, have you?'

'I have, actually.' I tried to keep my voice light.

'Well, that's a novelty,' she teased. 'Mind you, it's only Jon who has read every single one without fail.'

I couldn't bring myself to look at him, but whatever silent response he made to her statement provoked laughter around the room. I turned the pages of my book unseeingly, feeling increasingly hurt. So, he delighted in everybody else's interest in Suzanna, but not in mine. It was perfectly OK for everybody else to prompt discussion and to ask questions but not me. With hindsight, I was disappointed with myself for being so defensive and apologetic on the night of Eleanor Black's party. It was now clear that Jon didn't have a problem with talking about Suzanna. He simply had a problem with talking about Suzanna *to me*. Obviously, he had decided that I lacked the necessary depth and sensitivity to engage in that kind of conversation.

I was aware that discussion in the room had now moved on, but I was clueless as to the topic. I tuned back in only when Sophie gently placed her hand on the book in my lap. She disguised the action by leaning across me to talk to Miriam, but when I looked down, I realised that I had been neatly tearing the pages of Flaubert's *A Simple Heart* from their cover. I took a deep breath, closed the book, and refocused just in time to hear Abs asking if I would like to start the discussion.

I looked up. 'My basic conclusion was,' I began, 'that Felicité needed to pull herself together and get a life. She let herself be walked all over and I found her intensely irritating. She needed a good shake and a slap.'

'No, come on, Alice,' laughed Sophie. 'Don't mince words. Tell us what you really thought.'

And with objections being raised by both Miriam and Abs to my wholesale dissing of poor Felicité, a livelier and lengthier literary debate than usual ensued.

-

It was well past eleven by the time I got up to go. Spurred on by the enthusiasm shown for discussion of *A Simple Heart*, and taking into account a longer gap between meetings than usual, thanks to the anniversary dinner, we had agreed to Sophie's initially-shocking suggestion that we attempt a longer book as our next read. The proposal had at first been met with extreme scepticism as to the ability of anyone, other than Jon, to get through any novel over half an inch thick. However, when Sophie explained that her idea was that we should choose a book which, for most of us, would be a second-time read, we agreed. She suggested three novels which she thought most of us would have read: *Great Expectations*, *To Kill a Mockingbird* and *Jane Eyre*. I felt pretty sure that Harper Lee would have won the day had not Connie turned pink at the mention of *Jane Eyre* and quietly declared it to be her favourite book *ever*. Of course, everyone then voted for it, Jon being the only member who had never read it and, I'm sure we all suspected, the only member who would get through it in time for the next meeting.

Book selection at an end, Miriam and Sophie, who were car-sharing, said their goodbyes. A few minutes after they left, I stood up, thanked Abs for having us and went into the hallway to fetch my things. From there, I heard Connie saying that she too must be on her way, and then Jon declining her offer of a lift, explaining that he needed some exercise after a day behind a desk. Connie subsequently emerged from the lounge alone, just as I was buckling my helmet.

'Well, I did so enjoy that discussion,' she said, removing her jacket from the end of the bannister. 'Who would have thought that such a seemingly plain little tale could provoke such feeling?'

I smiled. 'I often think that the shorter the book, the better the chat, don't you?'

She nodded in agreement, before glancing furtively over her shoulder. 'Alice,' she said quietly, placing a hand gently on my arm, 'I've been meaning to call you. I wondered if you had had any more thoughts about Stephen.'

I frowned. 'Stephen?'

'Greg's work colleague,' she said, raising an anxious hand to her mouth. 'Do you remember? I've only met him once but he seems very charming and Greg speaks very highly—'

My expression cleared. 'Ah, Stephen. With the Morgan. I'm so sorry, Connie. Of course I remember.'

'That's right!' She smiled and looked relieved. 'Well, his flat is on the market now and he's looking forward to moving but has few friends here and I just wondered whether… whether you might like to meet him. But if you'd rather not…' She paused and looked over her shoulder as the sound of Jon's laughter escaped from the living room. She turned back to me and lowered her voice still further, '…that's totally fine,' she said, now barely audible.

There was another burst of laughter from Jon.

I took a deep breath. 'I'd be delighted to meet him,' I smiled. 'Perhaps Greg could give him my number.'

'Perfect,' said Connie. 'Thank you.'

'Thank *you*, Connie,' I smiled, turning away from her and beginning to open the front door before pausing with my hand on the latch. 'I'm looking forward to meeting him.'

'Ooh! Who?' I looked over my shoulder to discover Abs and Jon now standing behind us in the hallway. Abs beamed, as Jon reached for his jacket and Connie appeared pained.

Abs looked at Connie. 'Oops,' she said, her face falling, 'did we overhear something we weren't meant to? I've put my foot in it, haven't I?'

'No, you haven't,' I smiled. 'Greg has a work colleague who's moving to Bristol and we're going to meet up.' I glanced at Jon as he focused on buttoning his jacket. 'Maybe I should bring him along to *Oliver!*. I've got a spare ticket after all.'

'That would be just amazing!' gasped Abs. 'If you do, please bring him backstage!' She looked at Connie and Jon. 'You too. You must all come backstage.'

We of course promised that we would and then, having each kissed her goodbye in turn, we made our way down the short garden path, as she closed the front door behind us. I waved goodbye to Jon and Connie and then placed my abused book in my saddlebag and unlocked my bike. I had just wheeled it to the edge of the pavement and switched on my lights, when I jumped at the sound of my name.

'Alice.'

I turned quickly and put a hand to my chest. 'Oh it's you, Jon,' I exclaimed, laughing with relief. 'You scared me. I thought you'd gone.'

'Sorry.' He didn't smile. In fact, he looked incredibly serious. 'I know it's late but I'd like to talk to you, if that's OK.'

I felt a knot begin to form in my stomach. 'Sure,' I said, managing to maintain a smile.

He looked at me, his expression unreadable. 'I think there's a lot of tension and irritation between us at the moment, don't you?'

I blinked up at him, completely taken aback by this abrupt, unsmiling approach from someone usually so measured and warm.

'Well,' I said, recovering and bristling slightly at his tone, 'evidently you're irritated by me, or you wouldn't have made the statement. And,' I bent over and checked my newly re-inflated tyre, as a means of breaking the eye contact with which I was beginning to feel uncomfortable, 'you're certainly making me feel incredibly tense right now. So, yes,' I straightened up and shrugged, 'I agree.'

He didn't speak and I widened my eyes questioningly. 'Is that it? Or is there more?' I thought I saw his jaw tighten but still he said nothing. 'OK, well, can I just ask then if this is a recent thing for you? Or have I always been irritating and you've just reached saturation point?'

'I thought it might be helpful—'

'Oh,' I interrupted, 'so there *is* more.'

'I thought it might be helpful,' he began again, speaking more slowly this time, 'for us to discuss what you agree is a shared problem,' he said.

I spoke in deepened tones, mimicking his voice. '…to discuss what you agree is a shared problem.' I forced a laugh. 'I'm not one of your clients, Jon. You're not in the office now, you know.'

'I hoped we could discuss this calmly,' he said, 'and like adults.'

I stopped smiling. 'The implication being that I am not a grown-up?'

He turned to look for a moment at something unseen to his right, before returning his attention to me. 'I just thought it would help to talk about it.'

He exuded a cool calm, which had the unexpected effect of infuriating me even further. I remembered his total control of our conversation, and my failure to self-assert, at Eleanor Black's party. I decided not to make the same mistake twice.

'Yes, well, as you yourself have pointed out in the past, there are some things which it is better for us not to discuss. And I'm afraid that on *this* occasion, I'd rather not discuss the topic of why you find me irritating.' I looked up at him, pushing back my bicycle helmet. 'Because, as fun as listing my personality defects might be for you, I'm afraid it would all be a bit of a bore for me, because I can list them quite readily all by myself.'

He looked at me steadily. 'I've raised this at the wrong time,' he said. 'Let's just leave it. I think we both need to calm down.'

'I don't need to calm down,' I snapped, turning my back on him and climbing onto my bike. 'And this isn't anything to do with timing. It's simply that just as there are conversations you don't want to have with *me*, I don't want to have this one with *you*. And, you know what, Jon,' I added breathlessly, now forcing myself to look at him, 'if something is really that irritating, then discussing and dissecting and intellectualising doesn't actually help anyway. It just makes things worse. I think what you really need to do in that kind of situation is act: turn off the dripping tap, swat the mosquito, find yourself a new friend.'

He stood motionless, staring at me, clearly as shocked as I was by the conclusion to my sentence. I opened my mouth to say something, anything, which might retrieve the situation, but found myself either unable or unwilling to do so – I wasn't sure which.

'Ride carefully,' he said quietly. And, with that, he turned and walked away.

I watched as he headed towards the corner of the street and then disappeared out of sight. I continued to stare down the deserted road for a minute or two, with some desperate sense that he might return. When it was clear that he wouldn't, I put my hand to my face, wiped away newly-sprung tears with the sleeve of my jacket, and headed home.

Chapter 23

After a largely sleepless, night, I made up my mind to call Jon. Keen to make contact, but unable yet to face the idea of a conversation, I decided to phone him at home, while he was at work, so that I could leave the brief statement which I had perfected at around 4am that morning. Determined not to worsen the situation with a rambling off-the cuff message, my aim was to be concise and conciliatory, without apologising for a distressing situation which I still felt was entirely of his making. Both Sophie and David were out of the office all morning, allowing me ample opportunity to read and practise my three-sentence speech numerous times before actually dialling Jon's number. However, despite this considerable level of preparation, my A4 script still shook slightly in my hands, while I waited for his answer phone to kick-in.

The phone seemed to ring for an eternity before a pre-recorded Jon finally answered.

'I can't get to the phone at the moment, but if you leave a message, I'll call you back.'

I began to read. 'Hi Jon, this is Alice. I just wanted to say that I am disappointed that we argued last night. But hopefully now that we're both aware of a problem, we'll each think more carefully about how we behave and be able to move on. Bye.'

I pressed the hash key and listened to my message. Surprised at just how self-assured I sounded, I pressed '4' to deliver the message and flopped back in my chair, feeling emotionally and physically exhausted.

Unable to think of anything other than my argument with Jon, I spent the next few hours reliving it and hypothesising regarding his feelings and what he would say when he called. That he would call, I had no doubt; it was just a question of when, and of how that conversation might go. If he was apologetic, I was ready to be gracious. If, on the other hand, he called simply to say that the whole thing was best forgotten, then I would be non-confrontational, welcoming his statement and firm-up our arrangements for tapas that Friday after work. I both longed-for and dreaded his call, but by the time David and Sophie returned to the office at 3pm, I had accepted that he was unlikely to pick up home messages from the office, and would probably now call me at home that evening.

My colleagues had returned from their meeting somewhat subdued, although each had insisted it had gone well. They immediately began working on their return and, as I was still pre-occupied by the disagreement with Jon, the office was a much quieter place than usual that afternoon.

I left work on the dot at five, keen to discover whether he had left a message on my landline, as I had on his. However, a review of my messages when I got home at 5.30pm, threw up nothing more interesting than a reminder from a sash-window company of a visit the following week.

The evening dragged and I found myself checking either the kitchen clock, or my phone, every ten minutes. When Jon hadn't called by seven o'clock, I told myself that it was not at all unusual for him to work until seven or seven-thirty and therefore, allowing for travel time, he would be unlikely to call before eight. At eight-thirty, I began to wonder whether he had gone out with Suzanna or a client after work. At 10pm, I decided that must be the case and at midnight I assumed he must be too tired to call, or text, or was not alone. By 1am, I was thoroughly miserable, desperate to speak to him and wondering why on earth I had chosen to leave a message, instead of developing a backbone and phoning at a time when, no matter how distressing or uncomfortable, we could have had an actual conversation. I still felt hurt and angry about what he had said and wasn't at all ready to apologise or back down. But my overwhelming feeling was of a desperate need to make things better. As it was, the ball was well and truly in his court. I had served and now it was up to him to lob, volley or smash. Short of calling again, which a lingering reluctance to appear vulnerable or in the wrong prevented me from doing, I simply had to wait.

At 1.30am, I closed my copy of *Jane Eyre*, knowing that not one word of the thirty-two pages I had looked at had actually entered my consciousness. I switched off my bedside light as the alarm clock read-out changed to 1.33am, but it was at least another hour before my brain ceased whirring and I finally fell asleep.

Chapter 24

I was horrified to wake at nine-fifteen the next morning, having slept through my alarm; something I never did, unless aided by significant quantities of alcohol. The subsequent frantic and unthinking rush to shower, dress and get to work left me unable to focus on anything but the clock until I stumbled through the office door at just after ten.

'Sorry, sorry, sorry!' I called, as I hurried to my desk, flung my jacket at the hat-stand and switched on the Mac.

'Well, good…' Sophie paused theatrically and turned to look at the mantle clock, '…morning,' she concluded. 'Yes, it is still morning.' She looked at me and grinned. 'So what happened to you then? Ten more minutes and he,' she pointed towards David's office, 'would have had me calling the Bristol Royal Infirmary.'

'I slept through my alarm.' I ran a hand through my hair.

'And your phone,' she said.

'What?'

She pointed to the phone on her desk. 'I called you. Twice. Once on your landline and once on your mobile.' I picked my phone out of my bag. Two missed calls, one from the office and a second from a number I didn't recognise; no messages.

'I must have been really out for the count,' I mumbled.

'Must've been,' said Sophie. 'Heavy evening, was it?' She made a drinking gesture with her right hand.

'Didn't touch a drop,' I said. 'I guess I was just exhausted.'

'And everything's OK?'

I looked at her. She was still smiling, but the mischief had gone from her eyes.

I nodded. 'Everything's fine.'

'Ah, well, that's good to hear,' said David, emerging from his office.

'I'm so sorry, David…' I began.

He held up a hand. 'Oh my goodness, don't apologise. We're just pleased to see you. The number of extra hours you linger here in the evenings has earned you a late start. In fact, I think we should perhaps introduce official late-start days.'

Sophie shook her head. 'How you run a profitable business is completely beyond me,' she sighed. 'You pay us too much and now you're planning to add official being late days to our terms and conditions. Christ, David, you shouldn't be allowed out of the house without a minder. You're just way too…' she hesitated, searching for the right word, '…affable… too generous. I bet the woman with the Red Cross tin outside Waitrose has an orgasm every time she sees you coming.'

An increase in the rate at which David blinked, betrayed the fact that he was thrown by the sudden sexual reference. Nevertheless, he valiantly attempted a retort. 'Well, I think you two earn your salaries and as for charity,' he cleared his throat as he struggled to recover his composure, 'I do believe we reap what we sow.'

Sophie smiled but didn't look up from her computer. 'I bet you give her twenty quid a month.' she said.

He turned and headed back to the safety of his office. 'Closer to forty, and she's binned her vibrator,' he said, barely audibly, as he clicked the door shut behind him.

Sophie looked up and stared open-mouthed, first at David's door and then at me. 'Did you hear that?' she said. 'Did you hear what he said? He said the word,' she lowered her voice to a whisper, 'vibrator.'

'Yes,' I acknowledged. 'That was rather a departure.' I looked at my screen.

She paused. 'But he was being *bold*, Alice.'

'Well, you wouldn't be so surprised about that if you'd seen him put Eleanor Black in her place,' I said, absently, whilst looking in dismay at the long list of emails awaiting my attention. It had been my morning to open the paper mail and I noticed with gratitude that Sophie had taken care of a fair proportion of it. 'Thanks so much for doing the admin,' I said. 'I'll do the Monday log-in for you.'

She didn't respond and, when I looked up, I was surprised to find her staring into space.

'What?' I asked.

She looked at me. 'What?' she echoed.

'You're miles away.'

'Mm,' she said, returning her attention to her Mac. 'Just running through the day in my head. Oh and,' she looked up at me, 'before I forget. Jon called.'

Jon. The panic of my morning had temporarily freed me of my miserable pre-occupation with him. Now, at the mention of his name I experienced a sudden dip in mood, which was just as quickly replaced by an immense sense of relief that he had made contact – he wanted to talk to me. I don't know how this rapid succession of emotions was reflected in my facial expressions, but when I refocused my attention on Sophie, she was looking at me with a mixture of concern and fascination.

'Bloody hell, what was that?' she asked.

'What was what?'

She pointed at my face and made a circling motion with her index finger. 'You looked like you were giving birth to a Lego baby.'

'Did I?'

'Yes, you did,' she said. 'And it was *very* weird. So don't do it again.'

'OK,' I said and then, attempting nonchalance, 'So, does Jon want me to call him back?'

'Nope.' She began to tap at her keyboard. 'He's tied up all day. He was just phoning to say he can't make tapas with us tomorrow. Something's come up. And you'd have been very proud of me,' she added, smiling at her screen. 'I didn't pry.'

I slumped back in my chair, feeling numb, my mind a blank.

'Alice.' I heard Sophie but felt no need to respond. Instinct told me that the current sensation of emptiness and nothingness was definitely preferable to thought, and I wasn't ready to give that up just yet. 'Alice.' God, she was persistent. I turned towards her. 'Alice,' she said, 'what's wrong?'

I sighed. It was no good. I was going to have to think and speak.

I resolved to keep it shallow.

'I'm starving,' I said. 'I skipped breakfast.'

'Right.' She opened her desk drawer, removed a brown paper bag and peered inside it. 'Wholemeal raisin muffin or tuna mayo sandwich?'

'I can't eat your lunch,' I said.

'You can get me a replacement when you pop out later.' She looked at me questioningly. 'Come on. Choose.'

'Muffin, please,' I said, knowing better than to argue further.

She got up from her desk and brought the muffin to me, placing it in front of me with a smile. 'There you go.'

'Thank you.'

'My pleasure,' she said, returning to her desk.

I stared at the cake in front of me, trying to generate an appetite for it. But despite my best attempts to focus on the muffin, the whole muffin and nothing but the muffin, I couldn't prevent non-nutritional matters from dominating my thought processes.

So Jon didn't want to see me. But on the other hand, he had called the office knowing that there was the possibility that I would answer the phone. So at least he was willing to talk to me. He wasn't trying to avoid me completely.

This last thought was by far the most comforting to have so far entered my head during a morning of otherwise total gloom. I therefore focused my full intellectual capacity on it and clung to it in the same way I had witnessed Phoebe cling to a half-eaten lollipop she had found on the ground during a recent trip to the park with Miriam and myself.

'OK,' said Sophie suddenly, now standing in front of my desk and making me jump, 'so now we've established that you're not actually very hungry after all...'

I looked down at the muffin, which now lay picked apart and neatly piled in the shallowest compartment of my desk tidy.

'Sorry,' I said, whilst continuing to focus on my only positive; the fact that Jon had called the office. 'I'm just not quite with it yet.'

I picked up the desk tidy and popped a few of the larger chunks of the deconstructed muffin into my mouth, for which I was rewarded with an appalled, 'Yuck,' from Sophie. I then tipped the rest of the mutilated cake into the waste paper basket next to my desk.

'Anyway,' I took a deep breath, 'that's a shame about Jon.'

'I think he must be really busy at work,' she said. 'He called from his desk before eight. I was just getting in the car.'

I looked up from the pile of waiting correspondence, which I had begun to peruse. 'He called you on your mobile?'

She nodded.

'Oh.' I struggled to smile and felt my throat tighten, as the single grain of comfort I had managed to distil from events, was blown away.

Sophie walked round to my side of the desk, bent down and squeezed my arm. 'Are you OK? You don't look great.'

At that moment, David's office door opened. He emerged, engrossed in some drawings he held in his hand. 'Do you think...' he began, before looking up at Sophie and me and completing his sentence with, '...I should go back into my room for a little while?' He retreated back into his office and closed the door.

Sophie sighed and smiled down at me. 'Is there anything you want to talk about?' she asked gently.

I shook my head, aware that at that moment, any attempt to explain to her either the situation or my feelings would not only fail but also, quite possibly, result in personal disintegration and the loss of the entire working day. It was best for now, I decided, to retreat into denial. 'I'm just very tired and hormonal,' I said.

She looked at me sceptically for a moment, before straightening up and returning to her own desk. 'Well, if you decide that you do fancy a chat, just let me know.'

I nodded as David's door opened for a second time and he walked quickly across the office and towards the loo, without looking at either of us. 'Sorry,' he mumbled. 'I just need a...' He cleared his throat before continuing. 'So I had to come out,' he concluded, closing the toilet door behind him.

Sophie shook her head. 'What's he like?'

'He's lovely,' I said, just about managing my first genuine smile of the morning, before pressing on with the day.

–

What was left of the morning passed surprisingly quickly, thanks largely to the multiple emails which I had at first viewed with such horror. Most took a matter of moments either to bin or answer. But one or two required more thought, and they proved a more effective distraction from my personal problems than the muffin. I could only assume that both David and Sophie had similarly full inboxes as, other than the coffees we silently placed on each other's desks at regular intervals, there was nothing to distract us from our screens.

It was such a quietly intense morning in fact, that the sound of the telephone ringing at just before 1pm, made me jump and gasp. Sophie laughed, without looking up, as I picked up the receiver.

'Hello, Moore Interior Design. Alice Waites speaking. How can I help?'

'Hi, Alice. It's Stephen Powell.' He hesitated. 'Greg Golding's friend.'

I felt myself colour slightly. 'Oh hello, Stephen.' In my peripheral vision, I saw Sophie look up sharply from her screen. 'Connie said you would be in touch.'

'Great. Look, the first thing I have to say is that I'm sorry for calling you at work. I was given a mobile number too but there was no answer on that and I left quite a…' he hesitated again, '…quite a formal message because I wasn't sure whether it was the right number or not. The voicemail was just a standard *leave a message* job.'

I laughed. 'I must change that. But anyway, don't worry, I think you probably did call the right number. I just missed a lot of calls this morning.'

'Oh, OK, well, have you got two minutes now?'

I took a deep breath. 'Sure,' I said. 'Are you going to be in Bristol sometime soon?'

'I am actually,' he said. 'I'll be there after lunch tomorrow and I'm staying with friends overnight. So, I'm around for a coffee, or even a bite to eat, if you are.' Another hesitation. 'I know it's really short notice. I expect you're busy but I thought it was worth mentioning.'

'Oh, I'm afraid I can't take time out tomorrow afternoon,' I said. 'And I'm out after work with friends. What a shame.' I became aware of Sophie windmilling wildly at me. I looked at her.

'Invite him along,' she mouthed. I gave her a puzzled look, pretending not to understand.

'I see,' he sounded flatteringly disappointed. 'Well, don't worry. I knew it was a long-shot.'

'I'm so sorry,' I said.

Sophie ceased windmilling and now held up a sheet of A4, upon which she had written in large capitals: INVITE HIM ALONG.

I swivelled in my chair, turning my back on her. 'I'm sure there'll be another time,' I said, closing my eyes. 'When is your next visit?' Upon opening my eyes, I saw that Sophie was now standing in front of me, with a fresh piece of A4. On it, she had written: WHY NOT?

I stared at the sheet of paper and realised that, other than a general lack of enthusiasm for doing anything at all, due to combined sleep deprivation and ongoing angst over Jon, I couldn't actually come up with a why not. If there was anything else holding me back, it was impossible to pinpoint.

I became aware that Stephen was still talking. 'Hello? Are you still there?'

'Yes,' I said. 'I've just had a note passed to me. Sorry, Stephen.'

'That's OK,' he said. 'I shouldn't have called you at work.'

'No, don't worry.' I looked up at Sophie. She shook her piece of A4 and smiled at me, raising her eyebrows questioningly. I closed my eyes again. 'Stephen, why don't you come out with us tomorrow evening? We're going for tapas.'

'I wouldn't want to crash anything,' he said.

I resisted a significant urge to accept this as a refusal.

'Not at all,' I said. 'It's just me, my boss, David, and my friend Sophie. They're both great and you'd be making up a foursome and helping the whole thing be a lot less intimidating for David.'

He laughed. 'Well, in that case, I'd love to come. How about I let you get back to work now and we can sort out logistics later?'

'Sounds good,' I said. 'Speak to you later. Bye.'

'Bye. And I'll see you tomorrow.'

I opened my eyes, replaced the receiver and sat for a moment, unmoving, my hand resting on the telephone.

'Well done,' said Sophie.

I turned towards her. She was still holding the A4 sheet across her chest. She placed it on the table, in the process revealing a second sheet underneath the first. This one said: NOW GET ME A MUFFIN.

I smiled. 'Thanks.'

'No problem,' she replied, returning to her desk and sitting down. 'Now, off you go. I'm sugar hungry and that's not gonna be good for anyone.'

Chapter 25

The twenty-four hours or so in between inviting Stephen to dinner and finding myself sitting at my desk, checking my watch, waiting for him to arrive, passed surprisingly quickly and without any increase in anxiety levels. Unwilling, or unable, to think about the situation any longer, I succeeded in setting my depressing preoccupation with Jon largely to one side, allowing myself instead to fret mildly over a more immediate issue – that of meeting Stephen. Despite my new focus being not entirely stress-free, the prospect of an evening with him did offer the double benefit of being both a distraction from, and significantly less distressing than, a crumbling friendship. And I was pleasantly surprised to realise, several hours into Thursday evening, and after a second, more relaxed telephone conversation with Stephen, that I hadn't thought to check my landline for possible missed calls from Jon.

Of course, he was not entirely absent from my mind. Every now and then I found myself sighing involuntarily, or experiencing a fleeting sense of something worryingly close to panic but, on the whole, such negative feelings remained at bay.

I had agreed with Stephen that we would meet at our offices at six-thirty and then walk to meet Sophie and David for drinks, before all going to the restaurant at eight. Sophie was reluctant to accept the plan and, as she and David put on their jackets at six, she was still trying to persuade me to change my mind.

'What if he's a psychopath?' she asked.

'He's a friend of Greg's,' I reminded her.

'My point *exactly*,' she said. 'If I asked you to name one person we both know who might befriend a psychopath, who would immediately spring to mind?'

'David,' I said tonelessly.

David raised a finger. 'Er, excuse me but I—'

'OK, OK,' agreed Sophie. '*Obviously*, David. But if you had to name another.'

'The computer guy. The one with ears shaped like Quavers.'

Sophie sighed. 'I just don't see why we can't all head off from here *together*,' she protested.

'Because I don't want an audience,' I said.

'An audience for what?' she asked. 'You're just meeting a new person.'

'You know exactly what I mean,' I said.

She looked genuinely perplexed. 'I don't get it.'

I rolled my eyes at her. 'I just need fifteen to twenty minutes in his company, without feeling under scrutiny by you, OK?'

She looked thoughtful and then shook her head. 'I still don't get it,' she repeated, before turning to David. 'Do you get it?'

'Yes,' he said, 'as a matter of fact, I do.'

'Really?' She placed a hand on her chest, feigning surprise. 'I am all astonishment.' She walked towards him, buttoning her jacket as she went. 'Because you're not usually one to display any signs of anxiety.' She smiled up at him fondly. 'Well, come on then, Mr Darcy. Let us depart,' she said, linking his arm and acknowledging defeat. 'We can fetch ourselves a glass of refreshing punch, whilst we await the arrival of the Reverend and Mrs Bentley.'

'Am I to assume that you've never actually read *Pride and Prejudice*?' asked David.

'I only got as far as: "*It is a truth universally acknowledged…*",' she replied. 'I'm more of an *Adam Bede*, kinda gal.' He laughed and, with that, they disappeared down the stairs, each calling a 'goodbye' to me as they exited.

On hearing the outer office door slam, I sighed and wondered how to pass the next thirty minutes. Stalking Stephen on the internet was out. He had apparently shunned all social media and the only picture I had of him was an indistinct and, I hoped, unflattering, thumbnail on Greg's company website. I had considered asking Connie whether she or Greg had another photo, but decided against this in case she thought me superficial. I didn't like the idea of disappointing Connie.

Online research being a no go, I leaned back in my chair and tried to remember what I had been told about Stephen. He was, according to Connie, good-looking. However, I had already decided not to get my hopes up in that department, as she had once confided that newsreader Huw Edwards was her 'ideal man; both physically and intellectually.' I had additionally been advised that Stephen was thirty-three, spoke beautifully, held an MSc in Bioengineering from Imperial, dressed well, thought government foreign policy was misguided, had a face which lit-up when he smiled and, *of course*, owned a Morgan 4/4 with a walnut dash. The eclectic nature of these personal details was due to the fact that they were supplied by two people, each with a rather different set of priorities. My primary source of information was Greg, with a few supplementary titbits from Connie, based upon her one, relatively brief, meeting with Stephen at a corporate event. The upshot was that I had no real idea of what to expect.

So it was with some relief, when he finally buzzed the intercom at 6.25pm, that I opened the street door to a man who resembled neither his thumbnail photograph, nor Huw Edwards. Stephen Powell was a few inches taller than myself, had strawberry blonde hair, blue eyes and a face which lit-up when he smiled. He did the latter immediately upon the door being open wide enough for us to see each other.

'Alice?' he said.

'That's right. And you're Stephen?'

'I'm afraid so.' He beamed and shrugged apologetically.

'Oh don't be afraid,' I laughed. 'I'm afraid enough for both of us.'

'Are you really?' His smile remained in place, but I could tell he was slightly anxious.

I held up my right hand, and indicated 'a tiny bit', using my thumb and index finger.

He opened his arms to their full extent. 'Well, I'm way ahead of you. Never had a blind introduction before. Absolutely terrified.'

I laughed again, stepped out onto the pavement and closed the door behind me. 'Well, shall we head off in a mutually terrified fashion? It's a fifteen minute walk.'

'Great,' he said, popping his hands into his pockets in an appealingly boyish manner. 'I'll leave it to you to steer. Just tug on my sleeve as appropriate.'

Chapter 26

'So, how often do you get to be in Bristol, Stephen? You're based in Birmingham, aren't you? And do have some more bacalao. It's quite delicious.' David picked up the dish and passed it across the table.

'Oh, David, for God's sake, tapas is always stretch or starve.' Sophie intercepted the fish dish, depositing some of what was left onto her plate, before passing the remainder on to Stephen.

I sighed and realised that inviting Stephen to dinner with David and Sophie, was a bit like bringing a new acquaintance home to meet your parents – if your father was Bertie Wooster and your mother Julie Burchill.

Not that things were going badly. David and Sophie's contrasting personalities always made for an entertaining evening out; the steady diplomacy and reserve of one, balancing the engaging energy and largely unedited conversation of the other. But I had wondered what Stephen would make of it all – of Sophie in particular – and I was relieved to see that he seemed to be holding his own so far. He had even coped quite well when, after drinks and while walking to the tapas bar, she had grilled him in the style of Louis Theroux; vacillating between charmingly off-the-wall, and rug-pullingly direct and incisive. I recognised the inquisition as a positive sign; knowing that it was an effort she wouldn't have wasted on someone she didn't warm to. But I couldn't help thinking that to Stephen, it might appear quite the reverse.

'Thanks,' he said, accepting the plate of tapas from her with a smile. 'I actually live in Solihull and about fifty per cent of my work, up until now, has been Birmingham-based. The rest I travel for: London, Leicester, Aberdeen and, of course, Bristol. At the moment, I average three or four days here a month, doing consultancy work for Greg and another firm. But I've now signed an initial two-year, full-time contract with a Bristol company, and I'm already looking at property to buy. But the market is pretty dead right now. There's no doubt I'll be renting for a while.' He picked up his fork and made as if to eat. However, the interview was not quite at an end.

'Where do you stay when you're here?' asked Sophie.

He smiled amiably and lowered his fork. 'I generally commute during the week,' he replied, 'with the occasional overnight stay in a hotel. But tonight I'm with friends in Sneyd Park.'

'Very nice,' said Sophie.

'It is,' he smiled. 'And there's parking.'

'Ah, yes, parking,' said David. 'I hear you have a Morgan. I suppose that makes whizzing all over the country much more enjoyable.'

Stephen looked intrigued. 'How did you know I had a Morgan?'

'Greg,' I explained, 'has mentioned it. Repeatedly.'

He smiled in comprehension. 'I see.'

'I'm afraid I know nothing about cars,' I said. 'I can barely drive, to be honest. I'm on my bike most of the time.'

Stephen looked at me. 'It's a shame I have to be back first thing tomorrow, or we could have gone out for the day.'

'It's the kind of car which deserves a wicker picnic hamper and cold champagne, Alice,' said David.

'All I want to know,' said Sophie, turning to Stephen, 'is whether the top comes down.'

'Yes, it does,' he replied.

She nodded and sighed happily. 'My first car was a 2CV convertible with bubbles on the side. Driving along with the roof down was great. I've got a Beetle now,' she added, smiling at Stephen, 'and I love that, but the 2CV was the only car I've ever really been excited about.'

'What happened to it?' I asked.

'Well, the windscreen wipers kept catching fire, didn't they.' The statement had an 'of course' air about it.

David looked puzzled. 'Goodness, I wasn't even aware that could happen.'

'Lots of things happen,' said Sophie, adopting a 1940s BBC tone, 'of which you are not aware, David. And that is because you are so very posh.'

'To be fair to David,' I said, 'I've never heard of windscreen wipers catching fire either.'

'No,' said Sophie, 'but you *have* heard of Jason Orange and McDonalds, and you aren't closely related to anyone who sits in The House of Lords.' She turned to Stephen. 'David's life experiences are very,' she pressed her hands flat together and then moved them a centimetre or so apart, 'narrow.'

David closed his eyes, as if concentrating deeply. 'Jason was the most proficient dancer in Take That and I can tolerate the Filet-o-Fish but not the Big Mac. Oh and,' he opened his eyes and looked directly at Sophie, 'Lord Porter is not a close relative, he's my aunt's cousin.'

Sophie held up her hand, palm facing David. 'Kudos,' she smiled.

David returned the smile and then looked up questioningly at her hand, which was still hanging at head height. She rolled her eyes, took his hand and slapped it against her own. 'It's called a high-five, David,' she said. 'A high-five.'

-

We left the restaurant at ten-thirty, Sophie and David wandering off to find her a taxi, and Stephen offering to walk me the short distance home. I hesitated over accepting and considered instead sharing a taxi with Sophie, despite the fact that I could be home in less than ten minutes on foot. But realising that this would seem both ridiculous and rude, I said yes to Stephen; three glasses of wine helping to conquer any nerves over a one-on-one conversation, which, I knew, risked being more personal than the small-talk with which our evening had started. Additionally, of course, I would have to face the come-in-for-coffee dilemma.

'You're sure you don't mind?' I said to him, as we headed off. 'It's going to leave you with quite a walk across The Downs.

'It's not a problem,' he said, patting his midriff. 'I need to work off at least some of that tapas.'

'We always over-order,' I sighed. 'Mind you, I did wonder at one point whether you were going to actually get a chance to eat anything. Sorry about the grilling from Sophie.'

'She's quite something,' he said.

I looked up at him, expecting to see a hint of disapproval in his expression. I was relieved to find him grinning.

I smiled. 'You coped well.'

'There wasn't anything to cope with,' he said. 'She obviously thinks a lot of you and wanted to assure herself that I wasn't a predator. I don't mind that. I like her for it in fact.'

'She's such a good friend,' I said. 'Scarily frank, at times. But lovely.'

'And David?'

'He's lovely too,' I said.

'He seems very fond of you.' He raised a quizzical eyebrow.

'There's nothing between us, if that's what you mean,' I said quickly. 'David's type is more...' I searched for an accurate, but not too damning, description, '...assertive. *They* pursue *him*. He's certainly not one for the chase.'

Stephen smiled. 'Maybe he just hasn't met anyone he feels is worth chasing yet.'

'Well, I wish he would,' I said. 'He often ends up sticking with relationships when maybe he shouldn't. He's just terrified of hurting anyone's feelings.' I sighed. 'But then I guess we all are to some extent.'

'The idea of hurting someone is never great,' agreed Stephen. 'But, in the end, my view is that life is for living your way. Pleasing all of the people, all of the time, is an impossibility.' He paused and nudged me. 'Do you think maybe we're getting a bit heavy here?'

'Maybe,' I smiled.

He laughed. 'Well, how about I just say: David and Sophie seem very nice and you're very fortunate to get on so well with your work colleagues.'

I nodded. 'To which I shall uncontroversially reply: Yes – they're great and I am indeed very fortunate.'

He smiled and placed his hands in his pockets, an action which left me feeling as if he might be in search of a pebble to kick along the pavement, or an overhanging tree branch to jump up and touch. 'I really miss the banter of a familiar workplace. Contract work can sometimes make you feel like the perpetual outsider – forever the new boy.'

'But not for much longer,' I said. 'Are you looking forward to the move?'

He looked thoughtful. 'You know, I am,' he said. 'I really am. I enjoy change and I should have moved on before now, really. Do you ever feel like that? That you're aching for change?'

I thought about it. 'I'm not sure I do,' I said. 'I wonder if I'm rather afraid of it actually.'

'So you never wake up in the morning and want something different, something unexpected, to happen? A change for the better?'

'Ah, but,' I held up a finger, 'what if you're pretty happy with things the way they are? And what if change *isn't* for the better?'

'I see your point,' he said. 'But it doesn't always have to be an either/or situation. You can taste change and, if you decide it's not for you, then simply revert. It's a case of maintaining, rather than burning, bridges. But, in any case, *pretty* happy just isn't enough for me. I want *completely*.'

'And you don't feel completely happy at the moment?'

He looked at me. 'Do you?'

'No,' I admitted. 'But I'm not as miserable as sin either.'

'Not as miserable as sin,' he echoed. 'You aim high, then.'

'God, that sounds pitiful, doesn't it?' I laughed. 'Alice Waites, current status: not as miserable as sin.'

'So, what would it take to raise Alice Waites' status to completely happy?'

I shook my head. 'I don't know,' I said simply. 'I'm not sure I've really given it much thought.'

'Well, maybe you should.'

'Unless I think about it and realise that I can't have what I want.'

'If you want something badly enough, you can have it.'

I stopped walking and looked at him. 'You make it sound very easy,' I said doubtfully. 'But what about the other people, other factors, in the mix? What about circumstances beyond our control?'

'It's not easy,' he said, 'far from it. And other people and their feelings, and how you manage them, are something you have to take into account when deciding what you want. But,' he reached up and plucked a leaf from a low-hanging branch, before discarding it with a flick, 'in my experience, to achieve something, you have to want it. *Really* want it. And if you don't achieve it, then you simply didn't want it enough. Blaming someone else for your failure to achieve, is just a convenient excuse.'

I looked up at him and whispered, 'Getting heavy again.'

He grinned. 'OK, how about I keep it really light?' he said, as we started to walk again. 'Right now, what *I* really want is for you to decide whether you'll let me take you to dinner, or to a movie, or for a champagne picnic. Just the two of us. No one else. And not because I want to find out more about Bristol, but because I want to find out more about you. That,' he turned his head to look at me, all hint of boyishness now gone, 'is what I really want.' We walked on in silence, whilst I pictured the various scenarios in my head, none of them striking me as at all unpleasant. 'Sorry,' he said eventually, interrupting my musings, 'on reflection, that was actually quite heavy again, wasn't it?' He slapped a hand to his forehead and shook his head despairingly.

I looked up at him and laughed. I didn't know exactly what I wanted; I didn't know whether I could ever be completely happy – but I did know that my evening with Stephen Powell had made me feel better than I had in weeks. 'I think, in this instance,' I said quietly, 'I'm actually surprisingly OK with heavy.'

We stopped walking and he took my hand and turned towards me. 'I'm delighted to hear that,' he said, looking at me for a moment before bending down and kissing me gently and briefly on the lips. And then, as I smiled up at him and he took my face in his hands, kissing me again, this time slightly harder than the last, I couldn't help thinking that the prospect of inviting him in for coffee, didn't seem such a worrying one after all.

Chapter 27

It was 8.25am when Sophie's yellow beetle pulled up outside my flat. She beeped the horn and I grabbed my umbrella and laptop and hurried out to meet her. She leaned over to open the car door for me as I approached.

'God, it's wet,' she said, as I slammed the door and buckled myself in.

'I know,' I said. 'Glad I'm not biking it to this meeting.'

I waited for her to pull away and, when she didn't, I turned to look at her. 'Everything OK?'

'New dress?' she asked.

'What? Oh,' I smoothed the floral fabric, 'yes, it is. I just thought it might be nice to have something new to wear to *Oliver!* tonight.' She smiled but didn't say anything. '*What?*' I asked.

'Nothing,' she laughed, turning on the engine. 'You just look very nice, that's all.'

-

Our meeting with Henry Stern lasted approximately two hours. Clearly a very creative individual, he put forward lots of ideas regarding the renovation and listened attentively and enthusiastically to our suggestions as to how these might be practically interpreted and brought to life. As we sat there, exchanging ideas, drinking tea and looking at mood-boards, I felt that this would be a project wholly unlike the one recently completed for Eleanor Black, a feeling which was echoed by Sophie as we stopped off to grab a quick coffee in Clifton, rather than returning straight to the office.

'Well, at risk of sounding like David,' she said, as I returned to our table and placed a cappuccino in front of her, 'I'm feeling really good about this project. All the more because it comes hot on the heels of Mrs Melons.'

'Yes,' I admitted, sitting down. 'But I also really like Henry. Perceptive and receptive.'

'Perceptive and receptive? You're as slick as he is, with his stimulation through simulation.' She smiled briefly but I noticed her face fall as she picked up her coffee and took a sip.

'Everything OK?' I asked.

She looked up at me and her smile returned. 'Yes. Why?'

'You just looked very serious for a moment, that's all.'

'Oh,' she shrugged. 'It's nothing. I…' She hesitated, sighed and put down her coffee. 'Alice, can I ask you something?'

'Of course.'

'Do you think I come across as a slapper?'

'What?' I was horrified. 'Are you serious? What on earth makes you ask that?'

She stared absently into her cup. 'I was thinking about it the other day. I mean, I look at you, dithering over going for a drink with a guy and then there's David…'

I opened my mouth to voice an objection but she held up a hand. 'Hang on, hang on,' she said, 'just let me finish. I look at David and OK, so he doesn't enter into relationships for the best of reasons but, once he's in them, he sticks with it because… well, because he places such importance on people's feelings, I guess.' She looked thoughtful. 'Yes, I guess that's it. And I worry…' She paused. 'Well, I don't worry – but I wonder – whether maybe people think that because I date quite a lot, I don't place that same importance on people's feelings.' She picked up and sipped her coffee. 'Or maybe they think I can't. And maybe,' she shrugged, 'maybe that puts a certain kind of person off.'

I stared at her. In the four years I had known her, I had never heard her utter anything so heavy with vulnerability and self-doubt. I felt at a loss.

'Sophie...' I began, before realising that I had no clue as to how to continue, let alone conclude, the sentence.

She looked at me enquiringly but didn't speak. I tried again. 'Nobody and I mean *nobody* thinks you're a slapper.'

She managed a smile. 'I know *you* don't,' she said. 'But I think maybe I give the impression to some people of not being very... selective. In here,' she tapped her chest, 'I'm very choosy. No bloke gets in here very easily. And it's always been more fun like that. Because when they do get inside, well, then it's...' She looked as if she might be about to say more but instead fell silent for a moment, returning her attention to her coffee. When she spoke again, it was with a changed, more familiar, tone. 'Did you notice how Henry kept mentioning his workshop?' she grinned. 'It's either gonna be full of muppets, or a sadomasochist's dream. Stimulation through simulation.' She shook her head and laughed.

I felt unable to keep up with, and unwilling to accept, the sudden change in subject and mood. 'There's nothing wrong with your approach to relationships,' I said. 'You have fun and no one gets hurt – and if something more significant develops, then great.'

She nodded rapidly. 'I know, I know,' she said. 'It's just that someone interested in significant, might think I'm only into fun,' she added quietly. 'That's the problem.'

I shook my head. 'This isn't like you.'

'And that,' she held up a finger, 'is precisely my point. Even *you* don't expect me to be thinking deeply about stuff. If you don't, then what's everybody else's opinion of me? What judgements are they making?'

'I'm not surprised that you have depth,' I protested. 'You're one of the most thoughtful and insightful people I know. I'm just surprised that you're worrying about what other people think. And that you're so wide of the mark. That's what I mean when I say this isn't like you.'

'Wondering not worrying,' she corrected. 'And I only wonder about people I care about.'

'Well, stop wondering, because everyone close to you knows you are funny, clever, caring, supportive and *certainly* not lacking in depth.

Ask any of the book group lot. And if you're after a male perspective other than Jon's,' I continued, 'look at the respect David has for you. He told Eleanor Black that he valued you both professionally and personally.' I picked up my coffee and leaned back in my chair. 'You know he never says anything he doesn't mean and I remember thinking that that was a huge, across-the-board compliment. And I don't know what I'd do without you.' I tutted. 'No one thinks you're a slapper. I've never heard anything so ridiculous.'

'OK.' She sighed heavily. 'Anyway, talking of slappers, how are you getting on with Stephen?'

I laughed, in spite of the sombre context of her comment, and accepted that it was now time to move on to a lighter topic. 'Well, I haven't had much chance to be a slapper yet, have I?' I said. 'Just that walk home and a few snogs over a late-night coffee after tapas last week.'

'But he's down tonight for *Oliver!*'

'He is.'

'God help him. Have you told him about the trolley? Ooh and the punch-up last year when Peter Pan called his shadow a—'

'Yes,' I interrupted. 'He knows they don't always stick to the script.'

She smiled. 'Anyway, where's he staying this weekend?' The question was unmistakably loaded.

'He's not staying the weekend. He has to be back early Saturday. People are coming to view the flat during the day. But he'll be in Sneyd Park again tonight,' I said, refusing to acknowledge the implication of her enquiry.

'Of course he will.' Her tone was sceptical.

'He will!' I insisted.

She laughed. 'Well, I liked him,' she said. 'But, while I'm all for seizing the day,' she tapped her chest for a second time, 'don't let him in here too quickly.'

'Thank you for that advice, Dear Deidre,' I said. 'But we're definitely leaning more towards fun than significant for the time being.'

'Great,' she said. 'And what about Jon?'

My stomach lurched.

The truth was that I had barely thought about Jon, during a week which had past largely in a blur. Work and pleasantly flirty telephone conversations with Stephen had occupied most of my waking hours. Now, at the mention of Jon's name, I experienced a mixture of emotions and recollections, the combined effect of which was not nice.

I looked at Sophie; she was delving in her bag. 'What about him?' I asked.

'You'll meet up with him at *Oliver!*, won't you?' she asked. 'Shit. I think I've left my fake fag at Henry's.'

'I expect I'll see him there,' I said.

'You'd better.' She continued to rummage. 'Because I'll be well pissed-off if you come in on Monday without all the gossip on Suzanna. And Miriam will kill you if you turn up there tomorrow with anything less than a full dossier. You're seeing her tomorrow night, aren't you?'

'Just for a drink. We're staying in because Craig's off out and Miriam couldn't get a sitter.'

Sophie looked up from her bag. 'Call Jon.'

I ignored the suggestion and drank my coffee.

'Do you need to pop back to Henry's for your fake fag?' I asked.

She shook her head. 'No, it's OK. I've got another in my desk. I can hang on for a drag 'til we get back to the office. Anyway,' she replaced her bag on the floor, 'promise me you'll arrange to meet Jon and Suzanna.'

I put down my coffee and sighed heavily.

'Ah, come on, Alice,' she wheedled. 'I'm facing a crap weekend and am gutted to be missing out on the play. I seriously think it might be even more sweary than *Peter Pan*. And then on top of that, not to meet Suzanna… And besides,' she continued more seriously, 'I'm sure Jon will want to introduce her to you. It'll be much easier for her to meet a few of us at a time, rather than all in one go at the book group dinner.'

I looked at her. She was so thoughtful and absolutely put me to shame. I had no desire to make things awkward for Suzanna and, whatever Jon's thoughts and feelings, I could be grown-up enough to swallow my pride and send him a simple text. Besides, I thought, bumping into him without talking or texting first would be far worse than the effort of getting in touch. And it wasn't as if we were going to an arena event. I estimated the seating capacity of Abs' school hall to be approximately two hundred: the chances of not bumping into him would be very small indeed. 'OK,' I said to Sophie, 'I'll text later and find out where he's sitting.'

She appeared satisfied. 'Well done.' She drained her coffee and peered into my cup. 'Now, can we head back to the office before I run outside and mug some poor sod for a fag?'

Chapter 28

Stephen picked me up, in the Morgan, at 6.50pm. And, despite having no interest whatsoever in cars, I had to admit that this particular car was rather nice. What made it even nicer was that my chauffeur for the evening was more amused than flattered by my enjoyment of the experience; and more interested in talking about me than his car, politely dismissing my few equally polite vehicular enquiries with brief, closed-ended explanations.

'You know,' he said, after one such explanation, 'I love this car because I think it has character – personality even. And because I've worked hard on it. It's a part of me, of my history – a memory box on wheels. But I'm not interested in cars per se.'

'What kind of memories?' I asked, enjoying the evening sunshine on my face as we waited at traffic lights, the engine idling.

'People, conversations, days out. I remember my father's face the day I turned up with the car and asked him if he'd like to take my mother out in it. That was a really special moment.' He shrugged as the lights changed and we pulled away. 'Things change. Situations change. People change. We move on. I like that. But it's great to have a physical reminder of a certain time in your life – or of a certain person.'

I nodded. 'I suppose a house is like that for a lot of people.'

'I suppose so. But,' he tapped the steering wheel, 'for me, for now, it's this car.' He turned to me briefly and smiled, before returning his attention to the road. 'I'll always remember driving Alice to see her friend's production of *Oliver!*. I'll remember what she was wearing and how she looked enquiringly at me as she sat to my left.' He looked straight ahead and grinned. 'She looked bloody good, by the way.'

I laughed. 'You charmer.'

'Yeah, that's me,' he said. 'A cad in a convertible. Now, what time is it? Do I need to put my foot down?'

I checked my phone. 'No, we're fine. It's ten past and we're less than five minutes away and there's plenty of parking at the school.'

'And we're meeting Jon and Susan there?'

I cleared my throat and put my phone in my bag. 'Suzanna. Yes, that's right. I told them you were happy to drive but it was easier for them to make their own way.'

I had texted Jon a few hours earlier and passed on the offer of a lift. I was pleased when Stephen had made the suggestion, as it gave me a reason to get in touch, other than simply arranging to meet up at the play. I had kept my text brief but had made a definite, considered attempt at warmth. I had made no reference to our disagreement and I had described Stephen as "my friend". I had said I was looking forward to meeting Suzanna and had given him our seat numbers.

His texted reply was similarly pitched. He thanked us "both" for the offer of a lift, but explained that he was picking up Suzanna from Temple Meads mid-afternoon and, beyond that, their plans were unfixed. However, he added that their seats for *Oliver!* were next to ours, so there would be no difficulty meeting up. It hadn't occurred to me that Abs would give us four seats together but, on reflection, I realised that she was unlikely to have done anything else. The fact that I wasn't entirely comfortable with the arrangement, was a painful reminder of my changed relationship with Jon. But whilst I continued to regret that change, my excitement at the prospect of an evening out with Stephen at least took the edge off any sense of sadness or misgiving.

Stephen, I had decided, was good for me. We had talked daily by phone since the tapas evening, and I liked him more as a result of each conversation. He was both a listener and a talker, and over several hours of phone calls we had discussed family, friends, his relocation and work. The latter was the only issue over which he expressed any dissatisfaction, complaining that his current heavy schedule meant that he was often speaking to me from the office or car when, he said, a conversation from home, with a glass of wine in his hand, would have been his preference.

However, despite the relatively intense and wide-ranging nature of our conversations, no references had yet been made to, or questions asked about, previous partners. And I sensed that the subject of relationships in general – past and possible future – was, for the time being, if not exactly off-limits for Stephen, then at least something he was as equally willing to save for later as I was.

As we pulled into the school car park and Stephen reversed into a space, I leaned forward to retrieve my bag from the footwell. 'I'll just turn off my phone,' I said, reaching into my bag. 'I don't want Sophie's ringtone blaring out mid "*Food Glorious Food*".'

Stephen turned off the engine, got out and raised the roof. 'Sophie's ringtone?' he queried, as he got back in the car.

'She changes the ringtone on my phone, and on David's, every Friday at 5pm. The rule is that we're not allowed to check it, or change it, until we've received at least one call. I haven't had a call this evening – only texts – so it's still a mystery. Mine are usually fine. It's poor David who gets the more edgy ones. The worst was *Anarchy in the UK*. That went off during a private viewing at the RWA.'

Stephen laughed. 'And yet he still lets her do it?'

I nodded. 'He loves it. But he now always asks me to phone him at six if he's going anywhere *sensitive*.'

'I like Sophie and David,' said Stephen.

'So do I.'

He smiled at me. 'But I like you more.'

He leaned towards me, and gently stroked my cheek before kissing me. After a few seconds, he moved his lips from my mouth to my ear. 'Alice,' he whispered softly.

'Yes,' I replied, my eyes closed.

'I don't want to panic you, but there are two people standing in front of the car, staring at us. And,' his tone remained gentle as he kissed my earlobe, 'unless they are Jon and Suzanna, I'm slightly concerned that this area might be even dodgier than you described.'

–

It *was* Jon and, as we discovered upon introduction following our exit from the car, it was Suzanna. She was slim, slightly shorter than myself and undeniably attractive. The long, dark hair which had so caught Craig's eye at Hotel du Vin, was this evening loosely coiled against the back of her head, with the odd stray tendril adding to the casually sophisticated effect. She wore cropped jeans, pumps and a semi-sheer, cream, loosely-fitted blouse over a camisole. A fine beige jumper was draped around her shoulders. I guessed her to be around the same age as me and was disappointed that Craig had described her as considerably younger than Miriam.

'We didn't mean to intrude,' she smiled, as the four of us made our way through the car park towards the school. 'I spotted the car, so I suggested we walk across to meet you. It wasn't immediately obvious what was going on, because of the way the light was reflecting off the glass.' She looked up at Jon for corroboration and slid a hand around his waist as she did so. He reciprocated with an arm around her shoulders.

'That's right,' he said.

Stephen took my hand. 'It was only a peck,' he smiled, and then, giving my hand a quick squeeze, added, 'because I'm not overly comfortable with PDAs in car parks. I prefer to save the heavier stuff for shop doorways.'

I laughed and looked at Jon, who appeared not to have heard the comment and was instead searching his pockets for something. He took out his car keys, turned and pointed them towards his car, which was parked just a short distance from our own. 'I'm not sure I locked it,' he said.

'I think you did, Jon,' said Suzanna.

He didn't reply but turned, replaced his arm around her shoulders and kissed the top of her head. My smile dropped and I found myself unable to look away. He looked up, caught my eye and for a moment we looked at each other, with no attempt on either part to disguise negative feelings with a smile. I was aware that Stephen said something to which Suzanna replied, but I took in neither comment, unable to focus upon anything but the growing conviction that a friendship with Jon might soon be impossible.

Chapter 29

The first half of the show passed largely without incident, other than Mr Bumble repeatedly turning to the prompter and saying, 'Shit, what's next?' whenever a line escaped him. To his credit, he did lower his voice on each occasion. However, the sound system was excellent and, thanks to his radio mic, the audience caught every word.

Nancy's mumbled exclamation of, 'You ran into my leg, you fucker!' when Fagin's trolley at one point veered slightly off course, was equally well broadcast. Nevertheless, compared to the mayhem which had ensued the previous year, when Peter Pan had lost patience with his shadow, *Oliver!* was, as we hit the interval, going very smoothly indeed.

'Well,' smiled Stephen, as we enjoyed our half-time complimentary tea and biscuits, 'I, for one, am really impressed.'

'Me too,' I said. 'The singing is great. And,' I continued, looking round, 'tonight seems to be a sell-out. I can't remember that happening before. Abs must be very proud.'

'Teaching is such hard work,' said Suzanna. 'I know it's something I just wouldn't have the energy or patience for.'

'Me neither,' I agreed. 'But one thing which Abs does not lack is energy. You might just pick up on that when you meet her later. She wants us all to go backstage.'

She smiled. 'I'd love to.' There was a moment's pause in the conversation, before she spoke again. 'I've noticed some beautiful artwork along the corridors here.'

Jon nodded. 'And there's a small sculpture garden, with some rather impressive pieces, just beyond those double doors.' He gestured towards the end of the hall.

'Oh,' she said, 'can we go and look?'

'The doors to the garden will be locked,' said Jon. 'But they're glass, so you'll be able to see most of the garden through them. It might be best if we don't all go, though,' he said. 'Just in case it encourages others to wander.'

Suzanna looked hesitant. 'I'll come with you, if you like,' I volunteered.

'Thanks,' she smiled. 'I'd love to see.'

I handed my cup of tea to Stephen. 'You two chat. We won't be a mo.'

'We'll do our best to cope,' he said, grinning.

Suzanna and I headed to the exit at the far end of the hall, before continuing a short way along the corridor to the glass doors.

'These are just marvellous,' she said, as we stood, side by side, looking out into the garden; a space divided into small, irregular, gravelled areas by intertwining paved pathways, with a single sculpture occupying each area. There were seven or eight works in total; a central bench and a tree completing the picture.

'I love that one.' She pointed towards a ceramic of a kneeling woman, her face and arms uplifted to the sky. I remembered admiring it when Jon and I had sat in the cold, darkened garden just before Christmas, as we waited to take Abs out for birthday drinks. On that occasion, each sculpture had been illuminated by a light at its base.

'Yes,' I said. 'It's my favourite too. Although, they're all so good, it's hard to believe they're the work of children.'

'So,' said Suzanna suddenly, 'how do you know Abigail?'

I frowned, confused that she didn't already know the answer to the question. 'Well,' I said, as she looked at me with an expression of polite expectance, 'she is in our book group.'

It was her turn to look puzzled. 'Your book group? Do you mean the book group that Jon's in? Are you in that too? So is that your connection with Jon?'

I turned my head and glanced back towards the hall, unsure whether I wanted to cry, or to run back and pelt him with custard creams. He had clearly told her nothing about me. In an effort to conclude the conversation as quickly and as painlessly as possible, I said, 'Yes, I'm in the book group.'

'I'm so jealous,' she continued brightly, oblivious to the emotional storm now circling above us. 'I'd love to join a book group. So you must know Miriam then?'

I attempted a smile and nodded.

'She sounds lovely,' said Suzanna.

'She is.'

'She was a best friend of Jon's wife, wasn't she?'

'Yes.'

'And I know she has been so supportive of Jon. I'm really looking forward to meeting her. I'm coming to the book group dinner, you know.' She looked at me and smiled. 'I didn't realise you'd be there. I'm so pleased because although I know it will be lovely, it could also be quite nerve-wracking. Especially as you all knew Lydia, even if it was only for a relatively short time – with the exception of Miriam of course.' She turned back towards the sculptures. 'These are just wonderful.'

'They are.' I took a deep breath, whilst experiencing a growing, and almost unbearably painful, sense of being written out of Jon's past, present and future. 'But I wonder if we should be getting back now,' I said. 'There can't be much of the interval left.'

She looked at her watch. 'You're right,' she said. 'And we're in the middle of the row, aren't we? I don't want to tread on anybody's toes.'

–

By the time we re-entered the refreshments hall, Jon and Stephen, together with most of the other audience members, had already returned to their seats. We hurried to join them.

'We thought you two might have been planning to skip Act II,' smiled Stephen, as Suzanna and I squeezed our way apologetically along Row F. 'Here, I'll move up one,' he said, vacating the space next to Jon.

'Wouldn't miss it for the world,' I said, taking my seat. 'But I might need your hand to squeeze, if the trolley makes another appearance. It makes me very tense.'

'You feel free to squeeze anything you like,' he said quietly. 'Anything at all.' I smiled at him and was rewarded with a wink.

Suzanna leaned forward and, reaching in front of Jon, tapped my knee. 'I was just saying to Jon how pleased I was to discover that you'll be at the book group dinner.'

I did my best to smile.

'It will be great to have a proper chance to talk,' she continued. 'And maybe the four of us,' she smiled at Stephen, 'could go out to dinner sometime.'

'That would be lovely,' I said, sounding, I thought, rather stiff despite my best attempts. And then, unable to suppress a renewed surge of hurt and bitterness. 'What do you think, Jon? Does that sound like fun to you?'

He turned his head away from me and spoke to Suzanna. 'We'll have to compare diaries,' he said.

I felt unable to let it drop. 'As you say, it would be good to get to know each other better.' I addressed this comment to Suzanna, before sitting back in my seat, turning slightly towards Jon and adding in an undertone, '…especially as Jon is apparently so reluctant to tell you anything about me.' I focused on the stage and whilst I was aware that his head turned towards me, I couldn't bring myself to look at him.

Stephen tapped my left shoulder and I leaned gratefully towards him. He placed his hand, palm upwards on my lap. 'That,' he said, looking at his hand, 'is all yours for squeezing over the next hour or so. And, believe me, I'm hoping for a whole heap of trolley action.'

I smiled and encased his hand in both of mine. A moment later, the house lights dimmed, the band struck up and the curtains opened on Act II.

Chapter 30

Abs was waiting for us in the bustling corridor outside the various changing rooms when we went backstage.

'Here,' she said, handing each of us a visitor pass as we approached, 'just pop these on and then we're good. Now,' she said, turning first to Suzanna and then to Stephen, 'it's so, so lovely to meet you both. I'm delighted that you came to see our play. I hope you enjoyed it.' She looked around. 'Pete is here too somewhere. He's been helping side-of-stage. He so wanted to meet you. He's been excited about it all evening. Anyway,' she clasped her hands together and positioned them endearingly beneath her chin, 'what did you think?'

'Best ever,' I said. 'Truly, your best ever.'

She beamed. 'You really think so, Alice?'

'She does,' said Stephen. 'And, although I've not had the pleasure of seeing one of your previous productions, I can say that I don't think they could have surpassed what I saw here tonight. Here, have a congratulatory shake.' He held out his hand. Abs shook it enthusiastically. 'The performances were excellent. I loved every minute.'

I looked from Stephen to Abs. He was saying all the right things and she was clearly thrilled. I found his hand and squeezed it.

'It was really good, Abs,' said Jon. 'You should feel very proud.'

Suzanna nodded her agreement.

Abs turned to Jon and placed a hand on his arm. 'You're so kind,' she said, before pointing over his shoulder. 'Oh look! Here's Pete!'

We turned to see Pete walking slowly down the hallway. He was dressed entirely in black and I noticed that he seemed to be limping slightly. He raised a hand in greeting as he approached.

'Pete.' Abs placed a hand on each shoulder, stood on tiptoe and kissed his cheek. 'How are you?'

'I'm great,' he said with a slow smile.

'Just look at him,' said Abs turning to us. 'He's still on a massive high.'

'I am,' said Pete, nodding at half-speed.

'He just loves it. The smell of the greasepaint, the roar of the crowd. He insisted on helping again this year. You're buzzing, aren't you, Pete?'

Pete continued to smile and nod.

'I don't know what I'd do without him,' sighed Abs.

'Are you OK, Pete?' asked Jon, pointing at his foot. 'I noticed a limp there.'

'Trolley,' said Pete and we all nodded in immediate comprehension. 'A gash. But nothing my sock couldn't absorb. Might be a fracture. Not sure. Will get it checked tomorrow.'

My face contorted involuntarily at his description of the injury and I noticed Suzanna wince. Stephen's grip on my hand tightened slightly but Jon remained phlegmatic. 'I see,' he said.

'Pete,' said Abs, 'this is Suzanna.'

He held out his hand to her. 'Hi. Great to meet you.'

'And you,' said Suzanna, 'Jon's told me a lot about you.'

I clenched my teeth.

'And this,' said Abs, 'is Alice's Stephen.'

'Well, I'm not sure he's quite my—' I began, feeling my face flush.

Stephen held out his hand to Pete. 'Really pleased to meet you. I hear you're an expert in both anaesthesia and bicycle repair.'

Abs clapped her hands and laughed. 'Oh he is!'

'Er, excuse me, miss.' The interruption came from a teenage girl who had squeezed herself between Suzanna and Abs. I recognised her as Nancy from the show.

Abs looked down and smiled. When she spoke, her tone of voice was as gentle as ever but now had an added air of calm authority which I didn't recognise. 'Yes, Chantel?'

'Mum told me to come and see you,' said Chantel. She jerked a thumb over her shoulder, in the direction of a fearsome-looking woman who was standing a few feet away. She was about five foot tall and at first glance appeared to be almost as wide; however, the overall impression was not of obesity but of power. She wasn't, I decided immediately, someone to mess with.

'Oh, hello, Mrs Hartley,' said Abs, addressing the human cube, 'how can I help?'

Mrs Hartley shook her head and then made a gesture with her hand, as if hastening Chantel. The girl took a deep breath. 'I shouldn't,' she began, glancing anxiously at us, her small audience, before focusing on her feet, 'have called Darren a fucker. It's bad for you and I made myself look like a twat. Sorry.'

My eyes widened with the effort of not laughing. I looked at Abs. Her face showed no emotion and she nodded seriously.

'Well, thank you for that apology. You made a mistake but the circumstances were mitigating. That means that whereas that kind of behaviour would usually merit punishment, in this case, it does not. And, while you're here, I would like to say what an impressive performance you gave tonight. These people are some of my best friends and they go to the theatre regularly. They have all thoroughly enjoyed the show and you were a significant part of that.'

We nodded our assent and Chantel bit her lower lip.

'Now,' said Abs, 'I think, as one of the leads, you should head home and get as much sleep as possible. Thank you again for your apology.' She turned to Mrs Hartley and smiled. The latter nodded grimly, advanced, placed a hand on her daughter's shoulder and escorted her down the corridor.

When they were out of earshot, Abs' Tiggerish air returned. 'Isn't that child wonderful? What courage! And what a mother; gorgeous woman and perfect parenting. Just amazing.'

Jon smiled. 'You're amazing, Abs,' he said simply. And despite the ongoing, intermittent agony of our disintegrating friendship, and a growing, largely uninterrupted, feeling of resentment towards him, I had to agree.

Chapter 31

'Tea, coffee, wine, beer?' I asked, as I walked towards the kitchen, Stephen following.

The drive home from the play had been considerably quicker than the journey there, thanks to largely empty roads. Consequently, we were home by ten, and this evening I had felt no hesitation in suggesting that Stephen come in for a drink. Now, as we stood in the kitchen, in response to my question, he placed his hands in his pockets, shrugged and smiled affably; a regularly repeated boyish gesture with which I was becoming familiar.

'What are you having?' he asked.

'Well, I quite fancy a glass of red, but I'm happy to keep you company with a coffee, if that's what you prefer.' I thought about adding, 'because you're driving' but, for reasons which I chose not to examine, I stopped short of that.

Hands still firmly encased in pockets, he looked first at the floor and then up at me. 'I'd like a glass of red too,' he said.

'Right.' I took a bottle from the wine rack and pushed it along the work surface towards him. 'You can pour. The glasses are on up on that shelf to your left.'

He said nothing, instead simply retrieving two glasses, opening the wine and pouring two, very generous, glasses. Driving, I realised, was not on the cards. 'I'm happy to walk,' he said, as if reading my mind. He handed me my drink and I smiled, grateful for the provision of a get-out, which had the effect of lessening any lingering desire I might have felt for one.

'Let's go into the living room,' I said.

In the car on the way home, the conversation had centred largely on the play. We had laughed over the many expletives additional to the original script, but at the same time Stephen had been genuinely, and pleasingly, impressed. What's more, he had warmed as immediately to Abs and to Pete as they clearly had to him and his easy, relaxed charm, and his willingness to laugh, had been a welcome antidote to Jon's increasingly cold behaviour towards me. Jon, I realised, had decided that our friendship was not one he wished to continue – at least not at the same level – and in order to avoid any further hurt, I had to accept that and focus on other things.

However, as I sat down next to Stephen on the sofa, he introduced a topic of conversation which made focusing on other things, for the moment at least, impossible.

'So,' he said, placing his wine glass on the coffee table in front of us and executing a theatrical yawn-and-stretch manoeuvre in order to place an arm around my shoulder, 'tell me about Jon and Suzanna. What's going on there then?'

I laughed at the arm around my shoulder, rather than the enquiry. 'Oh, I don't know,' I said, as he leaned forward to retrieve his glass. 'Jon's playing that very close to his chest.'

He looked at me and smiled. 'He and Suzanna seemed very well suited.'

'You think so?' I found myself interested to hear his assessment. 'It's difficult for me because I knew Lydia so well and she and Jon were… well, perfect together.'

'And she wasn't like Suzanna?'

'I don't know Suzanna at all,' I said. 'I can't compare them.'

'Well, what was Lydia like?' he asked.

I smiled up at him and took a deep breath, experiencing the bitter sweet mixture of gratitude for a wonderful friendship and pain over its loss, which I always felt when I thought about Lydia. 'She was much quieter than either Miriam or I, but great fun. She laughed so easily. She was…' I hesitated, 'I think maybe serene is the best word. She was peaceful and a peacemaker. How she coped sharing a house with us, I don't know. She was the calm to our chaos.' I leaned my head against his shoulder, before adding in a rush, 'I found it very difficult to see Jon with Suzanna tonight.'

Surprised at my own confession, I sat up and looked at Stephen. 'I'm sorry. There was no need to tell you that.'

He shook his head. 'I've told you a lot. Much more than I expected to. Sometimes things just need to be said.' He squeezed my shoulder and smiled. 'Are you interested in an objective opinion of Jon and Suzanna? Admittedly it's based on only two hours' observation and approximately twenty minutes of conversation.'

I nodded. 'I am.'

'OK, well,' he began, 'they're very friendly and pleasant but also quite closed, neither of them give a lot away. And, if I'm honest, they left me uncertain as to whether there was anything much *to* give away.' He looked thoughtful. 'But they seemed really right together. I don't think they are going to challenge each other at all. And I mean that as a positive.'

I didn't reply, having already begun to consider his appraisal of Jon. Distilling it down, Stephen had found him bland and lacking in depth. Well, the judgement wasn't, I decided, an unreasonable one, based upon this evening. But it was unrecognisable as a description of the Jon I knew – or had known. My mind turned to the evenings of wine bar whinging and chick-flick cinema he good-humouredly endured, his brave participation in book group, his encouragement, his concern, his humour, his patience…

'I've upset you,' said Stephen suddenly.

'What?' I was puzzled for a moment.

'You look upset,' he said. 'I was too frank.'

'No, no, not at all,' I shrugged. 'I can see why you formed those opinions…'

He looked at me questioningly. 'But?' he prompted.

'Actually,' I said, 'there is no *but*. I didn't enjoy his company this evening and I don't think he enjoyed mine either.'

There was a moment's silence between us, during which I fought again to rid my mind of Jon. When Stephen finally spoke, it was with a different tone. 'Well, *I* enjoyed your company. Very much,' he said. 'So why don't we focus on that.' I looked at him. His expression was serious and the transition from boyish, to something approaching authoritarian, was so rapid that it left me feeling uncertain as to what might come next. 'You're fascinating,' he said quietly, 'but you don't know it. And that,' he ran his forefinger gently across my lower lip, 'is part of your fascination.'

'You hardly know me,' I said, a little breathlessly. 'Another week and you might not find me quite so fascinating.'

'Oh, I think I will,' he said. 'That's the problem.'

'Is it a problem?'

He smiled suddenly and the boyishness returned. 'I just didn't expect this.'

'I didn't expect it either,' I said impulsively. I took his wine glass from him and placed it on the coffee table along with my own. 'I really didn't.' Then I turned and kissed him. He sat up, put his arms around me and pushed me gently backwards until we were lying on the sofa. I felt his hand slide down to my hip and then further down to my thigh, before coming to rest slightly below the hemline of my dress. I was just wondering where it might go next, and whether or not I might object, when a Cockney woman began singing '*Oom-pah-pah! Oom-pah-pah! That's how it goes*,' at the top of her voice, from the small, blue armchair on the other side of the room.

Our heads turned simultaneously towards the armchair and, recovering from my shock at the rather surreal nature of the interruption, I began to laugh.

'You know what that is?' I said, raising my voice above the continuing east end serenade.

Stephen smiled down at me, his face just inches from my own. 'Not a clue.'

I pointed at my bag, which I had thrown down onto the chair. 'It's my phone. That's my Friday ringtone.'

He laughed. 'Sophie?'

'Yes.'

The singing ceased and his lips moved to my ear. 'Do you need to check who it was?' he asked softly.

'I'd better.' I sighed. 'Just in case it was Dad.'

'OK.' He hoisted himself back into a seated position. I got up and retrieved my phone.

I unlocked it and the words *Jon: missed call and voicemail* appeared onscreen. I felt no urge to listen to the message, or to return the call. I was in little doubt that whatever he had to say would be far from uplifting and I felt I'd rather not hear that this evening – perhaps not ever. I opened voicemail, pressed 'edit' and stared at the screen, my finger hovering over 'delete'.

'Everything OK?' asked Stephen. 'Anything important?'

I switched off the phone and slung it back into my bag. 'No,' I said. 'PPI.'

'They always call at the best times.'

'I know. Yesterday, I was…' I ground to a halt, struck dumb by a cacophony of thoughts and the mundanity of the anecdote I was about to recount.

Stephen smiled. 'Yesterday?'

I closed my eyes and forced myself to focus on the moment. 'You can stay,' I said. 'If you want to.'

There was no response. I opened my eyes and looked at him. His gaze was steady, his smile had disappeared and he now appeared to be studying me intently. 'And what do *you* want?' he asked.

'I want you to stay,' I said. And it was true. Regardless of an inability to completely and precisely define my feelings, I wanted him to stay. Of that I was certain.

He stood up and walked towards me. 'Then I will.'

'But is it what *you* want?' I asked, as he reached out and took my hand.

He looked at me, maintaining an unsmiling silence and causing me to experience a momentary dread that his response might prove to be a kindly, but crushingly humiliating, one. I held my breath and braced myself for the worst.

'Alice,' he said eventually, placing a hand on my cheek and moving his face close to mine, 'one thing you have to know about me is that I never, ever,' he kissed me, 'do anything I don't want to.'

Chapter 32

I held up the bottle and grinned as the door began to open. 'I've got Prosecco and I'm not afraid to use it!'

'Good to know,' said Craig, smiling and beckoning me into the wide, but cluttered, black and white tiled hallway.

I stepped inside, carefully avoiding some Lego and two rather forlorn-looking Barbie dolls, lying semi-naked and wild-haired on the door mat. 'I was expecting Miriam to answer,' I explained, giving him a kiss, as he closed the door behind me. 'I thought you were going out.'

'I am,' he said, removing his glasses and rubbing his eyes. 'Although I could do without it,' he added wearily.

'Why not stay in with us then?' I asked.

'I think we both know that would cramp your style and besides,' he replaced his glasses and began to walk away from me, down the hallway, 'it's business. I can't cry off.'

I followed him into the kitchen and he reached out to take the Prosecco from me. 'Here, I'll put that in the fridge. There's one already open and cold.'

I handed him the bottle and walked to sit down at the large, oak dining table in the middle of the room.

'So, where's Miriam?' I asked, surprised to see him pouring a glass of beer, in addition to my glass of wine. 'Not in any hurry then?' I nodded at the beer, as he placed both drinks on the table and sat down opposite me.

'Taxi will be here at eight.' He glanced at the kitchen clock. 'So I've got half an hour. Miriam's upstairs on the phone to her mother and

Phoebe's out for the count. She and Miriam have been at a barbecue all afternoon.'

I picked up my Prosecco. 'You didn't go?'

He shook his head. 'Working. And it was one of Miriam's mum friends. A dad friend, actually. I'd have been in the way.'

I had been absently admiring Miriam's new retro Smeg food mixer, but at the mention of a dad I refocused on Craig. 'I'm sure Miriam would have preferred you to go,' I said.

He looked at me over the top of his beer but didn't reply.

'And you're not coming to the book group dinner,' I continued. 'Couldn't you spare the time for that either?'

He placed his beer on the table.

'Am I being told off here?' he asked.

'Yes, you are,' I smiled.

He nodded. 'Noted.'

'Here I am!' Miriam bustled into the kitchen, hurrying towards me and enveloping me in a tight squeeze. 'I'm so sorry, Alice. That was Mum on the phone.' She straightened up and beamed. 'I've had such a lovely afternoon and now I'm going to have a lovely evening. I feel so spoilt!'

I looked her up and down, taking in the earrings, necklace, bracelet and rarely worn make-up. She had clearly gone to some trouble today.

'You look lovely,' I said and then, turning to Craig, 'Doesn't she look beautiful?' He said nothing, instead staring fixedly at his beer.

'Oh, don't,' protested Miriam with a delighted grin. She walked to the fridge and extracted the bottle of Prosecco. 'And I must smell like a giant sausage after the barbecue. Which is appropriate,' she added in an undertone, 'since Craig is forever telling me I look like one.' She held up the almost empty bottle. 'I'm sorry my husband didn't think to open a fresh one for you, Alice.'

Craig shot her a glance and then stood up, picking up his glass and pushing back his chair. 'Well, I'll leave you to it. Enjoy,' he said, saluting me with his beer.

'Cheers.' I smiled, raising my glass and, with Miriam ignoring his departure, he exited the kitchen, closing the door quietly behind him.

I looked after him, as Miriam returned to the table, champagne flute and bottle in hand. 'Shall we stay in here or do you fancy an armchair?' She seemed in high spirits, and I suspected that the drink she poured herself was not her first one of the day.

I looked up at her. 'I'm OK in here for now.'

Her smile faded and she sat down. 'What's the matter? You don't look very happy.'

'Craig was just telling me he's been working all day,' I said.

'Oh,' she waved a hand dismissively and her smile returned, 'don't you worry about him. If it makes him happy, then let him get on with it.'

'Yes, he seemed over the moon about it,' I said. She appeared not to hear and sipped her drink contentedly. 'Anyway,' I continued, 'you evidently enjoyed your afternoon at Eammon's barbecue.'

She placed her drink on the table and looked at me, her smile now taking on a fixed quality. 'Yes, I did. Phoebe and I both did.' She paused. 'So Craig told you whose barbecue it was then?'

I shook my head. 'Nope,' I said. 'That was just a lucky guess on my part.' I drank my Prosecco. 'Is that a new lipstick?'

There was silence between us, as she picked up the bottle and needlessly topped-up my glass. 'Don't judge me, Alice,' she said eventually, putting down the bottle and staring at her drink.

'Well, would it be OK if I judged Eammon?' I asked.

She shook her head and smiled sadly. 'I'd be disappointed if you thought there was anything going on,' she said quietly.

'As if I'd think that,' I said, leaning towards her and placing my hand on hers. 'And I'm not judging.' I paused. 'I'm just asking you not to give up on Craig. Don't cut him off.'

She turned her hand over and took mine, lowering her eyes as she did so. 'Sometimes I feel very cut off,' she said.

I sighed and squeezed her hand. 'I'm not blaming you for anything, or for one minute saying that Craig isn't at fault here. But one of you has to start a conversation about all this, or you may as well call it a day right now.'

'I think maybe he has already.' She tapped her forehead. 'Up here at least.'

I looked at her, feeling horrified at this starkest acknowledgement yet, of the trouble they were in. After a moment's hesitation, I managed a smile and shook my head. 'I'm certain he hasn't. He just seems exhausted by work and bewildered by home.'

There was a pause and then she heaved a sigh, released my hand and picked up her drink. 'Come on,' she said. 'Cheer me up by telling me about last night. How did it go?'

She looked up at me expectantly and I wondered what to do. My urge was to run upstairs, find Craig and drag him down to the wife who clearly believed she was losing him – or had already lost him. However, aware that my most impulsive actions often proved my most disastrous, I decided that it would, for now, perhaps be better to divert Miriam from her troubles with Craig, rather than locking her in the kitchen with him and forcing her to dwell on them. I therefore accepted the change of subject.

'The play went really well,' I said. 'It was a sell-out.'

'You know full well I wasn't asking about the play,' she tutted. 'Besides, I saw it on Thursday.'

'And did it go OK then?' I asked.

Her expression became pained. 'Well, naturally, there was lots of unscheduled swearing.'

I nodded. 'Naturally.'

'But also,' she hesitated and put a hand to her mouth, 'he came off the trolley.'

I put down my glass and laughed.

'Alice!' She made a commendable attempt at sounding shocked.

'Oh, come off it! I bet it was *really* funny.'

She smiled guiltily. 'Well, once it was clear he was OK.'

'What happened?'

'I'm not sure,' she said. 'He just sort of toppled off. The other kids seemed quite flummoxed and didn't move to help him. And then there was total silence while he rolled into the wings. He was in the middle of the stage at the time, so it took quite a while.'

'He rolled?'

'Yes. It was a linear roll – like a sausage,' she explained. 'Not head-over-heels.'

'Oh, well, that's OK then,' I said.

She giggled. 'I do love Abs' plays,' she said fondly.

'Me too,' I smiled.

'But,' she said, after a moment, tapping the table lightly with a forefinger, 'I want to know about *you*. You and Stephen.'

I tutted. 'I know. But you'll make me blush.'

'Ooh!' she said, pouring the last dregs of Prosecco into her glass. 'So there's something to blush about!'

I sighed theatrically. 'You're so shallow, Miriam.'

'Oh, come on,' she prompted impatiently. 'I need details.'

I stared at her. 'I genuinely, *genuinely* don't know what you mean by that. You're not honestly expecting me to describe anything, are you? Maybe you'd like a diagram?'

'Oh, you know what I mean,' she said, sounding exasperated. 'I want to know how you feel about it all. Happy? Regretful? Indifferent?'

I had asked myself the same question a number of times during the hours which had elapsed since Stephen left, just after breakfast. Unfortunately, I had been unable to provide myself with a definitive answer. It was no easier now.

'Well,' I said, picking up and sipping my drink, 'I'm not regretful.'

She leaned towards me conspiratorially. 'Is there a "*but*" looming?'

'I like him,' I said, 'a lot. He's funny and good-looking and we talk… a lot…' I ground to a halt.

'But…'

She was right, of course, there was a "*but*". I was aware of a reservation, but I couldn't put my finger on it. It was like a word on the tip of my tongue, or an item just out of reach at the back of a shelf.

'He's not your Mr Right?' Miriam persisted.

I would have to give her something. 'He's my Mr Right for now,' I offered. 'But I'm not head over heels.'

She seemed satisfied. 'Well, I think that's a very reassuring "*but*", actually,' she said. 'You've only known him a very short time. If you'd come here claiming to be in love, I'd have had to give you a good shake. But it'd be lovely if it works out,' she added brightly. 'I spoke to Sophie earlier in the week and she said he seemed really nice.'

I rolled my eyes and she held up a placatory hand. 'I was chatting to her about heels. You and Stephen just happened to come up in conversation.'

'I bet we did,' I said, injecting as much scepticism as possible into the phrase.

'It's true,' she insisted. 'And I'm just so pleased that you've met someone… well… nice.'

'Thank you,' I said. 'And you were right that I needed to give the idea of a relationship a chance.'

'And you feel completely free of Eddie?' She looked at me questioningly.

I shrugged. 'I felt free of Eddie almost as soon as he walked out the door.'

She looked surprised. 'Really?'

'Yes,' I said. 'The manner of his exit was devastating, but not the exit itself. I wasn't in love with him at the end.'

She looked thoughtful. 'So, your apathy about dating definitely wasn't anything to do with Eddie then?'

I shook my head. 'I'm not sure apathy is the right word. I think maybe I was just unconsciously assuming that something… someone… was ready and waiting to fall into my lap. Does that make sense?'

'Basically, you're saying you couldn't be bothered,' she said.

I laughed. 'You're right. I'm just glamming-up the apathy.'

She smiled. 'I'm just pleased it's all going so well.' She leaned back in her chair. 'Going so well, *so far* – in a relaxed, let's-see-what-happens kind of way,' she added. 'Ooh, but,' she turned her head towards the kitchen window as we heard an indistinct farewell from Craig, immediately followed by the front door slamming, 'I nearly forgot! Tell me about Suzanna.' She looked back towards me, her face falling as she saw my expression. 'Oh my goodness, you're going to tell me she's a cow.'

I shook my head emphatically. 'No, I'm not.'

'Well, why that face, then?' She gestured towards my head with her glass. 'Come on, spit it out.' There was a distinct, gossip-loving eagerness in her tone regarding the possibility that Jon's girlfriend might not be entirely without fault.

My shoulders sagged involuntarily, as I felt suddenly exhausted at the thought of trying to explain a situation to Miriam which I couldn't even explain to myself. 'I didn't dislike her at all. She was very lovely,' I began, 'very attractive and very keen to get to know us all. And she spoke *extremely* highly of you.' I concluded my statement with a brave attempt at a smile, keeping my fingers crossed that this brief, and scrupulously accurate, synopsis of the situation would suffice.

No such luck. Miriam's eyes narrowed in suspicion. 'There's something you're not telling me,' she said.

I shook my head. 'No. That's it.'

She remained sceptical. 'That's not what your face said.'

I sighed. 'It was just a bit strange seeing him with someone else.'

'Ah,' she smiled sadly and nodded. 'Of course it would be,' she said quietly, before adding, 'but as you've said before, we must try and set our own feelings aside – if he's happy.' She frowned. 'Is he happy?'

I took a gulp of Prosecco. 'I assume so.'

'Hasn't he said anything?' she asked.

I shook my head.

'Well, did he *seem* happy?' she pressed.

I slumped back in my chair. 'Miriam, I'm really not the one to ask.'

Her frown deepened. 'What do you mean? Why not?'

I stared at the table. 'I'll tell you another time.'

She said nothing more but instead rose to her feet, walked to the fridge and took out a fresh bottle of Prosecco. Then she returned to the table, uncorked it and looked at me questioningly. I held out my glass and she topped it up.

'So, has your dad invented anything good lately?' she asked.

I sipped my drink before replacing it on the table and resting my head in my hands. 'I don't think Jon and I are friends anymore.' I continued to stare at the table, while the simple truth of my own words sank in. 'We're not friends anymore.' It felt like the acknowledgement of a bereavement.

There was a pause before she spoke. 'What happened, Alice?' she asked quietly.

'I said something I shouldn't have at Eleanor Black's party,' I admitted, looking up at her guiltily. 'I mentioned that he was seeing someone. I know I shouldn't have,' I continued hastily, as she opened her mouth to interject, 'but it was just a single sentence and I did apologise. Repeatedly. But things have gone from bad to worse. I haven't discussed it with you because I didn't really want to think about it, or draw you into it,' I concluded miserably.

'What,' asked Miriam matter-of-factly, 'has he actually said?'

'Well,' I took a deep breath, 'he finds me irritating and—'

'He said that at the party?'

I shook my head. 'As we left the last book group meeting.'

She was immediately aghast. 'You've misunderstood,' she said flatly. 'It just sounds so unlike him. In what way did he say he finds you irritating?'

'I didn't let him go into detail,' I admitted, in the interests of being as honest as possible with my account. 'He wanted to discuss it, but I didn't.'

'Well, I can't blame you for that. It's not a nice thing,' she said gently. 'And has anything happened since?'

I took a deep breath. 'Last night, when I saw him, he was very distant and when I spoke to Suzanna I realised that he hadn't told her anything about me. And I mean nothing. She knew all about you and Abs and even Pete, but nothing about me.'

'Maybe she got muddled about names,' she suggested. 'I forget names all the time.'

I shook my head. 'She didn't know how Jon and I knew each other. She didn't know that I was a member of the book group. She didn't even know,' I concluded quietly, 'that Lydia and I were friends.'

At that, Miriam put a hand to her mouth. 'Oh, Alice,' she gasped. 'I'm so sorry. That's awful.'

I picked up my drink and took a gulp, desperate not to cry. 'I actually wonder at what point he told Suzanna I was even going to be at the play,' I said. 'Presumably as they pulled into the car park. Otherwise she would have asked a few basic questions about me, wouldn't she?'

'This just can't be right,' murmured Miriam. 'I'll talk to—'

'No,' I said abruptly.

She looked up at me. 'You can't leave things like this.'

'I don't want the conversation to go beyond this kitchen.' It was my turn to be matter-of-fact.

She nodded. 'I won't mention it to him.'

'Or to anyone else,' I insisted. 'Promise me, Miriam.'

'I promise. But Alice,' she said gently, 'hard as it may be, and I do accept that it's difficult, you should listen to what he has to say. Your friendship is such a long and a close one. If you think he's not going to be as upset as you are over this then you're wrong. I'm sure of that. And I also know that silence won't resolve this.'

I smiled sadly. 'So you're telling me to have a conversation?'

'I suppose I am.' She returned the smile with one equally as rueful. 'It's very good advice, actually.'

I looked at her and heaved a sigh. 'We're so good at giving advice, aren't we?'

'Yes,' she said. 'Now, if only either of us would take it.'

-

It was eleven-fifteen when the taxi dropped me at my flat and, feeling too awake and too low to go to bed immediately, I decided to pour myself a drink and call Stephen. I had no intention of burdening him with my concerns regarding the state of Miriam's marriage, or my friendship with Jon, but I felt a chat about how the flat viewings had gone, and what we each had planned for the rest of the week, might be a welcome distraction.

Within five minutes, I had settled myself on the sofa and, with a glass of wine in one hand and my phone in the other, I called him. His phone rang twice and then switched to voicemail. Disappointed, I didn't bother leaving a message but instead placed my phone down next to me and half reclined along the length of the sofa, propping myself up on one elbow and sipping my wine. Everything was, I thought, in flux: my relationship with Jon, Miriam's relationship with Craig, my relationship with Stephen, Jon's relationship with Suzanna – even Sophie seemed to be experiencing some sort of mild inner turmoil. And I suddenly, as never before, found myself looking forward to the upcoming weekend away with my father with a real enthusiasm – a longing even. I always enjoyed his company but, on this occasion, what I was most looking forward to was the status quo. My relationship with him was solid and unchanging and I just wanted some down-time from flux. Unlike Stephen, I decided, I was not a fan of change.

My musings were interrupted by the bugle blast which alerted me to text messages. I picked up my phone. The text was from Stephen.

> *Sorry I missed call. Been out with industry contacts for dinner. Just in and off to bed. Are you free to catch up tomorrow? Am working in Bristol a week Mon. Fancy getting together Sun evening when you get back from the Cotswolds? Think about it. Speak tomorrow. X*

I heaved a sigh, reassumed my semi-recumbent position and then, feeling in need of a friendly voice, I called Sophie. She picked up after a single ring.

'Hi.' She sounded sleepy. 'Are you with Miriam? Everything OK?'

'Yes, fine. I'm home but didn't fancy hitting the sack yet,' I said. 'I didn't wake you up, did I?'

'No,' she yawned. 'I'm just slumped on the sofa with a glass of wine, watching some total crap on TV.'

'Same here, except without the crappy telly.'

'An early-ish end to your evening with Miriam then?'

'Yes. But how's your weekend going?'

'Same old, same old,' she said. 'Another man, another mess. If she wasn't my sister, I wouldn't bother. She's a…' she sighed. 'She's a disaster.'

'I'm sorry, Sophie.'

'Mmm…'

'Is she there now?'

'In bed.'

'Right.'

'I do love her, you know, Alice. She just doesn't help herself.'

'I know,' I said. 'She's lucky to have you.'

'Not sure she'd agree with you. But anyway,' she paused and when she spoke again, her tone had lightened. 'So, how was Miriam? Any gossip?'

'I'm not sure that my Miriam gossip would cheer you up much actually.'

'Oh.'

'But I do have a trolley tale from *Oliver!*'

'Brilliant,' she said, sounding immediately brighter. 'Hey and don't worry, I won't be pushing you for any of the stressy stuff tonight. I don't think that would be great for either of us.'

Chapter 33

'And you're certain you're not too busy for all this, my darling?'

'Why on earth do you keep asking me that?' I closed the door, buckled myself in and stared at Dad. 'It's a day of walking and a night away, in a lovely hotel. I'm looking forward to it very much. I'm just sorry we couldn't have gone yesterday instead of this morning.'

He continued to look anxious. 'It's just that I know you're a very busy girl. And you have a boyfriend. This is a weekend you could be spending with him, instead of a boring old pensioner.'

I placed a hand on his arm. 'I have genuinely, *genuinely* been looking forward to spending this time with you; just the two of us. Everything has seemed a little up in the air lately and it'll be great to get away and slow down.' He offered me an uncertain smile. 'And, as for Stephen,' I continued, 'I'm seeing him for dinner tomorrow night. So you are not in any way cramping my style.'

He looked, I thought, slightly reassured. 'In that case,' he said, starting the engine, 'I suppose we should get going.'

'D'ya think?' I said and then, planting a kiss on his cheek, 'I love you. Let's go.'

-

Dad and I took at least one weekend break together every year and usually tried to keep the drive-time to under two hours, in order to allow us maximum quality time together. We had explored not only Devon but Somerset, The Gower and The Cotswolds, with walking, rather than sight-seeing, always top of the agenda. Our itinerary varied little, regardless of location. We always aimed to arrive late Friday or early Saturday and then, rain or shine, we would head out for a full day of walking, punctuated by frequent flask and photography breaks and a light pub lunch. Dad would have a nap early Saturday evening, before we headed out to dinner at around 8pm. I occasionally joked to friends about the schedules set in stone and elderly pace of our trips, but in fact, the familiarity of both company and itinerary was thoroughly enjoyable and extremely comforting.

This particular weekend, our destination was Moreton-in-Marsh and after a drive of just an hour and a half, we arrived at our hotel, The White Hart, at 10am.

My father's conversation in the car on the way up had proved as diverse and tangential as ever, with him touching on subjects ranging from global politics to neighbourhood news – namely Odd Bob using Hammerite to paint all his window panes black, after experiencing difficulty hanging blinds. He had, Dad told me, done this under cover of darkness, providing neighbours with little opportunity to intervene. Nevertheless, they felt bad for not having kept a warier eye on him, and Dad had felt particularly guilty over the incident as he had actually supplied the Hammerite, assuming Bob wanted it for his drainpipes. The good news was that the matter had led to Social Services being back on the case, so at least there was an all's-well-that-ends-well feeling to the tale.

On the whole, Dad seemed, I thought, well, and in good spirits. However, although for much of the drive-time he was his usual enthusiastic, optimistic self, there were also occasions when he appeared completely lost in thought, almost to the point of being unaware of my presence, until I reminded him of it with some comment or question. I asked him several times whether there was anything troubling him and, on each occasion, he insisted he was fine, re-iterating how blessed he felt to have me as his daughter and how important I was to him.

This pattern of happy interaction, interspersed with occasional distraction, continued into our walk and, as the day wore on, I told myself to accept it as a harmless consequence of aging, rather than allow my concerns to spoil the weekend.

We had decided to eat that evening at The Black Bear, which was located just opposite our hotel. A table had been reserved for 7pm, which I had thought a little early, but when Dad explained that he didn't want to be up too late, I had given in. So at six forty-five, after I had showered and treated myself to an hour of mindless magazine reading on my bed, I made my way to the hotel lounge to find him ensconced in an armchair, a copy of *The Times* open, but ignored, on his lap. Instead of the paper, his attention was focused on the street scene outside the quaint, 17th century bay of the hotel.

'You look great,' I said as I approached and bent down to kiss his cheek. 'Is this new?' I tugged admiringly at the sleeve of the casual red and white striped shirt, which he had paired with chinos. 'Ooh, and those.' I patted his knee.

He looked up at me, appearing pleased. 'Do you like them?' he asked. 'I wasn't so sure but Hil…' he coughed, '…but I got them anyway.'

'Well, I thoroughly approve.'

He smiled. 'So long as you do,' he said. 'That's all that matters to me.'

'Come on,' I said, holding out my hand, 'let's go and show you off.'

–

Despite the relatively early hour, the bar of The Black Bear was already quite busy when we arrived, with a mix of smartly dressed evening diners and slightly damp and bedraggled walkers, who had dropped in for a pint. We were offered a choice of two tables, one a quiet corner seat for two near a window and the other a larger, more centrally-located table. I suggested the window seat but Dad thought it may not quite give him enough room to stretch his legs, so we opted for the one nearer the main bar instead.

'I'm not massively hungry yet,' I said, as we sat down and I began to peruse the menu. 'Are you? Or shall we have a drink before we order?'

He glanced around the bustling bar. 'It's quite busy, isn't it?' he said.

I looked up from my menu. 'That's not a problem, is it?' I asked, noticing his concerned expression.

'No, no.' he smiled. 'Not a problem.'

'Good.' I returned my attention to the menu. 'I hardly need look,' I said. 'I already know that I want fish and chips and mushy peas,' I laughed. 'And I'll bet any money you're having the same.' He didn't reply and I looked up to find him twisting in his seat, scanning the room. 'What are you looking for?' I asked.

He turned to me bemused. 'Sorry, darling. What?'

I sighed and stood up. 'I'll go and get some drinks. Would you like a pint?'

'Donnington Gold, please. I'll just... er...,' he leaned back into his chair, 'sit here and wait.'

'Brilliant plan,' I said. 'And do you mind if we delay ordering food for a little while?' I asked. 'Or are you starving?'

'I'm happy to delay.' He patted his stomach. 'The wait will give me a little more room for all those lovely fish and chips.'

I smiled and then made my way round to the smaller bar on the other side of the pub, hoping that it might prove slightly less busy than the one closer to our table. I was right and within five minutes I was wobbling my way back to my father. I had a poor reputation when it came to carrying drinks and I kept a careful eye on his brimming pint.

'Well, will you look at that,' I said, when within a few feet of the table. 'I haven't spilled a drop. A first, I think.' It was only when I made to place the drinks on the table that I looked up and realised that Dad was no longer alone but was instead sitting with a small, slender woman, who was seated on a third chair which had been pulled up to our table. The woman was, I guessed, in her mid- to late sixties. She had greying, light brown hair, cut into a neat bob and she was dressed for walking, in a pink, short-sleeved polo shirt, grey trousers and brown hiking boots. What struck me most about her, however, was the sense of nervous anxiety she exuded and which the smile she now offered me did nothing to disguise.

I looked at Dad and he too gave me a similarly distressed grin. I returned my attention to the woman. 'Hello,' I said.

'Hello, Alice,' her voice was soft to the point of being almost inaudible. She held out her hand. 'I'm Hilary Radcliffe,' she said, 'a friend of your father's from the club.'

I shook her hand. 'The club?' I sat down and looked at Dad questioningly.

His eyes widened slightly and he maintained his grin as he spoke, giving him the appearance of a ventriloquist's dummy. 'My widow and widowers' club, darling,' he said. 'Hilary is in the same club.'

'Ah, I see,' I smiled in comprehension. 'Of course, yes, Hilary. I remember. You give Dad culinary tips,' I said. 'I only wish you'd give him a few more.'

'Indeed!' said Dad, laughing far more than the joke deserved. Hilary joined in the laughter, causing me to reflect that a disproportionate sense of fun was just one of the many delights of aging that I had to look forward to.

Once they had calmed down, there was a pause which I assumed one of them would fill with an explanation as to how Hilary came to be in The Black Bear on this Saturday evening, rather than at home in Chippenham. When no such explanation was forthcoming, I decided to request one.

'So, Hilary, you're visiting the Cotswolds too. Is it for the weekend, or as part of a longer holiday?'

Hilary cleared her throat and took a deep breath. 'Well, Alice, I have a brother here. His name is Terry. I visit him often,' she began, her eyes fixed on the ceiling, giving her the air of someone ticking off points in her head. 'I didn't know your father was coming, so this is quite a coincidence. I love walking. This is my third visit this year.' She redirected her gaze from the ceiling to Dad.

He smiled and nodded and then looked at me. 'This is Hilary's third visit,' he said.

'So I gathered,' I returned, rolling my eyes. 'Hilary is speaking English, you know.'

More elderly hysteria ensued. 'Oh you are funny, Alice,' said Hilary. 'Jim said you were.'

I looked at Dad. 'I take it he didn't mention my brains or beauty, then,' I said, before adding quickly, in an attempt to pre-empt any fresh outbursts of geriatric giggling, 'Are you here with Terry tonight?' I looked around the bar.

Hilary smiled. 'No,' she said, 'not tonight.'

I nodded and there followed yet another elderly conversational pause, which I eventually accepted would not be filled without prompting.

'You're meeting friends?' I ventured.

'No, no,' she said brightly. 'It's just me. I just thought I'd come out for a quiet drink.'

'That's right.' Dad nodded once again.

'Gosh, you're brave,' I said. 'I get anxious after just a few minutes of waiting on my own in a pub.'

'Ooh, yes,' said Hilary suddenly animated, smiling and touching my arm conspiratorially, 'I know just what you mean, Alice. I absolutely hate being on my own like that too. I feel so conspicuous and friendless. I always take a book if I think there's the slightest possibility of being on my own for even a minute.'

I blinked, feeling a little confused. 'Oh, well… well done for being so brave tonight.'

She beamed. 'Yes.' She looked at Dad. 'I just thought I'd pop out for a quick drink and a little time alone. That's what I thought.'

I decided to move on. 'Is this your brother's local?'

'Ooh, no.' She shook her head. 'It's a good twenty minutes by car for him.'

I frowned involuntarily. 'But this pub is a favourite of yours?'

She looked around. 'Do you know, I was just saying to Jim that I don't think I've ever actually been here before,' she said. 'Appalling really, because it's so lovely, isn't it?'

I picked up my spritzer, looked at Dad and weighed up the possibilities of the situation. I had so far formed three hypotheses, namely that:

> *i) this was all an enormous coincidence and that Hilary was an eccentric, wildly contradictory character, who deliberately travelled significant distances to test her own ability to endure loneliness in a crowd, or*

ii) Hilary was an aging, pink-polo-shirted stalker, who had tracked my father from Chippenham with unknown intent. Or the third and final possibility, towards which I was leaning heavily,

iii) that I was sitting with two elderly people who, for whatever reason, were ineptly trying to convince me that finding themselves in the same pub, in the same town, on the same evening was not at all by design but entirely by coincidence.

My dilemma, of course, was how to determine what was going on, without causing any offence to Hilary, given that dragging my father into a quiet back room, shining a bright light in his eyes and interrogating him at length was not currently an option.

I looked at him now, sitting in a way which I knew indicated he was not at all relaxed. However, whether this was because he wanted Hilary to leave, or was desperate for me to invite her to stay, I just didn't know.

In the end, I took a punt. 'Would you like to join us for a drink, Hilary?'

She took a sidelong glance at Dad. 'Ooh, I wouldn't want to interrupt your time together. I was going to pop off back to Terry's in a minute or two.'

'Oh, so you've been here a while then?' I asked. 'Have you got a drink sitting somewhere which you could bring over?'

'No,' she smiled. 'I've only just arrived.'

I found myself unable to stifle a laugh. 'Well, look,' I placed a hand on her arm, 'if you don't have to rush off, I think it would be really nice for you to stay and have a drink with us.' I looked at Dad. 'Don't you agree?'

His shoulders relaxed, he smiled at me – and I knew. 'Yes, I do, sweetheart,' he said.

I swallowed and felt my eyes prickle. 'Lovely,' I said, standing up. 'Hilary, what can I get you?'

Chapter 34

Hilary stayed for a drink and then, at my suggestion, and to Dad's obvious delight, she joined us for dinner. I discovered that she was sixty-eight years old, had been a widow for three years and had joined 'The Club' just over a year ago. Additionally, she had two sons: Luke, who lived in Oxford, and Simon, who was currently living in Canada, but who would be returning to the UK next year.

At no time during the conversation was the precise nature of Hilary's relationship with Dad defined or discussed. However, it was readily apparent from the number of shared stories that they had spent, recently at least, a significant amount of time in one another's company and that whatever time they had spent together, they had thoroughly enjoyed.

I liked her. She was warm, energetic, interested and interesting and, most importantly of all, she clearly made my father very happy.

Over dinner, she told us all about a daytrip to Winchcombe with Terry and then asked about our walk. I said a little bit about our route but then sat back and enjoyed watching and listening to Dad describe, with characteristic enthusiasm, unusual cloud formations and unexpectedly beautiful views – his own and Hilary's mutual absorption in the detail of the day, providing me with an opportunity to observe unobserved.

They were, without doubt, happy and relaxed in each other's company. But they were also, I realised, equally happy and at ease with the past. There was no sense that Hilary was either competing with my mother's memory or ignoring it. Far from it. She welcomed my mother to the table, laughing along and asking questions as Dad contrasted today's weather with the 'apocalyptic rainfall' which, he told us, had marked the occasion when he and my mother had celebrated their fifth wedding anniversary in Stowe-on-the-Wold, which lay less than five miles from Moreton-in-Marsh.

And Dad appeared similarly at peace regarding Frank, Hilary's late husband, whom she talked about fondly, frequently and without self-consciousness. Here, I thought, were two people rejoicing in a new relationship, whilst simultaneously celebrating past ones. They had the air of a couple who just couldn't believe their luck and, for reasons I couldn't fathom, that caused me to spend the evening perpetually on the brink of either laughter or tears, and occasionally both.

The evening flew and when I checked my watch, as Dad mooted teas and coffees, I was surprised to discover that it was well after nine.

'I'll have a coffee if you two do,' I said.

'I'd love a peppermint tea,' said Hilary.

'And I'd like an *actual* cup of tea,' said Dad, nudging Hilary and being rewarded with a tut and a smile, 'but I must just make a trip to the bathroom first, if you'll excuse me for one moment, ladies.' He stood up, briefly squeezed Hilary's shoulder and headed for the toilet.

I smiled and looked at Hilary. 'So you're teaching Dad to cook,' I said.

She smiled. 'He's actually very into his baking at the moment,' she said. 'And he's being ever so ambitious. Chelsea buns and millefeuille are top of his list to perfect. Chelsea buns because they were your mother's favourite and millefeuille because you so love custard slices.'

I smiled. 'That's nice but,' I leaned towards her and lowered my voice, 'I was thinking he might be better with a packet mix.'

There was a momentary pause and then she laughed. 'A packet mix, yes.'

'Seriously, though, Hilary,' I said, 'couldn't you try to talk him into having a bash at something simpler? Scones maybe?'

'Oh no, dear,' she said. 'The reason for his choice is so very lovely, that's the most important thing. Whatever he bakes will be baked with love, you see.'

She looked at me and smiled, clearly oblivious to the effect of her words. I was, I realised, going to have to bring a box of Kleenex to every future encounter with Hilary. I cleared my throat.

'Well, maybe practice will make perfect,' I said.

'I'm not overly hopeful,' she said, adding "realist" to a growing list of admirable character traits. 'His millefeuille are, I'm afraid, particularly dreadful and showing no sign of improvement. But, you know your father, he's still enjoying himself.' She smiled to herself, looked down, removed her napkin from her lap and folded it neatly, before placing it on the table.

'I'm so pleased he's met you, Hilary,' I said.

She said nothing but nodded, still focusing on the napkin. Then she turned to me, took my hand briefly in hers and gave it a squeeze. I managed a wobbly smile, which she returned with one as equally full of emotion, and it struck me again how useful some tissues at the table might have proved for everyone.

'Right,' said Dad, returning, pulling out his chair and sitting down. 'Have we ordered?'

'Not yet,' I said. 'We haven't managed to catch the waiter's eye. We've been talking about baking.'

'Oh yes,' he said beaming. 'You must try one of my custard slices, darling. Hilary says she's never tasted anything quite like them. Isn't that right?' He looked at her and winked.

She laughed. 'You are such a silly thing,' she said.

He took her hand and then reached across the table for mine. 'A silly, *happy* thing,' he said. 'And that's what counts.'

-

After our teas and coffees, I hugged Hilary goodbye and then, rather than bid her farewell at the table, Dad walked her to the door of the pub. It was several minutes before he returned and sat down opposite me.

He looked at me and smiled, somewhat sadly, I thought. I returned the smile but said nothing.

Eventually he spoke. 'I'm sorry, darling,' he said.

I reached across the table and took his hand. 'If you're apologising for not telling me sooner, or for that quite pitiful charade earlier this evening, I shall accept that. But if you're apologising in any way for Hilary, please don't. She's lovely.'

His eyes fell upon our hands and he nodded.

'I wanted you to meet her a good while ago,' he said quietly. 'But I didn't know how to do it. I didn't want to place you, or Hilary, under any pressure. I thought it might be better for you to meet her as if by chance, without any labels being hung around her neck and without you feeling you had to like her or approve of anything. I had arranged to bump into her on a walk after one of our lunches a couple of months ago. But I lost track of time and we missed her.' He looked up at me. 'In my defence,' he said, 'Hilary favoured the bumping-into approach also.'

'Hmm,' I said. 'Why doesn't that surprise me?' He looked at me uncertainly and I smiled. 'I like her very much,' I said. '*Very* much. You seem to be birds of a feather. And you know that I just want whatever makes you happy.'

He sighed. 'I was in a bit of a muddle for a while, darling,' he said. 'I love your mother utterly and that will never change. But Hilary did confuse things. She confused *me*.' He smiled sadly. 'At one point, I actually thought I wanted her to go away, you know. It felt like she was causing trouble, even though she hadn't done anything except exist. It was quite a jolt. I hadn't expected to feel those things again.' He returned his gaze to the table. 'It's all been weighing rather heavily,' he patted his chest, 'in here. I really needed to talk about it all. But who to discuss it with?'

I tutted. 'Well, why not me?'

He raised his eyes and met mine. 'I didn't want to upset you. Am I upsetting you now? You must tell me if I am.'

'Upsetting me?' I said exasperatedly. 'I'm delighted you have found someone you want to spend your time with, to confide in, to laugh with. And Mum...' I paused for a moment, steadying my voice and blinking back a tear, 'and Mum would be delighted too. I know that beyond a shadow of a doubt.'

His eyes filled with tears and I allowed my own to fall. 'I know that. I reached that same conclusion myself. Eventually.'

'Well, in that case,' I laughed and wiped my cheek, 'what on earth was all this nonsense about?'

'I don't know,' he said, now laughing too. 'I'm an absolute ninny, aren't I?'

I smiled. 'Well, I can think of one or two other words, but ninny will do,' I said.

'Dear me.' He extracted a handkerchief from the pocket of his chinos, blew his nose and then pointed at my empty glass. 'Now,' he said, 'are you for another of those watery wine things, or for your bed?'

'Not quite for my bed,' I said, checking my watch. 'I know I become immediately geriatric in your company, but it is a little bit early, even so. However,' I smiled, noticing him stifle a yawn, 'I am rather keen to give that enormous bath of mine a whirl. So I think I'll head up if that's OK?'

'That's fine, darling,' he said. 'Being genuinely geriatric, I am more than happy to retire.' He rose to his feet and together we walked slowly to the door. 'I'm so very blessed to have you, Alice,' he said, as I linked his arm and we stepped out onto the pavement. 'You are your mother's daughter, you know.'

Unwilling to risk speech, I replied instead with a squeeze of his arm and a kiss on his cheek, and then we headed back across the road to our hotel.

Chapter 35

Upon reaching my room, I sat on the bed, kicked off my shoes and flopped backwards; closing my eyes and reflecting on the day. It had, I decided, been a good one and my overwhelming conviction was that both Dad and I would go away from this weekend with a sense of relief regarding secrets and feelings shared and aired.

Resisting a significant urge to remain horizontal, I stood up and went into the ensuite. After taking a moment to admire the large bath, complete with a side tap designed to permit unhindered, full-length lounging, I began to run a bath.

Just a few minutes later, and with the tap still running, I was submerged up to my chin, letting the warm water and bubbles envelop me. I then extended an arm, turned off the tap and added complete silence to my current list of little luxuries. Holding my breath, I slid completely under the water, enjoying the sensation of weightlessness afforded by the extra deep tub.

I came up a moment later, to the somewhat disturbing sound of Sophie shouting, 'Answer the phone! Answer the phone!', the ringtone which she had popped onto my phone the evening before.

I grabbed the nearest towel, dried my hands and reached across to my phone, which I had placed on the tiled surround of the sink. I pressed *accept* just as it stopped ringing. *Unknown caller: missed call* appeared onscreen.

I tutted at the thought of my luxurious silence being shattered by an annoying cold call, placed the phone back down by the sink, and sank once more into the bubbles.

Moments later, Sophie was again insisting, at considerable volume, that I answer the phone. I sat up, dried my hands and picked it up.

There was again no caller ID but I answered nevertheless. 'Hello?' I said, not bothering to keep the irritation out of my voice. There was no reply. 'Hello?' I repeated, increasingly annoyed, but unsurprised, by the initial silence of a marketing call. I waited for the inevitable click, which would herald the return of the salesperson to the automatically generated call. However, no click came. Instead, I thought I heard an intake of breath, a gasp. 'Hello?' I said, a little less assertively. 'Can you hear me?'

Without warning, three beeps signalled the end of the call.

I put down the phone for a second time and tried to regain my earlier sense of relaxation and calm. But despite my attempts to reason away the call as one of those poor connections, in which only one party is able to hear anything, I just couldn't. It had unnerved me and no amount of telling myself not to be so melodramatic could change that. I lay amongst the bubbles, no longer enjoying them and wondering whether I should simply get out, get dressed and go and read *Jane Eyre* in the cosy snug, next door to the main lounge.

In the end I did neither. Instead, I picked up my phone again and called Stephen. After sighing with disappointment when his phone went straight to voicemail, I attempted a message. 'Hi, it's Alice. Hope you're having a good weekend. Dad and I have had a lovely day here – just having an after dinner soak. Looking forward to seeing you tomorrow. Don't forget to text me your ETA. I think I'll be home around two or three o'clock. Bye.'

I hung up, switched my phone to vibrate and climbed out of the bath.

Ten minutes later, I was pulling the duvet up around my chin and just wondering whether to watch telly or read when I was disturbed by the vibration of my phone on the small chest of drawers next to me. I picked up the phone as the screen lit up, revealing that while getting ready for bed I had a text from Stephen and also a missed call. The notification *unknown caller – missed call and voicemail*, leapt out at me.

I went immediately to voicemail and played the seven-second message. I was disturbed, but not entirely surprised, by the silence. I strained to hear anything but without success.

I clicked on Stephen's text.

> *Sorry I missed call – driving. Have thought about calling you a few times but haven't wanted to crash your time with your Dad. Busy day here – lots of viewings. One offer and a rival bid expected. Tired and up early tomorrow, so bed now. Looking forward to seeing you tomorrow. Will aim to be with you at 5pm. I've booked us a table for dinner – 7.30, hope that's ok. S x*

Still distracted, I returned to my voicemails and twice more played the anonymous message. This time, I thought I could perhaps hear a distant door closing but, frustrated by both the calls and my inability to glean anything of use from the voicemail, I deleted it. Now wide awake, I began, without thinking, to work my way down my extensive list of historic voicemails, deleting as I went. It was only when I had binned at least two screens' worth of messages, that I paused, my mind suddenly engaging as the notification of Jon's week-old, unplayed voicemail reached the top of the list.

I sighed, closed my eyes and leaned back against the headboard of the bed. There was no internal debate. I knew Miriam was right; I had to listen to what he had to say. I just needed a moment or two to brace myself for it, whilst being careful not to give myself long enough to worry about content or consequences.

I opened my eyes, touched "play" and pressed the phone to my ear.

'Hello, Alice, it's Jon.' His tone was, I thought, clipped. I re-closed my eyes. 'I know you have Stephen there. I was going to leave this call until tomorrow but felt I should make it now. I want to apologise to you for my behaviour at the play this evening.' There was a pause. 'For more than that. I want to apologise for the things I've said and done which have hurt your feelings. Your friendship could not be more important to me. I have assumed you know that, which isn't fair. I should have just told you. I'd really like to meet for a drink and we can either talk about this, or not talk about this, whatever is best for you. I'll leave it to you to think about it and let me know if a drink is something you'd want to do. Bye.'

I allowed my hand, still holding the phone, to slide down the side of my face and come to rest on my chest and I thought about Jon. I felt ashamed at my persistent, petulant refusal to listen to what he had had to say – and at my total failure to view his behaviour not only in the context of his current situation, but also in the context of our long friendship.

I opened my eyes and looked at the phone. I didn't trust myself to have a conversation with him and, besides, I guessed he would be with Suzanna. But I knew that I wouldn't be able to sleep unless I acknowledged his message. Without further pause for thought, I began to text.

> *I have only just played your voicemail. I hadn't wanted to play it in case you were going to tell me some things about myself, probably true, which I didn't want to hear. I'm sorry. I know there's a lot going on for you at the moment and I don't think I at all appreciated the enormity of that. I'd really like to meet up. Don't know if I can manage to talk about any of the important things and make any sense, but I don't think that matters. It would just be really good to see you. I'm in the Cotswolds with Dad – back tomorrow afternoon. Dad has a lovely girlfriend – I'm not sure that's the right word. He's baking a lot and I've had some weird phone calls. I'll call you tomorrow if that's OK. If you're busy, don't worry, I'll catch you in the week x*

I pressed send without review, threw the phone down on the bed, switched off the light and, for the third time that evening, cursed my lack of tissues.

Chapter 36

I woke at 7am and immediately reached for my phone. There was a text from Jon. It had been sent just fifteen minutes after my own the previous evening and I was surprised at how quickly I must have fallen asleep. I read it three or four times, enjoying the increased sense of relief each re-reading brought.

> *Hi, it was great to get this. Had considered texting when I didn't hear from you but you weren't alone in your fear re possible responses. Really good news about your dad, I'm happy for him. And no, I'm not sure girlfriend is the right word either but I can't immediately think of an alternative. Also interested in the baking and the phone calls. Are you saying there is some connection between the two? I'm around tomorrow. If I miss your call, I will call you back. Looking forward to a drink. And you're right – it doesn't matter if you don't make sense, I'm used to it.*

I smiled, put down my phone and headed for the shower, with a plan to then call Dad's room and bully him into an earlier breakfast.

As it turned out, he was already up, dressed and perusing the Sunday papers by the time I called his room at just after eight o'clock. He too, as he subsequently explained to me over breakfast, had woken up early and invigorated, as had Hilary, to whom he had already spoken at length.

Heavy rain beat down upon the grey paving of the inner courtyard visible from our breakfast table, leading us to discount the idea of a further walk before leaving. And so, after a leisurely breakfast, which was marked by levels of laughter and relaxation considerably higher than the day before, we gathered our things, checked-out and made our way back to Bristol.

Our conversation on the way home focused more on the weeks to come, than the weekend just gone, with Dad clearly revelling in his new-found freedom to talk about Hilary and what they would be up to. Not that they had any plans to cruise the Med, dine out in Paris or punt along a Venetian canal. But they had scheduled a day trip to Bradford-on-Avon, a pub supper, an evening at the theatre and, of course, lots of baking.

On arrival in Redland, he stopped just long enough for a cup of tea and a piece of cake, before heading home to Chippenham. Hilary was due back late afternoon and he explained that he wanted to have completed another batch of Chelsea buns for her consideration by the time she arrived. I suggested it might be prudent to have a sneaky packet from Tesco's to hand, in the unlikely event that his own were a total and utter inedible disaster, in response to which he laughed loudly and ruffled my hair.

I waved him off just after one o'clock, deciding to unpack, load the washing machine and tidy up a little, before sitting down to call Jon. That was something which, despite our recent uplifting exchange of texts, I still felt rather nervous about.

When I found myself plumping the pillows in the spare bedroom, I realised that I had reached the point of disgraceful procrastination and must now simply make the call.

I went and sat at the kitchen table, took my phone from my pocket and dialled, experiencing a mixture of disappointment and relief when, after half a dozen rings, Jon's mobile went to voicemail. I cleared my throat, whilst he asked me to leave a message.

'Hi Jon, it's Alice. I'm back from the Cotswolds and around now until five-ish. I was just calling to arrange going out after work one evening. I'm free this week, any evening except Friday, I think – I'm that popular. So just let me know. OK, well, bye.' I hung up, suddenly feeling oddly flat and at a loss as to how to pass the time until Stephen arrived.

I had just decided to go and tackle some long overdue weeding, when the sound of a bugle heralded the arrival of a text. It was from Jon.

In Waitrose. Nearly done. Just give me half an hour.

I looked at my watch; he would be calling about two. Or did he mean I should call him at two? Either way, I had half an hour. I went outside, fetched a trowel and small fork from the shed and began to attack the borders.

At 1.55pm, frustrated by the ongoing, low-level anxiety which I was still undeniably experiencing, I came inside with the intention of washing my hands, putting on the kettle and calling Jon for a second time. I had just begun the process by turning on the tap, when the doorbell rang, causing me to start slightly. I gave my hands an inadequate rinse, drying them on my jeans and turning to look at the kitchen clock; it was a minute off 2pm. I took out my phone and checked Jon's text. It hadn't occurred to me that he might mean he would be coming round in half an hour but I supposed it could be him. I sighed in dismay at my blackened nails, damp, mud-covered jeans and make-up free complexion, before taking a deep breath and walking from the kitchen towards the front door. It would probably, I reasoned, just be Sim, the sports-mad eleven year-old from next door, wanting one of her tennis/foot/cricket balls back.

But it wasn't Sim.

I opened the door to a man, visible only from the shoulders down, his face hidden behind a large cream and peach bouquet of roses, germinis and lilies. I gasped, surprised but delighted by the gesture. I guessed that it was Jon, even before I noticed the Waitrose care label, as he extended the huge bouquet towards me.

Instead of taking the flowers from him, I pushed his arm gently to one side, making his face visible and his neck accessible; I then experienced last-minute shock and hesitation, as I flung my arms around him.

'Well, that certainly wins welcome-of-the-week,' said Stephen, laughing.

'It's you,' I gasped, clinging to him and feeling as if I would crumple and collapse without his support.

He laughed. 'Well spotted.'

'I thought… I just wasn't expecting you… so early,' I said, my voice muffled, my head buried in his shoulder.

'Ah well, there you go. I'm full of surprises.'

I eased myself away from him and looked up into his eyes. 'Stephen, you know, I don't think—' I began, in unpremeditated fashion, before being suddenly interrupted by Sophie's ringtone, commanding me to answer the phone and, it seemed, to pull myself together. Stephen smiled.

'I've really got to change this one – and soon,' I said to him, extracting my phone from my pocket and beckoning him to come inside and follow me through to the kitchen. I looked at the screen. It was, of course, Jon. 'I just have to take this call.' I made an apologetic face. 'I'll be two seconds.' Stephen nodded and sat down at the kitchen table. I answered the phone. 'Hello.'

'Hello, Alice.'

'Hello,' I repeated, wishing I didn't have an audience.

Jon laughed. 'Well, I would say hello again, but I think I should probably try to move the conversation on a little.

'Yes,' I said.

There was a pause. 'Is everything OK?' he asked. 'Is this not a good time to call?'

'No, no, it's fine,' I said. 'Stephen's just arrived, though, so I just don't want to be rude by chatting for too long.' Stephen smiled and waved a hand at me to indicate that I shouldn't worry.

'Oh, I see,' said Jon. 'I was just wondering if we could arrange a—'

'Yes, tomorrow,' I said, quickly turning my back on Stephen and flicking the switch on the kettle.

'Er…' Jon sounded surprised or hesitant, I couldn't tell which.

'Or not,' I continued hastily. 'I don't mind.'

He laughed again. 'No, no,' he said, 'tomorrow's great.'

'Brill,' I said.

'You sound… busy,' he said. 'Let's sort out the details by text.'

'Yes.'

'OK.' There was a second pause. 'Well, I'll see you tomorrow, then, Alice. Bye.'

'Bye.'

I hung up the phone and, feeling slightly flustered, kept my back to Stephen whilst opening one of the wall cupboards.

'Sorry about that,' I said. 'Tea or coffee?'

He didn't reply, instead I felt his arms slip around my waist as he kissed my neck. 'I was rather hoping you might add "or me" to that list of possibilities,' he said, gently turning me round.

'Hmm...' I said, kissing him lightly on the lips and then holding up my grubby hands and gesturing towards my muddy attire. 'I think it might be an idea to save *me* for later.'

He looked down at me, smiled and then kissed my forehead. 'Maybe you're right,' he said. 'We have lots of time and besides,' he added, gesturing towards the flowers on the table, 'they could do with a vase and I,' he kissed me again, this time on the cheek, 'could murder a coffee.'

-

Five hours, one walk through Leigh Woods and a considerable amount of grooming later, and we were sitting in the tiny Cotham restaurant which was one of my favourite places to eat. I had mentioned it, fleetingly, a week earlier, and Stephen had noted it down and made the booking. It was the kind of thoughtful gesture which I knew I should value.

'Here's to moving on,' he said, toasting me with a glass of the Pinot Grigio the waiter had just deposited on our table.

'So, you've sold, then?' I asked, clinking my glass against his.

'Well, I'm as confident as you ever can be about these things.' He leaned back in his chair. 'Something could still go wrong but there are only three of us in the chain, which is good.'

I nodded. 'And apart from the sale, how is everything else in Solihull?'

'There's nothing except the sale in Solihull,' he said, sipping his wine.

'There must be some things about it you'll miss,' I said, slightly taken aback. 'No happy memories? No nostalgia?'

'Oh, of course,' he replied with a grin. 'I was just being flippant. There are lots of happy memories. But they are the past. And I can enjoy them while looking forward to new challenges and experiences,' he took my hand, 'and relationships.'

I shook my head. 'You always make change sound like such an exciting thing. It doesn't frighten you at all, does it?'

He squeezed my hand. 'Why should it?' he asked. 'You know, I think you assume that any change is going to be a sudden jolt to your existence. But it doesn't have to be like that, especially if it's a change of choice.' He paused, let go of my hand and picked up his drink. 'It's all about managing the transition; making it as smooth as possible, and leaving yourself as little opportunity as possible for looking back over your shoulder.' He looked at me and grinned. 'I know, I know. I'm getting heavy again. So let's just say that I have a few loose ends to tie-up and that I'm very ready to go. And, of course, I'm looking forward to being able to see you more,' he said. 'A lot more.'

'Yes,' I smiled, envying him his clear-sighted determination. He came, he saw, he conquered, and all in the most delightful, affably charming way imaginable.

'But anyway,' he continued, 'enough about me. You haven't told me much about the Cotswolds.'

'Oh, well,' I said, 'Hilary was, of course, the big news.'

'She sounds great.'

'She is,' I agreed. 'Dad is so happy at the moment. It's lovely to see.'

'No other weekend news of note, then?'

'No, not really, other than those phone calls.'

He replaced his glass on the table and looked puzzled. 'What phone calls?'

'I thought I'd told you,' I said frowning. 'I've had some weird phone calls; silent ones.'

He shook his head. 'You haven't mentioned them. That doesn't sound good. Have you blocked the number?'

'There was no number to block. But don't worry,' I attempted a reassuring smile, 'it's probably just an automated call.'

'But that's not what you think?' he asked.

'Well…' I hesitated, 'I thought I could hear someone on the line in a couple of the calls. But there haven't been many and I haven't had one today.' I reached into my bag and took out my phone. 'Ooh no, actually, I have. Look.' I turned the screen towards him to show him the notification of a call received since arriving at the restaurant. 'Let's listen.'

'OK,' he said.

I positioned the phone on the table between us, put it on hands-free and played the voicemail. There was no message; however, this time I heard a soft, but very definite, sigh.

'There! Did you hear that?' I asked. 'I wonder if it's a child.'

He shook his head. 'I didn't hear anything. You're probably right about being on someone's marketing list.'

'You didn't hear a sigh?' I asked, feeling disappointed. 'Why don't we listen again?'

He picked up the phone and handed it to me. 'I don't want you worrying about this,' he said. 'I'm going to call a friend of mine who works for EE and see if there's a way of blocking calls from unknown numbers. I'm sure there is. Let's look to the solution, rather than dwelling on the problem. And, in the meantime,' he picked up his menu and grinned boyishly, 'let's order.'

'Good idea,' I said, smiling and replacing my phone in my bag. 'I'm starving.'

–

Dinner was delicious, if, in my case, a little alcohol-heavy. Stephen stopped drinking after just half a glass of wine, saying he had drunk quite a lot the previous evening. But he encouraged me to keep going. I managed a couple of glasses but then refused any more. 'I'll never get up tomorrow,' I protested, when he tried to top up my glass as we waited for the bill. 'Let's just head home.'

'Ah, well, about that...' he said, lowering his head slightly and looking up at me guiltily. 'Sorry, Alice. I have a confession to make.'

'Hmm?' I offered him a slightly tipsy smile and touched his nose with my forefinger. 'What,' I said, tapping his nose lightly with each word, 'is... it? What... have... you... done?'

He took hold of my hand and kissed it. 'Well, I haven't been entirely honest with you about today.'

'No?'

'No,' he said, kissing my hand for a second time. 'As you know, I was originally coming to Bristol this evening because I had a meeting here tomorrow. But that was cancelled on Friday and I now have a meeting in Leicester tomorrow. And it's an 8am start. So...'

I understood. 'So you're heading back this evening.'

He nodded. 'And I'm sorry. I would have told you yesterday but I wanted to see you so much and I was afraid you might tell me not to make the journey. And, as I say, I wanted to see you.' He reached across the table, touched my cheek and smiled. 'Actually, it felt like more like a need than a want,' he said softly.

I smiled at his thoughtful concealment of the truth and at his willingness to undertake a lengthy round trip just to take me to dinner. And I was grateful to discover that three glasses of Pinot Grigio were enough to lessen any sense of disappointment I might otherwise have felt at his early departure. As it was, I found myself very much looking forward to the pleasant walk home, to the goodnight snog, and, best of all, to pulling my duvet up under my chin and going to sleep. I was, I realised, shattered.

Chapter 37

'So your dad and Hilary pretended that they had just bumped into each other accidentally?' Sophie screwed her features into an incredulous ball. She had wasted no time in demanding an immediate account of my weekend the moment I had arrived at the office that morning, and she now sat staring at me in bemusement as I concluded my summary.

I nodded. 'Yes.'

'Bumped into each other accidentally *in the Cotswolds*?' she clarified.

I continued to nod. 'Yes.'

'In a pub which was miles from where she was staying? Which she had decided to visit on a whim?'

'Yes and… yes,' I said.

'God, I love your dad,' she said, her face now relaxing into a smile. 'He's such value for money.'

I smiled. 'I know.'

'It is a very good story,' said David, from the armchair in which he sat next to Sophie's desk. 'And, you know, I can actually understand their reasoning to an extent.'

Sophie turned to him. 'And is the fact that you, Captain Harebrain, think their plan was a reasonable one supposed to carry some weight with somebody somewhere?'

'I am simply saying,' said David, 'that I can see why, to them, leading Alice gently into a realisation of their relationship, rather than declaring it to her outright, might have seemed like a good idea.'

'OK, well, thank you for your input and now shhhhh.' Sophie reached across, placed a finger briefly on his lips and then returned her attention to me.

'And did you,' she asked, 'at any time explain to Hilary that you hadn't been at all fooled by the ruse?'

I pondered the point. 'I don't think I did. Dad knows, of course. But no, I didn't say anything to Hilary and I'm pretty sure he didn't.'

'That's even better,' grinned Sophie, 'because now Hilary's gone away thinking that either she's a better liar than Mata Hari…'

'Or that I'm really dim.' I concluded the point for her.

She clicked her fingers. 'Got it in one!'

'I'm certain she wouldn't think Alice lacking in intelligence,' said David.

'Me too, actually.' Sophie smiled at David. 'You've just redeemed yourself there.'

He smiled, sighed and then hoisted himself out of the armchair. 'Well, I'm just delighted the pair of you had such a lovely trip,' he said. 'And now, I must move on with Monday.'

'Yes,' I said, looking at the pile of mail on my desk. 'It's me to log-in, isn't it?'

David paused by my desk en route to his office. 'If you're a little tired after your weekend, I'm more than happy to do the log-in today.'

'You're going to make somebody a lovely secretary one day, David,' said Sophie.

He ignored her. 'I actually find it quite relaxing.'

'Thank you, David,' I said, stealing a quick glance at Sophie who was now sitting in a despairing attitude, head in hands, 'but I'm feeling well-rested and raring to go this morning.'

He smiled. 'Well, that's super to hear and I feel much the same.'

'I don't,' muttered Sophie.

David walked through the open doorway of his office. 'What a surprise,' he said quietly, but audibly, before closing the door with an equally understated but definite click.

I looked at Sophie and she smiled broadly. 'He's getting so cheeky,' she said. 'Doubly happy I invited him to the book group dinner now.'

'Aw, did you?' I said. 'And I assume he can come?'

She nodded, looking pleased. 'He didn't even ask the date.'

'Really?' I said, feeling surprised. David usually liked to plan ahead – and a very long way ahead at that.

'I know,' said Sophie. 'It threw me a bit too. He just said yes, right away, and to let him know the date.'

'But he's usually so booked-up with Ascot and Queens and Wimbledon and Henley and goodness knows what.' I thought for a moment. 'You don't think it's because Romy is coming, do you?'

'What would that have to do with it?' asked Sophie, placing an elbow on the desk and resting her chin on her hand.

'Well, when I told him a while ago who was going, he did seem very interested in her.'

'Really? I didn't know they'd even met.'

'Yes, just briefly once or twice, when she's popped into the office with Miriam. Maybe you've not been around.' I picked up a pencil and began to tap it thoughtfully on my lower lip. 'I think they'd actually make a really lovely couple, you know, because she's so gentle and refined and—'

'Northern?' interrupted Sophie.

'I was going to say ethereal, actually. And besides, being born in Northampton doesn't make you northern.'

'OK.' She shrugged and turned to her screen. 'Anyway, are you bringing Stephen?'

I shook my head. 'He can't make it,' I said.

She looked over her shoulder at me. 'Oh no.'

I sighed. 'He's abroad on business. But it's OK. I'm going to text Hugh later. I think he might actually be quite chuffed to be invited and I think Abs would love it.'

'I think so too,' Sophie agreed. 'But it's still a bit,' she made a sad face, 'about Stephen, though.'

'It is a bit,' I agreed, taking the first envelope from the pile of waiting mail.

I opened it and turned to my screen to log it in, realising as I did so that Sophie was still staring at me.

'What is it?' I asked.

She gave up any pretence of work and swivelled her chair to face me. 'How are things with you and Jon?' Her face was serious.

I laughed. 'Gosh, you're to the point.'

'What can I tell you?' She held her hands out, palms upwards, and shrugged. 'It's a gift. And besides, don't think I haven't noticed that you haven't so much as uttered his name in days.' She leaned towards me, resting her chin on her hand once again. 'And it's such a little name,' she said. 'Tiny.'

'As usual, I haven't got a clue what you're on about,' I smiled. 'But things are fine with Jon.' I looked again at the sheet of paper in my hand before binning it as junk mail. 'I'm meeting him for a drink tonight, as a matter of fact,' I added, looking at her.

She sat up and smiled. 'Well, that's great,' she said.

'It will be nice,' I said, with affected nonchalance, reaching for and opening the next envelope. 'You can come if you like.'

'Thanks, but I can't.'

'Why? What are you up to?' I asked, consigning a second piece of junk mail to the waste paper basket, rapidly followed by a third.

She didn't answer and I looked up, to find her still smiling. 'Why are you looking at me like that?'

'I just think it's nice that you and Jon are sorting things out,' she said. 'I didn't like the idea of you being upset with each other.'

'Me neither,' I admitted.

'Right,' she turned to her screen once more, 'well, I'd better get on with this. And *you*,' without turning around, she extended her right arm towards me and pointed downwards, 'better start going through that bin of yours.'

I looked at the bin. 'Why?'

'Because you have just thrown away two cheques and an invoice from Riley Bathrooms. I don't know, Alice Waites,' she shook her head in a theatrically despairing manner, 'it's as if your mind is simply elsewhere this morning.'

Chapter 38

Jon's offices were situated on the top floor of a converted church, just off Whiteladies Road. For reasons I couldn't quite fathom, Synergy Solutions Ltd was accessible only via a basement entrance, located at the bottom of a long flight of external steps, which then necessitated climbing four internal flights of stairs to reach the office. On each occasion I met Jon straight from work, I entered the basement intending to question Geraldine, his longstanding PA, regarding this design anomaly. However, by the time I reached the top of the building, I was always tricked into forgetfulness by mild fatigue and Geraldine's motherly offers of tea and biscuits. And this evening was no different.

'Can I get you a cup of tea and some biscuits, Alice?' she asked, the moment I entered the office. I looked around, realising that she was the only member of Jon's four staff still at her desk.

'No thanks,' I said, 'I'm OK and besides,' I gestured at the clock on the wall, which was showing just after six, 'shouldn't you have gone by now? You haven't been waiting just to buzz me in, have you?'

She smiled. 'No, no,' she said. 'Our youngest is back from his travels tonight. His train gets into Parkway at six-forty, so I'm going straight there. There wasn't any point in going home first.'

'I bet you can't wait to see him,' I said.

'And his laundry,' she sighed. 'But you're right. We've missed him. Anyway,' she said, turning off her PC and leaning forward to pick up her bag, 'you two have fun tonight.' She turned in her chair to wave at Jon through the glass wall of his office. He was on the phone and when he didn't notice her, she stood up, walked to his door and tapped lightly, before waving again. He responded with a wave. She then gestured over her shoulder and I saw him lean to one side, in order to see me. He gave me a quick thumbs-up and then held up two fingers to indicate the anticipated length of talk-time remaining. Geraldine turned back towards me and glanced up at the clock. 'Poor thing has been on the phone to that client for a good half hour,' she said. 'Very needy. A lot of hand-holding required. Mind you,' she lowered her head and looked at me over the top of her glasses, 'she's female and rather a lot of them seek hand-holding from Jon. Not that they ever get anywhere, of course.'

I opened my mouth to say, 'Especially not now with Suzanna on the scene,' but closed it again, realising that it was perfectly possible that Geraldine was unaware of the relationship. I sighed, as it dawned on me just how many opportunities remained for me to put my foot in it all over again.

'But better for him to be happily single…' said Geraldine, almost to herself, confirming that she was indeed ignorant of the fact that Jon had a girlfriend – a situation which I found both surprising and a little sad, considering the length of time she and Jon had worked together, and how highly he thought of her.

She walked past me, patting my shoulder as she went. 'Enjoy.'

'Thanks, and have a lovely time with your son.'

'We will! We will!' she called, turning and giving me a wave as she exited the office.

I sat down in a nearby low, cushioned chair, leaned back and stared at the ceiling, aware that my exchange with Geraldine, as brief and seemingly innocuous as it had been, had left me feeling a little flat. I closed my eyes and wondered whether I might feel able to discuss any of it with Jon, or whether this evening would turn out to be one of light banter and safe small-talk. Not that that would be a bad thing. In fact, I reasoned, it might well be for the best.

'Asleep already?'

I opened my eyes and, with my head still resting on the back of the chair, I turned towards the voice.

Jon was smiling down at me, laptop case in one hand, jacket in the other.

All thought of small-talk evaporated, and without thinking anything beyond the fact that I had missed him, or feeling anything other than a huge sense of relief at seeing him again, I stood up and put my arms around him. I was aware of him leaning to one side to place his laptop on the chair and then, letting his jacket drop, he hugged me back.

'Hello,' he said.

'I know,' I replied.

He laughed and then neither of us said anything else for what seemed like a very long time.

'I'm sorry,' he said eventually.

'Oh, me too,' I mumbled into his shoulder. 'Me too.'

I felt his head press gently against mine and we stood there, neither of us making any attempt to move.

'I've never known you this quiet,' he said.

'I'm just so worried about saying the wrong thing.'

'Really? It's never bothered you before.'

I relaxed, eased away from him slightly and met his eyes.

He smiled down at me. 'I'm lightening the mood,' he said.

'Ah...' I bent down to retrieve his jacket from the floor. 'Thanks for explaining that because I thought you were crashing the moment,' I said, handing him his jacket.

'I've missed you,' he said quietly, 'very much.'

I took a deep breath. 'Well done for retrieving the moment. And, in case you were in any doubt, I have missed you too.'

He smiled. 'Shall we go and get a drink?'

'Absolutely,' I said. 'I'm starving. I only had half a wrap for lunch.'

'Is that your way of saying you want chips?' he asked, picking up his laptop and then gesturing for me to lead the way.

'Yes,' I said, as we headed for the door, 'it is.'

-

We opted for The Neath, a wine bar just a short walk from Jon's office, nestled below a long row of terraced Georgian houses. Although relatively large, it was divided into quiet, cosy rooms and quirky nooks and had the added advantage, in my opinion, of serving some of the best chips in Bristol.

'You can share if you like,' I said to Jon, when presented with my bowl of chips and a small dish of rhubarb ketchup, by a member of the bar staff. We were sitting at a table for two, next to a window which looked out onto a pretty walled garden, in the middle of which was a large, spreading tree. Jon had fetched our drinks: a large glass of red for himself and a similarly large white for me.

'I'm just going to pretend you didn't say that,' he said, 'because I know it's not a genuine offer.'

'Gosh,' I said, 'you're just so good at reading people.'

He smiled and picked up his glass. 'Cheers. So, what have I missed? How tangled is your current web?'

'Shockingly untangled, actually,' I said. 'Had a lovely time with Dad – and his girlfriend, of course,' I added significantly.

'Yes, you texted that he was in a relationship. But didn't tell me any of the details.'

'She's lovely,' I said, smiling at the thought. 'Her name is Hilary, she is sixty-eight, he met her at his widow and widowers' club and she's as bonkers as he is.'

'Sounds perfect.'

'Dad seems so happy.' I looked at Jon and smiled. 'And that's all I want.'

He nodded and smiled back at me. 'You look very well,' he said after moment.

'Do I?' I reached for my wine glass.

He cleared his throat. 'And you mentioned weird phone calls. What was all that about?'

'Oh, just some hang-up calls,' I said dismissively, whilst feeling an odd sense of disappointment that the conversation had moved on so quickly from my personal appearance. 'Stephen's sorting it out.'

'I'll cross that off my list of concerns then.'

'But did I tell you that Sophie and Graham had never been anything more than friends?'

He shook his head. 'No, you didn't. Is that significant?'

'I don't know why it feels significant, but it does,' I shrugged. 'And I want to talk to you about Miriam and Craig.' I picked up another chip and dipped it in the ketchup. 'I love this,' I said. 'They make it themselves.' I popped the chip into my mouth.

'You tell me that every time we come here,' Jon sighed. 'Now focus. What's going on with Miriam and Craig?'

I looked up at him. 'It's not great.'

His expression became suddenly serious. 'It's not?'

I shook my head. 'Miriam is looking increasingly glam, and I don't think it's for Craig's benefit. Which is just as well, because at the moment I don't think he'd notice if she grew a moustache and started calling herself Hercule.' I stared sadly at the chips. 'Have you seen him lately?'

'I ran into him in a restaurant a while ago.'

I felt myself tense involuntarily at this indirect reference to his date with Suzanna.

'I suggested then that we go out for a drink,' he continued, 'but I haven't followed it up. Perhaps I should.'

'Oh, would you?' I looked up, feeling relieved at the thought.

He smiled. 'I'll phone him tomorrow,' he said.

I pushed the chips towards him. 'Have one,' I said. 'It's a genuine offer.'

'Thank you.' He took a chip. 'So, tell me more about Sophie.'

I sipped my wine. 'She asked me if I thought she was a slapper.'

He blinked and paused mid-chip. 'A slapper? I assume that was her word.'

I nodded. 'She thought she might come across as "a slapper"', I drew the inverted commas in the air, 'because she has short-term relationships.'

He looked bemused. 'But she doesn't have that many, does she?' he asked. 'And never more than one at a time.'

'I know. I told her she was talking nonsense. I don't know what prompted it.' I sipped my wine. 'Maybe she made the mistake of comparing herself to her work colleagues who are both, of course, freaks of the dating world; one an emotionally masochistic, serial monogamist and the other… well…' I leaned back in my chair. 'Go on – your turn now. Précis all your exciting news.'

'I'm not sure I have any news which would qualify as exciting,' he said.

'Hopeless,' I tutted and we returned our attention to the chips.

'There's Suzanna, of course,' I ventured after a moment.

He looked up. 'Yes, there is.'

I hesitated and then decided that I must try to address the horror that had been Eleanor Black's party. 'I am so sorry about… about the thing that happened… at Eleanor's,' I said haltingly.

He began to speak, almost before I had finished the sentence. 'It was my fault,' he said. 'I was just taken by surprise and handled it badly.'

I shook my head. 'I shouldn't have said what I said. It's as simple as that.'

'It's been far from simple,' he said. 'And I was so focused on my feelings, that I forgot about other people's.'

'Same.' I smiled sadly. 'Plus, I have really bad timing, of course.'

He looked down at his wine glass. 'Same.'

'But you're feeling better now?' I asked.

'I am,' he said quietly, without looking up. 'Because I know it's OK for me to fall in love; whoever the person and whatever the past.'

The statement, uttered so unexpectedly and unselfconsciously, prompted a rush of thoughts and feelings which left me unable to do anything but stare blankly at him, my mouth hanging wordlessly ajar. Half-recollected conversations and half-acknowledged emotions whirled around my consciousness, refusing to arrange themselves into any meaningful train of thought. But despite this rapid-onset internal chaos, I knew instinctively, and without a doubt, that of course he was right.

I managed a nod and then, on impulse, half stood and very awkwardly leaned across the table to hug him, at enormous risk to our drinks.

'Ungainly,' he laughed, returning the hug, 'but very welcome.'

'I have no words,' I said eventually. 'Apart from those words.'

I felt him nod.

'I'll sit down now,' I said, releasing him and settling back in my chair, whilst feeling strangely out-of-body. It was a moment or two before I could raise my eyes to look at him. When I did, I saw that he was again focused on his wine glass.

'I'm so pleased,' I said quietly. 'Suzanna is lovely.'

His expression flickered. 'She is,' he said simply. 'And Stephen…' He paused and looked up. 'You seem very happy.'

I knew I should agree, but for some reason I couldn't bring myself to. So instead, I offered him a hesitant smile. He offered me one in return and as I watched it briefly form and then fade on his lips, my thoughts at last ordered themselves and I realised two things. Firstly, that here was a man from whom the pain of separation had been immense, and from whom I never wanted to be distanced again, by either situation or person. And secondly, that I was, at that moment, experiencing a significant urge to express those feelings of affection for him physically, by risking a second stretch across the table – not this time to hug him – but to take his face in my hands and kiss him. And as I sat there, still staring at his mouth and evaluating the situation, that idea seemed both perfectly reasonable and absolutely unthinkable. I waited for my head to explode.

'Are you OK?' he asked, taking another chip.

I tore my gaze from his mouth and back to his eyes. He was looking at me steadily. 'Stephen, Suzanna, you and I,' I began slowly, reminding myself of all parties with an immediate interest in the current situation, 'must go out to dinner – the four of us.'

'Your syntax was very interesting there,' he said.

I inhaled deeply and pressed on. 'Shall we try to fix a date?'

'I'll mention it.' He smiled and I leaned back slightly in my chair, desperately trying to restore some sort of natural order to my feelings, whilst at the same time subconsciously putting a healthy distance between my lips and his.

I took a second deep breath. 'I'd like to get to know Suzanna better.'

He nodded.

'But maybe I can do that at the book group dinner,' I said, desperate to divert both the conversation and my thoughts, whilst still very aware of an ongoing desire to kiss the close friend sitting opposite me.

'Are you bringing Stephen?' he asked.

I shook my head. 'He's in France that weekend – so I'm bringing Hugh,' I added, grateful for the opportunity to focus on a man other than my boyfriend or Jon. I formed a mental image of Hugh, dressed in a pristine white coat and pale green wellies, advancing towards a waiting corpse with a small circular saw. It was comfortingly unerotic.

Jon raised an eyebrow. 'Battle re-enactment Hugh?' he said. The idea clearly intrigued him.

I nodded. 'I'm really pleased he's coming. And so is Abs. I think she feels vindicated, because she was right; we do get on well.'

Jon smiled, sipped his wine unhurriedly and then replaced his glass on the table. 'What do you like about him?'

'Well, he's frank, but kind and that's a rather valuable combination,' I said, relieved by the conversational shift. 'And he's funny too,' I continued, clinging desperately to the new, safe subject of Hugh. 'Although, you do have to keep explaining to him why he's funny. That's a negative point – in *my* opinion. But I suppose someone else might find it endearing. Could it be endearing?' I paused, aware that I was beginning to gabble. 'What do you think?'

'Having never met him,' he said, 'I'm afraid I can't comment. I'll let you know if he's endeared himself to me after the dinner. Any other observations on any of the other attendees you'd care to share?'

I sighed and managed a smile. 'You can step in any time with your own exciting chit-chat, you know.'

'I'm genuinely interested,' he laughed.

I frowned at him.

'*Genuinely*,' he insisted.

'OK, well, Miriam's bringing Romy and Sophie's bringing David,' I said. 'That could be interesting.'

'What could? David and Sophie?'

I shook my head. 'No. David and Romy. He seems really pleased that she's coming and whenever she's visited the office, it's been obvious that he thinks she's gorgeous.'

Jon's expression remained impassive. 'He'd have to be made of marble not to think that,' he said.

'I know but it's not as if he looks like the back of a bus, is it?' I protested. 'Women turn in the street for him. And in wine bars. Sophie pointed that out to him just the other day.'

He smiled and there followed a pause in the conversation, during which I drank my wine and attempted to regulate my thoughts by studying the various couples sitting at the tables closest to our own. Two were clearly work colleagues, deep in business-like conversation, another pair appeared to be on a date, enjoying the evening, but not yet entirely relaxed in one another's company. A third couple, sitting immediately to my left, was harder to categorise. Maybe, I thought, they were like Jon and me: the best and oldest of friends – one of whom had just considered kissing the other as the most natural and complete way of expressing and conveying her feelings.

'You're thinking,' said Jon.

I started slightly and turned to him. 'Sorry?'

He gestured towards my hands; I was twisting my mother's wedding ring, my fingers interlinked around the stem of my near-empty wine glass. 'What are your thoughts?'

'Confused,' I said, looking at my hands and placing them on my lap under the table.

'Business as usual then,' he said.

'Yes.' I looked up and found myself once more disconcertingly fixated upon his mouth as he smiled mischievously.

A combined ringing and buzzing sound interrupted my latest, increasingly confused, thoughts. Jon reached into the pocket of his jacket and retrieved his phone. 'Sorry,' he said, glancing at the screen, 'I have to take this.' He turned slightly in his chair to face the window and smiled. 'Hi, how are you? No, it's fine. I'm out with Alice. We're in The Neath… Yes, that's right, the one with the tree… Of course.' He turned to me briefly. 'Suzie says hi.'

Suzie. I managed a smile. 'Say hello back.'

'Alice says hello… Yes, she's looking forward to it too.'

There then followed an extended pause, while Jon listened. When it was clear he was going to be tied up for a few minutes, I decided to distract myself with my own phone. I took it from my bag. There was a text from Stephen, wondering whether I wanted go away over summer and asking whether I had had any more silent calls. It was his third text of the day about the calls. He was so sweet. I looked at Jon, smiling over something *Suzie* was telling him, and then tapped out a quick message to Stephen, replying in the negative regarding the phone calls and in the effusively affirmative regarding summer. My finger hovered over *send*. Meanwhile, Jon's conversation was ongoing.

'Yes, that's great,' he said and then his tone changed. 'I know,' he said softly. 'I feel the same way.'

I smiled and pressed *send*. Jon, I told myself, was my friend. What's more, he was in love with Suzanna, and I was as happy for him in that new relationship as I was for my father in his. Any feelings of physical affection towards him this evening were, I reasoned, a muddled, over-emotional reaction to seeing him again, following what had been a very difficult, stressful and painful period in our relationship.

'Yes, bye.' He replaced his phone in his jacket and turned to me. 'Sorry,' he said.

I shook my head and smiled. 'I'm fine. I mean, *it's* fine,' I corrected. 'All sorted with Suzanna?'

'Yes. She was booking her train for next week and just needed a few timings confirming.'

'I see.' I picked up my wine glass, and drank the last mouthful. 'Will she be staying the weekend?'

'Yes.'

'That'll be nice. And Stephen's just texted to suggest going away over summer,' I added. 'I'm pleased about that because I was starting to wonder what I'd do. Will you be going away?'

'I hope so.' He pointed at my wine glass and the now empty bowl of chips. 'Some more of everything? Or would you like to go somewhere for dinner?'

I smiled, pleased not to have been presented with going home as an option. 'Well, you know I'm more than happy with chips. What would you like to do?'

Never one to make a hurried decision, he took a moment to consider our options. 'I think,' he said eventually, turning and looking at me in a way which prompted a fleeting, but distinct, internal ache, 'it's easier if we just stay as we are.'

I smiled, took an extra little steadying breath and then nodded. 'I agree,' I said quietly. 'That's definitely the most sensible option.'

He looked at me for a moment and I thought he might be about to say more. But instead he simply returned my smile, rose to his feet and headed for the bar.

Chapter 39

'I'm jealous,' said Stephen.

'*You're* jealous?' I responded incredulously. 'You're in the south of France!'

'I'm in an office, sitting in front of a computer.'

'*In the south of France*,' I repeated. 'And besides, won't you be off out to dinner soon?'

'I'd just rather be there,' he said, 'coming to your book group dinner with you. I haven't seen you in weeks.'

'Twelve days. And you're here next weekend,' I said, 'for dinner with Jon and Suzanna.'

'I just hope nothing crops up and gets in the way.'

'Why should it?' I smiled into the phone. 'And if you get stuck in Solihull, we'll cancel dinner and I'll come there.'

'I couldn't let you do that,' he said. 'I'm packing everything up. It'd be like camping.'

I laughed. 'I have been camping before, you know.'

'But still,' he said. 'I don't want your first experience of staying in my home to be one of sleeping amongst boxes. Anyway,' he said, 'I'd better let you go. What time are you eating?'

'Drinks at seven-thirty, dinner at eight. Hugh and I are being picked up by Greg. He's got a seven-seater.'

'It'll be a lot of fun.' He sounded flat.

'You'll have a great evening too,' I said. 'And I'll text you as soon as I'm home.'

'I'll look forward to it,' he said. 'Enjoy.'

'I will, bye.'

'Bye.'

I hung up and then turned to my computer, with a view to logging out.

'All well?' asked Sophie.

'Yes,' I replied. 'He's just not having the best time.'

'Is he missing you?'

'I think he would like to be coming tonight,' I said.

She turned off her computer and leaned back in her chair.

'Are you looking forward to him moving?'

'Of course,' I said.

'How often do you phone him?'

'We speak every day,' I said absently. 'Often more than once.' I reached down for my bag.

'Does he phone you or do you phone him?'

I straightened up and looked at her.

'What?' she asked.

'You're interrogating me,' I said. 'And you don't do that without purpose. So spit it out.'

'OK,' she said, before continuing in typically direct fashion. 'I was just wondering if he's a little more into you than you are into him.' She held up a hand. 'Which, let me just say, is a very good thing in my book.' She smiled. 'I just wondered if maybe you felt that too.'

'I like him very much,' I said. 'Let's just see where it goes.'

'Absolutely. See where it goes,' she said.

'Talking of which,' I rested my arms on the desk and leaned towards her. 'Any men on your horizon?'

She smiled and ran a hand through her hair. 'I think I probably need a little break from men actually.'

I was about to ask why, but she anticipated the question.

'Not sure why,' she said, 'although, of course, my sister does a pretty good job of putting me off them.' She smiled ruefully.

'Well,' I said, 'you're going out with a lovely man tonight.'

She looked at me for a moment, then got up from her desk, came round to mine, leaned over and enveloped me in an unexpected hug. 'You're brilliant, you know that?' she said.

I hugged her back. 'Ditto,' I said.

She straightened up and I realised that she was a little emotional.

'You OK?' I asked.

She cleared her throat. 'Yeah, yeah. I'm just going to go and get changed,' she said, looking towards David's office.

I checked the clock on the mantelpiece. 'What's your plan?'

'Frock's there, of course,' she pointed towards a suit bag hanging from the hat-stand. 'I'm just going to pop that on and apply a bit of slap, while David finishes off, and then we're off out for pre-drink drinks.'

'Sounds like fun.'

'Doesn't it just,' she said. 'Right.' She walked to the hat-stand, unhooked the bag and began to make her way to the bathroom. 'I shall see Uhu there,' she said.

'Uhu?'

'You and Hugh,' she explained, pausing for a moment, before continuing on her way. 'It's my new mono-name for the pair of you. I'm quite proud of it,' she called. 'It's like Samneric.'

The bathroom door clicked shut behind her.

'Samneric?' I echoed questioningly.

'It's a reference to *Lord of the Flies*,' said David, appearing in the open doorway of his office. 'The twins.'

'Oh yes,' I said. 'Anyway,' I stood up, 'I shall leave the pair of you to swap literary references over cocktails and see you a little later.' I looked at David. He was now staring at the floor, hands in pockets. 'Everything OK?' I asked. 'No project problems?'

'What?' He appeared momentarily bemused.

'You look a little pensive,' I said. 'I was just wondering whether everything is OK?'

'Oh, yes,' he said smiling. 'I was just reflecting on… on a thing. A work thing. Not a personal thing.'

'Anything you want to bounce off me?' I asked.

'Maybe…' he hesitated. 'Maybe when I've thought it over a little more.'

'OK,' I said, beginning to make my way to the door. 'In that case, I shall run home, fill in the cracks and then see you at seven-thirty.'

'That's right,' he said, 'seven-thirty. I cannot wait.'

I turned to offer him a final wave, but he had already resumed his study of the carpet and now had the appearance, somewhat ironically, of a man who just might be prepared to wait his entire life. 'David,' I said, jolting him out of his reverie.

'Oh yes, Alice. I'm sorry. Goodbye,' he said, smiling and removing a hand from his pocket to return the wave.

'Bye, Sophie!' I called. I waited a moment but received no response, which was unsurprising as she had just started singing '*Should I Stay or Should I Go?*' very loudly indeed, punctuating her vocals with enthusiastic da-na-nas, in lieu of a guitar.

I sighed and headed off down the stairs, smiling to myself at the eclectic mix of characters the book group anniversary dinner always threw together and wondering, with a strange mixture of excitement and, for some reason, slight trepidation, what the evening might hold for us all.

Chapter 40

An additional advantage of being chauffeured to dinner by Greg was, I thought, as I squeezed into the Sharan next to Romy and Miriam, that Hugh would meet my friends in small waves, rather than as a single, potentially overwhelming, social tsunami. By the time we arrived at the restaurant, the journey would have halved the number of necessary introductions.

He settled himself into the front seat next to Greg and held out his hand for the latter to shake.

'Hello, I'm Hugh,' he said.

'Pleased to meet you, Hugh,' said Greg amiably. 'I'm Greg. You've been dragged along by Alice, have you? Well you're a brave man, that's all I can say. She is trouble, with a capital T.'

'Oh dear,' sighed Connie quietly from the back row of seats, before clearing her throat in preparation for speech. 'Now, Greg, Hugh does not know you and your sense of humour as yet and—'

Greg laughed loudly. 'Oops, there I go again, Hugh. In trouble with the wife already and we haven't even reached the restaurant yet. But you know I'm joking, don't you? Alice is more muddle than trouble, aren't you, Alice?'

I forced a laugh for Connie's sake and then decided to press on with the introductions. 'Hugh,' I said, twisting in my seat 'meet Connie, Miriam and Romy.'

Hugh reached round awkwardly, in an attempt to shake their hands.

'Not to worry, Hugh,' said Miriam from her window seat behind Greg. 'I'll settle for a wave. I wouldn't want you dislocating anything.'

'Me too,' said Connie, waving.

Hugh raised a hand. 'Hello,' he said.

Romy unbuckled her seatbelt and edged forward, adjusting her turquoise, embroidered shift dress as she did so. 'Hello, Hugh,' she said, extending a hand. 'I'm Romy. I'm not a member of the book group and I've never been to one of their dinners before either. I'm here as Miriam's guest. We can be newbies together.'

Hugh smiled and, whilst he remained unspeaking, I saw for the first time what Sophie and Miriam had meant; he was actually, I had to admit, a rather handsome man. He shook Romy's hand. 'Thank you, Romy,' he said, 'for that welcome. I believe you were at university with Abigail, were you not?'

She nodded. 'That's right. She's so lovely and I didn't manage to see her last time I was in Bristol, so that will be an additional treat for me this evening.'

'I very much enjoy catching up with old friends,' said Hugh, his attractiveness maintained, enhanced even, by his deep Edinburgh tones. 'And I also enjoy making new ones. Maybe over dinner you could tell me a little about your personal history and interests.'

And, with that, he became about as sexy as a dead fish once more.

Miriam threw me a sidelong glance, whilst Romy, in typically saintly fashion, managed to appear thrilled at the prospect of sharing her personal history and interests with Hugh, as if it was the very thing for which she had been creating a personal history and developing interests over the past twenty-nine years.

'I'd love to, Hugh,' she said and then as she sat back in her seat and re-buckled her belt, we headed for the restaurant.

-

We arrived at Primrose in less than ten minutes and the length of the journey would have left me with some guilt over not walking, were it not for the fact that Hugh had chatted happily all the way, having discovered shared passions for mountain climbing with Romy, and for all things chemical with Greg. I was delighted to see him at ease so early in the evening.

On arrival, Romy and Miriam detoured to the ladies, while the rest of us made our way upstairs to the room Abs had booked for us. Approximately two thirds of the space was taken up by two heavy wooden oblong tables, pushed together to form a single square and laid for twelve. Because the evening was warm, the French doors onto the terrace were open and we discovered Abs, Jon and Suzanna already outside, each holding a glass of the pink Cava which sat in ice buckets on a small table in one corner of the dining room.

'Alice and Hugh!' cried Abs, as we stepped out onto the terrace. 'Oh and Greg and Connie too! Brilliant!' Effusive at the best of times, she seemed this evening to be beside herself with excitement. 'Oh, gosh, look at Alice and Connie! Connie, that blue dress matches your eyes perfectly,' she said, reaching out and gently touching Connie's arm, as the latter smiled and blushed slightly at the compliment. 'And you look positively radiant, Alice,' she continued, turning her attention to me. 'Doesn't she, everyone? Don't they both look gorgeous?' She turned to Jon and Suzanna, each of whom responded with polite nods.

'Looking dressed to kill, even when you're *not* on the hunt eh, Alice?' laughed Greg, elbowing me hard. 'Grrrr...' he clawed the air.

I laughed, finding the joke funnier now than I had the first time; presumably because I now heard it from the security of a relationship, rather than as a needy single woman who had just thanked all her friends, in writing, for offering to set her up with men. I looked down at the purple, patterned sheath dress, which I had excitedly purchased a week earlier. 'Thank you. It is a new dress actually.'

There were murmurs of approval, following which Jon turned to Suzanna and smiled.

'Well, everybody,' he said, 'this is Suzanna. She has—' At that point, whatever he was about to say was cut short, as Greg lunged forward, grabbed Suzanna's hand and began to pump it vigorously up and down. 'Ah, yes,' he beamed. 'We've been looking forward to meeting you, haven't we, Connie?' Connie nodded her agreement and as Greg rambled on, I looked from Suzanna to Jon. It was the first time I had seen him since our drinks in The Neath and I had thought little in the busy intervening days about my sudden urge to kiss him that night. But I recalled it now, and was unsettled to once again find myself appreciating his appearance, and his mouth in particular, in a way which didn't sit comfortably within the bounds of friendship.

He had just turned to look at me with a puzzled smile, when my thoughts were suddenly, but thankfully, interrupted by a gentle nudge from Hugh. 'You look beautiful,' he said quietly. I turned and looked up at him in surprise.

'My sister told me to say that to say that to every woman in the room,' he murmured.

'Great advice,' I whispered.

'I'm joking,' he said, without cracking a smile.

I laughed. There was hope for him yet.

'Oh look!' said Abs. 'There's Romy!' She dipped inside the room to welcome the newcomers who had paused on entry to pour themselves some wine.

'I'll go and get us some drinks,' said Hugh. 'You stay here.'

'OK.' I turned to Suzanna, as Jon distracted Greg with a business enquiry. 'It's lovely to see you again,' I said. 'I'll introduce you to Hugh when he gets back.'

'Abigail has just been telling me all about him. He sounds quite fascinating,' she said.

I laughed. 'Abs has a tendency to make us all sound fascinating. But yes, Hugh does have a lot of strings to his bow.'

'It's lovely to meet him, but I thought you'd be with Stephen,' she continued. 'Jon says he's away.'

'Yes, in France.'

'And whisper on the wind,' said Greg, suddenly listening-in, 'is that things are going very well indeed with Stephen, Alice. And I think I'd like to take a little bit of the credit for that. Cash'll be just fine.'

Connie turned from her conversation with Jon and looked anxiously first at me, then at Greg. 'Now, Greg,' she said quietly, 'let's not discuss Alice's personal life at a party.'

Greg rolled his eyes. 'I don't know, Connie, you tell me off for discussing business at parties and now I'm not allowed to discuss personal matters.' He looked at Jon and laughed. 'Women, eh?'

I stifled a sigh, Connie didn't bother to stifle hers and I noticed Suzanna frown slightly.

Jon smiled and placed an arm around her shoulders. She looked up at him fondly. I was grateful for Hugh's return with my drink.

'Thanks,' I said, taking it from him. 'Now Hugh, this is Jon and his partner, Suzanna.' Hugh nodded and transferred his glass to his left hand, making his right hand available for shakes.

'Lovely to meet you, Hugh,' said Suzanna, taking his extended hand. 'I'm actually—'

'At last!' Abs' excited screech reached us through the French doors. 'A full house!'

I turned to see David and Sophie entering the upper room. David was smiling broadly, and looking very relaxed, and Sophie appeared equally serene in a thin, slightly shimmering blue dress. Her arm was through David's and they looked, at that moment, picture perfect. I smiled at the thought of two such contrasting personalities, so at home in each other's company and felt suddenly sentimental regarding my riotously harmonious place of work and my colleagues who were also my friends.

'You know, I hardly feel as if introductions are necessary,' said Hugh, following my gaze. 'Abigail has told me so much about everyone.

'Did she tell you how fascinating they all are?' I asked.

'She did.'

'Yes, well, she told me that about you and…' I pulled a face and looked him up and down disparagingly.

He remained stony-faced. 'You're being amusing again, aren't you?' he said.

'She's attempting it,' said Jon.

'I'm learning to spot it,' sighed Hugh. 'I'm also learning to laugh along.'

'That's easily the best approach,' said Jon. 'If you don't laugh along, she just tries harder, and that's not great.'

Greg laughed loudly and slapped me hard on the back, as if we were navvies sharing a joke on the railway. 'Are they teasing you, Alice? Well, don't you worry, it's a sign of affection.'

Hugh turned to me and smiled and Jon raised his glass in salute.

'Where's Pete?' asked Hugh, looking around. 'Has he made it this evening?'

'Dear Pete,' said Abs, returning to the terrace, with Miriam trailing. 'He's been looking forward to this for weeks. Like a child waiting for Christmas. I didn't think he was ever going to get to sleep last night.'

'Where is he, Abigail?' Hugh repeated. I had noticed during occasional drinks with Abs and Pete, that Hugh, fond as he clearly was of Abs, seemed to treat most of her conversation as not unpleasant white noise. He appeared to sieve it, honing in only on the salient and rarely acknowledging the hum of the rest.

'He's with the manager, double-checking our orders and costings,' she explained. 'He loves figures and food. Two of his very favourite things.'

It occurred to me to ask if these interests were up there with mending punctures and helping side-of-stage, but I stifled the urge by taking a sip from my drink. I noticed Jon do the same and he lowered his glass and offered me a smile as his eyes met mine.

Miriam coughed lightly.

'Ooh, Miriam, I'm so sorry. Suzanna, this is Miriam,' said Abs.

'Hello,' said Miriam. I detected a note of tension in her smile.

'Miriam.' Suzanna stepped forward and hugged her warmly, an indication I thought of the way in which Jon must have described her.

Miriam looked slightly taken aback but also, I thought, rather touched. 'Lovely to meet you,' she said and a quiet conversation immediately ensued.

Abs began talking to Connie about main courses and Greg sought Hugh's advice concerning a pain in his lower back. I touched Hugh's arm. 'Sorry to interrupt. I'm just going to pop inside for a moment.'

Hugh nodded. 'That's fine.'

'Don't worry, Alice,' said Greg. 'I won't grill him regarding medical matters for too long.'

'You do realise that he specialises in dead people, don't you, Greg?' I said.

'If he knows how my back bone connects to my tailbone,' laughed Greg, 'that's good enough for me.'

I looked up at Hugh. He was smiling and I judged him to be happy with the conversation. 'Fair enough,' I shrugged. 'Back in a mo.'

'I'll come with you,' said Jon. Suzanna looked over her shoulder at him and smiled. As she did so, Miriam took the opportunity to catch my eye and wink. I looked at her questioningly, as she put her hand to her mouth, feigned a cough and mouthed the word *gossip* at me, her hand still positioned to hide her mouth from the rest of the group. In response, I frowned and attempted what I hoped was a brief but disapproving thinning of the lips at her shameless lack of discretion. I then turned and walked with Jon towards the open French windows, through which we could see David and Romy laughing, as Sophie concluded an anecdote, inaudible to us. She turned as we approached.

'Hello, you two. After more booze?' she smiled. 'And where are your dinner guests? Why haven't you brought them in for a meet and greet?'

'Miriam's got one and Greg's got the other,' I explained.

'Well,' said Sophie, 'I don't fancy being able to crowbar myself into either of those conversations.'

'You underestimate yourself,' said David. 'You're rather an expert with a conversational crowbar. Although you do tend to whack, rather than lever.'

Romy laughed and Sophie looked simultaneously shocked and amused. 'When,' she said, 'did you get so bold, David Moore?' she asked, nudging him. 'We were just saying last week how cheeky you'd become, weren't we, Alice?'

'*You* were,' I said. 'I was actually very busy.'

'Busy chucking a cheque and two invoices in the bin,' she returned with a smirk.

David snorted in an attempt not to laugh. She had clearly shared the incident with him.

I tutted. 'Two cheques and one invoice, *actually*.'

Jon looked at David. 'I admire your fortitude,' he said.

'They have their upside,' smiled David.

Romy sighed. 'I wish my working environment was such a happy one,' she said.

'How are things professionally?' I asked.

'Well,' she smiled, 'I've got a job interview in Bristol next Friday.'

'Wow,' I said. 'Miriam must be over the moon.'

She laughed. 'I've told her not to get her hopes too high. But it would be lovely to be nearer her and Phoebe.' She sipped her drink. 'And Craig, of course,' she added quietly.

I glanced at Jon, making a mental note to enquire at some point how his evening with Craig had gone. We had texted and emailed regularly since meeting for drinks, but the topic of Craig had barely been touched upon. I knew that he and Jon had gone to the pub, and that Craig had been "OK" but, beyond that, nothing.

'You could join book group!' exclaimed Sophie.

Romy smiled. 'That was the first thing Miriam said. But I'm not sure I would – or should. You're such an established group. I wouldn't want to upset the equilibrium.'

'Equilibrium my arse,' said Sophie. David coughed lightly. 'You've met us all. We couldn't achieve equilibrium if we tried. And we don't try,' she added with a grin. 'I love our lack of equilibrium. Don't you?' She looked at Jon.

He smiled at her and then turned to Romy. 'If you do move to Bristol,' he said, 'we'd love to have you.'

'I think you would be very happy here,' said David. 'Bristol has much to offer.' He looked at Romy and she flashed him a grateful smile, which succeeded in making her appear more beautiful than ever. David returned the smile with one equally as charming and I nudged Jon, his only reaction to which was to emit a light sigh.

'He's back!' cried Abs, rushing in from the terrace and looking beyond us to the stairs. I turned to look over my shoulder and saw Pete.

We all said hello, while Pete raised a salutary hand, at the rate of a leaden flag going up an extremely tall flagpole.

'Is everything sorted, Pete?' asked Abs.

He nodded slowly. 'All sorted,' he said, his features gradually arranging themselves into a smile.

Abs clapped her hands. 'Brilliant!' she exclaimed. 'Now, Pete, do you have the place cards?'

'I do,' he said, extracting cards from every pocket of his chinos and handing them in batches to Abs.

'Splendid,' she said. 'You get yourself a glass of fizzy stuff, Pete, and take a moment to calm down, whilst I just pop these on the table. I thought it would be rather exciting if we started off *not* sitting next to the people we brought.' There was a general murmur of agreement. 'And then we can swap around with each course as usual.' Abs began to lay out the cards, reading the names aloud as she went. 'Sophie, Hugh, Romy, Jon...'

I sipped my drink and waited for it to be revealed that I would be sitting next to Greg.

'...me and Greg and... Alice!' concluded Abs, triumphantly. 'There. Isn't that fantastic?' she said, standing back and admiring the table. 'Come on, everybody. Let's eat!'

Chapter 41

It was with some surprise, given my early sense of mild despair at finding myself sitting next to Greg, that I found myself enjoying the evening, Greg and all, from the off. The reason for this unexpected turn of events was that he, I discovered, was genuinely proud that his matchmaking on my behalf had met with some success. And his eagerness to discover the exact nature and extent of that success meant that he was, for once, more keen to talk about pleasure than business. Connie, who was sitting directly opposite us, had, I suspected, shared my initial concerns regarding our pairing and threw us several nervous glances, the frequency of which increased upon her hearing Greg mention Stephen. However, I attempted to reassure her, by means of cheerful nods and smiles, that all was well, and after a few minutes she relaxed enough to appear fully absorbed in her conversation with Miriam.

Of course, Greg conducted *our* conversation with a total lack of sensitivity and diplomacy, treating me, as he always did, as some sort of charming village idiot. However, keeping his voice lowered, and resisting all urges to play to the gallery, he revealed a more sentimental side to his character, never before apparent to me. And this, together with my enjoyment of no longer playing single white female to his confident family man, made his habitual lack of tact seem entertaining, and even endearing, rather than annoying.

'I'm pleased it's all going so well,' he said, upon learning that I would be spending the following weekend with Stephen. 'OK, so you've cocked-up with your choices in the past,' he punched me not-so-lightly on the arm, 'but now it's onwards and upwards. Stephen is a nice bloke and is very keen. I'm keeping my fingers crossed for you.'

'Me too,' I said, holding up my hands to illustrate the point.

'I've got a good feeling about it – like I did when we developed the ceramics side of things,' he said, unable to resist a commercial analogy. 'I thought you and Stephen might click from the start, you know.' He gestured across the table towards Connie. 'I said so to Connie. You're a very attractive lass, Alice, and while you may not be the sharpest tool in the shed by any means, you're not stupid either.' He tapped his forehead. 'It's always been clear to me that there's a brain up there, should you choose to use it.'

'Thank you.'

'And Stephen does have a lovely car,' he said. 'It sort of purrs, doesn't it?' He gazed dreamily at his wine glass.

'It is nice,' I agreed.

'Yes,' he said. 'I could have bought a Porsche when I was twenty-five, you know.'

'No, I didn't know that.'

'Well, it's true,' he sighed. 'But, of course, I chose Connie instead.'

I decided it best simply to accept, rather than request an explanation of, the statement. 'Of course.'

'And,' he said, 'it was the right choice and I've never regretted it for a minute.'

I looked at him and, to my astonishment, thought I detected a twitch of emotion in his jaw line. 'That's a lovely thing to say,' I said.

He looked across at Connie, smiled fondly and then seemed to recover himself. He cleared his throat and turned to me. 'Of course,' he said, turning up the volume, picking up his glass and draining the contents, 'if it had been a choice between Connie and an Aston Martin, it might have been a different story.'

I rolled my eyes and nudged him. He winked and nudged me back with inappropriate force, causing a significant amount of the wine I had just picked up, to slop from glass to tablecloth – but I didn't mind.

As our plates were removed at the end of the first course, Abs leapt up and collected all the place cards. Then, consulting a table plan extracted from a pale blue plastic wallet, she redistributed the cards in preparation for a seat-swap. When she had finished, she remained standing and tapped her wine glass lightly with a spoon to gain our attention.

'Right, everybody,' she said, as a hush descended, 'I don't know about you, but I have *so* enjoyed my first course discourse.' She smiled down at David who had been sitting to her left. 'David has been telling me all about his latest work projects and his plans to re-plumb at home.' David shifted awkwardly in his seat, perhaps aware that Abs' synopsis of their conversation didn't make him sound like the greatest of raconteurs. 'However,' Abs continued, 'it is now time for the main course shuffle. Yay!' She smiled broadly and clapped her hands. 'And for this course, you will be sitting next to the person you came with.' This announcement prompted a light, but undeniably weary, 'Oh,' from Connie, which in turn prompted a loud guffaw from Greg, as he offered me a nodded farewell and made his way to the other side of the table. I watched, as he bent down to kiss his wife on arrival, and as she smiled up at him affectionately.

'Hello, Alice,' said a voice to my left.

'Well, hello,' I said to Hugh, as he sat down. 'How was your starter?'

'Very good,' he replied. 'I had the crab beignets and I don't regret the choice.'

'Good to know,' I smiled. 'And you got to know Sophie and Romy a little?' I asked.

'I did,' he said. 'Romy in particular was very interested in pathology.'

I was unable to prevent my upper lip from curling slightly. 'Over dinner?' I asked. 'Are you positive she wasn't just being polite?'

'Yes, I am,' he said. 'I didn't press the subject, or return to it. And I asked numerous questions regarding her personal history and interests. It was she who pursued the subject of pathology.'

'Can I just ask something, Hugh?' I asked quietly.

He sighed. 'Go on.'

'Well, you know this personal history and interests thing?'

'Yes.'

'Is that something your sister has suggested you talk to people about?'

He nodded. 'It is, yes. Why? Do you not think it's a good idea?'

I held up a hand. 'No, I think she's spot on. It's just that I don't think she would have intended you to repeat the phrase *personal history and interests* every time you ask someone about—'

'—their personal history and interests?' He completed the sentence for me.

'Yes.'

He raised his eyebrows, as if bemused but nevertheless willing to give the matter some consideration. 'OK,' he said eventually, 'I'll stop doing that. Now,' he glanced under the table, 'can I ask you to move your bag, because it's vibrating against my leg.'

'Ooh, sorry,' I said, reaching down and delving into my bag. 'It's my phone. It's in the front zip pocket and on vibrate. It has quite an aggressive pulse.'

'I'll let you check it,' said Hugh, picking up a bottle of red wine and leaning away from me, across the corner of the table, to offer some to Suzanna.

I took my phone from my bag. Three missed texts from Stephen. All identical and sent at five-minute intervals – the result, I assumed, of a glitch in overseas texting.

> *Hi, hope you're having fun. Would be great to hear that you're having a good time and all going well x*

There was also a missed call from him but no voicemail. I smiled and texted a reply, confirming that I was enjoying myself and that I would call him when home. I then returned my phone to my bag and sat up, just in time for the waiter to present me with my main course of sea bass.

'This looks great,' I said looking at my plate. 'It was such a good idea to come here,' I added, raising my voice slightly and directing the comment towards Abs. And, as my declaration was echoed generally around the table and translated by Pete into a kiss for Abs, we all tucked in.

The second seat-swap of the evening was effected with much less efficiency than the first, for two reasons. Firstly, there were no place cards to guide us; Pete had collected these in, whilst Abs instructed us to, 'sit next to two people you haven't yet sat next to.' The second hindrance to completion of the set task was the significant amount of alcohol which had been consumed by almost everyone during the first two courses. Consequently, locating a seat between two entirely new neighbours, when we had each already sat next to four of the twelve attendees, proved a huge intellectual and logistical challenge. It led to several minutes of us all wandering round the table, like a crowd of Goldilocks in search of a suitable chair. In the end, having moved twice, I decided to sit down, stay put and let the mountains come to Mohammed.

My first mountain was Miriam, a result which delighted me; although I was having such a lovely time that I decided there was no outcome with which I would have been disappointed.

'I'm going to sit here and stay here,' she said, flopping down next to me. 'I've already had to move on from Romy and then again when Connie sat down and I'm not moving again. 'Where's the wine?' She glanced around before stretching for a bottle of white and topping up her glass. 'Want some more?'

I placed a hand over the top of my half-full glass. 'I'm fine for now, thanks.'

She leaned towards me and smiled. 'I've got something *very* interesting to tell you,' she said conspiratorially. 'You know how—' She stopped abruptly and looked over my shoulder.

'Hello,' she beamed. 'Would you like some?' She held up the wine bottle and I turned to see that Jon had now occupied the seat to my left.

'I'm on red,' he said, pointing towards his glass. 'I'll help myself later.'

'OK,' smiled Miriam. 'How about you, Greg?' she asked, turning to her right as he sat down next to her. Top up?'

I looked at Jon and smiled. 'Well hello, Mr Durham,' I said.

'Well hello, Ms Waites,' he replied, returning the smile. 'How's your evening going?'

'Really well,' I said. 'And yours?'

'Getting better by the moment and,' he paused, 'I have some gossip for you.'

I laughed. 'Not you too? I'm already on a promise from Miriam. What's yours about?'

He turned and looked across the table at Romy and then back at me. 'It's about why,' he said, lowering his voice, 'you are wrong about David and Romy.'

'Ooh, why?' I asked, leaning towards him, my eyes widening.

'Because,' he whispered, 'she's got her eye on someone else.'

I put my hand to my mouth and waited for him to continue but he said nothing more. 'Well, come on,' I tugged at his shirt sleeve. 'Who is it? Tell me.'

'Wait a moment,' he said, 'while I pause to build up the excitement.'

I groaned and was about to demand immediate further details, when Greg reached behind Miriam and prodded my arm. 'Look, Alice, here comes dessert. Every woman's favourite course. But as I always say to Connie,' he wagged a cautionary finger, 'a moment on the lips, a lifetime on the hips.'

Miriam tutted and smiled at me, before turning in her seat to address him. 'I'm surprised Connie hasn't brained you, you know.'

'Me too, Miriam,' he said, nodding his thanks to the waitress as she presented him with a sizeable summer pudding. 'Me too.'

-

It was eleven o'clock, and we had eaten dessert, drunk coffee and enjoyed an impromptu, enthusiastic and expletive-riddled vote of thanks to Abs from Sophie, by the time the waitress placed the final bill on the table.

I had spent most of the dessert course chatting to Miriam and Greg, whilst eavesdropping every now and then on Jon's rather serious discussion with Abs regarding education. I turned to him now, as I added my debit card to the pile forming in front of Pete.

'So,' I asked, 'what's your weekend?'

He ran a hand part-way through his hair.

'Ah,' I said, gesturing at his hand resting on top of his head, 'still thinking about it, I see.'

He laughed, lowering his hand. 'Yes, I am – or rather, we are,' he corrected, looking towards Suzanna. She was laughing with Romy, together forming a tableau which put me in mind of an advert for posh coffee.

'That reminds me,' I said in a whisper, with a nod of my head towards Romy, 'you haven't told me your gossip.'

'True,' he said. 'But how about I call you with all the details, rather than trying to hiss them at you now? Or perhaps we could discuss it over a drink next week.'

I laughed. 'You're really bigging this up, you know. It had better be good.'

He said nothing but instead turned to look again at Romy and Suzanna.

'They seem to be getting on well, don't they?' I said.

He smiled and nodded. 'I think they might actually be quite similar, you know.'

'Both very beautiful, certainly,' I agreed, 'and I don't know Suzanna very well but if her personality is anything like Romy's, then you're extremely lucky.'

I felt a hand on my right shoulder and then a wet kiss was planted on my cheek. 'I heard that,' said Miriam. 'You are so very lovely and my very, *very* best friend.'

I wiped my cheek. 'And you,' I said, 'are very dribbly.'

She giggled. 'I've just put on some lip balm.'

'Marvellous.'

'But they are boofitul, aren't they?' Miriam directed her gaze towards Romy and Suzanna. 'Ooh!' She put her hand to her mouth and giggled again. 'Listen to me! Boofitul! I've had so much to drink! I meant beau…ti…ful,' she concluded, enunciating the word syllable by syllable and causing Jon to laugh.

'And you're beautiful too, Jon,' she sighed, beaming up at him and then nudging me. 'You think so too, don't you, Alice? You're always saying how handsome he is.'

I looked at Jon. He raised an eyebrow and smiled. I was horrified to find myself beginning to blush.

Miriam rested her head sleepily on my shoulder and I gratefully turned my face towards her and away from Jon.

'Yes, Jon,' I said, prodding Miriam, aware that her breathing was slowing and beginning to sound an awful lot like snoring, 'I think you're very handsome.'

Miriam jolted upright, before shifting her chair and repositioning herself to lean against an uncomplaining Greg.

'Look at that,' I muttered, pointing at a patch of drool on the shoulder of my new dress.

'Never mind,' said Jon. 'You're still beau…ti…ful.'

I smiled and dabbed at the drool patch with my napkin. 'Thanks for no…ti…cing.'

'It's hard to miss.'

I turned towards him, with the intention of delivering a flippant response but, in the end, I decided to allow myself the pleasure of accepting his comment as a compliment.

'Thank you,' I said simply.

'You're welcome,' he replied, before standing up suddenly and pushing back his chair. 'Now, I'd better go and talk to Suzie about how she wants to get home.'

'Oh, right,' I nodded, slightly taken aback by the abruptness of his decision to leave. 'A nice night for a walk, maybe?'

'Maybe,' he said, bending down to kiss me on the cheek. 'How about you?'

'We're sharing a taxi.' I gestured towards Miriam, still semi-conscious against Greg. 'I think a walk is out of the question for us.'

He nodded and then, after a moment, sat back down.

I laughed. 'Are you not leaving after all, Mr Indecisive?'

'I was just about to ask the same thing.' I turned my head to find Suzanna standing behind me. She smiled, walked towards Jon and placed a hand on his shoulder.

He looked at me for a moment, before standing up again and turning towards her. 'I thought you were chatting to Romy,' he said.

'I was.' She looked up at him, still smiling. 'But I've finished now. And how about you?' she asked gently. 'Have you finished the conversation with Alice?'

He smiled at her but said nothing.

She sighed and then turned to me. 'Bye then, Alice,' she said. I thought she looked rather emotional and wondered how much she had had to drink. 'It's so lovely to have met you.'

I stood up and gave her a hug. 'I'll be seeing you next weekend for dinner, don't forget.'

She kissed my cheek and we separated. 'Right,' she said, taking a deep breath and turning to Jon, 'I think I'm ready to exit.'

He nodded and, after a general goodbye and wave to the room, he took her hand and accompanied her down the stairs.

Chapter 42

'Don't you dare dribble on me again,' I said to Miriam as I climbed into the taxi.

'I'll go in there on my own, if you want me too,' she said petulantly, gesturing towards the boot.

I shrugged. 'Could be quite cosy with a blanket.'

'I won't dribble, I promise.' She grinned and slid across the back seat towards me. Romy climbed in after her, while Hugh opened the front passenger door and took his seat next to the driver.

'What a perfectly lovely evening,' said Romy. 'I thoroughly enjoyed that.'

'Who did you sit next to?' I asked.

'Well,' she furrowed her brow in thought, 'I ended the evening between Suzanna and Pete. Before that I was between David and Miriam and I started the evening between Jon and,' she leaned forward and touched Hugh's arm, as he finished giving the driver instructions, 'of course, Hugh.'

He turned and offered her a smile which once again made me think how very attractive he would be if only he never actually spoke.

'Indeed,' he said. 'I very much enjoyed our conversation, Romy.'

'You kept me in absolute stitches, Hugh,' she laughed.

'Did he?' I asked.

'Did I?' echoed Hugh. He looked as doubtful of his comedic talent as I was, but was also clearly delighted. 'That's good to hear,' he said.

'Yes,' she said. 'And so interesting.' She turned to me excitedly. 'Hugh's description of how to peel the skin away from the skull was riveting.'

I shuddered involuntarily.

'Is everyone in the back buckled in, please?' asked the driver. And upon being answered by yes's from Romy and I, and one light snore from Miriam, he pulled away.

-

We arrived at my flat in just under ten minutes. By this time, Miriam was fast asleep and not only snoring loudly but also occasionally talking in her sleep. Her mumblings related largely to the food she had eaten that evening, with the odd reference to Craig's stupidity thrown in for good measure. Having each shared a home with her, neither Romy nor I were surprised by this behaviour but Hugh found it highly entertaining, and his amusement was contagious. Consequently, we were distracted and laughing loudly as I slid open the car door and began to bid them all goodnight.

None of us spotted the woman waiting at the top of the steps which led down to my flat, until she actually spoke.

'Alice Waites?' she said, advancing slowly towards me.

I started at the sound of her voice and all laughter inside the car immediately ceased. She stopped just a few feet from me, her features thrown unflatteringly into relief by the internal light of the car. She had dark brown, almost black, hair and was, I guessed, about my age. She was slim, bordering on thin, several inches shorter than myself and, in normal light, and different circumstances, I suspected she might have been attractive. However, her hair hung ragged onto her shoulders, escaping from what I could see had, at some point that day, been a business-like up-do, and her sharp cheekbones were stained with streaks of mascara. As she addressed me, she appeared perfectly calm. However, this air of serenity, juxtaposed with clear evidence of prolonged crying, served only to unnerve me further.

I was aware of the passenger door opening and of Hugh climbing out. 'Can we help you?' he asked her.

She didn't appear to hear him and stared unblinkingly at me. 'Alice Waites?' she repeated.

I nodded. 'Yes, I'm Alice,' I said. 'Is there a problem?'

'I'm Catherine.' She forced her mouth into a smile which didn't quite make it to her eyes. It had the same effect on me as Romy's reference to face-peeling. 'And yes, there is a problem,' she said, her smile widening to deranged proportions, 'because I'm Stephen's fiancée.'

And, with that, she covered her face with her hands and began to wail.

Chapter 43

Catherine came into the flat – and so did everyone else – the taxi having been sent away. Hugh had been adamant that he wouldn't leave me alone with her, and Romy and Miriam, when the latter woke up, also refused to leave. And so it was, as midnight approached, that the five of us sat in my living room drinking or, in the case of Catherine and myself, staring at mugs of tea prepared and distributed by Romy.

'I had guessed you didn't know,' said Catherine suddenly, looking up at me, her voice still wobbling from the latest bout of hysteria, in what I suspected had been a long day of crying.

I looked across at her from where I sat next to Romy on the sofa, but didn't speak.

'Clearly,' said Romy, 'this is a dreadful situation for both yourself and Alice, Catherine. But I wonder whether there's anything to be gained from talking about it at this time of night. Alice is very tired and you're clearly very...' she hesitated, 'upset.'

Catherine turned her head, transferring her attention unblinkingly from myself to Romy.

'Is there someone,' Romy continued, smiling kindly, 'a relative or friend, nearby we can call for you? How did you get here?'

'I drove,' said Catherine. 'I don't know anyone here.'

'Well, you can't drive home,' said Romy. 'So we can either pop you to a hotel...' She hesitated again as Catherine continued to stare at her, '...or we could call Craig and tell him to make up the spare room.' She turned to Miriam. 'What do you think, Mim?'

Miriam nodded slowly. 'We can't dump her at a hotel,' she said in a tipsy and, unfortunately, perfectly audible stage whisper. 'She's completely unhinged.' She pointed to the side of her head and made a circling motion with her index finger.

I looked with disinterest at Catherine. She was still focused on Romy and appeared not to have heard. I wondered if she even knew where she was.

'I'll call a taxi,' said Hugh, standing up and heading out into the hallway.

'I'm sorry,' said Catherine quietly.

Nobody spoke. Two people drank their tea.

It was Miriam who broke the silence. 'Are you OK, Alice?' she asked, punctuating the gentle enquiry with a hiccough. 'I'll stay with you and look after you. I don't want you to be on your own,' she said, her lower lip wobbling and her eyes now brimming. 'I'll take care of you.'

'I can stay, Mim,' said Romy gently. 'You need to help Hugh in the taxi and then help Craig sort things out at home.' She glanced at Catherine and then at me. 'Shall I stay, Alice?'

I stared into my mug of tea and Miriam answered for me. 'Yes, Romy, you stay.'

'Taxi will be five minutes,' said Hugh, re-entering the room and placing a roll of toilet paper next to Catherine.

Romy smiled up at him, as he sat back down in the armchair.

'How did you find me?' I looked at Catherine.

'I saw lots of long calls to one number on his bill.' She lowered her eyes and gazed at the carpet, her voice barely above a whisper. 'He'd been… different. I called the number.' She paused and looked up at me. 'I called you. Then I Googled the number and found your company website.' Her face suddenly crumpled and she began to cry again. 'I've never done anything like this before,' she said. 'You must all think I'm some crazed stalker.'

'That's right,' said Miriam, as if to herself, whilst nodding solemnly in supportive agreement. Romy extended a hand, placed it gently on her arm and shook her head.

'I thought he was here,' sobbed Catherine, still apparently oblivious to everything except herself and me. 'He said he was in France.'

'He is in France,' I said.

'He's just told me so many lies,' she said.

'Does he know you're here?' I asked.

She shook her head and dabbed her eyes with a piece of toilet paper, torn from the roll. 'But I left him a message saying I knew all about you.'

I got up and fetched my bag from the hallway. Returning to the living room, I took out my phone. Three texts and two missed phone calls. I put the phone back into my bag and leaned back on the sofa.

'Has he called?' she asked.

I nodded.

'Right, Catherine,' said Hugh, 'let's get you to Miriam's house. We can wait for the taxi outside and if you give me your phone, Miriam, I can call Craig in order that he may prepare himself.' He stood up, an action which everyone, with the exception of myself, copied.

There followed a flurry of departure, during which I was hugged and kissed and Hugh did a final, thoughtful check of the living room and hallway, *in case anyone had left any personal belongings or items of outerwear*. And then, very suddenly it seemed, the flat was empty, save for Romy and myself.

She came and sat next to me. 'Do you want to talk about it?' she asked after a moment.

I shook my head. 'Not tonight.'

'OK,' she said. 'I'm just so sorry, Alice.'

I looked at her. 'Unless she's a lunatic, there's only one person who should be sorry.' My bag, lying in my lap, began to vibrate. 'And I suspect that's him calling right now,' I said, reaching down to extract my phone. I looked at the screen. 'Yes, it's him.'

'Do you want to take the call?' asked Romy.

I nodded and pressed *accept*. She squeezed my free hand and then left the living room, closing the door behind her.

I put the phone to my ear. Stephen was already talking, enquiring after my evening.

'I've just met Catherine,' I interrupted.

There was a lengthy silence before he spoke. 'I can explain.'

'She claims to be your fiancée,'

'Let me explain to you what I—'

'Is she your fiancée, Stephen?' I asked.

'My relationship with her is over,' he said.

'Does she know that?'

'We haven't yet had that conversation. But—'

'So, she's currently your fiancée then.'

'I can explain everything.'

'Explain it tomorrow,' I said. And with that, I ended the call, put my phone back in my bag and went to fetch some towels and a pair of pyjamas for Romy.

Chapter 44

I woke the next morning at nine, to find Romy already up and dressed and breakfast laid in the kitchen. She stayed just long enough to assure herself that I was of sound mind and to run through with me my plans for the day. Miriam had called her an hour earlier, telling her that Catherine had already headed back to Solihull and insisting that Romy bring me home with her. But I declined the offer, assuring Romy that I would certainly call Miriam, and may even pop round later, but that I first needed to talk to both Stephen and Catherine. Romy accepted this without argument and, after helping me to clear away the breakfast things, she left me alone to shower, dress and, for the first time since Catherine's dramatic arrival, to think.

At ten o'clock, I went outside into the sunshine of the garden, carrying a mug of coffee and my phone. Sitting down at my small patio table, I tried to organise my thoughts and excavate some feelings; for at that moment, I felt nothing. The numbness which had descended the previous evening had not yet lifted, and whilst the basic facts were not pleasant: Stephen had betrayed his partner with me – I was his bit on the side – I felt no anger, no bitterness, no sadness. All I could drum up was a feeling of extreme weariness and a contorted, but undeniable, sense of déjà vu. Perhaps, I thought, this was my lot in life; forever destined to be either single, or unwittingly part of a threesome.

I picked up the coffee and sighed. Today, I knew, was going to be one of difficult conversations. Apart from the two most obvious calls, I would also have to think of something reassuring to say to Miriam – and sooner rather than later, not least to stop her picking up the phone to Dad. And I would, of course, have to talk to him too, because I knew that if he thought I had hidden anything from him, it would cause him far more upset than if I simply told him the truth from the outset.

But first, however distasteful and potentially distressing the prospect, I had to discuss the events of last night with my fellow protagonists. I couldn't imagine that either of them would have anything to say which might change my bit-on-the-side perspective but, nevertheless, it had to be done. I put down my coffee, picked up my phone and after a moment's hesitation upon seeing half a dozen missed calls from Stephen, I dialled Catherine's number, with which I had been supplied by Miriam, via Romy.

-

My conversation with Catherine took just ten minutes, with her sobbing throughout and me maintaining my involuntary, ice-maiden cool. She and Stephen, she told me, had been together for two years and engaged for six months. They had shared a home, her home, for just over a year because he had actually sold his flat some time ago. She had been told that the move to Bristol was a temporary one of three to four months, but on Friday evening she had found a bundle of estate agent brochures and scribbled viewing times in a clothes drawer, which made it clear that he was looking to buy. And whilst she had no actual proof that he was having an affair, there had been a suspicious number of late meetings and, of course, all those calls to my number. The brochures, coupled with his refusal to answer her calls, had pushed her over the edge and she had climbed into her car and driven to Bristol.

She asked me only one question; whether I loved him. I told her that I didn't and then, with a sense of foreboding for her, as she seemed to brighten on hearing that, I just wanted the call to be over. When it was, I retreated into the kitchen, made myself a second cup of coffee and, with total sangfroid, sat down and called Stephen.

He answered within half a ring. Quite a contrast, I mused, to the days when he could never answer a call, presumably because his wife-to-be, or rather not-to-be, was hovering.

'Hello, Alice,' he said, sounding as calm as I felt. 'It's so good to hear from you.'

'Hello,' I replied. 'I'm calling to let you explain your behaviour.'

'Great,' he said. And then, after first confirming that he and Catherine had been a couple for two years, he began his explanation, whilst I listened patiently and with detached interest.

'It was always my intention to end my relationship with Catherine as organically and painlessly as possible,' he said, his tone that of a kindly teacher, eager to convey information clearly and concisely to a promising student. 'And I knew that the physical separation of relocation would provide me with the perfect opportunity to do this, smoòthing the transition and underlining the finality of the situation for her.' He paused. 'But then I met you and my additional, in fact my *main* focus,' he said gently, 'became to protect you from a situation you had nothing to do with, and over which you had no control. My relationship with Catherine was no longer emotionally relevant to me,' he continued, 'and it had *never* had any relevance to you. And much as I would have liked to share the situation with you, to offload, it would have been selfish of me to burden you with it. And so I kept it from you.'

'Right,' I said, my ongoing emotional coma freeing me from any urge to point out the more obvious reason for not telling me about Catherine – namely that I would have told him to get lost had I known that he was already engaged to someone else.

'My only regret,' he sighed, 'is the unforeseen situation which arose on Friday evening.'

'Yes,' I said, assuming that he was referring to his unforeseen unmasking as a complete bastard and the unforeseen arrival of his temporarily deranged fiancée on my doorstep at midnight.

'But I hope you can see,' he continued, 'that I did my best to protect you. And I hope you can also see just how important you are to me. We have so much potential and we mustn't let this spoil things. I know Friday was a shock. And I hate the thought of you being upset by that. But I also know that we have to see beyond Friday to the future we can have together. I still want that future,' he concluded quietly, 'more than anything.'

'I don't,' I said. 'So please don't try to contact me again.' And then I hung up the phone, blocked all further calls from his number, stretched myself out horizontally on the sofa and took to studying the ceiling.

I then lost all track of time, because when I checked my watch at the sound of the doorbell it was well after midday. I sighed, wondering if it was Miriam, worried about my failure to call and impatient to check on my welfare. I hauled myself to my feet and trudged down the hallway, opening the front door just in time to see my visitor reach the top of the stone steps which led up to ground level. He, for it was a man, turned, offered me a smile more anxious than any I had ever seen and then made his way back down the steps towards me.

'I was just dropping those off for you,' he said, gesturing towards a large bouquet, lying to the left of the front door. 'I thought you must be out or...' He hesitated. '...or resting.'

'Thank you,' I said, stooping down to retrieve the flowers. 'That's very kind but you didn't have to do that.'

'Oh,' he said, scratching his ear and studying his feet, 'I think I did, you know. I feel a right idiot. I *am* a right idiot. And it's led to you getting hurt.' He looked up. 'I'm so sorry, Alice.'

I shook my head. 'Don't worry about it, Greg,' I said. 'I'm absolutely fine.'

And then I started to cry.

Chapter 45

'Here you go,' said Greg, handing me a mug. 'I hope I've used the right teabags. You've got quite a collection in there.' He smiled and sat down in the armchair opposite me.

'Thank you, I'm sure it's lovely,' I said, resting the mug carefully on the arm of the sofa, to enable me to blow my nose. 'I'm so sorry for crying, Greg. I'm really embarrassed.'

'Nonsense.' He shifted in his seat. 'It's me who should be embarrassed. And I am embarrassed, actually. Very.'

I picked up my tea. 'None of this is your fault.'

He looked doubtful. 'Well, I'm afraid Connie doesn't agree with you on that. And, much as I'd like to, I can't agree with you either. I should have taken more care over who I put you in touch with. I should have vetted him more thoroughly.' He sipped his tea. 'You see, I didn't know him *that* well, did I? I mean we had a professional relationship. But I didn't know him *personally* – on a personal level – that's what I mean. Connie's ever so cross with me, you know.'

This latter statement gave him the air of an eight year-old schoolboy, caught doing something unintentionally naughty. He looked thoroughly miserable and I felt immediately sorry for him.

'Well, I don't hold you at all responsible,' I said. 'I didn't expect anyone to run background checks.'

He smiled sadly. 'That's very kind of you,' he said. 'But he had mentioned a girlfriend in the past. The thing is, when he said he was moving to the area and didn't mention anyone else, I just assumed they'd split up. And so I never mentioned a girlfriend to Connie.' He stared forlornly at his tea. 'And then when she said how desperate you were to meet men… well…'

I didn't say anything, finding myself more troubled by Greg's turn of phrase regarding my desperation for male company, than his failure to check out Stephen's backstory.

'But, of course, they hadn't split up, had they? They were engaged,' he continued more anxiously, unsettled, I guessed, by my lack of response. 'Dear God. Engaged,' he said quietly.

'You weren't to know that,' I said. 'I would have made the same assumption as you. You'd expect someone to mention something like that. And you were just trying to help,' I added.

He looked up at me and seemed momentarily relieved. 'Thank you,' he said. 'But Connie is furious with me.' His face fell once again. 'Absolutely livid.'

I struggled to form a mental image of Connie being livid. But even trying to picture her mildly ticked-off was a stretch; livid was impossible. 'I'm more than happy to talk to her, Greg. If that would help.'

He held up a hand. 'You've got quite enough on your plate without me adding bother,' he said. 'Although, I know Connie would love to talk to you at some point, when you're feeling up to it. She's a worrier about people at the best of times but she was beside herself about you this morning when Miriam phoned.' He heaved a sigh and when he spoke, his voice cracked slightly. 'We both were, if truth be known.'

I felt tears begin to sting my eyes again and I swallowed hard. 'I'm actually feeling fine, you know,' I said. 'I mean,' a tear escaped and Greg's face fell another inch, '*obviously* I'm not *totally* fine or I wouldn't be sitting here sobbing into my tea. But I'm fine about him. It was very early days and I wasn't head over heels or anything...'

'I can sense a "but" coming,' said Greg gently.

'But,' I put a hand to my forehead, 'I'm just so embarrassed, Greg. It was all so public and I hate the thought of everyone worrying about me and feeling sorry for me. Plus, you know, it just makes me feel a bit...' I shrugged, 'unappealing. I think that's the best word for it. I feel like I don't hold sufficient appeal.'

'Now, hold on moment,' he said, leaning forward in his chair. 'You're not being logical there, Alice. Let's back up and think about what you just said, because I think you'll find you're being entirely contradictory.' He placed his mug on the small table to his left and folded his arms. We were suddenly, I felt, at a board meeting. 'So, to sum up: on the one hand you're saying you feel unappealing; whilst on the other, you are acknowledging that there are an awful lot of people concerned about you. Is that right?'

It felt like some sort of kindly trap. 'Well, yes,' I said warily.

'Well, people aren't generally concerned about unappealing people, are they?'

'I suppose not,' I conceded.

'*Absolutely* not,' he said, making a fist with his right hand and slapping it against his left palm. 'People don't get upset about unappealing people over breakfast and then come round with bunches of flowers for them, do they?'

I shook my head.

'And they don't phone each other anxiously all morning to see if anyone has heard from an unappealing person, do they? Well, not unless they're parole officers of course.'

'I guess not.' I smiled and he broke into a grin.

'That's better,' he said. 'And, Alice, I would just like to add one thing.' There was a pause whilst he cleared his throat and then looked around the room, as if for inspiration. 'I don't know what my opinion is worth anymore,' he said eventually, 'or whether it has ever been worth anything, but on the occasions Stephen mentioned you, I felt he was smitten.'

I tutted but smiled again. 'Oh, Greg.'

'I mean that,' he insisted. 'I came home and said so to Connie at the time. You can ask her if you don't believe me. Of course, I know it's of little or no comfort to you at the moment. The idiot bastard, pardon my French, went about everything in completely the wrong way, and I shall certainly tell him that, possibly with my fist, when I get the chance. But,' he unfolded his arms and reached for his tea, 'I'm pretty confident that he's feeling worse about this than you are.' He saluted me with his mug. 'And I can't say I'm unhappy about that.'

There was a pause, whilst we finished our tea.

'Thank you, Greg,' I said at last. 'You've made me feel better.'

'Have I?' he said. 'Have I really?' He looked both surprised and delighted. 'Well, perhaps there's hope for me yet.'

'Hope for us both, maybe,' I said, rising to my feet. 'Now, would you like a top-up of your tea? Or are you anxious to get home?' I asked.

His mouth stretched to a worried grimace. 'If you don't mind, Alice,' he said, 'I'll just send Connie a quick text telling her that you're OK and then I would love another cuppa. You know, just to give her a chance to, er, cheer up.'

'Very wise,' I said. 'Pass me your mug.'

He stretched back into the armchair and, for the first time since arriving he looked relaxed. 'Thank you,' he said holding his mug out towards me and smiling. 'Hey and I tell you what.'

'What?' I asked.

He winked at me and grinned. 'I'd absolutely kill for a biscuit.'

–

As Greg rose to leave after his second cup of tea, we were both, I felt, in a much better state than on his arrival. Connie had replied positively to his reassuring text and I had told her, via him, that I would call her for a chat later in the day.

'I've got an awful lot of phone calls to make,' I sighed, as I opened the front door for him.

'Well, don't you worry about the one to Connie,' he said. 'She'll be happy with my assurances. You just call her when you come up for air. I'll explain.'

'OK,' I smiled, hugging him goodbye. 'And thanks for coming, Greg. You really have cheered me up.'

He smiled, appearing simultaneously proud and bashful. 'I have to say, I didn't think I was going to, but I've enjoyed my visit,' he said. 'It's a sad business but I can tell you it's given me a few things to think about.'

'Really?'

'Hmm...' he said, looking down. 'I'm going to work on a bit more of this...' He tugged at his ears. 'And a lot less of this...' He tapped his mouth. 'Especially where my wife is concerned,' he said. 'She talks a lot of sense and I don't always take heed as I might.'

I smiled. 'I often let my mouth run away with me,' I said. 'So we could work on that together.'

He turned to walk up the steps. 'You're lovely the way you are,' he said. 'And don't you forget it.'

He offered me one last wave and then he was gone. I closed the front door and leaned against the hall wall for a moment. I had been telling the truth when I said that Greg had made me feel better. However, I remained somewhat daunted by the prospect of the various phone calls which still lay ahead. Connie's I could perhaps delay, Hugh, I knew, would prefer a text, but Miriam had already left a voicemail to say she was looking forward to hearing from me and, of course, I had to phone Dad. He, I decided, was the priority. I had heard nothing from Abs, Sophie or Jon which, I supposed, meant that bad news didn't always travel fast. I was pleased about this and had no urge to bring any of them up to speed. I had enough people to reassure as it was; everybody else could simply find out as and when.

I went into the kitchen, fetched myself some cheese, crackers and salad – primarily because I knew I should eat, rather than because I had an appetite – and then, after a deep breath, I picked up the phone. It rang three times before he picked up.

'Hello?'

'Hello, Dad, it's Alice,' I said.

'Oh darling, whatever's wrong?' he asked.

'Actually,' I began, feeling the tears begin to well, 'I think something has been put right.' And then, in between sobs, I told him the tale.

Chapter 46

With breaks for coffee, *Jane Eyre* and a long afternoon stroll, I hung up on what I hoped was my last phone call of the day at just after 6pm. I was, I decided, all talked-out – in a good way, but talked-out nevertheless. Feeling emotionally and physically exhausted, I poured myself a glass of wine and ran a bath, with the intention of perhaps watching a movie and being in bed by nine. It was with a weary sigh then that, just as I turned off the taps, I heard my phone ring and saw Sophie's name appear on the screen. Much as I wanted to ignore the call, I knew I couldn't. I pressed 'accept' and began my reassurances even before she had said hello.

'Before you say anything – I'm fine,' I said. 'Yes, he's a bastard, or something worse according to Miriam, but I'm fine.'

'Who's a bastard?' asked Sophie, sounding bemused. 'What are you talking about?'

'Stephen,' I said. 'I'm talking about Stephen.'

'Why is he a bastard? What's happened?'

'Oh, I thought that's why you'd phoned.'

'You thought what was why I'd phoned?' She was starting to sound tense. 'Start from the beginning and tell me what's happened.'

I explained events, with no interruption from her, save for the odd gasp and, of course, four-letter word.

'And anyway,' I concluded. 'I'm blocking his calls and won't be having anything more to do with him. The end.'

There was silence for a moment. 'Jesus, Alice,' she said eventually. 'I'm sorry.'

I sighed. 'Absolutely everybody is sorry – except him.'

'No apology?'

'No,' I said.

'Bastard.'

'He doesn't think he's done anything wrong,' I explained. 'He thinks he's been protecting everybody from the situation and themselves. Like some weird psychiatrist, superhero hybrid.'

'Captain Crazy-Crap,' said Sophie.

'Exactly,' I agreed.

'And how are you?' she asked quietly. 'Honestly.'

'I'm honestly OK,' I said. 'This isn't an Eddie situation. In fact, I'm totally the other side of the fence. I'm Pip. Oh, God, I'm Pip.' I groaned at the thought.

'You're not Pip,' she protested. 'You were clueless. She wasn't clueless.'

'I was clueless,' I repeated. 'Now, why doesn't make that feel any better?'

She laughed. 'Sorry,' she said. 'Poor choice of words. But you know what I mean.'

'Yes, I do.'

'Are you sorted for the rest of the weekend?' she asked. 'What are you up to? Do you fancy getting together?'

'Well, I've been on the phone for most of the day…'

'Sorry.'

'No, no, I'm not complaining,' I said. 'It's all been very helpful, very cathartic, but I'm done-in. I've just run a bath and then I'm going to watch a movie and go to bed.'

'Sounds good,' she said. 'And what about tomorrow?'

'Off to Dad's for lunch.'

'That'll be nice. Well,' I heard a sigh, 'I'll let you get on with your bath. We can catch up properly on Monday. Perhaps a drink after work?'

'I've just arranged one with Miriam. The three of us can go.'

'Hmm…' There was a pause. 'I'll think about it but maybe I'll drag you out another evening.'

She sounded a little flat. 'Are you OK?' I asked.

She laughed. 'Am *I* OK? God, you're priceless. Yes, I'm fine.'

'So, what were you calling about?'

Another pause. 'Oh… no… nothing. You've got enough going on.'

'What do you mean?' I asked. 'What's the matter?'

'Nothing at all,' she said. 'I just meant you've got enough going on without me spouting trivia. I was just phoning for a general chat. Go and get in your bath before it goes cold. I'll see you on Monday.'

'And there's nothing wrong?'

'For God's sake, Alice, no.' She laughed again.

'OK,' I said, though still unconvinced. 'Your sister isn't causing problems for you?' I added, guessing at possible reasons for her weary tone.

'Alice…'

'Sorry.'

'And no, she's fine. Everything is fine.'

'And Friday was fun, wasn't it?' I said. 'Or at least the first half,' I added ruefully.

'It was a lovely evening,' she said. 'One of the best.'

I smiled. 'I'll have to tell you about some of my conversations.'

'Yes, you will. But tell me on Monday,' she replied. 'When you've had a bath.'

'OK. Bye then.'

'Bye, Alice. Lots of love,' she said and then hung up.

'Lots of love,' I said into the silent phone and then headed for the bathroom, certain that Sophie was keeping something from me and not entirely looking forward to finding out what that was.

Chapter 47

Sunday with Dad proved the perfect antidote to the trauma of Friday and the emotional wringing-out of Saturday. He focused on all the right things; immediately expressing relief at the fact that Stephen's bad character, as he put it, had been revealed sooner rather than later, and saying how sorry he felt for Catherine, who had invested so much more time in a relationship with him than I had. Other than that, he told me, in an unrelated fashion, how wonderful, beautiful, intelligent, kind-hearted and popular I was and, of course, how much he loved me. After a long lunch, he took me for a walk and, wisely letting the matter of Stephen drop, distracted me with an account of his most recent baking tutorials with Hilary. These, along with all other things Hilary-related were, it seemed, going very well indeed, and I was relieved that my *hiccough* with Stephen, as he put it, didn't seem to put too big a dent in his obvious happiness. He appeared to accept fully my assurances that I was coping with the situation and his overwhelming response seemed to be one of relief that I had escaped a dreadful situation before greater damage was done.

My weekend therefore passed off remarkably well in the circumstances, and by the time I opened the street door of Moore Interior Design on Monday morning, I had to admit that there was a significant part of me already sharing Dad's sense of relief at the passing of Stephen Powell and this helped to mute the ongoing twinges of a heavily dented ego.

I closed the street door behind me, glanced at the busy shapes visible through the frosted glass door of Lewis Twinney Legal, and started to climb the stairs. The door into our offices was ajar but as I entered, I was greeted only by silence. I walked across to my desk, registering that the door to David's office was closed. Sophie was nowhere to be seen and I at first assumed that she had gone for coffee, before spotting her bag on the armchair next to her desk. I looked back towards David's office but, short of standing in front of it and peering through the small circle of glass near the top of his door, I couldn't see who, if anyone, was in there. I assumed he at least must be, as he habitually left his door open whenever he wandered off.

I put down my bag, hung up my jacket and sat down. Maybe Sophie had gone to the loo, I thought. I remained still for a few moments, listening for the sound of a flush, before tutting at myself and turning on the Mac.

A few minutes of staring unseeingly at my screen later and curiosity got the better of me. I walked over to David's office, raised myself onto tip-toe and peered through the glass porthole.

They were both in there; David sitting behind his desk, his face expressionless, looking at Sophie who was sitting opposite him, with her back to me. Neither was speaking.

I stood for a moment, transfixed by the rather odd scene and then returned to my desk and sat down. I couldn't imagine what was going on. David's response to any work crises was invariably to encourage, support and resolve; silent reproach was not his *modus operandi.* So I could assume only that the problem was a personal one.

Motivated by a mixture of curiosity and concern, I was just considering knocking and entering when the door opened and Sophie emerged, closing the door gently behind her.

She said nothing, offering me only a brief and exceptionally weary smile, before sitting down at her desk.

I opened my mouth to ask the obvious question but was distracted from doing so by David's door opening once again and the man himself walking out into the main office.

'Hello, Alice,' he said, in a tone which reminded me of his authoritative exchange with Eleanor Black on the night of her party. 'I'll be back at eleven.'

'But—'

'If Henry calls, please tell him that I've sourced the slate and delivery will be this week.'

And with that, he was gone.

I stared after him, my mouth hanging ajar, still desperate for an opportunity to interrogate.

'I've resigned.'

I turned towards Sophie. She was sitting, staring at the half-open door to David's office. 'What?'

Rather than turn her head, she swivelled in her chair to face me, her upper body remaining still and automaton-like. 'I've resigned,' she repeated.

'Why on earth have you done that?' I was appalled.

'Lots of reasons,' she said tonelessly.

'Have you got another job?'

She shook her head.

'Then why resign? Are you unhappy here? Have we done something wrong?'

She closed her eyes and slumped forward, resting her elbows on the desk in front of her and cradling her head in her hands; suddenly human again.

'I love it here,' she said. 'I love you and David. I love working with you both. I just need a change.'

'But why do you need a change if you're so happy?' I exclaimed. 'I don't understand. It doesn't make sense. Explain it to me.'

'I can't, Alice,' she said quietly. 'Not yet.' She looked up at me, clearly now on the verge of tears. She plucked a tissue from the box on her desk and blew her nose.

'I just don't understand,' I repeated quietly.

'I keep telling myself, it's not like I won't still see you,' she said. 'There's still book group. And I'm planning to stay in Bristol.'

I nodded, completely at a loss and feeling the benefits of Dad's moral boosting efforts slowly sliding away. 'When?' I asked. It was all I could manage.

She dropped a crumpled tissue into the bin under her desk and took another from the box. 'I'm going to work a month's notice,' she said, now dabbing at her eyes.

'I'm sure you'll have found something else by then,' I said, seeking refuge from bewildered misery in a platitude.

She nodded. 'I'm sure I will.'

There was silence for a moment before she spoke again. 'I was going to tell you on Saturday,' she said. 'But…' Her voice trailed away.

'I wish you had,' I said. 'I would have talked you out of it.'

She looked at me sadly and shook her head. 'I've been going round in circles up here for ages.' She put a finger to the side of her head. 'You're not cross with me, are you, Alice? You know how much I love you.'

I looked at her and, whilst completely unable to fathom her motives, and feeling undeniably stung by her decision, I had no wish to make anything more difficult for her than it clearly already was. I sighed. 'Actually, I'm taking it *very* badly and *utterly* personally,' I said.

She smiled. 'Thank you,' she said. 'I knew you would.'

I attempted to return the smile. 'Why don't you come out with Miriam and me tonight?' I asked.

'That's really kind but I think I'll pass,' she said. 'Another evening would be good, though. Any other evening actually. My calendar is that booked up.'

'Mine too,' I said. 'The weekends are looking pretty empty. And don't even get me started on summer.' I rolled my eyes.

'Oh, I wouldn't worry,' she said, still teary but feigning brisk and turning towards her screen. 'I'm sure book group will have you hooked-up with another hunk before the summer is out.' She looked over her shoulder at me. 'Too soon for jokes?' she asked.

'Not at all,' I said, standing up and reaching for my bag. 'I'm just disappointed it was a joke. I'd hoped you'd be lining them up for next week. Now,' I said walking towards the door, 'latte or Americano?'

'Espresso, please,' she said. 'Triple. It's that kind of day.'

'It certainly is,' I said and headed off down the stairs, now fully-focused upon the sanctuary and sanity of a strong cup of coffee.

Chapter 48

'Crikey', said Miriam, clearly drained of expletives by the events of the weekend. 'And Sophie won't say why she's resigning?'

I shook my head. 'And she's so upset about it, I can't press her.'

Miriam inhaled deeply and then exhaled an enormous sigh. 'Gosh. It's all gone a bit oo-er since Friday, hasn't it?'

'To put it mildly.' I picked up my wine glass and relaxed back into the cushioned window seat; we had managed to secure The Cambridge's cosiest alcove, with most other pub-goers this evening opting for the late sunshine of the beer garden.

'And how long is her notice?' asked Miriam.

'A month.'

'Golly. And how is David taking it?'

'His reaction can best be described as variable.'

She looked surprised. 'I would have thought he'd be devastated.'

'There have been distinct phases,' I said. 'He looked like he'd been hit by a truck when they were in his office. Then he was all masterful immediately afterwards.'

'Masterful?' queried Miriam. 'David?'

'Oh, he can do it, you know,' I said, nodding. 'It doesn't happen very often – in fact I've only seen it once before – but he can do it.'

'I wouldn't mind seeing that. I've often thought he would be extremely attractive, minus the trust fund dither.'

I laughed. 'And you a married woman.'

She sighed. 'So, is he still being masterful about it?'

I shook my head. 'By the time he got back mid-morning, he was bordering on chipper.'

'Chipper?'

'Yes. But when I left to come here he seemed to be back in shock.'

'Blimey.'

'He's a one-man lexicon of emotion at the moment.'

'And Sophie?' Miriam was eager for detail.

'Well, she's just morose beyond belief. It's like working with Eeyore on a particularly down day.' I drank my wine. 'I just hope she hasn't stopped to buy a fake fag on the way home. She hasn't had a puff on one for weeks.' I looked at Miriam and sighed. 'You know, if someone had told me yesterday, that I'd be the most consistently cheerful person in the office today, I'd have thought they were insane.'

She laughed. 'And talking of insane,' she said, 'how are you? You look amazing. I expected to be greeted by a gibbering wreck. I know I would have been.' She took a handful of peanuts from the bag open between us on the table. 'Or are you still in shock?'

I thought about it. 'Well, Dad has been drumming it into me that I've had a lucky escape and that I should be thankful for that. And he's right. So that's where my focus is.'

'Very wise.'

'Plus,' I said, joining Miriam in her assault on the peanuts, 'there's something else that until this afternoon I hadn't quite admitted to myself, or to anyone else.'

'Ooh, what?' She leaned forward, her inner teenage surfacing, eager for secrets.

'Well, when we went to Eleanor's party and there was that business with her and the waiter...'

'Yes?'

'When we got outside, David said something like...' I dredged my memory. 'He said, "That's me off the hook."'

'And you feel you're off the hook with Stephen?'

I nodded. 'I don't really understand it, but,' I leaned back in my seat, 'today, I felt relieved that it was over, and not just because of Catherine.'

She eyed me intently. 'That's interesting.'

'It is,' I agreed. 'Because I liked him, I enjoyed his company, I was looking forward to seeing him.' I took the final peanut, which she had politely left for me. 'But something wasn't right.'

'It certainly wasn't. The rotter.'

I laughed. 'The *rotter*?'

She smiled sheepishly. 'Craig told me off for swearing in front of Phoebe on Saturday and now I'm trying not to swear at all – otherwise they just keep popping out.'

'Oops,' I pulled a face. 'Was that while you were on the phone to me?'

She nodded. 'I didn't know she was standing there but apparently she wandered off and asked Craig what a wanker was.'

I put my hand to my mouth and laughed. 'No!'

'Isn't that awful? But he was very quick thinking. Told her it was *winker* and that it was someone who can wink really quickly with both eyes.'

'Isn't that just blinking?'

'You know what I mean.'

I grinned. 'Genius save on his part.'

'Yes, apart from the fact that she now keeps telling everyone Craig is a winker.' She sighed and picked up her drink. 'A woman in the park asked me if she was Australian.'

'Oh dear,' I said absently, my mind now on Craig. 'So how is he? Craig, I mean.'

She shot me a suspicious look over the top of her wine glass. 'He's fine,' she said, somewhat defensively, and then, putting down her drink and softening her tone. '*We're* fine.'

'Are you?'

She looked at me. 'I didn't say perfect. But he came home one evening and said he thought we should talk and so...'

'So?'

'And so we did.'

'And?'

'And now,' she took a deep breath, 'we're still talking and we'll see how we go.'

'I'm pleased,' I said.

She smiled. 'So am I.'

She sipped her drink and when she spoke again, it was to introduce a new topic of conversation.

'Do you know what you're doing for summer yet?' she asked.

I groaned. 'Well, I had been planning to go away with Stephen.'

She looked at me guiltily. 'Sorry.'

I shook my head. 'It's OK. I have an open invitation to go with Jane Crane to a villa in Spain.'

'Which would be poetic, if nothing else,' said Miriam.

'True,' I nodded. 'But other than that – nothing planned.' I laughed humourlessly. 'And I mean *really* nothing. Even my weekends are now social deserts. I was supposed to be having dinner with Suzanna—'

'Oh my goodness! Sh, sh, *shhhhhh*,' Miriam interrupted, flapping a hand and quickly swallowing a large mouthful of wine. 'Friday!' She placed her glass hurriedly on the table. 'We haven't talked about Friday.'

'Well, not—'

'Did you know that Jon and Suzie are just good friends?'

The question hit me as if fired from a crossbow. I looked at her, opened my mouth to speak, realised I had nothing intelligent to say and so closed it again.

'Did you?' pressed Miriam excitedly.

I remained mute and simply shook my head.

'Me neither!' she exclaimed, before adding, as if to herself, 'And if you didn't know, I don't think anyone can have known.'

She looked up at me questioningly and I responded with a simultaneous nod of the head and shrug, which I hoped pretty much covered the situation.

'Anyway, with all the horrid things happening on Friday night,' Miriam continued rapidly, 'I completely forgot about it. Well,' she said, prodding me with a forefinger, 'aren't you going to say anything? Don't you think that's interesting?'

I nodded again.

There was silence for a moment and then Miriam gasped. 'Oh, I'm so sorry,' she said, now reaching out and gently rubbing my upper arm instead of prodding it. 'I expect the last thing you want to gossip about is relationships.'

I took a large gulp of wine, followed by a deep breath.

'No, no,' I said. 'I'm just thinking it through. It's very interesting.'

'I know!' Miriam's eyes widened, her excitement returning. The effects of a single glass of wine were already beginning to tell and she clapped her hands in the manner of a sea lion at the zoo.

I took another deep breath and then threw her a fish. 'Tell me more,' I said. 'When did he tell you this?'

She finished the small amount of wine remaining in her glass and shook her head. 'Jon didn't tell me, Suzie did – almost as soon as we arrived at Primrose.'

'I see.' I recalled Miriam's animated conversation with Suzanna and her increasing maternal warmth towards her, now reflected in the use of the shortened version of her name.

'They were in a relationship only for a short while and then…'

I frowned, smiled and nodded as felt appropriate while Miriam chattered on, but I wasn't really listening. I knew at some point I would have to ask her to repeat everything, but at that moment, I was content to focus on the simple fact of Jon's newly-discovered single status. That was as much as I felt able to absorb for now.

'…had a long and difficult conversation after *Oliver!* but she said she understood completely and…'

Miriam's words continued to wash over me.

'…to give him space and stay friends.'

She adjusted the position of a large cushion to her left and leaned back, which I recognised as a signal that she had finished.

'Interesting,' I said.

She nodded. 'But do you think I'm right?'

'Hmm…' I put my hand to my mouth and attempted a contemplative look. 'It's actually a very complex situation, isn't it?'

She eyed me coldly. 'You haven't listened to a single word I've said, have you?'

I smiled sheepishly. 'Don't get tetchy with me, Miriam,' I said. 'I listened to an awful lot of your words. I was just a little taken aback by the news.'

This was obviously the right thing to say. She leaned forward and grasped my left hand, which was resting on the table. 'I know,' she said. 'It was the most interesting, unexpected revelation I'd heard in ages,' she said. 'Until we got to your flat, of course.'

I sighed. 'God, what a night.'

'What a night indeed. Now,' she said briskly, bum-shuffling along the bench and then rising to her feet, 'I'm just going to pop and get us each another drink, and then, when I get back, I'll go over it all again.' She began to make her way to the bar but stopped and turned after just a few feet. 'Oh but this time,' she said, jabbing her purse in my direction, 'you just bloody listen.' She shook her head and tutted. 'Bugger. I meant *blooming* listen,' she corrected. 'You just *blooming* listen.'

Chapter 49

It was with some trepidation that I climbed the stairs to Moore Interior Design the next morning. My ascent took place in silence, exactly as it had the day before; however, just as I braced myself for an icy atmosphere, the morose peace was shattered by a cackle of explosive laughter. I pushed open the door, which was already slightly ajar, and although I was a little disappointed to discover that Sophie's entertaining exchange was not with David but with someone on the other end of the phone, it was still good to see her smiling.

She waved as I approach, mouthing 'Henry,' and pointing to the receiver, as I hung up my jacket.

I nodded and then pointed at David's office, the door to which was slightly ajar. She shook her head and mouthed 'out', before continuing her conversation.

'Yes, that's right,' she said into the receiver. 'Either Thursday or Friday, so just pick whichever suits.'

I pulled the pile of mail on my desk towards me.

'That's great, Henry.' There was a pause and then. 'Yes. It will be me there next week.' Another pause. 'You charmer… OK, I'll see you then… Bye.' She hung up the phone and turned to me. 'Hello,' she said. 'That was Henry.'

I gave her my best knowing look. 'Evidently.'

'Hey, you, don't go getting any ideas.' She wagged a finger at me. 'Purely platonic.'

'Well,' I said significantly, 'there's a lot of it about.'

She looked up from the plans she had just called-up on screen. 'What?' she asked, her eyes narrowing. 'You've got gossip, Alice Waites. Come on. Spit it out. Is this via Miriam last night?'

I nodded.

'Ooh,' she said. 'Is it armchair quality?'

'If Miriam were here, she would say yes.'

She rose to her feet and solemnly walked the few steps to the armchair next to her desk. After theatrically plumping the cushions, she sat down, crossed her legs and folded her arms. 'I am ready,' she said. 'Begin.'

'Well,' I leaned forward across my desk, 'Suzanna told Miriam on Friday that she and Jon are no longer going out together,' I said, attempting to keep my tone light.

Sophie's smile vanished immediately. 'It's all OK,' I reassured. 'Suzanna is fine about it. They've just agreed to be friends and see what happens.'

'And what does Jon say about it?' Sophie asked, sounding unexpectedly serious.

I frowned at the question. 'I don't know. He hasn't mentioned any of this to me and Miriam has been very restrained and made no attempt to fish.' Sophie made no response but instead sat staring at the floor.

'There's nothing to worry about,' I said. 'You saw them on Friday; they get along really well. It's not sad – just interesting or, if you're Miriam, wildly exciting.'

'I'm not worried, I'm just thinking,' she murmured.

'Personally, I wouldn't be surprised if they get back together. I mean, it's obvious Jon cares a lot about her, isn't it?' I continued, sharing the conclusion I had reached in the hour or so between saying goodnight to Miriam and climbing into bed. 'He's pulled back from a relationship – not out of it. Anyway,' I sighed, tapping the pile of mail in front of me, 'better go through this lot.'

'So when did they break up?' asked Sophie, apparently not taking on board my intention to get on with some work.

'Not sure,' I said, now sounding deliberately vague and pressing on with the mail. 'A month or so ago, I think. Maybe longer.'

'But Jon hadn't mentioned it to you?'

I looked up at her. 'No. But,' I gestured at the mail and tried again, 'best get on.'

She looked bemused. 'It didn't come up when the pair of you went out for a drink?'

I sighed again and leaned back in my chair. The matter clearly fascinated her as much as it did Miriam, and she wasn't going to let it drop. 'No, it didn't come up,' I said, thinking back to my night out with Jon. 'But then they're still sort of together, aren't they. Just not...' I hesitated. '...just not *together* together. I mean, she's staying with him this weekend.' I groaned at the sudden recollection of our planned evening out and slumped forward, resting my head on my hands. 'Must cancel dinner with them actually.'

Sophie shuffled forward in the armchair, until she was literally on the edge of her seat. 'You mean you haven't told Jon about Stephen?'

I shook my head.

'Why not?' She sounded appalled.

'Because,' I said, unable to keep a note of exhausted exasperation out of my voice, 'I haven't seen him since Friday and, surprising as it may seem, it's not that much fun phoning round telling everyone that your boyfriend has, yet again, turned out to be a bit of a shit.'

She ignored my irritation. 'Call him now,' she said.

I raised my head to look at her. 'No,' I said flatly. 'I'll tell him before Saturday, but there's no rush.'

She frowned disapprovingly. 'I think it would be polite to give him as much time as possible to sort something else out for the weekend. If you don't hurry up, that's everybody's Saturday night ruined – not just yours.' She pointed at the phone on my desk. 'Go on.'

I glared at her, stung and surprised by her lack of tact. 'I'm not going to phone him *at* work and *from* work.'

'I'll leave.' She hauled herself out of the armchair. 'You can have the whole office to yourself.'

'You're being ridiculous,' I said.

She sighed, walked round her desk and sat down in front of her computer. 'I know you. You'll leave it and leave it. Whereas, if you let him know today, he can sort something else out.'

'Right,' I said, somewhat icily. 'Well, thank you for spelling that out for me. I certainly wouldn't want to inconvenience anybody with my personal problems. I'll call him when I get home tonight.'

'Great,' she said and turned towards her screen. 'Although right now would be better.'

I stared at her back, considering for a moment screwing up an empty envelope and aiming it at her head, before instead contenting myself with a mouthed expletive. Sophie, I told myself, had her own life issues to deal with right now, and I had to assume that these were temporarily impacting, rather negatively, upon her sensitivity levels.

'Potty mouth,' she said, without turning round.

I laughed in spite of myself, she joined in and the working day began.

Chapter 50

Just over nine hours later, I kicked off my shoes, dumped my bag in the hallway and headed for the kitchen. A glance at the clock revealed it to be 6.00pm and although I usually made myself a cup of tea whenever I went straight home after work, this evening I decided it was not too indecently early for a glass of wine. While it hadn't been a terrible day, it hadn't been a great one either and it had certainly been far removed from the days of happy creativity, in a convivial working environment, with which I had been spoiled for so many years.

David was continuing to alternate between listless and jolly to the point of mania – and it was a tough call as to which state I found most wearing. Sophie, meanwhile, whilst pretty much her usual self when it was just the two of us, was clearly now less than comfortable when David was present. As colleagues, they were an increasingly depressing pair, and as friends I was increasingly concerned for them.

I poured myself a glass of white wine, took it into the living room and flopped down onto the sofa. Forcing the issue of work from my mind, I picked up the phone, with the intention of taking Sophie's advice and calling Jon. I had decided to make the call, not to assist him in the scheduling of his social life but because I realised that I wanted to retain what little control I had over the situation and, besides, our friendship was such that I didn't want him to find out about Stephen from anybody else.

I dialled, his phone rang and a few seconds later, his recorded voice invited me to leave a message after the beep.

'Hi Jon, it's Alice,' I began uncontroversially. 'Just a quick call to say that I'm going to have to bow out of dinner with you and Suzanna this weekend. Stephen and I broke up on Friday, and three's a bit of a crowd.' I inserted a light laugh. 'Anyway, I'm fine – sort of relieved actually. Isn't that strange? But yes, all's well. All's well *now*, that is. On Friday night there was a crazed woman on my doorstep – and it wasn't me! Ha, ha! Hope to see you at book group. I've only got twenty pages left to read of *Jane Eyre*. I know! How did that happen? Bet you've read it twice.' More laughter. 'Bye.' I hung up and then immediately regretted failing to vet the recording. I ran through it again in my head: *can't make dinner... broke up with Stephen... feeling fine... see you soon*. I was pretty sure it was OK.

I sipped my wine and decided to phone Abs. With everybody else knowing what was going on, I didn't want her to feel out of the loop.

I picked up the phone again and dialled her landline.

'Hello?' A male voice answered. It didn't sound like Pete.

'Pete?' I said nevertheless.

'No, it's Jon.'

'Jon?' I felt momentarily at a loss. 'How weird. I was trying to call Abs.'

'Yes,' he said. 'You were dialling in my ear.'

'Oh.' He must have called just as I picked up the phone to call Abs.

'I got your message,' he said after a moment. 'I'm sorry.'

'I'm not,' I said quickly; perhaps too quickly, I thought, immediately concerned that I might sound as if I was protesting too much. 'I said that very quickly, didn't I?' I continued. 'But I promise you it's not a case of protesting too much. Although, now I've said that I'm not protesting too much, it sounds as if I'm protesting even more than I was, or wasn't, in the first place.' I took a breath. 'It's just really difficult to deny that you're protesting too much, without actually protesting... quite a lot... possibly too much...' My voiced trailed away and I made a tight fist with my right hand and pushed as much of it as possible into my mouth.

There was a pause before he spoke.

'Am I allowed to laugh?' he asked.

'Please do.'

He did.

'Perhaps we should begin again,' I suggested, smiling into the receiver.

'Let's do that,' he said. Then, after another pause, 'Hello, Ms Waites.'

I felt a need to take moment before replying. 'Hello, Mr Durham,' I said eventually. My smile wobbled. 'I'm so sorry not to be able to make dinner.'

'Do you want to tell me the background to that situation?' he asked.

'Can I save the gory details for another time?'

'Just tell me you're OK,' he said.

'I'm OK,' I confirmed. 'It was my decision. I'm just sorry I can't make dinner.'

'It's funny,' he said, 'because I was going to call you about dinner anyway.'

'Oh?'

'Yes. Suzanna and I talked over the weekend and we agreed that, although we enjoy one another's company, we want different things. And so we've decided… well, we've decided that we want different things.'

'I see,' I said hoarsely, before clearing my throat and repeating more loudly, 'I see.'

'So,' he continued, 'I was going to phone you to say that Suzanna wouldn't be coming to dinner. But, well, you got in there first.'

I nodded but said nothing.

'I wonder if you're nodding into the phone,' he said.

I laughed. 'I was actually.' And then, without pausing for thought or consideration, which I instinctively feared might prove detrimental to my future happiness, I said, 'Perhaps we could still go to dinner. Just the two of us. If you like.' I closed my eyes and, with a sense of *in for a penny in for a pound*, added, 'I'd like that. Very much.'

'Now *that*, Ms Waites,' he said, 'would have been a genius plan, if only Romy wasn't already my date for the evening.'

I opened my mouth to reply but no sound came out and I realised that I was completely crushed by his response. 'Ah,' I said after a moment. It was all I could manage.

'She'd told me she was going to be in Bristol this weekend,' Jon continued, sounding buoyant, 'so I texted her this morning, explained about Suzanna, asked if she was free for dinner and she said yes, without knowing any other details. I was just about to call her and fill her in when I got your message actually.'

'Ah.' I stared unblinkingly across the room, no longer listening to Jon, but instead thinking about Romy. So, she had accepted his dinner invitation, no questions asked. In my book, that made her quite keen and perhaps, I mused, that shouldn't come as a surprise. After all, they always got on very well whenever they met. I heaved a sigh as I remembered them laughing and chatting together in the pub several months earlier, whilst I had sat opposite them, enduring Miriam and Craig's endless bickering. And, of course, they had enjoyed each other's company again at dinner on Friday. Jon had even invited her to join book group.

I nodded absently into the phone and, as Jon continued to talk, it suddenly occurred to me that this was the gossip he had wanted to share on Friday night. Romy wasn't interested in David – because Romy was interested in *him*. And her feelings were clearly, to some extent, reciprocated – or why call and ask her to be his dinner date? I knew Jon better than to think he would ever toy with somebody like that. I raised a hand slowly to my forehead, as I remembered his response to my claim that David was attracted to Romy: *He'd have to be made of marble not to be.* Of course he would.

Meanwhile, Jon was now concluding his explanation of the situation.

'...and so we can still go ahead if you want to...'

'Ah.'

'...if you invite someone too.'

Deciding to play it safe and stick with monosyllables, I this time opted for an *ooh*, in preference to a fourth *ah*.

'So you'll do that?' he asked.

I nodded.

'I wonder if you're nodding again,' he said.

I made a sound, which I hoped approximated to laughter.

'What was that?' he asked.

I took a deep breath. 'My saliva went down the wrong way.'

'OK.' He sounded impressively unperturbed. 'Well, I'm looking forward to Saturday and,' he paused, 'I'm glad you're OK,' he added gently.

'Yes,' I said. 'Anyway, I'll let you go and call Romy.'

There was another pause before he spoke again. 'Bye, Alice,' he said simply.

'Bye then.'

I hung up the phone and continued to stare miserably into space, reviewing and reflecting upon what had just happened.

Jon, who was single, had invited Romy, who was also single, to dinner. And Romy had said yes. These were simple and uncontroversial facts, which should have prompted nothing more from me but happy acceptance. And yet, they had instead devastated me to the point of speechlessness. So why was that?

I paused my thoughts, gazing down at my mother's wedding ring, sensing an answer to the question I had posed myself, but reluctant to acknowledge it.

Instead, I twisted the ring, focusing intently on it and thinking about my long friendship with Jon: a friendship which began with our love for Lydia, and her love for us. And, after Lydia, a friendship which was maintained and strengthened because of our love for one other.

Yes. We loved one other. He loved me and I loved him.

I stopped twisting the ring, held my breath and, at that moment, in a whispered but unstoppable thought, I finally told myself the truth.

I not only loved Jon – I was in love with him.

Letting out my breath in something halfway between a gasp and a sob, I covered my face with my hands and, resting my head on the back of the sofa, I experienced a car crash moment of relief and anguish: relief at having finally acknowledged the truth of my feelings, and almost unbearable anguish that those feelings were not reciprocated. I might happen to want Jon, to at last know that I was in love with him, but what use was that when he simply didn't want me? He loved me as a friend, of that I was certain, but he had never shown any interest in me beyond friendship. He had dated Suzanna and, now that she was off the scene, he had the peerless Romy on speed-dial.

I removed my hands from my face and sat up, remaining completely still, until an awareness of tears dripping from my chin forced me to look around for something within reach which approximated to a hanky. Finding nothing, I wiped my eyes on the sleeve of my blouse and then hauled myself off the sofa. There was nothing for it, I told myself as I headed off in search of tissues, but to attempt to woman-up and face facts: Mr Durham was my friend, but he was not, and never would be, my Mr Right.

Chapter 51

'No, I can't,' said Hugh, with characteristic bluntness. 'I have a college dinner this Saturday.'

'Oh, well, not to worry,' I sighed. 'I realised it was very short notice.'

'Have you recovered from Friday night?' he asked. 'That was an unusual experience.'

I leaned forward on my desk and experienced a sudden urge to massage my temples. 'Yes,' I said, 'it was quite unusual.'

'Well,' he said, 'I hope you manage to rearrange your Saturday evening. Who else is going to dinner?'

'As of last night, Jon and Romy. I was going to take Stephen but obviously...'

There was a pause before he spoke. 'Obviously what?' he asked.

My grip tightened on the telephone. '*Obviously*, Hugh, I can't take Stephen because I've told him to piss off.'

'I see, yes.'

'Sorry,' I said, rubbing my eyes, 'I'm just a bit tired.'

'Hmm,' he sounded distracted.

'Go on. You must be busy, with patients to see,' I sighed. 'I won't keep you.'

'All of my patients, as you call them, are dead,' said Hugh. 'They're in no hurry.'

I smiled but it was beyond me to reward him with laughter. 'That's funny, Hugh,' I said. 'And I'm being sincere.'

'You sound disgruntled,' he said.

'I am disgruntled,' I replied.

'I'll come,' he said.

'What?'

'I'll come to dinner with you on Saturday.'

'But what about your thing?'

'I've thought about it and I would rather come to *your* thing,' he said. 'Now, I have to go because, although all my patients are dead, there are several people waiting for me who are not. Text me all the details and I'll arrange a taxi for us from your flat.'

'You don't have to come just to be nice, you know,' I said. 'I don't want you cancelling something important just because I'm being moody.'

'I wouldn't do that,' he said. 'I would rather come to dinner with you than go to the college dinner, so that's what I'm going to do.'

'Oh… OK.'

He said goodbye and, before I could reciprocate, I heard the dialling tone.

I put down the phone, lowered my head and placed my cheek on the cool surface of the desk. It was a surprisingly calming sensation. I took several deep breaths and reflected upon my conversation with Hugh. Perhaps I should be more like him; more straightforward, simplistic, direct. He judged a situation, considered the options, reached a conclusion and then told it like it was. Yes, he could do with a little more humour and tact at times but he had acknowledged these shortcomings and worked hard to address them. Hugh had a clarity of purpose and approach which I envied. He spotted problems and potential problems early and sought speedy, or even pre-emptive, solutions. In contrast, my issues seemed to crash down on me like pianos from first floor windows. By the time I spotted them and thought about dealing with them, they were usually crushing the life-breath out of me.

I lifted my head as I heard Sophie and David climbing the stairs: no conversation, just footsteps.

I smoothed my hair and attempted to appear busy and brisk. 'Good morning,' I said brightly as they entered. 'How did that go?'

David looked at me. 'Very productive, thank you.'

I looked at Sophie. She offered me a smile and nodded.

'Marvellous,' I said.

David went into his office and closed the door. Sophie turned on her computer. I suppressed a rising urge to scream.

'Your Saturday's sorted then,' said Sophie suddenly.

I looked at her. 'Who told you that?'

'No one,' she shrugged. 'I was just wondering.'

'Oh.' I took a deep breath. 'Yes, it's all sorted.'

'Good. So you found someone to take?'

I frowned at her. 'How did you know that I was looking for someone to take?'

'I didn't,' she smiled. 'It was an enquiry not a statement. God, I really must work on my intonation.'

I had a sense that she hadn't quite answered the question posed, but as I didn't have the energy for arguing semantics, I let it go. 'I'm taking Hugh, and Jon is taking Romy because he and Suzanna are no longer together.' Sophie nodded. '*In any sense*,' I added significantly. 'She will not be visiting him this weekend.'

She nodded again. For someone so intrigued by the topic just twenty-four hours earlier, she now seemed to be teetering remarkably close to the edge of disinterest.

'Well,' I sighed, turning in my chair to face my screen, 'I'll be getting on then.'

'Nothing else to report?' she asked.

I looked up to find her now peering at me intently. I knew I could trust her implicitly, both to give sensible, considered advice and to be entirely discreet and maintain a confidence. I could, if I chose, confess to her my feelings for Jon, and share the crushing sense of defeat and disappointment I felt upon realising that they weren't reciprocated. But what would be the point of that? She couldn't change the situation any more than I could and besides, she had enough worries of her own.

'Nothing else,' I said, shaking my head and forcing a smile. 'Just business as usual.'

Chapter 52

I hesitated for just a moment before picking up the phone from my bed. 'Hi, Miriam.'

'Hello!' she replied excitedly. 'I'm so glad I've caught you.'

I smiled. 'OK, but before you start, you should know that I'm still in my bathrobe and that Hugh and the taxi will be here in less than twenty minutes.'

'I know, I know and it's only a quickie, I promise,' she laughed. 'It's just that I haven't heard from you all week and I'm itching for a gossip about your dinner this evening!'

I experienced an immediate, and highly uncomfortable, mixture of guilt and dread. Miriam had texted me three times during the week with various bits of news, each time also telling me how excited Romy was about her evening out with Jon, Hugh and myself. I, meanwhile, had been doing my best to forget about the event and to stifle wholly unjustified feelings of negativity towards Romy – with distressingly little success. And I was now starting to dread the evening to such an extent that if Hugh hadn't been missing an important dinner engagement to keep me company, I would have cancelled without hesitation. The last thing I therefore wanted right now was to be having this conversation with Miriam. Despite my feelings of guilt, I cursed myself for answering the call.

'Look, I'm sorry for not calling, Miriam, but work is insane at the moment,' I said.

'Oh, that's OK,' she said generously. 'I know you're really busy and I know you're rushing now, but you will tell me how it all goes, won't you?' Her voice had reached squeak pitch.

I heard Craig say something in the background. Miriam laughed. 'Hang on a moment, Alice… I am *not* turning into my mother, Craig!' she called. I heard another indistinct response and then more laughter. 'Sorry, Alice,' she said. 'Craig doesn't quite share my enthusiasm for romance. Although, to be fair, he did buy me flowers yesterday.'

'That was nice,' I said, grateful for an opportunity to change topic. 'What kind of flowers?'

'A bouquet. I'll text you a pic. But anyway, call me as soon as you can for a debrief.'

I sighed and flopped down on the bed. 'Why not just let Romy tell you herself?'

'Oh, she won't tell me anything,' she huffed. 'She's forever accusing me of being nosy and interfering.'

'I wonder why,' I murmured.

'I know I'm dreadful,' she giggled. 'But I can tell she's really excited about this evening. She's usually as cool as a cucumber but she's just not today. It took her quite a while to decide whether to wear her green dress or a floral one.'

'Ooh,' I said, 'call the fire brigade.'

She laughed again. 'I know you think I'm silly, but she's my little sister and I just want the very best for her.' She sighed audibly. 'If it was just about looks, they're a match made in heaven. They look like something out of a magazine when they're sitting next to each other, don't they?'

'Yes,' I admitted, 'they do. So does Romy think he's keen?' I asked after a moment, steeling myself for the reply, aware of the internal agony it might cause.

'Oh,' Miriam sounded disappointed, 'I was hoping he might have had a chat with you about it.'

'No,' I said, with a certain amount of relief. 'I haven't had a chance to chat with anyone about anything all week.'

'Well, you know what Romy's like,' tutted Miriam. 'She'd never declare it if she thought he liked her. But at the same time, I don't think she'd be this excited if she thought there was no hope. Besides, how could he *not* be attracted to her?'

'Yes,' I agreed. 'He'd have to be made of marble, wouldn't he?'

'Exactly!' she exclaimed and then sighed again. 'I know I'm biased. Alice, but she is lovely, isn't she?'

'She is,' I acknowledged sullenly, now desperate for the conversation to end. 'But I must go, Miriam, or *I* shan't look lovely in the least. At the moment,' I stood up and inspected myself in the full-length mirror which hung on my bedroom wall, 'I look like a crack addict.' I leaned towards the mirror and homed-in on the dark circles under my eyes. 'A crack addict with a heavy cold. There isn't enough *Touche Eclat* in the country to hide these bags. They're more suitcases than bags actually.'

'Oh, Alice,' Miriam went into mother mode, 'you've been so brave about everything that I forget what you've been through. I'm sorry. Are you sleeping OK?'

I came over all Hugh. 'No, I'm not,' I said. 'I am sleeping *really* badly.'

'Gosh,' said Miriam, 'you must be exhausted.'

'I am,' I said petulantly. 'Anyway, I'd really better go or I'll be wearing aged towelling to dinner. I know no one will be looking at me, but I'd better make some sort of effort.'

There was silence for a moment before she spoke. 'You'll look beautiful,' she said quietly. 'You always do. And you don't realise it, which just adds to it. Romy was saying earlier this evening how very beautiful you are. We both loved that dress you wore to the book group dinner. Apparently Jon commented on it too. Romy was wondering if you'd mind her buying one like it – but in russet, I think. She'll probably ask you about it this evening.'

I bit my lip, feeling both anguished and complimented, as well as guilty for my lack of patience with Miriam, who was always so supportive and well-meaning. 'Of course, I wouldn't mind. I'd be flattered.'

'Lovely,' she said. 'Anyway, I'll stop pestering you and let you go and gild the lily.'

'Bye, then. Oh and it'll probably be too late to run through my notes with you tonight. But I promise I'll call tomorrow.'

'You're a star,' she laughed. 'Have fun.'

'I'll try. Bye.' And with that, I hung up the phone, pulled both myself and my bathrobe together, and headed into the bathroom in search of cosmetics.

Chapter 53

'I am considering inviting Romy out and I should be grateful for your thoughts.'

We had left the restaurant, said our farewells to Jon and Romy, and Hugh was walking me home when he made the shock announcement. It took me completely by surprise and for a moment I was lost for words.

'Inviting her out?' I managed at last.

'Yes,' he said. 'And I would be grateful for your thoughts.'

I decided some clarification was required. 'Do you mean you are considering inviting her on an outing for two people who share a common interest? Or on an outing for two people who are attracted to each other?'

'I mean the latter,' he said. 'I find her very attractive.'

I resisted an urge to slap my hand against my forehead and groan. Romy had, that evening, looked particularly stunning. She was often described as effortlessly beautiful, but I realised that Miriam had perhaps been right about the importance with which she viewed her date with Jon, as an effort had clearly been made. Dressed in an understated, but impeccably fitted, olive-green silk shift dress, her long red curls had been swept up and held in place by invisible pins and five or six visible diamante flower clips. The result was quite breath-taking and, at the same time, strangely and unexpectedly calming. I had left home with Hugh, fearing that I would spend the evening consumed by feelings of bitterness and rivalry towards one of the most lovely people I knew. However, immediately I set eyes on her, all sense of resentment and competition fell away. How could I compete with that? She was a worthy winner. And so I had shrugged internally and retired gracefully, without even approaching the start line.

I sighed. 'Look Hugh, lots of men find Romy very attractive. She gets *a lot* of offers,' I added, in preparation for trying to dissuade him from chancing his arm.

'I have no doubt,' he said. 'So, what would you advise?'

'Well,' I said, feeling increasingly out of my comfort zone and conscious of a growing sense of responsibility, 'as I say, she's very popular but I'm aware of only two serious relationships. And I'm not sure those men were quite like you. Not quite as thoughtful, or as intellectual as you, I mean. It's hard to say what her type is. Although, I do wonder if she and Jon might be quite attracted to each other. Did you notice that?' My heart sank a little at the recollection of the numerous, unmissable knowing looks and smiles which had been exchanged by Jon and Romy during the meal, together with a certain shyness and awkwardness I had not seen in her before.

Hugh shook his head. 'I detected nothing.'

I stifled another sigh. 'Really? Because it seemed to me that they were getting on very well indeed and well, you know, I think there's potential there. So I just wonder…' I heard myself beginning to gabble and took a deep breath before continuing more slowly. 'I just wonder if it might be best to hold back for the moment and give yourself a chance to work out the lie of the land.' I turned and smiled up at him, feeling that despite my aversion to this kind of discussion, I wasn't doing too badly.

He looked down at me, his face registering no emotion. 'When I said I wanted your thoughts,' he said, 'I meant regarding where I should take her on a date.'

'Oh.'

'Not whether you thought I was too boring for her.'

'I see.' Only the fact that we were walking quite briskly prevented my toes from curling.

'I believe she is attracted to me.'

'Ooh.'

'You clearly do not,' he said.

'Hmm, well, it's so difficult to say, isn't it? I'm absolutely rubbish at that kind of thing.'

'I very much suspect you are,' he said.

'Well, why ask me, then?' I said, feeling affronted.

'I've just told you. I wasn't asking for personal advice. I was asking for recommendations regarding days out. You know her quite well. You must have an idea of what she would enjoy.'

'Well, if you're determined to go for it...'

'And I am,' he said flatly.

'Well, why don't you offer her a tour of the abattoir, or whatever it's called, and then take her to the theatre?' I suggested, giving the matter genuine thought, despite knowing full well that his chances of success were hovering around the zero mark. 'See if there's anything on at the Old Vic – she loves theatre. Or do the harbour walk if it's fine, then have a drink outside – or on one of the boats.'

We walked on in silence for a short way, whilst he considered his options and I reflected that my main concern was not that Romy would turn Hugh down flat but that she would accept the invitation, failing to recognise his romantic interest, cloaked, as it almost certainly would be, by his on-the-spectrum manner. That situation, I thought, would be painful for everyone. I decided not to beat about the bush but to instead voice this concern with Hugh-like candour.

'You must be clear with Romy that this is a date,' I said. 'As opposed to a matey walking tour of death, followed by food.'

He nodded. 'I'll be clear,' he said. 'But I have asked women out on dates before, you know.'

'Any of them ever said yes?' I asked.

'Not one,' he said.

I looked at him and smiled.

'In fact,' he said, 'they all said yes. I never ask unless I'm certain to my own satisfaction that they'll agree to a date,' he said. 'I wouldn't want to risk their embarrassment, or my feelings.'

I looked up at him and it occurred to me that whenever I thought I had Hugh's personality type pegged, he threw something in to upset the Myers Briggs applecart. 'And you're certain about Romy?' I asked gently. 'You wouldn't like me to do some fishing first?'

He smiled. 'I hope you won't be offended, Alice, when I say that I suspect you would be either highly ineffective, or highly unsubtle, when it came to fishing. So, if you don't mind, I think I'd like to handle this one by myself.' And with that, he held out his left arm for me to link, and the last Myers Briggs apple tumbled into the gutter.

–

Hugh stayed for coffee, calling a taxi at just after eleven. I waved him off fifteen minutes later, reflecting that, overall, I had enjoyed the evening, and the company of all three friends, despite the slightly painful circumstances.

I had brushed my teeth and was just climbing into bed when the phone rang. It was Miriam. I sighed wearily but answered nevertheless.

'Hello, Miriam,' I said.

'Hello, it's me… Miriam,' she giggled, making it immediately apparent that she had been drinking. Probably no more than a glass or two, but with Miriam that was all it took to prompt either giggling, gross indiscretion – or both. 'And I'm whispering, so Romy can't hear.'

'Cunning like a fox,' I said. 'You after details?'

'No need,' she replied. 'I was phoning to say that Romy came home full of it. Couldn't stop talking about him.'

I lay back on the pillow and closed my eyes. 'Really? You didn't expect that, did you?'

'No,' she said, sounding suddenly subdued. 'She likes him *a lot*, Alice. Could you tell?'

I took a deep breath. 'Well, there was nothing too obvious; just the odd smile, as if they had a shared secret.' With my eyes still closed, I was unable to keep an image of Jon smiling from entering my mind and I sighed over an evening spent constantly keeping myself emotionally and physically in check. More than once, I had found myself leaning involuntarily towards him, watching a mouth I desperately wanted to kiss, forming words, rather than listening to the words themselves.

I opened my eyes, dragging myself back to the conversation with Miriam. 'I think I spotted something between them because I know them both so—'

'She had a lovely, *lovely* time,' Miriam interrupted. 'I've never seen her like this and I just hope it's all reciprocated. I'm trying not to stress about it. You know, I said to Craig I wonder if I worry and fuss about everyone else because I don't want to look too closely at myself.'

'I don't think it's—'

'We just have to sort out our own relationships and then listen and support where we can, don't we, Alice?' She paused. 'Because what will be, will be. I think there's enormous comfort in that. I just hope he feels the same. I'd hate to see her hurt,' she continued quietly. 'He hasn't suggested anything. And modern woman though she is, I can't see her asking him out on a—'

I suddenly remembered Hugh, opened my eyes and sat up. 'Ooh, sorry to interrupt, Miriam, but I must tell you quickly that Hugh is planning to ask Romy out.'

There was what sounded like a horrified gasp at the other end of the line. 'He's not!' she said breathlessly. 'He told you that?'

'Yes, on the way home. He plans to take her to see either dead bodies, or a play, or maybe both.'

'I must tell her!' she said, sounding panicked. 'Or is that too interfering? Do you think I should tell her?'

'Well, I'd want to know if I was her,' I said. 'I'd want to be prepared for something like that, if I could be, wouldn't you?'

'Yes, I would,' she said and hung up.

I sat there with the phone to my ear for a moment or two, before registering that she'd actually gone. I considered calling her back, but it was approaching midnight and judging by the panic in her voice, and her inebriated haste to be gone, she would be too busy hammering down Romy's bedroom door to hear the phone ringing anyway.

I placed my phone on the chest of drawers next to my bed, switched off the light and lay back down. I wondered momentarily if I should call Hugh and pass on the bad news about Romy's feelings for Jon. However, I quickly came to the conclusion that Miriam was right:

getting involved in other people's relationships was not a good idea. Things must just be allowed to happen. Hugh would suggest a date, Romy would refuse Hugh with compassion, and everyone would recover in time.

And with the chorus of *Que Sera, Sera* playing on a soothing loop in my head, I drifted off to sleep.

Chapter 54

For the next week or so, work dominated my life like never before. And although the primary reason for this was Sophie's imminent departure, the distractions of the office were, in some respects, very welcome. They meant that I had little, or no, time to think about Stephen or, most crucially, about Jon and Romy.

I had had one reminder of them, in the form of a text from Miriam, saying simply:

> *I know you're hard at work but quick Romy update... It's dinner for two! Everything's coming up roses! xx*

I sent a brief, appropriately positive, response consisting of a smiley face, three exclamation marks and four kisses and left it at that, unable to bring myself to request details.

The only direct contact I had had with Jon since our foursome dinner, was a number of light-hearted texts from him, suggesting possible dates for a drink. I wondered if he wanted, amongst other things, to talk to me about Romy, and while I was braced for that, and increasingly determined to feel good about it, work offered me a genuine excuse for postponing an evening out until such time as I could express complete, rather than muted, happiness for the pair of them.

Personal struggles aside, the process of trying to find Sophie's replacement was, meanwhile, proving depressing. Not because of the quality of the candidates – most were very pleasant and came with glowing references, and every single one of them was as well, or better, qualified than Sophie on paper. But none of them *was* Sophie – and

Sophie was what we wanted. After a week of interviews, and almost three weeks after Sophie had handed in her notice, I was beginning to despair of us ever appointing.

'We've got to pick someone, David,' I said, as we sat in his office one evening, staring at a meeting-table strewn with CVs, interview notes and letters of recommendation. It was almost half-past seven and Sophie was hard at work in the main office, catching up on time missed due to an interview earlier that day. There was a book group meeting at Miriam's that evening and we had eaten dinner at our desks, with a view to going straight there.

David leaned back in his chair. 'I know,' was all he said.

We looked at each other and sighed simultaneously. 'Look,' I said, 'I can't think of anything cheerful to say about this but people do move on.' He nodded. 'And if we pick the right person, we can still have a great working environment.' He nodded again and I picked up a CV. 'What about Merrin?' I asked, placing the stapled sheets in front of him. 'She's bright, qualified, smiley, shares a lot of your interests…' He continued to nod. 'Oh for goodness sake, David, stop nodding and say something.'

'I'm not sure Merrin would speak her mind,' he said.

'In what context?' I asked. 'In the context of the job?' I looked over my shoulder at the half-open door and lowered my voice. 'Or in the context of your annoying cough and your insistence upon dating harridans?'

His expression remained unchanged. 'The latter, obviously,' he said.

'Well,' I said, gesturing in frustration at the paperwork littering the table, 'you might as well set fire to this little lot then. Oh and why not throw the business on the bonfire while you're at it? Because unless you start to drop projects, you and I cannot manage alone.'

'Give me until close of play tomorrow,' he said.

I threw my hands up. 'But then it's the weekend and we can't start any balls rolling until Monday. We've been going over these for days already. There's nothing more to think about. She leaves in just over a week, David. Every one of these applicants, with the exception of Smelly Jeremy – and I am not working with him – has to give at least a month's notice.'

He stared fixedly at the table. 'I will make a decision tomorrow,' he said. 'Remind me of your preferences.'

'Well, I'd be happy with any of these three,' I indicated the relevant CVs. 'But I warmed to Merrin more than to the others.'

He nodded. 'I think we're on the same page. If I reach a different conclusion, I shall of course run it past you.' He looked at the clock. 'You'd better go,' he said, attempting a smile. 'You don't want to be late.'

I nodded. 'You do know I'm just as miserable about this as you are, don't you?'

'I do,' he said. 'But thank you for keeping a steady head.'

I smiled. 'I might add "steady head" to my own CV.'

He stood up and walked back to his desk. 'If you ever try to leave, I'll give you a terrible reference,' he said tonelessly.

'And yet you gave Sophie a fabulous one,' I replied, rising to my feet.

'This is true.' He sat down in the brown leather chair behind his desk. 'But then, as you know, I am completely and utterly terrified of her.'

Chapter 55

'Do come in,' said Craig, opening the front door and waving us into the hallway, with a graceful sweep of his arm.

'You on the door tonight then, Craig?' said Sophie.

'I am indeed,' he said, 'and serving drinks. What can I get you?'

'Waiter service,' Sophie grinned. 'I'm just disappointed Miriam didn't get you a little bow tie and a pinny.'

'They're upstairs,' said Craig, 'for later.'

'Love it,' Sophie laughed. 'And I'd love a red wine too, if there's one going.' Craig nodded.

'Hello!' Miriam bustled out into the hallway, beaming. She slipped her arm around Craig's waist and he reciprocated with an arm around her shoulders. She looked up at him. 'Do you need a hand carrying drinks?'

'Why don't I come into the kitchen and help?' I suggested.

Craig nodded and smiled. 'Thanks,' he said.

'Great,' said Miriam, reaching out and taking Sophie's hand. 'And you come through with me. I've got tales to tell.'

She headed off with Sophie, whilst Craig and I made our way into the kitchen. Once there, he opened the fridge, took out several bottles and began to pour various drinks.

'What can I get you?' he asked.

'I'll have a hug for starters,' I said.

He put down the bottle in his hand, turned and hugged me.

'You're looking better,' I said.

I felt him sigh, before we released each other. 'We have started to prioritise,' he said, recommencing pouring drinks. 'And it might be that a house this size,' he looked around, 'just isn't a priority.'

I felt suddenly anxious. 'How is work going?'

He glanced up at me, before returning his attention to the drinks. 'Don't panic. The work is still there. I've just eased up on it a bit,' he said 'and that has to have consequences. But Miriam and I are much better and that's our focus. We both want it to work.' He shrugged philosophically. 'As far as everything else goes, we'll just have to wait and see.' He looked up at me again. 'What did you say you wanted to drink?' he asked. 'I've forgotten.'

'I didn't say,' I replied, and then, accepting the change of subject, 'I'll have a red wine, please.'

He poured the wine. 'Right,' he said, pointing at the drinks on the table, 'red for Sophie, red for you and a beer each for Abigail and Jon. Hey, hang on,' he said, as I attempted to pick up two glasses of wine and a beer. 'You just take your wine and Jon's beer, I'll bring the other two. I know what you're like.'

'OK,' I said, slowly exiting the kitchen, focusing particularly upon the brimming glass of red wine in my left hand.

I entered the living room to a chorus of 'hellos' and a hasty dash from Miriam to relieve me of the red wine. 'Here, let me. I'll hand it to you when you're sitting down,' she said, taking the wine and following as I headed towards Jon, who was sitting on the sofa next to Connie. The latter stood as I approached and gave me a crushing hug, nearly causing me to quite literally fall at the last with the beer. She then sat back down on the sofa, moving up and patting the vacated space between herself and Jon. It was the first time I had seen her since splitting with Stephen and although we had talked a number of times on the phone, she looked, I thought, a little anxious.

I sat down, smiling at both her and Jon and handing him his beer.

He returned the smile. 'Thanks,' he said.

Miriam handed me my wine. 'There you go,' she said, in the mummy voice she usually reserved for Phoebe, 'now do be careful with that.'

'Are you sure you wouldn't like to put it in a tippy cup for me, Miriam?' I asked.

She ignored the comment and returned to her seat across the room, immediately continuing her conversation with Abs and Sophie, as

Craig handed out the rest of the drinks and then exited, with a grin and a wave to Jon.

'Are you well, Alice?' asked Connie, her tone even more diffident than usual.

'I'm really well, Connie,' I said turning towards her. 'Everything is really good; busy, but good. The only cloud on my horizon is that,' I glanced across the room and then lowered my voice, 'Sophie is leaving,' I said, keen to imply that Stephen was no longer a concern.

'Oh, my goodness, I know,' she whispered. 'How sad for you and David.' She placed a devastated hand on her chest. 'Although, of course,' she added, 'you won't lose touch. She's not moving home, is she?'

I shook my head. 'She's job-hunting in Bristol.' I looked again at Sophie who, along with Abs was listening intently to the conclusion of some breathless anecdote or other from Miriam. 'What's Miriam so animated about?' I asked, gesturing towards the group with my wine glass and looking first at Connie, then at Jon.

'Romy has a job interview here next week,' said Jon.

'Oh, I see,' I said.

'Miriam is so excited about it all,' said Connie. 'She would just so love to have Romy nearby.' I nodded whilst focusing determinedly on Connie, unwilling to look at Jon. 'And, of course, Romy has a date this weekend. Isn't that right, Jon?' Connie continued, leaning in front of me and smiling at Jon.

I heard him sigh. 'Sometimes,' he said, 'just sometimes, it would be nice to have another Y chromosome in this book group.'

I forced myself to turn towards him and managed a smile. 'Has there been a little too much girl talk about it already this evening?' I asked.

He smiled and Connie laughed. 'We're all just excited, that's all,' she said. 'It's a nice thing.'

'It is,' I said, again looking at Jon and surprised to discover him so relaxed about the conversation. 'It's a very nice thing.'

He shrugged. 'I'm not disagreeing with you.'

'I'd be slightly worried if you were,' I said.

'Hey, Connie,' Sophie called to her from across the room. 'I'm thinking of an American road-trip this summer.'

'That's news,' I interjected. 'Since when?'

'Since right now,' said Sophie, fixing me with a stare.

'You've never mentioned it,' I said.

'Yeah, well, I've never mentioned that I've got a liking for cold baked beans mixed with mayonnaise, but it's still a fact.' She looked at Connie, beamed and beckoned her over. 'Can I pick your brain for two minutes, Connie?'

Connie looked both flattered and thrilled. 'Oh my goodness, yes,' she said, rising to her feet. 'And depending upon where you visit, Sophie, I could put you in touch with any number of friends who would be delighted to show you around. Excuse me, Alice... Jon.' She walked over to Sophie and sat down next to her.

I leaned back on the sofa. 'I did know about the cold baked bean thing, *actually*,' I muttered.

Jon laughed. I looked at him and smiled. 'I'm ridiculous, I know,' I said.

He shook his head and opened his mouth to speak.

I held up a hand. 'Don't say any more. Just let me take the head shake as a compliment.'

'Feel free,' he said, before adding more quietly. 'So, how are things with you?'

I looked at Sophie. 'I'm quite down about that,' I said.

'I can imagine.'

'But I'm sure it will all work out.' I took a deep breath. 'Things do, don't they?'

'I don't like seeing you unhappy,' he said.

Both tone and sentiment struck me as unusually serious. I turned to look at him, unable to think immediately of an appropriate response.

'Don't you?' was the one I eventually settled for.

'I hope that's not a genuine query,' he said.

I shook my head. 'Of course not. I just didn't really know what to say, so I said something inane. I do that a lot.' I paused. 'As you know.'

He didn't reply.

'Ironically, that was itself quite an inane thing to say,' I mumbled, unsettled by his silence. 'And now,' I closed my eyes, 'if you don't say something quickly, I'll just carry on becoming more and more inane until you feel compelled to smother me with a cushion.'

'Square or round?' he asked. I opened my eyes and looked at him. He was smiling now. 'I thought you might have a preference.'

I sighed and sipped my wine. 'Hexagonal box-edge, please.'

'Are you free for a drink tomorrow?' he asked suddenly.

I looked at him and hesitated, taken by surprise and wondering for how long I would be able to put off the inevitable discussion about Romy. 'Work is just so full on,' I said, after a moment.

He nodded. 'OK. Well, let me know when it's not.'

'OK.' I looked down at my copy of *Jane Eyre*. 'I've actually read the whole thing, you know,' I said.

'Really?'

'Really. And that's despite having read it twice before.'

'I'm impressed,' he said. 'Do you enjoy it every time?'

I nodded and continued to stare at the book in my hand. 'I do.'

'Tell me what you like about it.'

'The equality of feeling,' I said immediately, more to myself than to him.

'That sounds like a title,' he said quietly. 'Now I need to hear the essay.'

I looked up at him again. His expression was one of serious interest. For just a moment, the ache of feelings not reciprocated subsided and I smiled, picturing myself leaning towards him and kissing him, untroubled by any consideration of the possible consequences. As I continued to gaze up at him, his expression softened and he smiled back at me. I took a deep breath. 'Probably best for me to stick to *Jane Eyre* tonight,' I said.

'Absolutely,' said Miriam. She was standing over me with a wine bottle. 'Do you want a top-up before I start the book chat?'

Grateful for the distraction, I looked away from Jon and gestured at my still-brimming glass of red. 'Only if you're thinking of pouring it directly into my mouth.'

'Wouldn't be the first time,' she said and then turned to Jon. 'Another beer, Jon?'

'No, I'm fine, thanks,' he smiled.

'Right.' She turned and placed the bottle of wine on a table by the window before returning to her seat. '*Jane Eyre*. I think I'd first just like to say thank you to Connie for encouraging us to choose it.'

Connie smiled self-consciously.

'I was about fifteen or sixteen last time I read it,' continued Miriam. 'And I remember really enjoying the sexual tension, the shredded wedding dress and the night-time arson. This time, I suppose I read it from a different perspective: as a mother and as a wife.' She paused. 'I think that's why Jane's childhood had much more of an impact on me and I felt for little Adèle, who seemed rather disposable and incidental. Also, I thought more about Rochester's relationship with Bertha; that was a marriage, they had history.'

'So this time,' I said, leaning towards her, 'you were drawn in by the drama in the domesticity, rather than by the melodrama.'

'What a great précis from the English graduate.' She looked at me and smiled. 'Yes, that's it exactly. What did you think?'

'Well, I can relate to the changed reading perspective,' I said.

'In what way?' asked Abs, smiling at me with teacherly interest and encouragement from across the room.

'Well, I was more judgemental of Rochester and his choices.' I looked at the book on my lap. 'And a lot less impressed with him than I used to be.'

'You're kidding!' laughed Sophie. 'I still fancy him rotten. What was your issue?'

I opened the book. 'I was just much more uncomfortable about him hiding his marriage and his feelings from Jane. I know he says he thought a governess wouldn't want to stay in a house with a lunatic, but what about as he came to love Jane? Why not tell her everything then?'

Sophie opened her mouth to reply but, unusually, was beaten to it.

'Because he was afraid of losing her,' said Jon.

I turned to him. 'Too afraid to be honest with her?'

'I'm not saying it was the most selfless choice,' he smiled, 'but I think I'm going to allow him his selfishness.'

'God, me too.' Sophie sat forward in her chair and nodded. 'If you don't think someone could love you back, crap and all, then of course you're going to hide your crap, or hide your feelings, or both. The only other option is to walk away without telling them about the crap and the feelings, so you don't have to hear them say that they don't want you. But walking away is fucking painful too.' She reached for a handful of nibbles from the table in front of her. 'So let's give the guy a break.'

The use of the f-word, which had never before made an appearance at book group, was an immediate indication to us all of how strongly she felt. I flicked a sidelong glance at Connie to see how she was coping with the bad language but, although she had coloured slightly, I saw that she was nodding in enthusiastic approval of Sophie's impassioned, if somewhat foul-mouthed, defence of Mr Rochester.

Abs was nodding too. 'That's the beauty of the book for me,' she said. 'The humanity of it. The mistakes, the imperfections, the misconceptions. There are no easy characters or situations. You can pick holes in all of them. It's what makes it relatable, despite all the wild-eyed Gothic horror.'

'I agree,' said Jon.

'You found it relatable?' I asked.

'Yes,' he said, 'I did.'

'And such ground-breaking feminism,' said Connie suddenly. 'I love that Brontë made her protagonist female and small and plain and insignificant but then gave her a voice and such strength. *So frail and so indomitable*. She takes control. I love that.'

I looked at Connie, the feminist, and smiled.

'I love that,' she repeated quietly.

'And I love *this*,' I heard myself say.

I looked up at the sound of my own voice, expecting to be met with quizzical looks and bemused enquiries.

But there were none.

'Me too,' said Sophie quietly. 'We're so lucky.' And everyone else just nodded.

-

Jane Eyre, to Connie's obvious delight, proved a universal hit. But as an uncharacteristically lengthy and in-depth discussion on the nature of feminism within the novel concluded, I couldn't help experiencing a certain initial sense of relief when Miriam said she wanted to suggest a shorter, lighter read as our next book. This was subsequently revealed to be a romantic comedy Romy had lent her several weeks earlier – a proposal which was met with enthusiasm from Abs and also from Connie. However, the response from Sophie and myself, despite my eagerness for something light, was more equivocal.

'I'm just not sure,' said Sophie.

'And I'm not entirely sold,' I echoed.

'Why not?' asked Miriam, sounding affronted.

'I just tend to prefer a little more realism,' I shrugged.

'There's lots of realism in it. And besides, you're always going on about loving *The Hitchhiker's Guide to the Galaxy*,' said Miriam witheringly. 'Where's the realism in that?'

'I'm not going to veto it,' I said. 'I'm just saying I suspect it's not going to be my cup of tea right now. And,' I turned to Jon, 'what about Jon?'

Miriam pursed her lips. 'Some might infer sexism there, Alice. But OK.' She looked at Jon. 'Are you OK with women's fiction, Jon?'

'Now you ask me,' he laughed. 'But Romy has mentioned the book to me. She enjoyed it and found it funny, so I'll give it a go.'

I was disappointed to feel myself deflate at this favourable reference to Romy's literary taste.

'Well, if Jon's prepared to give it a go, then so will I,' said Sophie. 'It's just that when your love life isn't exactly soaring, that kind of thing can feel a bit like being beaten up by someone who's reeling off the gags while kicking the shit out of you.'

'But it can also cheer you up,' argued Miriam. 'It really cheered me up. It had me laughing on the same evening that Phoebe came down with norovirus and projectile vomited on Craig from her loft bed.'

'Oh dear me,' said Connie, gasping and putting an anxious hand to her mouth.

'I know,' said Miriam. 'But the real downside was that only about eighty per cent of the sick landed on Craig. The rest ended up on the new carpet.' She reached forward, picked up a nacho and scooped up a generous helping of hummus from a bowl on the table in front of her. 'We scraped up the worst with a fish slice and then shampooed it silly but her room still smelled like Sainsbury's cheese counter for a month.' She popped the nacho and hummus into her mouth. 'Yum,' she said.

Connie nodded in an empathetic manner and I thought I saw Sophie gag.

'Well, I'd like to read it,' said Abs, thankfully dragging the conversation back to literature. 'It sounds fun and it might make you feel better, Sophie.' She turned and smiled at me. 'And you might find something uplifting in it, Alice. Remember *A Simple Heart*? Remember how much you enjoyed hating Felicité? You loved that!'

I smiled and rolled my eyes. 'Oh, go on then. Let's try it.'

'Great,' said Miriam, placing her hands palm down on her lap in a job-done kind of way. 'I really enjoyed it and, as Jon said, Romy loved it too.'

My jaw clenched involuntarily.

'Ah, but,' said Sophie, 'Romy's love life wasn't on the down and is now very much on the up, isn't it?'

I looked at her, surprised that she had made the comment in front of Jon.

'Let's not count chickens,' said Miriam, looking like she had not only already counted her chickens but also entered the figures onto an Excel spreadsheet. 'But it all looks promising.'

I opened my mouth, but no words came out. I turned to Jon. He was smiling at Miriam in the manner of a despairing, but doting, parent.

Abs clapped her hands. 'It's just so lovely knowing both parties.' She looked around the room and was rewarded with nods of agreement from Miriam, Connie and Sophie and another smile from Jon. She then leaned forward and touched Miriam's knee. 'I'm keeping everything crossed.'

'Me too,' said Miriam, 'but,' she held up a hand, 'as I said to Alice recently, what will be, will be.'

'I agree totally,' said Abs. 'We'll just wait and see. No pressure.'

I sat there, unable to decide whether I was the only sane, or the only insane, person in the room. In the end, I felt a need to know.

'Sorry but do you think we should be discussing this with Jon here?' I said, attempting both a smile and to keep my voice light.

They each looked at me and then at Jon.

'Sorry, Jon,' said Miriam, 'are we boring you?'

'I didn't mean we were *boring* him' I said, frowning at her. 'I meant that the conversation is going on as if he's not here.'

It was Miriam's turn to frown. 'He knows he can join in if he wants to.' She looked at Jon. 'You're not feeling left out, are you?'

I groaned in exasperation and turned towards him. 'If you object to a personal relationship being discussed like this, you should say so.'

His expression was one of puzzled amusement. 'You've lost me,' he said.

'And me,' said Miriam, her bemused expression mirroring my own. 'Why should Jon object? It's not as if it's *his* personal relationship under discussion. And you don't object to a little bit of happy gossip, do you Jon?'

She smiled at him and he sighed. 'I'm loving it,' he said. 'Almost as much as the lengthy Spanx price comparison discussion at Christmas.'

Everyone laughed and I felt myself beginning to redden.

'There,' said Miriam, smiling at me, 'nothing to worry about.'

I smiled sheepishly, pushing myself backwards on the sofa, hoping that by some miracle it might swallow me up. 'I think I got the wrong end of the stick,' I said quietly.

'Like that'd surprise anyone,' murmured Sophie, before winking at me and asking Miriam a question about projectile vomit, which prompted gasps and giggling and had the immediate, and extremely welcome, effect of distracting all female attention from me.

I hung my head and closed my eyes.

'Romy is going out with Hugh on Saturday night,' said Jon quietly.

I nodded. 'I worked that out a moment ago,' I whispered, keeping my eyes closed. 'Just too late to save me from acute embarrassment.'

'She's very happy,' he said. 'She told me she liked him at the book group dinner and we talked about it again on our way to meet the pair of you last week.'

'Thanks for sharing that,' I groaned, opening my eyes and turning towards him, 'just too late to save me from acute embarrassment.'

He smiled. 'Sorry, but Miriam gave us the impression that you and she had already discussed it all.'

'I thought…' I looked up at him and put a hand to my forehead. 'Never mind. I'm just so embarrassed.' He didn't reply but instead opened his copy of *Jane Eyre*. 'Aren't you going to say anything to try and make me feel better?' I asked.

He shook his head. 'That was pretty bad,' he said, 'even for you.'

I tutted. 'You can go off people you know.'

He looked at me. 'I really hope not,' he said.

'Alice, can I give you a lift home?' asked Connie, now standing next to me.

I looked at Jon. 'Me too,' I said.

'You too what?' asked Connie.

I looked up at her. 'Sorry, Connie. I'm afraid I don't understand the question.'

'Alice, how many have you had?' sighed Sophie, now standing next to Connie. 'Hey, everybody, I reckon Alice has been sneaking drinks tonight.'

Jon stood up. 'I'd better be going,' he said. 'Thanks, Miriam. I hope all goes well for Romy and Hugh at the weekend.' He walked over to her. 'Be sure to text me the moment you hear.'

She laughed and gave him a hug. 'I hope we haven't been too female for you tonight, Jon,' she said.

'Not at all,' he smiled. 'It's always an education.'

'You're not coming back in the car with me, Jon?' asked Connie.

'No thanks, Connie,' he said. 'I could do with the walk.'

Sophie and Abs stood up to leave and I decided that I didn't want everyone to go before I had offered some sort of apology.

‘Sorry about the misunderstanding,’ I said.

They turned towards me and I was aware that everyone in the room was now looking down on me simultaneously, their faces registering concern, puzzlement, pity and amusement in varying degrees.

I stood up. ‘I just got a bit muddled.’

My statement was met with a general murmur of unsurprised, philosophical acceptance. Then I was warmly hugged and kissed five times, and we all went home.

Chapter 56

'No, but thank you,' I said.

'Why not?' asked Sophie, at the same time gesturing me towards the stairs. 'It's too crowded down here,' she said. She turned to the barista behind the counter. 'We'll be up there, OK?'

The woman smiled in acknowledgement and we headed upstairs to the largely deserted upper floor of the café.

'They've discontinued the fabric Frances McGirr chose for those curtains and softs,' I said, as we flopped down in two armchairs, beside a low table. 'I've sourced a last batch but I'm not sure there'll be enough.'

'Why won't you come out with me?' asked Sophie, ignoring my attempt to change the subject.

I sighed. 'OK, well if you want me to be really honest, it's because it sounds a lot like a pity invite.'

She looked at me blankly. 'I don't understand.'

'Yes, you do.'

'I don't ever,' she said, leaning forward in her chair, 'and I mean *ever* sully my Friday nights with pity invites. Friday nights are for fun. Wednesday nights are pity invite nights.'

'We go out quite a lot on Wednesdays,' I said.

She shrugged and held her hands palm upwards, in a *point proven* kind of way.

I laughed. 'You're lovely – and thank you for inviting me out – but I'm exhausted.'

'And you're not still worried about last night?'

'See!' I said, throwing up a hand. 'I knew it was a pity invite.'

'Oh, don't talk bollocks,' she said. 'Me wanting to go for a drink and you making an idiot of yourself at book group, are wholly unconnected.' She nudged me. 'It was funny though. I keep laughing every time I think about it.' She laughed raucously as if to illustrate the point. 'The best bit was when you—'

I glared at her.

'Oh, don't be a misery about it,' she said. 'Just come for a quick drink.' Her smile faded a little. 'You'd be doing me a favour,' she added more quietly.

'In what way?' I queried this new spin with suspicion.

'Well, you know, I've got a lot of stuff going on and it'd be nice to have a proper chat – one where we're not rushing to get back to the office, or to see other people, that's all.'

'I honestly don't think I'll be of much use conversationally,' I said. 'I'm exhausted,' I slid down in the chair, 'in every possible way imaginable.'

'Me too,' she said.

I experienced a rush of guilt. 'How's the job hunting going?' I asked. I had determinedly avoided the topic for days, telling myself Sophie wouldn't welcome it being raised. But, in truth, I had been sparing my own feelings as much as hers.

'Two cappuccinos.' The waitress placed the drinks in front of us. We nodded our thanks and she disappeared.

Sophie reached for her coffee. 'Two job offers within an hour of each other this morning,' she said miserably.

'That's wonderful,' I said, matching her tone.

We looked at each other and smiled ruefully.

'Please come out,' she pressed. 'Not for you – for me.'

I picked up my coffee. 'Of course I'll come out. But don't moan if I fall asleep at the bar.'

'Fab.' She toasted me with her cappuccino and we drank our coffee. 'I'm going to really miss working with you, Alice,' she said suddenly.

I attempted a smile and resisted the urge to beg her not to leave. 'Well, we can still go out every Wednesday,' I said. 'And invite David.'

She laughed and checked her watch. 'And talking of David…'

'I know,' I said. 'Let's drink up and get back before he starts to worry.'

–

It didn't surprise me that David took making a decision over Sophie's replacement right down to the wire. It was 5pm when he called me into his office to say that he agreed that Merrin was the most suitable candidate. He explained his decision with the air of a doctor tasked with delivering a terminal diagnosis and I kept expecting him to open a drawer and hand me a black arm band.

'Well, it's good that we agree,' I said, attempting positivity.

'Yes.' He offered me a tired smile.

'We should think about a gift for Sophie,' I said.

'Yes. I'm going to give her a golden handshake, naturally.' He rubbed his eyes. 'But something personal would be nice. I am, as you would expect, hopeless at that kind of thing. Any ideas?'

'I'll have a think,' I said. 'Was there anything else you needed to discuss?'

He said nothing, his elbows resting on his desk, hands now interlaced in an attitude of deep contemplation.

'David,' I prompted.

He looked up. 'Sorry, yes?'

'Was there anything else?'

He smiled and shook his head. 'No, Alice, I think that's everything.'

I remained seated for a moment. 'Are you busy tonight?' I asked.

'No,' he said.

'Well, why don't you come out with Sophie and me?'

He blinked and I was unsure whether this was due to pleasant surprise, or mild distress at having to come up with a polite refusal.

'Don't feel you have to,' I said. 'I'm just going for one drink, to keep Sophie happy, and then I'm going home.'

He smiled. 'Thank you but I think I'm going to say no. I'm very tired and I…' He paused before continuing. 'I'm very tired.'

I nodded, rose to my feet and walked to the door. 'Another time then.' I opened the door and looked back, with the intention of wishing him a good weekend, but he had turned his chair towards the window, and appeared once again lost in thought. I exited and closed the door quietly behind me.

'All sorted?' asked Sophie, looking up as I approached my desk and sat down.

'Yes,' I said.

'Merrin?' she asked.

I nodded.

'I'm pleased,' she said. 'She was nice. And I don't think she'll take advantage of him.'

'No,' I said. 'Anyway, shall we go?'

She checked the clock on the mantelpiece. 'Yes, come on, we better had.'

'We're not in a hurry, are we?' I asked, surprised by the haste with which she was now switching off her computer and gathering her things.

'What?' She looked up. 'Oh… no. But if you're tired, I don't want to keep you late.'

'I'm not the only one who's tired,' I said, checking my desk. 'David looks done-in.'

'Is he OK?'

'I hope so. I invited him to come out with us; I assumed you wouldn't mind.'

She smiled. 'Of course not.'

'But he's—'

At that moment, the door of David's office opened and its occupant emerged.

'Sophie,' he said authoritatively, 'I wonder if I may speak with you.'

'Er…' she looked momentarily disconcerted. 'Well,' she said, 'Alice and—'

'Yes, I realise you are going out with Alice,' he said. 'But perhaps she could go on ahead and buy some drinks.'

'Or, alternatively, David, I could just wait at my desk for five minutes,' I said, stating the obvious.

He looked at me. Clark Kent was nowhere to be seen: this was man of steel.

'Or,' I said, bending down and picking up my bag, before standing up, 'I could go on ahead and buy some drinks.'

'Thank you,' he said.

I looked at Sophie. She was staring at David with a look of wariness, mixed with fascination, as if he was a newly-discovered species, with hitherto untested behavioural patterns. 'Right, well…' she mumbled, placing her bag and jacket on her chair and walking towards him. As she reached the doorway to his office, she seemed to gather herself a little. 'See you later,' she said, turning to me. 'Mine's a white wine.' And with that, she and David disappeared into his office, closing the door behind them.

Chapter 57

I walked into The Neath, bought our drinks and, without thinking, headed to the back of the wine bar and sat down at the same table Jon and I had chosen when we had met a month earlier. I looked forlornly first at my spritzer and then at the white wine I had bought for Sophie, before swapping the drinks and taking a large gulp of the wine and replacing it miserably on the table. I then removed my phone from my bag and placed it next to the wine glass. I stared at it, willing Sophie to make contact. I had ambled to The Neath at a leisurely pace, gazing into shop windows as I went, and had left her a message to text as soon as she was on her way. It was now a good half-hour since I had left the office and yet there was still no news.

Another five minutes passed and I was just beginning to become concerned, when a bugle sounded, indicating the arrival of a text. It was from Sophie. My sense of relief was immediate.

But very short-lived.

> *Sorry but can't make it. Am going out with David. Your date will be with you in 5. Have fun x*

'Oh, what?' I exclaimed at full volume. I looked up. Only the couple immediately next to me appeared to have heard.

I picked up the phone and called Sophie. She didn't answer and it went to voicemail. I hung up and began to text furiously.

> *Are you joking? Because I'm not laughing. What have you done?*

I pressed send and waited. A bubble on the screen told me she was replying.

> *Calm down. I'm just introducing you to a friend. Connie and Abs had a bash – now it's my turn. I was going to come and help things along but I think it will be better without me. Just have a drink and if you're not keen you can leave.*

I replied again.

> *I'm actually really pissed off about this. Get here right now. Bring David with you.*

Another bubble.

> *Can't. I'm on a date too. David and I had a huge snog in his office and now it's a romantic dinner for two.*

I flopped back in my chair; misery totally suffocating any sense of shock, curiosity, amusement or delight which I may otherwise have felt at Sophie's announcement. And my mystery date, whoever he was, was not my main point of misery. I was a grown-up. It was an embarrassing situation but I could cope with half an hour of awkward conversation, followed, no doubt, by an equally awkward exit. What was more difficult to cope with was the realisation that one of my best, supposedly most insightful, friends didn't actually know me at all.

I texted again.

> *Who is he?*

I waited for the reappearance of the bubble before tapping the caps lock impatiently.

> *WHAT IS HIS NAME?*

The bubble appeared, followed immediately by the text itself.

Wesley.

I reached for Sophie's wine, took another gulp and began to run through the seemingly innocuous chain of events which had resulted in me being out on a Friday night, against inclination, and facing the prospect of having to make polite conversation with a man whom I had never met, whom I had never wanted to meet and who, knowing Sophie, might not even be expecting to meet me.

And just when I thought I couldn't feel any worse, I was suddenly gripped by an icy terror.

I began to text again.

Wesley? The plasterer? The convict?

Her reply was immediate.

Ex convict

I was staring at the screen in open-mouthed horror, when what was to prove to be her penultimate text of the evening arrived.

But that's Wayne – not Wesley. So just relax, have fun and please, please trust me. xx

'Hello.'

At the sound of a man's voice, I took a deep breath and looked up, bracing myself for an unwelcome stranger.

'Jon,' I said, uncertain whether to laugh or cry with relief. I stood up and threw my arms around his neck. 'Are you meeting someone here? Even if you are, could I sit with you for half an hour? Wesley is coming and we're on a date arranged by Sophie, which I knew nothing about. Meanwhile, she's gone swanning off with bloody David and left me here to face the music. I can't believe she's done this to me. But I'm so pleased you're here. Who are you meeting?'

He put his arms around me and said nothing. I turned my head to one side and rested it on his chest.

There was silence between us.

'Are you here to meet *me*?' I said at last.

'The penny drops,' he replied.

'Are you…' I took a deep breath and hesitated, 'my date?'

'Apparently so.'

'You didn't know?'

'No. I found out about five minutes ago, at around the same time that I discovered that Sophie was no longer coming and that my name is Wesley.'

'And do you mind?' I asked, enjoying the feeling of holding and being held, but agonised by the possibility that he might not feel the same way.

'Well, Wesley's not my favourite name, but the rest…' he paused. '…the rest I'm definitely OK with.' I exhaled, closed my eyes, and realised that I was smiling. 'And you?' he asked.

'I'm definitely OK with it too,' I said quietly.

I felt him relax. 'Good,' he said simply.

'And I even quite like the name Wesley,' I added, 'if you shorten it to Wes. But Sophie's insane.'

He laughed. 'I'm putting it all down to a twisted sense of humour and an overdeveloped sense of theatre.'

I thought for a moment. 'Maybe she thought I wouldn't have come if she'd said you were coming.'

'Well, you have refused me twice.'

'I've genuinely been really busy,' I said. 'Plus, I got a bit muddled,' I murmured.

'Yes,' he said, 'I know. I was there.'

'Hmm…' I opened my eyes and realised that the couple at the next table were staring. 'I'm still hugging you,' I whispered.

'I can tell,' he said.

'It's nerves.'

'Stay nervous,' he said. 'It's working for me. Although, I could do with a drink. I'd offer to get you one, but it looks like you're lining them up.'

'You go to the bar,' I released him, 'while I try to calm down.'

'I'll be back in a moment,' he said.

I sat down and watched him walk away. Then I texted Sophie.

He's here. Honestly, Sophie, you're such a nutter x

I waited for a moment and was rewarded with a smiley face and a kiss. I returned my phone to my bag.

A minute or two later, Jon returned, placed a glass of red wine on the table and sat down opposite me. Wearing a dark suit, with a white shirt unbuttoned at the neck, he looked, I thought, intimidatingly good. He offered me a smile, which I attempted to return.

'Are you OK?' he asked.

I nodded and focused on my glass. 'If I seem subdued, it's terror, not misery.'

'That's...' he hesitated '...nice.'

'I just don't want to say the wrong thing.'

'Neither do I,' he said calmly. 'But we should probably try to clarify a few things.'

I nodded again. 'OK.'

'Such as your feelings, for example.' He looked at me questioningly.

I recoiled at the prospect. 'Why don't *you* clarify *your* feelings first,' I said.

He looked amused. 'A somewhat cowardly, suggestion.'

'I prefer prudent to cowardly,' I said.

'OK, I'll go first.' He smiled, looking at me in a way which made me reach hurriedly for a steadying sip of wine. 'And I'll start by saying that I am very happy to be here, with you, and even happier to discover that we are on a date.' Suddenly finding myself unable to maintain eye contact with him, I instead watched his mouth forming each word. 'That I love you,' he continued, 'and that I have loved you for a long time is, I hope, a given.' I nodded slowly and found myself involuntarily leaning towards him. 'That I wanted you as more than a friend was harder for me to come to terms with.' He paused before continuing. 'Accepting that our relationship could change was difficult for me. I hurt you in the process and you already know how much I regret that. I want us to be more than friends and I hope you feel the same way. But, if you don't, I can accept that. Whatever happens, I don't want to lose your friendship.'

I remained silent; wholly focused upon his mouth which, as I continued to stare, formed a smile.

'Your turn,' he said.

I nodded, my mind racing as I recalled the wonderful highs and heart-breaking lows of our long friendship; a friendship now on the brink of becoming so much more. I wordlessly opened and closed my mouth several times, clueless as to where to start. 'Actually, I really like what you said,' I said eventually, barely audibly, suddenly finding myself unable to raise my voice above a whisper.

His smile broadened. 'That's quietly – *very* quietly – promising.'

'So, can I just copy that?' I asked, still in an undertone.

He sighed. 'I suppose so.'

'OK – what you said then,' I whispered.

He picked up his drink. 'A little disappointing in terms of effort and audibility, but a relief nevertheless. I think—'

'I love you, Jon,' I interrupted loudly, surprising myself with the sudden increased volume of my voice and causing him to jump and almost spill his wine. The female half of the couple next to us groaned. 'I have loved being your friend, but I want more than that,' I continued, loudly and undeterred, moving my gaze from his mouth to his eyes. 'And I now know that being in love in the present, doesn't mean we can't still hold precious the past.' I blinked up at him. 'And also your mouth is very nice,' I concluded in a rush.

'Impressive projection,' he said, raising his eyebrows, 'and also an unexpected twist at the end there.'

'I know,' I said, finally gaining control of my vocal chords and lowering my voice to a more acceptable conversational level. 'And I'm not usually very good at public speaking.'

He put down his wine glass and smiled. 'Thank you, Alice,' he said quietly.

'You're welc—' And then, without thinking, or attempting to finish the sentence, I was kissing him.

How long I kissed him for I wasn't certain. But eventually regaining a sense of time, place and decorum, I went to move away, only for him to reach out, place his hand gently behind my head, and pull me back towards him.

And then *he* was kissing *me*.

Only a light cough from the table next to us prompted separation.

We looked at each other and smiled. Neither of us spoke for a moment.

'It's been an odd few months, hasn't it?' I said eventually.

He nodded slowly. 'It certainly has.'

I stared at the table. 'You know, I told Miriam that I hadn't been looking for a new relationship, because I felt that the one I wanted was already there – just waiting for me.' I looked up at him and frowned. 'I just didn't let myself see that it was you.'

'If it's any comfort, I didn't really know what was going on either,' he said quietly. 'Everything between us just seemed suddenly very complicated.'

I nodded. 'It did.'

'And then, of course,' he sighed and picked up his wine glass, 'just as I slowly began to make sense of everything, and tried to come to terms with how I felt… you shredding books and advising me to find new friends seemed to indicate that perhaps my feelings might not be *entirely* reciprocated.' He smiled at me over the top of his wine glass.

'I would like to point out,' I said, raising a finger, 'that you had previously reduced me to a quivering wreck at a party and then followed that up by telling me how irritating I was.'

'Minor details,' he said. 'And besides, before *any* of that there was your email.'

'My email?'

'Your finding-Mr-Right email. The one in which you welcomed all-comers and promised not to stand anyone up. That wasn't exactly what you'd call encouraging either.' He tutted and rolled his eyes.

'I was actually very confused and feeling quite low at the time,' I protested. 'As I said to Sophie, I was *trying to be positive*.' I frowned at him across the table and he offered me a slow smile in return; one which left me feeling in need of a little extra oxygen.

I took a deep breath and smiled ruefully. 'To be honest, even when I stopped being confused, it didn't feel great,' I said. 'It was so awful, understanding my feelings for you, but being absolutely certain that you didn't feel the same way.'

'I can relate,' he said.

I sighed and turned to gaze unseeingly out of the window. 'I still wanted you though,' I murmured. 'I couldn't help it. I wanted your conversation, I wanted your company and worst of all I wanted to kiss you.' I shook my head despairingly. 'Every time I saw you, basically. It was quite an issue for me,' I concluded a little breathlessly.

'Again, I can relate,' he said.

I turned back towards him. 'You can?' I asked, envying his relaxed tone, in contrast to what felt like the sudden onset of mild hyperventilation.

He nodded. 'I mean, I can't claim to have always been as comfortable with the thought of kissing you as I am at this moment,' he said, leaning towards me. 'But it crossed my mind frequently: in pubs, in taxis, at parties, in my office…' I took a deep breath and held it as he looked at me steadily. 'Even when you've been shouting at me whilst wearing a very unflattering bicycle helmet.'

I exhaled. 'Is that true?'

'Yes, it's very unflattering,' he said. 'Are you sure it's the right size?'

I smiled and placed my elbows on the table, resting my chin on my hands and continuing my attempts to regulate my breathing. 'You're so Ethan Frome,' I said quietly, my face now just inches from his. 'Perhaps if you'd just kissed me in a taxi, in an act-now-think-later kind of way, it might have saved us a lot time and trouble. But actually,' I said, sitting up, 'I don't think I can talk about…' I inhaled deeply through my nose and exhaled slowly through my mouth, '…that at the moment.'

'About Ethan Frome?'

I shook my head. 'About kissing in taxis.' I took another deep breath. 'About kissing anywhere, actually,' I added, leaning back in my chair and placing my hand on my chest. 'Because thinking about it is making me feel breathless, as if I'm asthmatic, even though I'm not asthmatic.' I continued the deep breathing.

He smiled and shook his head, as the muffled strains of *The Divine Comedy*, began to drift up from beneath the table.

Everybody knows that I love you
Everybody knows that I need you
Everybody knows that I do, except you.

Jon frowned, I reached into my bag to retrieve my phone, and the couple next to us got up and moved to a table on the other side of the bar. 'It's my Friday ringtone,' I explained, 'courtesy of Sophie. And this is her now,' I added, looking at my phone and pressing *accept* just as the singing ceased.

Jon laughed. 'I wonder how their date is going.'

'Well, I've just missed her,' I sighed, still looking at my phone and waiting in vain for a voicemail. 'Do you think she was being serious about it being a date? I think she was. I hope she was. But you just never know with her.'

'She sounded pretty serious about it in her texts to me,' he said. 'And very happy too.'

I looked up and smiled. 'I think they're perfect together,' I said.

'I agree.' He reached out and tucked a stray lock of hair behind my ear. 'Now, would you like to go to dinner, Ms Waites?' he asked.

I nodded and smiled. 'Yes, I would, Mr Durham,' I said.

'Come on then,' he stood up and held out his hand to me.

I took it and rose to my feet. 'Where shall we go?' I asked, as we walked across the bar, and through the stone-lined archway, towards the exit.

'How about,' he said, holding the door open for me as I stepped out onto the pavement, 'I cook for you? We will have privacy, we won't be forced to whisper and you can relax and hopefully feel less asthmatic.' He turned, looked down at me, seemed suddenly amused and then, taking my face gently in his hands, he kissed me. 'What do you think?' he said after a moment, his hands moving to my waist.

'I think I might actually end up feeling more asthmatic,' I said, reaching up and placing my arms around his neck. 'But I'm willing to risk it. So,' I continued, 'what are you planning to cook this evening?'

'I'm not sure,' he said, smiling down at me. 'Any thoughts?'

I nodded.

'Any of them to do with food?' he asked.

I shook my head.

'Glad to hear it,' he said.

And then he took my hand and we walked up the hill.

Epilogue

There are, of course, many different approaches to change. We can accept it, resist it, or even, as in the case of my feelings for Jon, fail to recognise the possibility of it. But Stephen Powell was, for all his flawed thinking, right about one thing: there was no need for me to fear it. Because embracing change, I learned, doesn't mean the loss of what has gone before. Situations, people and relationships may change, but the family, friends and loves of the past remain just as real and precious, and hold just as much relevance, as they ever did. Jon and I didn't trade our friendship for something else, we built upon it. And we didn't forget a past which was so important to us both; we remembered and celebrated it.

As it turned out, the evening of my breathless first date with Mr Durham heralded significant change not only for Jon and myself. Because on that night, at the age of thirty-seven, David Moore finally asked a woman out. And he was fortunate enough to choose a woman so smitten with him that she had resigned from her job under the ridiculous misapprehension that she simply wasn't good enough for him. Sophie and I had talked many times since about what might have happened had David not nailed his colours to the mast that fateful Friday evening. And such conversations always concluded with mutual shudders at the thought of opportunities for happiness so very nearly missed, due to a fear of taking a leap, and the lure of a safe status quo.

And as I watched Sophie and David now, through the open doorway of The Albion, standing side by side at the bar, looking as happy and perfect together as they had on the evening of the book group dinner three months earlier, I was delighted that these two people, whom I loved so much, had not missed their moment.

'There you go,' said Sophie, returning to our table in the cobbled courtyard and placing my drink in front of me. 'White wine for you, a nice glass of red for me and,' she turned to David as she flopped down on the bench opposite me, 'a beer for Clark. Perfect.'

David sat down next to her, looked at me and sighed. 'I so wish you hadn't mentioned the Clark Kent analogy, Alice.'

'Bollocks,' said Sophie, leaning towards him and kissing his cheek. 'I mean rubbish. You love it.' She winked at me and kissed him again, as he coloured slightly and laughed.

When in the office, they were utterly professional, or at least as professional as they ever had been. Sophie still shouted at David for being too nice and coughing oddly and he still expressed quiet dismay at her man-language, but there was nothing to indicate that they were anything other than close work colleagues.

Outside the office, however, Sophie was what David termed *demonstrative*. The level of this demonstrated affection was never such to cause embarrassment to anyone other than the person upon whom it was bestowed and, although he sighed and rolled his eyes when made victim to her kisses, embraces and compliments, he clearly adored them – as much as he adored her and as much as she adored him.

'Are you not helping Jon prepare for the book group meeting this evening, Alice?' asked David, picking up his pint and taking a first appreciative sip.

'And why should she?' Sophie frowned. 'Just because she's got ovaries doesn't mean she's any more adept at putting crisps in a bowl than he is, does it?'

'Not at all,' said David. 'I merely thought that they may want to spend a little time chatting over the canapés…'

'Crisps, David,' said Sophie. 'We eat crisps. Wotsits, Pringles – that kind of thing.' She looked at me. 'I bet he's never had a Wotsit. Have you ever had a Wotsit, David?'

He ignored her. '…chatting over the canapés, before everyone else arrives,' he continued. 'Sophie and I had a very nice early evening last weekend, stuffing a ballotine before mother arrived.'

'And sadly that's not even a euphemism,' sighed Sophie. 'But it was fun,' she admitted. 'David's a very good cook, you know. Takes after his father, apparently. So his mum says.'

'Jon is a good cook too, actually,' I said, 'which is great because...'

'Because you are not,' concluded Sophie on my behalf. 'We know.' She beamed and nudged me. 'So, are there still lots of lovely romantic dinners then?' She threw me a wink. 'Lots of sleepovers?'

'Alice should be allowed some privacy,' said David disapprovingly.

'Oh, she knows I'm only teasing, don't you, Alice?'

'No,' I said.

She laughed. 'Oh but I'm just so happy for you both.' She sipped her drink and smiled. 'But God knows it's been a bloody long haul. When I think back to Eleanor Black's party...'

'Let's *not* think back to Eleanor Black's party,' said David.

I nodded. 'I agree.'

'When I think back to Eleanor Black's party...' repeated Sophie, gazing into the middle distance and shuddering. 'I just couldn't believe it when you said he was dating Suzanna, when I knew – I just *knew* he wanted to be with you.'

David closed his eyes and pinched the bridge of his nose between thumb and forefinger. 'So, you've told us,' he said, 'many times.'

'Many, *many* times,' I echoed. 'If only you'd been so perceptive regarding David's feelings for *you*,' I added brightly.

'And then I realised that he was trying to *not* be with you, because of history and uncertainty and fear of change and,' she continued, our interjections having had no effect, 'then when you said that you hadn't even bothered to tell him you'd split up with Stephen! I thought, oh for fu—' At this point she paused and glanced at David before continuing. 'I thought, oh, for goodness sake and then I had to find an excuse to phone him and check that you'd made the call. I tell you – it was never bloody ending.' She shook her head. 'I don't know. You two nearly drove me back onto the fags.'

David picked up his pint, emitting a theatrically weary sigh, whilst looking at her with undisguised affection and amusement.

'Oi, you,' she said, prodding him gently. 'Stop avoiding the question.'

'There was a question?' he asked, looking genuinely bemused.

She groaned. 'Have you ever had a Wotsit?' She reached into her bag and took out her phone. 'Hang on,' she said, 'let me get the list up.'

I looked at David. His face registered no emotion.

'What list?' I asked. 'I don't think I've heard about this.'

'I started it on Tuesday,' Sophie explained. 'It's a list of common people things which David has never done.'

'When you say common people…?' I queried.

'I mean normal people, obviously,' said Sophie. 'I just didn't want to make him feel bad.'

I looked at David; he hid a smile in his pint.

'So what's on the list so far?' I asked.

Sophie looked at her phone. 'Never played pool in a pub.'

David held up a finger. 'Although, I did point out to Sophie that billiards is very—'

She didn't pause for breath. 'Never watched an episode of *any* soap opera, never had arctic roll, never played Buckaroo, never had sex outdoors. Ooh, no, actually…' She pressed some buttons on her phone, 'I'll just delete that one…'

I refused to look at David.

'Never been to Alton Towers and,' Sophie began to type, 'never… had… a… Wotsit.'

'That's quite a list,' I said.

Sophie smiled. 'We're ticking them off.'

'So I gathered,' I said quietly.

She looked at me and I frowned disapprovingly.

'Ooh, sorry,' she said, looking at David.

'It's fine,' he said. 'I know you were just thinking aloud. Again.'

She bit her lip and smiled. 'Working on it,' she said and kissed him. 'Maybe you should start a "to do" list for me.'

'I'll show it to you later,' said Superman, looking at her over his pint. 'But I should warn you, it is of quite considerable length.'

–

'Hello!' said Abs. 'Come in, come in. Jon said you were going out first. Hope the pair of you aren't roaring drunk. Actually,' she held up her hand to her mouth and continued in a stage whisper, 'I met Pete and a couple of his friends after work for a very quick G&T. It's a leaving do and Pete's not at work tomorrow, so he'll be bouncing off the walls later. He's such a fizzer.'

Sophie laughed. 'Like David,' she said.

'*Just* like David,' agreed Abs. 'Two fizzers! Anyway, come on in.'

I hung my bag over the end of the banister and we followed Abs through to the back of the house. Everyone was there, seated on sofas in the L-shaped living area.

Sophie and I offered the room a general, 'Hello!'

'I'm just waiting for the day Alice Waites is not last to book group,' said Miriam, putting her arm around me and giving me a squeeze as I sat down next to her.

'Is that my new flaw to cure?' I asked. 'Now that I've actually started to read the books?'

'Three books in a row,' said Jon, appearing with a bowl of crisps and a tray of salmon blinis. He added the food to the selection already on the large, low coffee table in front of us. 'Hi.'

'Hi,' I smiled.

He turned. 'And hello, Sophie. Help yourself to drinks.' He gestured towards the kitchen, where glasses were laid out on the work surface. 'Cold stuff is in the fridge.'

'These are so fantastic, Jon,' said Abs, picking up something made of puff pastry. 'You always have the best hors d'oeuvres.'

'Thanks,' he said, sitting down next to her.

'Bit of a half-hearted host on the drinks front, though.' Sophie rolled her eyes at him and stood up. 'White wine, Alice?'

'Please,' I nodded and she headed for the kitchen area, grabbing Connie by the hand as she went and dragging her with her.

'Come with me, Connie,' she said. 'I want to hear all about how your interview for that part-time job went. I bet they loved you.'

I smiled after them and then, as Abs began to describe to Jon the jumper she was secretly knitting for Pete as a birthday surprise, I felt Miriam gently nudge me. 'How are things?' she asked quietly.

I leaned my head back on the sofa and turned my face towards her. 'Things are very good indeed,' I said. 'And you?'

'Looking forward to Cornwall next week,' she beamed.

I smiled. 'Great.'

'We're keeping our fingers crossed for the weather. It's later and closer to home than we'd usually go, but, you know, I'm not a great traveller and it's so much cheaper once the schools go back.'

'And it's often hotter in September,' I said, noting this further example of the belt-tightening which I knew was currently taking place in the Marshall household. 'How long are you there for? A week?'

She shook her head. 'No. Believe it or not we're going for a whole ten days. Craig insisted.'

'Well, good for him,' I said, keeping my fingers crossed that Craig's adjustment to his work/life balance would prove sustainable. 'Don't forget to send me a postcard.'

She laughed. 'You can have one of the unwritten ones I'll bring home with me. Ooh, but,' she squeezed my arm excitedly, I forgot to tell you. Romy's found a flat in Cotham.'

'Does that mean you won't have a lodger after all?'

'Just for three weeks,' she said. 'And I'll feel better for having her with us when she first moves. That way I can…' she hesitated '…help her settle in.' She gave me a guilty, side-long glance.

I wagged a finger at her. 'No prying, no spying and definitely no interfering.'

She gasped and placed a hand to her chest. 'As if I would!'

'Well done for managing to sound affronted,' I said.

She smiled.

'Anyway,' I said, 'I hear Romy's adamantly refusing to join book group.'

I enjoyed her look of surprise. 'Who told you that?'

'Hugh,' I laughed. 'Jon and I met him for a drink last week.'

Miriam nodded. 'Truth to tell,' she said, 'I didn't argue with her. She said we were a settled little group and that a new member would upset the dynamics and well,' she looked around and shrugged, 'I thought maybe she had a point.'

I followed her gaze around the room. Jon was now telling Abs about our forthcoming trip to Florence, whilst Sophie loudly reeled off her "common people" list to Connie – the latter nodding politely, if looking a little anxiously wide-eyed.

I turned to Miriam and smiled, remembering the moment, years earlier, when she had first suggested that we form a book group; an idea I had so very nearly trounced. I sighed, closed my eyes and saw and heard Lydia gently saving the day. *How about we just read short books... you'd be OK with a novella or two, wouldn't you, Alice?*

Aware of Miriam placing her hand on mine, I opened my eyes. 'Are you OK?' she mouthed. 'What's wrong?'

I shook my head. 'I was just thinking about us, about the Short Book Group,' I said quietly. 'Remembering.'

She smiled sadly. 'I understand.'

'I know you do,' I whispered.

'I think about it a lot,' she said, giving my hand a squeeze. 'Where we started and where we are now.' She turned her head towards Jon, as he glanced up, caught my eye and smiled, before returning his attention to Abs. 'She only ever wanted him to be happy, didn't she?' she murmured, as if to herself. 'And job done, I say.'

I looked down at her hand, still holding mine, and smiled. 'Thank you for caring about me, Miriam,' I said, 'whether I like it or not.'

She laughed and then, 'Same,' she replied.

'There you go.' Sophie patted my knee and handed me a glass of wine, before turning to sit next to Connie. 'So, yes, anyway,' I heard her say as she sat down, 'it was a warm evening and there was no one about, so we were able to cross that one off the list as well.'

'Well, how very lovely, Sophie,' said Connie, now looking commendably relaxed.

'Anyway,' said Miriam, suddenly brisk, tapping the book on her lap, and addressing the room, 'what did everybody think of this book?'

She turned to me, with a look of mischievous confrontation in her eye. 'Why don't you start us off, Alice? Did it compare favourably to *The Hitchhiker's Guide* in terms of realism?'

'Miriam,' I said, putting my arm around her, 'it was the perfect book choice. It made me laugh a lot, think a little and kept me hooked. I loved it.'

'I knew you would,' she said, grinning.

'Well, evidently you know me better than I know myself then,' I said, smiling.

'God, who doesn't?' said Sophie.

I turned towards her and she offered me a sly wink before laughing.

I rolled my eyes and sighed, but I knew she had a point.

-

I heard the front door close and then Jon's footsteps in the hallway, as he returned to the kitchen. I turned as he approached and enveloped me in his arms. 'Hello, Ms Waites,' he said.

'Hello, Mr Durham.' I placed my arms around his neck and leaned my head against his chest.

We remained like that for some time before he spoke again.

'So, have you lost your key or just forgotten it?'

I didn't reply.

'I'll get you another,' he said.

'Thank you.'

'Another another, I mean.'

'Sorry.'

He kissed the top of my head. 'Your father phoned,' he said.

'Oh?'

'He says he's left a message on your landline, but wanted you to know that he's entered a bake-off.'

'Dear God.'

'We had quite a conversation.'

I looked up at him. 'A good one?'

'Yes,' he said, 'a good one. We have a lot in common.'

'I know.' I replaced my head on his chest. 'You'll have to tell me about it some time.'

'I will.'

'I enjoyed book group,' I said.

'Yes.'

'Things are definitely still improving for Miriam and Craig. Oh and Connie had so much to say, didn't she?' I smiled. 'You know, I think she's getting used to being listened to. Both at home and at book group.'

'Hmm…' he said absently.

'And talking of being listened to…' I prodded him gently in the ribs. 'Are you listening to me, or is your mind elsewhere?'

'What?'

I looked up and pointed to his right hand, which was now resting on top of his head. 'You're mid run-through,' I said.

He smiled and put his arm back around me.

'I was thinking about the past and the future,' he said.

I sighed. 'That's a sizeable topic.'

'It is.'

'And your conclusions?'

'I am very happy,' he said.

I held him tightly. 'Me too.'

'And the other thing I was thinking,' he continued, 'is that maybe I need some new cushions.'

I looked up a second time, this time to frown. 'That joke is wearing *so* thin.'

'And I was wondering if you…'

'Really. Stop talking, Jon.' I reached up to place my hand across his mouth.

He took my hand and kissed it. 'And I was wondering,' he smiled, 'if you might share some of yours with me.'

'My cushions?'

'And some of your other furnishings,' he said, 'at some point. What do you think?'

I took hold of his shirt collar and pulled him towards me. 'I think,' I said, 'that you should never mention cushions ever again. But I also think…'

'Yes?'

I kissed him. '…that I would be delighted to share my furnishings, both hard and soft, with you.'

'Long term?' he asked.

'Extremely.' I smoothed his ruffled hair, as he began to trace the neckline of my blouse with his finger. 'Careful,' I said, 'you're making me feel asthmatic.'

He lowered his head and kissed me. 'Really?'

'Ye…s.'

He laughed. 'Come on,' he said, taking my hand and leading me towards the hallway. 'If you're feeling so out of breath that you can't even enunciate a one syllable word, then I think it's definitely time for bed.'

I smiled up at him. 'I'm sorry.'

He paused momentarily to turn off the living room lights and then looked down at me and returned the smile. 'That's OK,' he said, kissing me again, whilst extending an arm and flicking the switch. 'But just try not to calm down at all on the way up the stairs.'